Kyla Shinder grew up and currently lives in New York City. She is a graduate of Sarah Lawrence College. She has won multiple awards for her writing when she was 15 years old. *Until the Last Drop* is her first published novel. Kyla is the proud mother of a beautiful cavachon puppy named Tippi, to whom this book is dedicated.

To T, my real life muse.

Kyla Shinder

UNTIL THE LAST DROP

AUSTIN MACAULEY PUBLISHERS™

LONDON • CAMBRIDGE • NEW YORK • SHARJAH

A CIP catalogue record for this title is available from the British Library.

ISBN 9781398480117 (Paperback)
ISBN 9781398480124 (ePub e-book)

www.austinmacauley.com

First Published 2022
Austin Macauley Publishers Ltd®
1 Canada Square
Canary Wharf
London
E14 5AA

I want to start by thanking Austin Macauley Publishers for taking a chance on me and this book. There was a long while where I wasn't sure if this would ever happen for me. I will be forever in your debt for believing in us enough to grant this dream.

Thank you to Myra Goldberg, Carolyn Ferrell and Jonathan Sabol for helping me hone my writing over the years and always having faith that this day would come.

Jessica Renz, Atara Stahl and Julie Spain, thank you for saving my life on more than one occasion. You made sure I didn't give up on myself, so I share this special moment with you all. Thank you for making sure I was still here to write this book.

Alma Pres, thank you for being the Pessy to my Tympany since that first day of kindergarten.

To my sweet dog, Tippi, who can't read this, but who sat on my lap the entire time I wrote this book and gave me the strength through the whole process. Your essence lives inside Tympany and will be forever immortalised within these pages.

I would be remiss if I didn't thank my incredible family, the Adelsons and Shinders, but particularly my mother, father, and amazing sisters. Alex (aka. Tooie, Alextania, and the best twin ever), thank you for helping me come up with Kylantis when we were just toddlers, creating worlds on the floor of our bedroom. To my Elsie, the best big sister a girl could ask for, thank you for convincing me in third grade that Hadestia was actually the Greek Goddess of the Dead and pretending she possessed you to scare the shit out of us. Al and El, you are both massive influences in my life and work, who mean the absolute world to me. How lucky I am to call you my sisters and best friends.

To my incredible parents, who have always believed in me: saying "thank you" doesn't feel strong enough to portray how appreciative I am for all you've given me, but I'm going to say it anyway and hope the sentiment is sufficient. Thank you for making me who I am. Thank you for suggesting, I start writing down my stories instead of speaking them out loud, so I wouldn't embarrass myself around my second grade peers. Thank you for every journal you ever bought me. Thank you for instilling in me my love of reading and for never invalidating my imagination. I am as creatively confident as I am because you've given me the space all these years to be true to myself and never doubt my talent. There aren't enough words for me to express how much I love you both or how grateful I am for your support and love. I promise to never stop telling you how much you mean to me. I am lucky beyond measure to be your daughter.

Lastly, I want to thank little seven-year-old Kyla, who fell in love with Super Paper Mario and decided to write fanfiction for her favourite couple, thus beginning this lifelong love of writing. For the little girl who sat in the middle of the baseball field at camp, acting out her stories and not giving two shits who heard her, this book is for you more than anyone else. It's a love letter for all the progress you've made these last twenty-three years to get to this point. It hasn't been easy for us, but because you never gave up, even in the hardest, darkest times, we're now here, seeing our dream realised. I dedicate every accomplishment to you from here until the end of time.

Table of Contents

Chapter One

The two soft knocks followed by a louder one let me know right away who wished to enter.

"Come in, Pess," I called out, taking a seat on my bed.

Pessy poked her head through the door, her butter blonde hair trickling down over the length of her chest, curled away from her face. She wore a red off-the-shoulder gown, the material crushed velvet with long flowing sleeves in burgundy chiffon. The dress had ties of satin ribbons on the back, finishing off with a small train. It was rare to see Pessy wear anything other than leggings and a large tunic.

She looked glorious, but she was the kind of beautiful that would look striking even with a paper bag plastered over her head.

"Glad to see you didn't flee overnight," she said by means of greeting, closing the door behind her.

"I tried," I joked, "but I couldn't fit through the window with this dress on."

"It is a beautiful dress. It'd be a shame to ruin it." I glanced down, as though I'd forgotten what it looked like. Each God and Goddess had a specific colour assigned to them, one they were obligated to wear in public so they could be easily identified. Mine was grey. If I'd had a say, I would've chosen blue, which already belonged to my brother, Caspian, God of Water and Rain. I would've even settled for silver, but that was my sister, Luna, Goddess of the Moon's shade. The dress fashioned for tonight was long-sleeved, with a square neck, a natural waistline, and a sweeping train, as well as a corset back. The dress fabric was embellished throughout with tiny diamonds that twinkled when seized by the light.

Each time I'd tried on this dress, I felt like my ribs were being squashed, but Roara had insisted the feeling would recede throughout the night as I moved around in it more.

I was convinced the only way that feeling would subside now would have to be when I lost circulation and passed out.

"It would've been worth the destruction," I declared, simulating the motion of tearing the gown off and running away.

Pessy shook her head at me. "You're not funny, Tympany."

"I'm hilarious. I'm your own personal comedian. You're lucky I don't charge you for private viewings of my content."

She rolled her eyes, but eventually succumbed to a smile. "All jokes aside, you look outstanding, Tymp."

"I can't breathe," I groused, stroking my abdomen. "Seriously, how do my sisters do this every day?"

"You're lucky your mother's never insisted on you wearing gowns unless you're in public. You're so obviously her favourite."

I did my best not to stiffen. Pessy didn't know my mother told me I would need to wear gowns every day once I became Queen of the Gods. It was one of the things underscored on my *no* list.

"I don't think that's true," I protested, panic flaring in my throat. Pessy lifted her brows with incredulity.

"Seriously? Tymp, I'm sorry, but your mother lets you off the hook for *everything.* She let you train to fight with the Kylantian army, which is unheard of. She never reprimands you when you're late to meetings, or when you use your powers. You're *absolutely* her favourite."

All of this was true, and deep down, I knew it—but what accompanied favouritism was pressure to take a crown I didn't want. Sometimes, I felt I would willingly trade that with being overlooked. This made me sound ungrateful, so I kept that thought to myself.

"Am I allowed to wish you a happy birthday, or will I be punched in the throat?" She clutched her neck for dramatic effect.

"Just this once, I'll try to control myself," I teased.

"Well, in that case..." She set a hand on my shoulder. "Happy birthday, Tympany. I'm so glad you were born. My life would be utterly colourless if not for you."

The corners of my eyes stung with emergent tears. "I don't know what I'd do without you, Pess."

"You'll never have to know. Especially after tonight." Her sweet smile held so much love for me, even after all these centuries.

Pessy and I had the kind of relationship that was instinctual. I never doubted that, if I needed her, she would be there before I even opened my mouth to ask for help.

She was the main reason I debated leaving Kylantis right away, if at all.

Of course, leaving my parents and siblings would be difficult, but I knew they'd all still be here when I returned home. What if something happened to her when I was gone?

I felt guilty even considering not bringing her with me, but Kylantians rarely left the dominion of Kylantis. In the occasional instance a God travelled down to the Realm, their bonded Kylantian would accompany them, but that was only on visits sanctioned in the name of the Gods.

I didn't think Roara or Isaias would permit Pessy to leave Kylantis for a leisure visit, even after we were bonded.

So, I would have to leave her behind.

"Tymp? You okay?"

"Mhm," I mumbled, not wanting to alarm her of the direction my thoughts had taken. "Just dreading tonight." Her face softened with understanding, then sympathy, before she set her hand on my shoulder.

"Don't worry about tonight. I won't leave your side. I promise." She proffered her arm. "Ready to go?"

"Ready as I'll ever be." I looped mine through hers and let her shepherd me out of the bedroom.

I caught a glimpse of myself in the mirror before we exited the room. My hair was the hue of chestnut, chopped to shoulder length that, when struck by the sun, unearthed natural blonde highlights, which I always called a "hint of my father peeking through." Roara gave me a hard time when I wanted to cut my hair short, making me promise I'd keep it long enough to still fit within a bun. Tonight, the brunette locks were unfettered and falling to my shoulders in tailored, burnished waves. I blinked, and a pair of amber-green eyes set in an almond frame mimicked me in the glass. The diamonds on the dress drenched my brown skin in tiny streaks of silver that bounced off my flesh and returned to the opposing wall, following in my wake on the floor as well.

The woman in the mirror looked beautiful…and depleted. I doubted anyone would notice.

"Do you think your mother will open the gates to Kylantis tonight?" Pessy asked, trying to be conversational. She had this thing about silence—she said it made her feel like someone was dragging nails down the inside of her skin, clawing at her sanity.

"I hope so." I never got to see any mortals, unless Roara opened the gates. And even when she did, we were never allowed to communicate with them. Still, I relished the scarce moments in their close vicinity, their innocence and mortality fascinating to me. With the limited time they were gifted in their various worlds, they salvaged every moment they could of living. I'd been alive five thousand years, had the same routine, did the same thing every single day of my life, and it was *mind-numbing*. I envied mortals for taking advantage of every instance of life to explore and try new things and make mistakes, to learn and grow and thrive and love, even to lose.

To lose something means you had it to begin with, and that, in itself, is a gift not everyone is blessed with.

I was surprised when Pessy started steering me towards the throne room. "We're not going to the party yet?"

"You mother wants to speak to you before the ball."

"Of course she does," I muttered, repressing a groan. I had a pretty good idea of what Roara wanted to discuss, but tried to keep an open mind. Pessy kept close at my side, sensing my unease.

As we strolled through the hallway, I studied the nine paintings for each of my siblings hanging on the walls. Lucius, as the eldest son, was first—the God of Sun and Light was painted with a lustrous sun floating above his right shoulder, and a beam of light hovering over his left, sprinkling luminescence over his sharp features. Next to him was my sister Calliope, the Goddess of Music. Her dark, almost black hair was curled off her face, her eyes like dollops of chocolate surrounded by caramel skin. The symbol of a clef note hung above her right shoulder. Next to Calliope was Eira, Goddess of Snow, bleached white hair pulled away from her face and braided down her chest, snowflakes raining behind her. Luna's was next to Eira, her silver eyes piercing a hole through you even in her portrait, a crescent moon in the background. Caspian stood in the centre of a raging ocean in his painting, the roaring waves encircling him like a cape.

Beside Caspian was Benjen, God of Food and Harvest. His was my favourite—Ben was eating a slice of chocolate cake in his painting, which he'd refused to part with when he was forced to sit for his portrait. He was captured with a crumb in the corner of his mouth, and a conceited smirk on his face. It made me laugh every time I passed it.

Then came Jaxith's, whose painting made me happy for a different reason. The God of Kindness's portrait encapsulated his most sincere, sensitive smile in a frozen moment, the kind of smile that made you feel like someone was spilling warmed honey into your chest. After Jax was Nox, God of Night. When they were deciding the concept of his portrait, Nox and Luna, who were twins, argued over the usage of a moon, since that was Luna's domain. Lucius added fuel to the fire by decreeing stars as a symbol of light, so Nox couldn't use them. In the end, one of them had to give, and that would *never* be Lucius, so Nox's portrait contained no stars and a tiny moon, smaller than Luna's. The whole thing was strange looking, considering how purposeless and sad a night sky looks without stars. The painter also made his dirty blonde hair look too dark, juxtaposed with the black backcloth, so he almost appeared bald. We'd given him a hard time about that for centuries.

The last portrait was of Hadestia, Goddess of the Dead. Hadestia was the oldest of us all, and the only God or Goddess who didn't live in Kylantis. She resided in Nekropolis, the land of the dead. I'd never met my eldest sister, but if her portrait looked anything like her, I was sure I would've been afraid of her— eyes as black as coal with hair to match, the painter portraying her with an unequivocal scowl.

I didn't have a painting…yet.

The week before my birthday, I'd posed for five hours for mine, and tonight, at my celebration, it would be revealed.

Entering the throne room, I took a moment to admire the opulence of the scene before me, the high ceiling, the walls and floors of immaculate white marble, and the ten huge limestone chairs for each of Roara's children. Two rows of five flanked either side of Roara's massive throne, situated in semi-circles around the room. Roara's throne was carved from the same marble as the rest of the room, but the chair was delineated with clouds, the granite hidden beneath the billows.

When she sat in it, it looked like she was floating on air.

Roara let me sit on it a few times, when I was much younger, but it'd been years since I'd asked for or wanted to sit on her throne. No part of me felt a calling towards it, not the way Lucius felt when he saw it.

Occupying the seat now was Queen Roara in the flesh. Everyone told me I looked like a duplicate of my mother at this age, and if that was true, then it was a compliment of the highest order. Roara was a vision. Brown hair limned with slight accents of red when the light dribbled over it, large coffee eyes that complimented her dark brown skin. There was a unique regality to the way her chin was always raised, her posture aligned with boundless confidence. Tonight, she wore a gold off-the-shoulder gown, with short sleeves and a lace, glitter tulle material over the chest and skirt.

Her hair was blow-dried, twisted back into an elaborate bun that probably took hours to perfect.

Her gold crown lay peacefully on her head.

She wore it with such purpose, such certitude, that sometimes, I forgot it wasn't drilled into her skull.

Mergona, Roara's right-hand, as well as Pessy's mother, stood at her side. She was dressed in the customary Kylantian uniform—the bodysuit, harness, and shoulder armour were doused in gold, with black leggings, boots, and a waist cape. Her blonde hair, identical to her daughter's, was woven back in a tight braid that spilled down her spine, allowing her prominent jawline to take center stage.

Roara rose from her throne at the sight of me, hands outstretched. I left Pessy's side to slip my fingers through the slots between hers.

"Angel," she cooed, her special pet name for me. "You look radiant."

"Hi, Mother." Despite our differences, I revered Roara. She was my Queen, my sovereign, my idol.

"Happy birthday, Tympany." When she cupped the side of my face, I swallowed the lump developing in my throat, feeling guilty for entertaining the thought of leaving her. "I wanted to be the first to say that to you, as well as show you the portrait we'll be presenting for you at the gathering tonight."

She led me by hand over to where the painting rested on an easel, shrouded in a cream sheet. She waited for my nod, then signalled for Mergona to pull the cover away, revealing the artwork.

I gasped.

The portrait, objectively, was stunning. The Kylantian who'd painted it had managed to capture all my little intricacies, like the two freckles near the corner of my left eye and the one closer to my ear, the odd shape of my thin lips, the gold flecks speckled in my green eyes, the delicate slope of my jawline, and my

Adam's apple. If anyone wondered about the accuracy, I could confirm, it looked like me, which was a relief after seeing some of the botched work of my siblings.

But that's not what my eye caught first, what initiated my gasp. It was the gold crown sitting atop my head.

Chapter Two

I stared at the painting in absolute horror.

I couldn't believe the audacity of my mother to have this added to my portrait without consulting me first. A monstrous rage overrode my system, an untameable beast that snatched the reins and guided me down a path of demolition.

"Well? What do you think?" she asked, beaming.

"I think you must be losing your marbles if you actually thought this was okay," I barked, and heard Pessy gasp behind me.

"I beg your pardon?" Roara, when she wanted to, had a quiet intensity to her that was even more frightening than if she bellowed. I knew this from experience, but it didn't stop me from contesting.

"I want this redone, Mother. There is no way I will allow you to hang this portrait up as it is now."

"Tympany—"

I turned to Pessy and Mergona. "I wish to speak to my mother in private, please."

Mergona's eyes swung to Roara, checking to see if this was okay. When Roara nodded, she turned on her heel and marched out of the room, leaving the door cracked open.

Pessy loitered a moment, mouthing *are you okay?*

I sent her a tight smile and succinct nod, mouthing back *I'll explain later*. At this point, she'd already seen the portrait with the crown on my head. I couldn't keep her in the dark any longer.

Her eyes flickered fleetingly to Roara before she headed for the exit, closing the door behind her.

Once we were alone, I faced my mother.

"That was incredibly disrespectful, Tympany," Roara admonished, taking a seat on her throne, where she held the upper hand. "I thought I raised you better than to speak to your Queen with such impertinence."

"What's disrespectful is you thrusting this crown upon me when I've told you numerous times, I don't want it."

"It is your birth right."

"That I've told you, I don't want!" I didn't know how to be any more direct. "You have a son who's made it abundantly clear he wants to be next in line. Lucius is way more capable of running Kylantis than me, and he *actually* wants it."

"Your brother is incredibly endowed, in his own way, but he's too vain. You have the ability to not only inspire, but influence the actions of others by tapping into their hearts and minds. It's an extraordinary gift, Tympany, one that would aid you greatly as Queen, as well as your humility."

"That's all great, Mother, except *I don't want it.*" We'd had this same conversation so many times before. I felt like we were running up the same damn hill. It was becoming wearisome to keep explaining this to her. "Why are you trying to box me in? Don't you want me to grow? To flourish on my own?"

"Of course I do!" she cried, leaping out of her throne. She reached for my hands, insisting, "Tympany, I'm not trying to box you in to anything."

"Then what is this?" I pointed at the painting. "Why would you do this? Why would you have the painter put a crown on my head?"

"I don't know...wishful thinking? A self-fulfilling prophecy?" *Was she trying to be funny?* I'd said it before to be cruel, but now I was genuinely concerned about her mental state. "I know you say you don't want it, but you could change your mind."

"Putting a crown on my head in a painting that will live forever is not giving me space to change my mind. It's forcing it upon me. If you present that portrait tonight, you're practically announcing me as the new Queen of the Gods. I'm saying *no.*" Sensing her growing displeasure, I dampened my ire and edged closer, placing a hand on her shoulder. I considered for a half-second using my compulsion on her, but I'd never done so before. I figured, even if it *did* work on the Goddess of Life, she would be *furious* if she found out I'd manipulated her by stealing her free will.

In this regard, she had raised me well.

So instead, I just spoke the truth.

"I'm flattered you think I'd make a great queen. Really, I am. But I'm not ready for this right now. I don't know how to be any more clear. There's so much I still want to do, so much I still want to see. I haven't *lived,* Mother. Let me live. If you need someone to take the throne now, give it to Lucius. In a couple of years, maybe I'll feel differently…but not now. Please, understand. Respect that."

If there was one thing I couldn't stand, it was disappointing someone, particularly my mother. Anger, I could manage. Anger made sense to me and felt familiar, like an old friend. Sadness was erratic, a distant cousin that's awkward to be left alone with. It could come out of nowhere and engulf your senses, physically and mentally, leaving behind the kind of scar that lacerates you on the inside, never to be reached or mended. While anger eventually passed, sadness felt eternal.

"What will I say to the kingdom tonight?" she whispered to herself, picking at her eyebrow, an anxious gesture I'd adopted from her.

"I don't know. You don't have to say anything, but you can't present that portrait with a crown on my head. I'm sorry, but you can't." She nodded, finally seeming to accept what I was saying.

"I wish you would just consider," she continued. I bit my tongue, letting her finish so her disappointment wouldn't fester for the rest of the evening. "You know you'd make an excellent ruler, but I understand you're not ready. We will have to revisit this conversation in the future."

"*Distant* future," I mumbled, then shrunk back at her glower.

"Let's not spoil your birthday. I suppose I'll tell the public your portrait is still being finished, so it's not ready to be displayed." She lifted a strand of my hair, twirling it around her finger. "Let's enjoy tonight, and let that be tomorrow's problem. Alright?"

If I'm still here tomorrow.

I gulped, then gave her an acquiescent nod.

Roara wrapped her arm around mine, shuffling us towards the exit. Mergona and Pessy were waiting in the hall, shadowing our every step as we began strolling towards the upper level courtyard, where the party was being held. The palace was a massive structure that resembled a colosseum on the outside, divided into different wings for each of the Gods, the servant quarters, the dinning and ballrooms, and the throne room, which was located at the top of the edifice. The palace sat at the zenith of the Geddesia Mountains, which seeped down into Sleotha. Despite their close proximity, no mortal had ever dared to try and enter the citadel, because if they did, they would no doubt be struck down on sight.

The upper level courtyard in the East Wing, which everyone called Tympany's Province because of the amount of time I spent there, easily had to be my favourite place in all of Kylantis. The flowers there were like dancing rainbows, as if light and music had coalesced to find a new way to blossom together, delicate works of art that were medicine for my soul. I spent most of my days there lounging, journaling, sometimes doing nothing but staring up at the clouds, submerged in florae, daydreaming until I passed out. The garden offered protection and comfort from the claustrophobia being trapped in the castle caused, the closest I got to being transported somewhere far away, my safe haven.

Normally, Roara held birthday celebrations in the ballroom, but I'd managed to convince her this year to hold the gathering in the courtyard, in honour of this being such a monumental birthday.

On the way there, I asked her, "Are you opening the gates tonight?"

I classified her smile as mischievous. "You'll just have to wait and see," she replied, patting my hand.

When we entered the courtyard, I felt my heart swell at the sight of almost all my siblings waiting for me under the arch. It was rare for the nine of us to gather together outside of council meetings, and it warmed me from head to toe to see my brothers and sisters here to celebrate me.

Even though I'd hated the idea of having a party, this sight made it all worth it.

"There she is!" Jax cheered, clapping for me. He was dressed in his signature colour of red, donning a velvet maroon petticoat, a black and gold vest, and black slacks. His blonde hair was brushed back and braided, secured at the bottom with red silk.

"Who put this in your hair?" I asked, fiddling with the ribbon. His expression screamed distaste.

"Don't ask," he grumbled, scowling at Roara's back.

"Of course Tympany would be late to her own party," Calliope teased, reaching for me next. She looked breathtaking in her signature colour of purple, dressed in a gown the hue of grapes, with swirling beading and sequin shimmers extoled throughout. It gathered at the waist, the flowy A-line chiffon skirt spilling down to the floor like liquid.

Her dark hair was curled to perfection, her tan skin radiant, and her lips were painted a vibrant red.

"You look beautiful," I told her.

"So do you." She turned to Pessy and greeted, "Hi, Pess," in a soft, coquettish voice.

"Hi, Callie," she said back, her cheeks swept with colour. "How's the world of music treating you?"

Calliope answered, "Melodious," and Pessy snorted on a giggle, even though what she said wasn't that funny.

I'd teased Pessy for years over her crush on my older sister. She always insisted it was all in my head, but we both knew better. In recent years, the feelings seemed to be reciprocated.

"Always one to make an entrance," Caspian approved when he joined us, leaning down to kiss my cheek. His cerulean eyes were further accentuated by his all blue apparel. "Happy birthday, littlest sister."

"Begrudging," I reminded him, which earned me a laugh.

"How can anyone forget when you keep reminding us every four minutes?" Eira groaned, then winked to show she was kidding. Her white hair, coiled in ringlets, flowed down her chest, her matching gown a one shoulder sweep, with a brush train of chiffon. Leave it to Eira to wear the puffiest gown ever created on a night not about her.

"I remember the day you were born," Nox mused, looking dapper in all black as he slung his arm around my shoulder.

"Mother screamed so loud, I thought she was dying," Luna teased. Her silver dress matched her sparkling eyes, a sweetheart neckline with narrow straps and a pattern of sequins embellished throughout the silhouette. While I spent more time with Calliope and Jaxith than any of my other siblings, there was something about Luna I'd always respected. She marched to the beat of her own drum, never letting Lucius or any of our other brothers push her around. She was the only one of us who chopped nearly all her hair off, her dark pixie cut a message to our mother about not wishing to be oppressed by the usual expectations that burdened women. I'd been inspired to cut my hair because of her, though I didn't have the courage to cut it quite as short as she had.

"Hey, birthday girl," Benjen greeted, wrapping his arms around me from behind and lifting me off my feet, spinning me in circles.

"Ben! Put me down!" I shrieked. "I'm going to be sick." Lucius emerged from behind Benjen.

"I told you not to have that glass of nectar," he chided. He was referring to earlier on the roof, when he caught me and Jaxith with two flutes of liquor we'd stolen from the kitchen. I'd compelled him to leave us alone until the party. He didn't even realise I'd used my powers against him—Lucius was so self-centered that he thought it was his own idea.

My eldest brother was sporting his signature yellow, which made his brown skin glow in comparison. His jacket, however, was the colour of gilt, a colour usually reserved special for Roara and Isaias. It had to be a deliberate power move to wear gold, a message somehow about his desire to take the throne. I wondered what Roara would think when she saw him in this coat, if she'd force him to change.

I met his eye and declared, "I regret nothing," which even Lucius smiled at reluctantly.

"You should," he replied, his eyes flaring. Something was off about him tonight—I couldn't put my finger on it, but I sensed genuine indignation in the underbelly of his words, directed at me.

Perhaps he figured out I'd compelled him earlier?

Whatever was bothering him, I decided it wasn't my problem. If this was potentially my last night in Kylantis, I was going to take advantage of every moment and enjoy myself, not stress all night about what I'd done to offend him. It took a lot of mental power to do this, though, as my natural inclination was to try to assuage anyone's distress, especially if I was the one who caused it.

Lucius and his wounded ego, however, were the exception to that impulse.

I skimmed through the throng of Kylantian soldiers assembled in the garden, disappointed to see that Hadestia, once again, was nowhere to be found. While I understood her obligations were elsewhere, I'd always secretly hoped that one day, she'd randomly show up, so I could finally meet her. She almost didn't feel real to me, more like a mythic legend than my sister.

I perked up again when I caught sight of my father. Isaias had coordinated with his wife in a gilded ensemble that somehow made him appear blonder, his eyes the colour of gunmetal, glinting like pewter in contrast to the gold. They softened at the sight of me.

I found myself in his arms before I even realised I'd rushed towards him, folded tightly against his chest.

"Happy birthday, darling," he cooed, stroking a hand down my hair. He sighed. "I cannot believe you're already five thousand. Feels like just yesterday, you were an itty bitty thing that wouldn't let go of my finger long enough for me to feed you."

"You always say that, but that doesn't sound like something I'd do. How do I even know it's true?"

"Because I *lived* it, honey. I have the scars to prove it." He lifted his index finger as if to show me.

Whenever I was in my father's embrace, I was brought back to infancy. To him, I would always be his baby who couldn't withstand two feet of distance and clung to his leg during council meetings. I found reprieve in knowing she existed somewhere, that someone would keep that little girl's memory alive, even as I entered adulthood and worked to rid myself of her looming shadow.

"And now we're getting drunk off nectar together," I rejoiced. "It's life coming full circle." He laughed, shaking his head like he still couldn't believe he actually agreed to get drunk with his youngest daughter.

"Are you going to hold my finger as we do?"

"Of course. We must honour tradition." I looped my arm through his, allowing him to drag me to where the servers were passing out glasses of nectar. The only two reasons I looked forward to this party were Pessy's initiation into the Kylantian army, and Isaias's promise that we'd get drunk together.

"Your mother told me what you discussed in the throne room," he admitted, passing me a glass. I took a sip, the saccharine substance dancing on my tongue, invading my mouth with the flavour of molasses and honey. I internally groaned at the mention.

"I take it you agree with her." While Roara and I discussed me taking the throne on several occasions, I'd never spoken to my father about it. I assumed he agreed with her, as he did with most things.

"If I have to pick one of my children to succeed your mother, I agree with Ro. I would pick you."

"Why not Lucius?" Roara claimed it was because Lucius was too proud, but that never made any sense to me.

He wanted the throne—*wasn't that enough?*

"Lucius would be a very practical, hard-headed ruler, which is not necessarily a bad thing. If I was basing who I thought would be the best ruler on pragmatism alone, it would be him, but he lacks the emotional quotient. To be ruler of the Gods, you need to care about all elements of humanity, and Lucius…I love your brother, but he doesn't have the capacity to be considerate to all. He values what relates back to him more than anything else. He couldn't embrace all of humankind in its entirety."

"If that's what's holding him back, then why isn't Jaxith a contender?" As the God of Kindness, he was the best of us when it came to looking at something holistically, acknowledging both sides of the same coin.

"Jax is much more open-minded than Lucius, but he leads solely with emotion. You, on the other hand, are a perfect balance between the two, partly due to your gifts, but also just who you are at your core. You've always been that way, since you were a baby. You know when to use logic, or, when to follow your heart. You need both to be a great ruler, and out of all your siblings, you're the only one who's mastered the art of recognising when the appropriate time to favour one over the other may be."

"So I'm right, and you agree with Mother."

"I didn't say that." *Oh?* "I agree, out of all our children, it should be you to take the throne next. But you're only *just* turning five thousand. That might seem like a lot of years, but for a God, you're still so young. When your siblings turned that age, they were given the chance to explore the Realm, get a sense of the kingdoms we reign over, actually interact with mortals. You can't be Queen before you've seen what's out there. You need to understand what it is you have to care about and protect. That's our job as Gods…we protect and assist the mortals. They may worship us, but we exist to be a symbol of guidance and security for *them*. Once you understand that, you will make a great queen, Tympany, but not yet. You need time to live first." He dabbed the corner of my eye with the sleeve of his jacket, apprehending a fallen tear.

"You have *no* idea how much that means to me," I squeaked, trying to pull myself together before I turned into a blubbering mess.

"Can I ask you something? You don't have to answer if you don't want to." I nodded. "Do you plan on leaving Kylantis right away? Or waiting a while?"

I wasn't sure why I found the question so shocking, after what he'd just said about me exploring the Realm.

25

"I'm not sure. I haven't decided yet. I wanted to give Mother tonight, and figure it out tomorrow."

I couldn't pinpoint any one emotion in his face. He nodded impassively, tapping the side of his glass while he absorbed my answer.

"May I ask one favour? Give me a heads up before you go. I'd rather not wake up and discover you left without saying goodbye. I'll be pissed." I let out a hearty cackle, loud enough that I attracted the attention of my mother.

"I promise," I swore as she approached us, beaming at her husband when he leaned over to kiss her cheek.

"Tympany, come with me. There's something I'd like to show you."

I glanced at Isaias, who sent me a private wink of acknowledgement, surrendering me to Roara.

I followed her lead towards the corridor, which was half inside, half outside, shielded by stone with tiny slits as windows.

"Look," she said with a joyful smile.

I peered down past the lower level of the palace, to where the gargantuan golden gates of Kylantis stood tall in the distance, and gasped. The gates were opened, and a swarm of thousands of mortals were congregated beneath us. They were dressed in grey, waving streamers with the symbol of a brain inside of a heart—my emblem. They were cheering, chanting my name, boisterous with excitement. There were so many of them overhauling the square that they were overflowing, expanding all the way past the gates to the Geddesia Mountains, where I suspected there were even more mortals lined up, hoping to squeeze their way through the crowd to join the fun. I'd never seen so many humans before, not for any of my other sibling's birthday celebrations.

"There's so many of them," I mumbled under my breath, in awe.

"They're celebrating the Goddess of the Heart and Mind reaching the full age of adulthood," Roara explained, then said, more softly, "They're celebrating *you*, angel." Tears pricked the corners of my eyes.

Somehow, down there, I mattered.

Though I'd never visited the Realm, to the people of Sleotha and Esteopia, I'd still made an impact.

Roara left me alone in the corridor, gazing down at the jamboree happening below in my honour. I felt a twinge of longing, wishing I could join their celebration, rather than remain up here with the people I'd known my whole life and saw on a daily basis.

As I scanned the mob, taking in the mortals who'd travelled near and far to commemorate me, one human caught my eye. Even from all the way up here, I could tell he was incredibly attractive, his beauty resembling that of the Gods. He wore a gleaming grey vest under a black petticoat, with matching slacks tucked into black boots. His short brown hair was coiffed, the bridge of his nose low.

His jawline was so sharp, it looked like it could cut through glass.

He raised his head, and I could've sworn he saw me, even though that was impossible from where I was standing.

I jumped when I felt something graze my shoulder, swivelling around with my fists outstretched, my default when I thought I might be in danger. It was only Pessy, raising her hands in surrender.

"Hey, it's just me. I promised I wouldn't leave your side, remember?" I sighed with relief, then twisted my arm around hers, bringing her flush against my side. I glanced down, trying to locate the human again, but he'd dissolved somewhere into the crowd, where I could no longer find him.

She peeked down at the mass, exclaiming, "Holy shit. I know it's not custom for us to curse, but…"

"Since when have you ever cared about being mannerly?" She giggled, nudging me in my side.

She looked me up and down, then asked, "How're you doing in that dress? Still feel like you can't breathe?"

"My ribs ache so much, I worry they're going to pop out of my chest." I rubbed my abs for further emphasis.

"Overdramatic grouch," she teased, rolling her eyes. There was a pause before she muttered, "Are we going to talk about what happened in the throne room?"

I'd wondered when she would ask, if she'd wait until after the party. Pessy, like me, didn't have a lot of patience.

"I've wanted to tell you for months, but Mother made me swear not to," I started, so she'd understand why I hadn't confided in her, when usually, she was the first person I told anything to. I took a deep breath, then confessed, "Roara wants me to take the throne. I keep telling her no, that I'm not ready. I didn't know she was going to put a crown in my portrait, which is why I got so upset."

"Holy shit, Tympany." Her hand flew to her mouth to keep more blasphemies from leaking out. "I mean, I knew something was going on with you and your mum. You've been so tense around her these last few months, but I didn't know it was because of *this*." She shook her head in disbelief. "I don't mean this offensively, but I always assumed Lucius would take the throne after Roara."

"Me too. He wants it bad enough, but Mother and Father both want it to be me. I'm just not ready, Pess," I squeaked in a trembling voice, on the verge of bursting into tears now. "I've spent my whole life in Kylantis. I've never seen or been anywhere else. I can't commit to being Queen without experiencing what else is out there. I don't...I just don't want to be sheltered anymore."

"You don't have to explain it to me, Tymp. I know how restless you get." She smudged a tear that dripped down my cheek with her knuckle. "I'm proud of you for sticking up for yourself with your mum. I know how shy you get about asking for what you need, but if you're not ready, no one should force you."

"Thank you, Pess." My heart ached at the prospect of leaving her behind in Kylantis when I travelled to the Realm. "I wish you could come with me."

"Who says I can't? Once I'm inducted as an official Kylantian and made your personal guardian, I'll petition my mother and see if she'll let me accompany you when you go down to the Realm, since it'll be your first time visiting."

"Oh, Pess. I would *love* that." I honestly couldn't imagine experiencing the Realm and humanity for the first time without Pessy. It would feel wrong to go anywhere without her.

"Let's just get through tonight. Tomorrow, I'll speak to my mum, and we can go from there and start making plans. Alright?" I clasped her hand, lifting it to my lips, and planted a kiss in the center of her palm.

"You're amazing," I told her.

"No. *You're* amazing. Now, dry your tears, Miss Future Queen of the Gods. Let's go get bonded."

I cackled as she pulled me out of the hallway.

Because Pessy was being inducted to the Kylantian army as my personal guardian, there would be a bonding ritual between her and I. Every God was given one bonded Kylantian of their choosing. The chosen Kylantian's lifeline would then be linked to theirs for all of eternity. Nothing too extreme would occur. Roara would read out a set of oaths, which Pessy would recite back, and then, she would be imprinted with the symbol of the Goddess of the Heart and Mind on the back of her neck. It was the part of the ceremony I hated the most—

the idea of Pess being branded made me sick, and as I knew from the few other Kylantians who'd experienced the ceremony, the process hurt.

Pessy always insisted she was excited about the whole thing, even the marking part. Through that symbol, she would be able to communicate with me even if we weren't physically together, and track my location if I was ever in peril.

We'd joked for years we were practically already bonded. This would only make it official.

As we re-entered the party, Pessy's eyes strayed to where Calliope stood with Luna, mid tossing her head back with a forceful laugh. The sense of yearning was pungent in Pessy's soft sigh.

"Pess." Her gaze shifted back to me. "You know I love you and have always thought of you as a sister…but I wouldn't go there with Callie. She kind of flirts with everyone."

"I know that," Pessy claimed, but the defensive edge underneath the assertion suggested she hoped she was a rare case.

"I'm just looking out for you." As much as I loved Callie, she had a streak for being a bit unreliable with people's hearts.

"I appreciate the concern, Tymp, but you have nothing to worry about." Pessy patted my hand. "I'm big and ugly and can take care of myself." I opened my mouth to object to her calling herself ugly when Roara's voice rang through the courtyard so vociferously, I wondered if the mortals below heard and jostled at the sound.

"Pessoranda Whitereaver," she boomed, settling under the arch. "Come forward to take your place."

"That's you!" I squealed, nudging her in the ribs. "Try not to scream when they brand you. It'll live in infamy if you do."

She flipped me the middle finger behind her back, then headed to where my mother was waiting for her.

Once it was empty, Jaxith stole Pessy's place at my side. He'd torn the red ribbon out of his hair, his long blonde strands now flowing to his shoulders.

"I like you better this way," I joked. He lifted a strand of his hair and swatted me with it.

Roara's brown eyes were clouded with affection, smiling at Pessy. Mergona's glazed over with tears as she watched Pessy kneel in the florae, her head bowed respectfully. She pulled her hair over her right shoulder to expose the back of her neck.

With the variegated petals encircling her and her burgundy dress making her hair appear even blonder, she looked like a nymph.

"Repeat after me," Roara said with a softness reserved for those she considered family. Pessy nodded without raising her head. "I, Pessoranda Whitereaver."

"I, Pessoranda Whitereaver," Pessy repeated, my heart swelling with pride.

"Promise to dedicate my life to the protection and well-being of the Goddess of the Heart and Mind."

"Promise to dedicate my life to the protection and well-being of the Goddess of the Heart and Mind."

"Until the last drop of my blood."

"Until the last drop of my blood." Pessy lifted her eyes to me, then added, "And even after that."

Pess.

I nearly choked on a sob.

Mergona peeled off from Roara's side, gripping in her hand a metal rod with my emblem at the top, which had been dipped in fire and singed a flaming, sizzling orange. She hovered over her daughter, taking a moment to marvel at the whole ordeal, then lowered the steel to Pessy's skin and pressed the seething crest into the back of her neck.

Pessy's shoulders tensed up. I heard her suck in a breath, but other than that, she didn't move a muscle.

Mergona kept the heated metal against Pessy's neck for a full minute. It was torture to stand there and watch. I didn't feel anything through the process, but I knew Pessy felt the bond flood her senses through the symbol embossed on her neck, her every thought, feeling, limb and organ adhering themselves to me. I was clutching Jax's hand the whole time so tautly that his fingers were red.

"Pessoranda Whitereaver, please rise as the newest member of the Kylantian army," her mother announced, beaming with pride.

The sea of Kylantians behind us roared as Pessy rose to her feet, releasing her hair from within her grasp and letting it trickle down over her shoulders. She turned back to look at me, where I stood a few feet away crying, her eyes filled with tears that I knew weren't because the ritual had injured her. She was feeling inundated with the honour of officially being bonded, as was I.

We'd waited a long time for this moment, and it had finally arrived.

I was the first person, rightfully, to grab her after, throwing my arms around her in a very unladylike manner. She was taller than me, so when I jumped on her, I wound my legs around her thighs and glommed on to her like a barnacle on the side of a ship, which was hard to do with this bulky dress.

"Did it hurt, Pess?" Calliope asked, moving Pessy's hair to the side to get a better look at the mark.

"Only a little." When she glanced at me, I knew she was minimising the pain to appear tough.

"She's mine now, folks," I cheered, raising her hand and shaking our intertwined fingers in the air.

"She's *always* been yours," Callie assured me, then winked at Pessy, who turned as red as her gown.

"We're so proud of you, Pess," Isaias said, joining our group by the arch and wrapping his arms around Pessy in a somewhat awkward, yet sweet embrace. He lowered his eyes over me, adding, "Both of you."

"Thank you, Isaias," Pessy mumbled softly, lifting the ends of her dress and curtseying before my father.

"You're like another daughter to us," Roara told her, as if Pess's cheeks couldn't get any rosier.

"Alright, don't inflate her ego more than it already is," I teased, Pessy sticking her tongue out at me.

I left the group to get more nectar, a bit drunk off the liquor and the effervesce threaded through the air. Everyone seemed to be in great spirits tonight. I could still hear the sound of merriment from the mortals below, entrenching itself deep in my soul. This night was something I wouldn't forget for as long as I lived.

"Are you having a good five thousandth?" I braced myself before spinning around to address my eldest brother.

"I am," I replied, watching Lucius down his glass of nectar in one gulp. Alarm sirens went off in my head. "How many of those have you had?" Lucius was irritating in general, but he was a dangerous, belligerent drunk.

"Relax, Mum. You've had more to drink than I have." I highly doubted that was true. He was bigger than me, and had a higher tolerance. For him to be swaying and slurring his words, he had to have had at least ten glasses already. "I noticed your portrait painting is nowhere to be seen."

31

Remembering what Roara said she'd use as an excuse, I lied, "Mother said it's not finished yet."

He surprised me with a snort.

"You're a terrible liar, Tympany. You want to know how I know? When you lie, your hands ball up into fists, and you get really still after, like you're just waiting for someone to call you out." He mimicked me by going completely rigid, then reached out to pat my shoulder. "No need to be a thief *and* a liar."

"Thief?" *What's he talking about?*

"I had an interesting conversation with Mother this morning." I raised my brows, waiting for him to get to the point. "I stole a peek at your portrait. You know…where you're wearing her crown."

Oh.

My mouth instantly dried, my skin pimpled with goosebumps. Now, I understood why he'd been such an ass all day.

His rage emanated off him in ripples.

"Can we go somewhere private to talk?" I didn't want any of the Kylantians, or our other siblings, to hear the content of our squabble.

"Let's." He gesticulated with his hand for me to go first, his smile nasty, littered with inebriation.

I lead Lucius over to the corridor, where the hum of the mortals below was encouraging against the apprehension stitching its way through my veins. I didn't want to be having this conversation at all, but especially not with an already furious, drunk Lucius. It was a disaster waiting to happen.

"I can explain," I started, but Lucius didn't give me the chance.

"You know, when *I* turned five thousand, Tympany, I was still a fetus. I didn't understand anything about the worlds. I'd never seen the Realm, or spoken to any humans. I'd never used my abilities outside of Kylantis. I was just like you, hungry for more, and yet, I was *still* more mature than you will ever be."

I blinked back tears, his words internalising, spilling fire into all the hollowed places of insecurity inside me.

"I've always thought you were so innocent. Sweet, kind of naïve about the worlds around you, but it was endearing, for a while. Now, I know it's all been an act. A mask you wore, so I wouldn't notice you stabbing me in the back."

"Stabbing you in the back?" That *had* to be the nectar talking. "You know me, Lucius. You think I planned this? Pretended to support you, just to steal the throne out from under you? I don't want it. I've never wanted it. I've told Mother that."

"Oh, please," he groaned, rolling his eyes. "There's no way you just turned down the crown like that."

"Not all of us are power hungry, like you." His laugh was bitter and callous. "I don't want to be Queen. I want to see the worlds. I want to explore the Realm, interact with humans, everything you just said. I've never wanted to be Queen. If you want the throne, Lucius, take it. It's yours."

His expression somehow sharpened with even more ire, which I didn't know was possible.

"You think I want your sloppy seconds, Tympany? Don't insult me."

"I'm not trying to. I'm trying to make you see, I'm not a threat to you. I've never wanted to be Queen. That's what Mother and Father want, not me."

"But they chose *you*. They back *you* as next in line, not *me,* their eldest son. *You,* their pathetic, immature, weak youngest daughter." He raked a hand through his brown hair, tugging at the strands. "Do you know what it feels like to be second best all the time? Always Mother's second choice. Never first. It's a *death sentence.*" He shook his head, spitting, "Of course *you* don't. You're Mummy and Daddy's perfect little *angel.*" I flinched at how he wielded that nickname as a weapon against me.

"That's not fair, Luce. And when have you ever been second best?"

"Every day of my *fucking* life, Tympany. I'm the most qualified, *literally* the brightest, and yet they *still* chose you."

"Have you ever stopped to consider if maybe that's *why* they chose me?" He jerked his head back in shock. "You think you walk on water. You think you're perfect, that you have no room to grow. Your main focus has always been *you*, what furthers *your* agenda. Now, I'm not saying I'm qualified to be Queen, but I have a hell of a higher EQ than you do. At the end of the day, *that* matters more."

"Is that so?" His words oozed derision.

"I thought you always say sarcasm says more about the one deflecting than the person it's aimed at," I fired back. His mouth sewed shut. "Governing Kylantis means more than just *this* domain. It includes the whole Realm, Sleotha *and* Esteopia. I'm sorry, Luce, but you have never been the type to take a step back and think about anything universally, not just the portions that benefit *you*. That doesn't exactly scream *sovereign* to me."

"Fuck you, Tympany," he growled.

"No, fuck *you*, Lucius. Fuck you for throwing a temper tantrum on my birthday. Fuck you for insinuating I've stolen this from you, when *nothing* belongs to you yet. Fuck you for calling me pathetic and weak, when I'm stronger and more emotionally mature than *you* will ever be. If you have a problem with Mother and Father's decision, take it up with them. It's not my fault Mother chose me over you."

Shit.

I shouldn't have said that. The minute the words escaped past my lips, I wanted to take them back.

Lucius's eyes, normally an amalgamation of orange and yellow, darkened to a burnt umber. One minute, he was in front of me, and the next, he'd leapt forward, seizing me by the throat, and shoved me against the wall. His hand glowed golden, sunlight pouring out from the tips of his fingers as he crushed my windpipe. The light blazed through my bloodstream, scalding me from the inside out.

It felt like someone lit a match in my organs and left the flame unsupervised to torch everything in its path.

"Lucius!" I wheezed, clawing at his fingers.

"It's supposed to be *me*," he roared, squeezing harder. "*I'm* the future of the Gods. Not you. *Me.*"

"Lu..." My words crumbled to ash in my mouth.

His grip around my throat was so blistering, I worried he'd permanently blemish my skin with his imprint.

"You're not fit to run Kylantis. You're barely fit to be a Goddess. You're *nothing*, Tympany. *Nothing.*"

I locked eyes with him and summoned my compulsion forward, demanding, **"LET ME GO."**

He immediately dropped his hand, backing away from me. He seemed startled by the way he'd capitulated, then put the pieces together. "You compelled me earlier. On the roof," he uttered in horror.

Once I regained the ability to breathe, I replied, "Not so pathetic after all. **Now go back to the party.**"

He turned on his heel without a moment's more hesitation, making his way back to the courtyard.

Once I was alone, I let out a strangled sob, sliding down the wall.

I clutched my enflamed throat, sucking precious air into my lungs and struggling to pace my breaths. I still felt like my insides were on fire, the lingering effects of his powers writhing in my tissue.

"Are you alright?" someone beside me asked.

"I'm fi—" I stopped myself from finishing, the voice not one I recognised.

I lifted my head, stifling a gasp. It was the man from the square, the mortal I'd spotted below.

He had to be the most beautiful creature I'd ever seen. His eyes were as dark blue and profound as a midnight sky, his pupils like orbs of onyx in an intemperate sea. Now that he was standing before me, I could see his cheeks were dusted with faint freckles. I had to catch myself from staring with my mouth open like a fool, clambering to my feet and putting a safe amount of distance between us.

"You're not supposed to be up here," I blurted, instantly regretting not saying something more threatening.

After all, I was a Goddess—he was just some feeble mortal poking around somewhere he didn't belong.

He took a step closer, then murmured, "I won't tell if you don't." His voice was deep and sonorous, but also strangely soft. There was a humorous edge to his statement, like he found this whole situation amusing rather than terrifying.

"How did you get up here?" Again, another stupid remark.

"I scaled a wall," he answered with a shrug, making it sound like that was something everyone was capable of doing.

"What wall?" *Seriously, Tympany? Could you sound more idiotic right now?* He chose not to acknowledge that.

"Are you okay? That looked like it hurt." It took me a moment to realise the implications of what he said.

He'd heard what Lucius and I talked about.

He'd watched the whole thing, which meant he knew exactly *who* I was, and *what* I was.

"You're not allowed to be here." My fingers closed into fists. I thanked my lucky stars Roara had allowed me to train with the Kylantian army, for now, that training would finally come in handy.

I dashed forward, dipping to the floor, and wrapped my foot around his ankle, tugging it towards me and forcing him down onto his back. He caught himself before plummeting to the ground, impressively flipping off his hands and straightening up in front of me. He fixed his cufflinks, dragging his eyes down my body rather brazenly.

Until this moment, I'd forgotten I was wearing a gown, which was especially fitted around the chest area.

"Try again, sweetheart," he goaded, grinning the kind of smile that would win any argument it provoked.

I spun, catching him in the abdomen with my foot, the heel of my shoe digging into his stomach. The man doubled back, gliding several feet away from me due to the force of my kick. He groaned, rubbing the spot I'd punted him. While he struggled to stand, I leapt off my feet, soaring in the air until I was right in front of him. I bent down and coiled my fingers around his throat, lifting him off the ground. He kicked his feet as he dangled, trying to rip my fingers off him, but to no avail.

"How's that for round two?" I said in my flattest voice. He stupefied me by flashing an alluring row of criminally white teeth.

"Stunning." He breathed.

My grip around his throat loosened fractionally in surprise, which was a mistake. He snatched my wrist, twisting it back, and hauled me to him after his feet landed on the floor, our chests pressed together. We ended up crashing into the stone wall, his weight pinioning me beneath him. He thrust his knee between my legs, pinning my arms on either side of my head. When I tried to lift up and heave him off, he surprisingly wouldn't budge. He shouldn't have been able to hold me down.

"I don't want to hurt you," he promised. I tasted the earnestness in his plea. "I just don't want you to hurt *me*."

This shouldn't have been possible. I was a Goddess—I had immortal strength, yet this human rather easily incapacitated me. There was only one explanation for this.

"You're not human," I realised.

"Neither are you," he stated, midnight blue eyes dancing waywardly.

I commanded, **"Forget what you've seen and walk away,"** watching his pupils enlarge, then shrink in response to my compulsion. But oddly, instead of following the order, his lips twisted into a wicked smile.

"You know what?" he replied, his grin widening further. "I think I'll stay."

What the fuck?!

It didn't work.

This had never happened before.

I was disturbed to my very core, every inch of me that had previously been on fire hardening to ice.

"Who are you?" I stuttered breathlessly.

"Me? I'm nobody," he said, his thumbs tracing the inside of my wrists. My stomach fluttered at the sensation, which unsettled me more than him being impervious to my compulsion did.

"I highly doubt that," I refuted. The man chuckled, licking his lips, and now, I couldn't tear my gaze away from his mouth, how his bottom lip was fuller than his top one, how his breath smelled of lilac.

"You're nothing like I imagined you'd be." I tensed, which only made this position more uncomfortable.

"If you meant that as an insult, I will tear you limb from limb. You have no idea who you're dealing with."

"Actually, I do," he reminded me, then leaned in closer, his warm breath on my face sending a shiver down my spine. I noticed then that he had a tiny birthmark in the shape of a teardrop on the back of his left ear. "And I swear, I meant that as a compliment. You are…magnificent." At last, he released my wrists and stepped back.

I straightened my posture to reach my highest height, raising my chin the way my mother did when she exuded confidence.

"Leave while you still can," I ordered, not bothering to use my compulsion again, since I knew it wouldn't work on him. He spread his hand out over where his heart beat in his chest, then bowed.

"Your wish is my command." I watched him walk down the corridor, head held high. When he reached the end of the hall, he twirled back around, leaving me with one last outstanding smile. "I hope we meet again…*angel*."

Then, he jumped off the balcony.

Chapter Three

I rushed down the corridor as fast as my legs could carry me, then gripped the railing and flung myself off the edge. I hurdled down the length of the palace, landing on my feet on the ground floor. There was no body. I searched all the rooms in the East Wing for the man, checking in the servant quarters, the kitchen, and the ballroom, but didn't find anything. I made my way back upstairs, peeking through one of the slit windows for any sign of him in the crowd of mortals.

He was gone.

Disappeared, as if he'd never existed at all.

I unconsciously rubbed my wrists, still itching from his touch, as I sagged against the wall, trying to wrap my brain around what just occurred.

A mortal somehow made it past the guards, into the palace, and was immune to my compulsion.

What *was* he?

No one was immune to my abilities, not even the other Gods. I'd never tried them on my mother and father, but always assumed they'd work if I did. Perhaps only the weak-minded were susceptible, those who didn't have the strength to resist being influenced. But that didn't explain why they'd worked on people like Pessy, Jax, or any of my other siblings, who were the opposite of spineless.

The more I thought about it, the more frustrated I became. I hadn't been able to defend myself. I took pride in being a skilled fighter, in having trained with the Kylantian army and being more adroit with my fists and a sword than Jax or Benjen.

But none of that had aided me when it really mattered.

I remembered what Mergona told me during one of our training sessions: "*Never* freeze, Tympany. You're only vulnerable when you're not moving." When that man had me pinned to the wall, I just…froze.

Magnificent.

That's what he'd called me. I looked down at my hands. I didn't feel all that magnificent right now.

I felt like a failure of a God.

Maybe Lucius was right about me after all.

"Tympany?" Pessy stood in the entrance of the corridor, radiating concern. "Hey. I've been looking for you everywhere."

"Sorry. I didn't mean to worry you." I came out of my miasma of despair, dashing to meet her.

"What happened? Are you okay? You look like you've seen a ghost." I contemplated lying to her, but remembered what Lucius said about my lack of proficiency when it came to being dishonest.

"There was a human," I told her, her eyes growing to the size of saucers. "He scaled a wall to get up here. I tried to fight him, but he was…stronger than me." I felt disgraced admitting that to her.

"That's impossible," she contested. I wished that were true. "Maybe it was because you were caught off guard. I've fought you before, Tymp, when you're completely focused and at full power. I *promise* you, you're stronger than *any* mortal would be. I have the scars to prove it."

"But that's just it. I don't think he was mortal. I tried to use my compulsion on him, but it didn't work."

She was stunned into silence—a first for Pessy.

"Can I try something?" Maybe my abilities were weakened when Lucius used his against me. After she'd given me permission, I stared deep into her eyes and commanded, **"Raise your right hand in the air."** She immediately submitted, lifting her arm up over her head.

Huh.

So that wasn't it.

"At least they still work," she said. I smiled half-heartedly at that. "Where did the man go, after you fought him?"

"He jumped off the ledge and disappeared. I looked for him all over the East Wing. I don't know where he went." I left out the part about him calling me magnificent, knowing she'd only tease me for it later.

"Wow. I would've loved to see that." Pessy may have wished she'd been there, but I was glad I hadn't had an audience for my epic flop. She inspected me closely, then asked, "Was he attractive?"

"Why would you ask me that?"

"Because you're all flushed." My cheeks burned hotter. I didn't even want to know how red I'd become.

"*No*," I asserted, but knew I wasn't convincing.

"Alright. Just wondering." She snickered at my frown. "Maybe we should look for him when we visit Sleotha."

"I'm not sure locating the one person my abilities don't work on is a good idea."

"Probably true…" Her voice trailed off when her eyes drifted over my neck. Her amusement evaporated in an instant, replaced with fierce rancor. "What happened here? Did he get his hands around you?"

I blanched, clutching my throat.

When Lucius was strangling me, I'd been concerned about his sunlight leaving behind an impression.

"I got into a fight with Lucius. He found out about Mother wanting to make me Queen and attacked me. I used my compulsion on him so he'd leave me alone. That's why I fought the human. He saw what happened."

"What?!" Her sky blue eyes flared, her fingers dancing over what must've been burn marks in the shape of his fingers. "I don't care that he's a God, and I'm supposed to worship him. I could kill him right now."

"I'm alright," I swore, half meaning it. While I was okay physically, that didn't extend emotionally. "Do you think I should be worried about what the human saw? That he'll tell someone about me becoming Queen?"

"I doubt it. He has to know, if he says anything and it gets back to the Gods, you guys will crucify him." She had a point there. "We'll deal with Lucius later," Pessy decided, linking her arm with mine. "I promise. Now, let's go have some much needed fun. It's still your birthday, after all."

Something happened then.

Before I could respond, I felt the most disconcerting feeling quiver down my spine, like someone was spilling ice into the back of my dress. I pulled Pessy back towards the festivities, surveying Jax, Callie, then the rest of my siblings to see if they felt it too. They looked just as frazzled.

Roara was trembling as well, while Isaias cringed.

The fact that the unsettling sensation had passed between all of us could only mean one thing.

Someone had prayed to the Gods.

The sound of fast paced footsteps grabbed my focus. My father's bonded Kylantian, Adam, emerged from the corridor. He beckoned Mergona over, and we all stood there barely breathing, just watching.

They conversed for a few moments before Mergona returned to us.

She looked more ashen than usual, the gravity of whatever it was he'd told her weighing down her every step.

"I apologise, Tympany, but the party will have to end now." My shoulders lowered, not from disappointment, but from concern.

"What about the mortals below?" Pessy asked.

"They've already been sent back down the Geddesia Mountains. The gates have been closed."

"What has happened, Mergona?" Roara demanded, wrapping her fingers around Isaias's wrist.

"The Queen of Sleotha has prayed for the Gods' intervention. There's been an attack."

Roara was already in her rightful seat at the heart of the space when we filed into the throne room one by one. Isaias stood behind her, as he always did during council meetings, his hand placed on her shoulder in a quiet show of support. The seating arrangements went in order of oldest to youngest, the left side reserved for the males, the right side for the women. Lucius's chair sat directly at Roara's left, followed by Caspian, Nox, Benjen, and last, Jaxith. On the right side, the first chair was always kept empty in honour of Hadestia—then Calliope, Luna, Eira, and lastly, me.

Lucius was already seated when I entered the room. He'd sobered up, but looked no less indignant than before. His head swung to me, ochre eyes scorching.

I clutched my still throbbing throat in reflex.

"Tympany. Come sit by me," Roara said, gesticulating to the vacant seat at her right side.

I knew what me sitting there would indicate to my other siblings, particularly Lucius, who was watching me like a hawk. But I couldn't say no to the Queen of the Gods, not in front of all these Kylantians, so I swallowed my qualms and headed for the chair I knew didn't belong to me.

I lowered down into it slowly, aware all eyes were on me.

The chair felt cold and incongruous, the shadow of Hadestia lingering over the limestone, rejecting my presence against it.

I glanced over at Jaxith, who looked confused, but also disappointed. I was too. I liked being directly in front of him during these meetings because we always made faces at each other. I was now sitting across from Lucius, the last place I wanted to be.

Pessy, as my official bonded guardian, was allowed to stay for the meeting, a first for us. She remained at my side, hands folded in front, glowering at Lucius and not being the least bit subtle about it.

Adam and Mergona stood in the center.

"Esteopian soldiers entered the capital undercover," Adam informed us, voice sounding out clear despite the distress I knew was simmering under the surface. "They were dressed in the Sleothian colours to gain entry. The crops that were about to be reaped for the winter were completely destroyed, as well as many of their livestock. They've prayed to the God of Food for help restoring the harvests that were lost."

"I can do that," Benjen said with a nod.

"They've also prayed to the Goddess of Snow to delay the start of winter, in order for them to have time to assemble enough crops for the off season." Eira didn't look happy about that request.

"I can hold off for a month, but no more than that."

"They will still appreciate thirty days of extra time," Adam replied, which didn't help remove Eira's frown.

"Was anyone injured in the crossfire?" Calliope asked.

"The city of Dennard was hit the hardest. It borders the countryside, where the fields are. Seventy lives were lost. Even more were severely wounded."

"Seventy?" Isaias repeated in dismay. Roara reached behind her, tangling her fingers with his.

"They believe the Esteopians were aiming for the produce. Those slaughtered were just in the way."

"Good Gods," Pessy muttered under her breath.

"Why did Esteopia attack? Were they provoked?" Everyone's eyes oscillated to me. I usually kept quiet during these meetings, only speaking when I was called upon, but it didn't make sense that Esteopia would destroy their crops and pillage their towns randomly without cause.

"Why does that matter?" Lucius snapped, the acidity of his tone making me shrink back. "What they did, regardless of the reason, was immoral. They deserve to be punished."

"I'm not saying they don't. What they've done is horrible. I just don't understand *why* they did it to begin with."

"Because they're at *war*. This is what people do at war, Tympany." I was *really* growing tired of his snobbish attitude. "If you paid any attention, you would remember the armistice between the kingdoms disbanded ten thousand years ago, after Esteopian soldiers raided the capital of Sleotha and slaughtered thousands of lives. If you're to sit in Hadestia's chair and pretend like you're the next heir to the throne, you should know this, *Tympany*."

I was shocked by his shameless admission, especially in front of our mother. I didn't have to look at my other siblings to know my jaw wasn't the only one that had dropped to the floor.

Roara was *not* having it.

"Tympany has not been included in conversations about the war," she snapped, sterner than I'd ever heard her. "This is her first time being involved in these discussions. Curb your impudence and give her time to catch up."

Lucius looked like he'd swallowed his tongue. "Yes, Mother," he murmured, sinking a bit in his chair.

"These actions clearly show they're gearing up for another battle," Nox stated, the air still crackling with the tension between Roara and Lucius.

"For them to target Sleotha's main source of sustenance is a pretty major sign," Callie concurred.

"We can try to stop them by cutting off their food supply," Luna suggested. "Casp can deny them access to the fish in the ocean by creating massive waves, or Eira can freeze the water."

"We can't deny them food," Benjen exclaimed in horror.

"I have to agree with Ben," Caspian piped up. "I'm not doing that."

"Why not? That's what they did to Sleotha, cutting them off at the source. It's an eye for an eye."

"You can't deny them food," Jaxith pressed. "That's unethical, no matter what they've done."

"No one asked you," Lucius grumbled, evading Roara's glare.

"Someone has to be the voice a reason." That made me smile. "I know we support Sleotha, but there has to be another way to aid them than starving all of

Esteopia. They're still our people, or have you forgotten." Jax directed his scowl at Lucius, who flipped him off.

While everyone began bickering over ways to assist Sleotha, Roara inclined towards where I was fiddling with my fingers in my lap, pulling at my knuckles to the point of nearing disjoining them.

"Tympany? Do you have anything to add?" A blanket of silence swept over the room when she addressed me.

I hated how she put me on the spot like that, but I had given this some thought. The ways everyone was suggesting were only solutions that would hold them off temporary, but not for forever. If we wanted to assist Sleotha in the war, the real way they'd win would be by knowing exactly what Esteopia was planning beforehand.

"I...I might have an idea." Roara waved her hand, willing me to speak. I took a deep breath, then described my plan. "Cutting off their food supply would slow them down only temporarily. It wouldn't stop them from striking eventually. It's inevitable. I think, the best way to help, would be for one of us to go to Esteopia. They can go undercover, disguising themselves as godly support for the war, and gather intel, learn what they're planning, so we can give Sleotha the advantage."

I wasn't used to having this many eyes on me, or having the floor during a council meeting at all.

It was actually pretty empowering.

"I think that's a wonderful idea, Tympany," Roara esteemed, reaching over to squeeze my hand.

"I can go," Caspian offered. "I spend the most time there due to the ocean. The King and Queen know me."

"No offense, Casp, but I don't think it should be you." He cocked his head at me in surprise. "Not that I don't think your personal relationship with the crown could be beneficial, but...they've prayed to you before, many times. They'll question why you haven't intervened sooner. For them to believe we're backing them seriously, I think someone who they haven't met should go."

"She's right," Jax chimed in. Caspian nodded, not putting up a fight, like I'd expected him to.

"And who might that be, then?" Lucius's voice was contemptuous.

I suppressed my nerves, straightened my posture to match our mother's stance, and declared, "Me."

A compilation of gasps echoed from all corners of the room, from both the Kylantians and the Gods. Roara's face plummeted—she hadn't expected my plan to include me leaving Kylantis.

"I've never been to either of the kingdoms. The King and Queen of Esteopia would know this. They'd recognise that as a sign of good faith, someone willing to heed their call who hasn't been to Sleotha and isn't tainted by the stories told of them."

"It's too dangerous, Tympany," Roara argued, trying to find any excuse to deny my request. "You can't go alone."

"I wouldn't go alone," I said, inspiration striking. "Pessy would come with me." I didn't have to see her to know she was beaming behind me.

"You would need more protection than just Pessy. No offense, Pess," Roara directed at my best friend.

"None taken," she replied with a smirk.

"We can travel with as many Kylantians as will make you feel comfortable, Mother," I conceded to appease her.

"That is a horrible idea," Lucius, of course, had to refute.

"Actually, it could work." Caspian's approval was essential to my argument, considering he was the most familiar with Esteopia out of all of the Gods. "The King and Queen would be ecstatic Tympany chose Esteopia as her first kingdom to visit. It'll make them more inclined to believe she's serious about backing them. It's kind of brilliant."

"*Thank you.*" I wanted to hug him.

"I think Tympany is the perfect person to go," Jax agreed from across the room, warming my heart.

"Is everyone forgetting she's a *muse?*" Lucius yelled. "Just her mere presence stimulates motivation. She might inspire Esteopia to strike sooner."

"But I can also—"

"We'd be handing them a victory by sending her there," he interrupted, and then I *really* had enough.

"Let me TALK."

Lucius's lips glued together and wouldn't unfasten, no matter how hard he tried to rip them apart. His eyes enlarged with panic at the realisation he wouldn't be able to speak until I was done.

I didn't mean to use my abilities on him. My wrath summoned my compulsion all on its own, which had never happened to me before. Usually, I needed to be looking at the person to compel them. I hadn't been looking at Lucius when I'd said that.

"Tympany, don't compel your siblings," Roara admonished, but I think she secretly loved that I'd used my powers on Lucius.

"Sorry. What I was *going* to say was that I can also control them." While I despised the idea of abusing my power that way with mortals, I wasn't going to let Lucius take this opportunity away from me on a technicality. "As you can *see*," I gestured to Lucius's current state, "I can stop them from attacking, keep them at bay until Sleotha has all the information they need to beat them." I deliberately waited a second, watching Lucius squirm, then declared, "*Now* I'm done."

The moment he was free, Lucius sprang out of his chair.

"Can't you see she's *dangerous?* Not to mention she's still young, and could be easily influenced. She's a liability."

"Just because she compelled you to shut up when you were being an ass doesn't mean she's a liability," Luna scoffed.

"She compelled Jax this morning to steal nectar from the kitchen. She compelled *me* to leave the roof when I caught them, then compelled me again at her party. She just compelled me without even looking at me! Her powers are clearly growing stronger." I wasn't sure that was true—the man I'd failed to compel came to mind, but I kept that to myself. "She's out of control."

"Out of control?!" I was good at keeping quiet, but when someone tried to call my character into question, someone who was describing *himself,* not me, I wouldn't be docile. "*I'm* not the one who attacked one of my siblings tonight!"

"Wait, what?" Roara shifted to me in horror. "What're you talking about?"

"Tympany, *don't,*" he threatened.

I lifted the strands of my hair off my shoulders, exposing Lucius's birthday present to the room.

"What my brother failed to mention was that he strangled me tonight with sunshine. I only compelled him so he would leave me alone."

"Lucius!" Isaias cried, while Roara tilted over, skimming the tips of her fingers over the marks. When her palms radiated a silver light, I knew she was healing the wounds so they wouldn't scar.

"You're one to talk about who's in control, and who isn't," I snarled at Lucius, leaning back in my chair. "Now, I motion to take this debate to a vote. Majority wins. All those in favour of me traveling to Esteopia, raise your hand."

Jaxith was the first hand that shot up, Caspian's second. Callie was third, Luna, Benjen, and Nox following shortly after. Eira was too busy stewing about having to delay winter a month to notice what was happening around her. I wasn't sure she'd even been following the conversation.

The vote that counted the most to me was Isaias's. His hand soared above his head, his smile laced with pride.

"All those opposed." Lucius raised his hand high, as if that would multiply the influence of his singular vote.

I turned to my mother, who had yet to make a decision. I seized her hand, giving it a gentle, entreating squeeze.

I repeated my words from earlier.

"Let me live. Please." Her eyes softened with maternal love before she exhaled a conceding sigh.

"Alright. Effective tomorrow, Tympany will go to Esteopia and gather intel on their plans for Sleotha. She'll report back to us, and we will help Sleotha win the war."

I bit my lip to stifle a squeal, channelling all of my excitement into Pessy's proffered hand.

Victory never tasted so sweet.

"You should expect to leave early in the morning, so you can make the ride in a day's time," Mergona recommended. It made me realise—I didn't really know anything about Esteopia.

"This might be a stupid question, but...how do you *get* to Esteopia?" I only ever knew the route to Sleotha, since it was directly accessible to us through the Geddesia Mountains.

I noticed, from the corner of my eye, Lucius roll his eyes.

"You go down the Geddesia Mountains, through the Dream Forest, and enter Esteopia through its capital, Acadia," Mergona explained. "You'll know you've reached it when you spot their massive gates."

"You don't want to spend a night in the Dream Forest," Jaxith inserted, bristling from memories. "It's not fun."

"Good to know," I mumbled, though now I was curious to learn what he meant.

"Before you go, I think you should be armed with everything there is to know about Esteopia, so you're prepared." Caspian then offered, "I can answer any questions you might have."

Gods, where do I begin? "Tell me about the royals." I felt like that was a good place to start.

"Demetrio and Seraphina are the King and Queen. They have two children, Blekket and Raevon."

"Who's next in line?"

"Blekket, but he doesn't want to be king." *That sounds familiar.*

"Are the royals mortal, like the villagers? Or are they of a special bloodline?" I'd always wondered about that.

"The Elrods live a mortal lifespan, but they're not mortal. You know Esteopia borders the Argent Ocean, right?" I nodded. "The Elrods have been around since the creation of the kingdom. They're linked to the sea. They're actually classified as Neraids, not humans. They're born in the ocean, but can also live on land. They look human, but they pull their strength from the water."

"Kind of like you?" All at once, he got smug.

"*Nothing* like me," he fired back, annoyed at the suggestion that his abilities were in any way comparable to theirs. "I can bend water to my will. I can summon floods with my mind, can cause rainstorms with the snap of my fingers."

"I don't need a history lesson on your powers, Casp. I know what you can do. I didn't mean to wound your precious ego by suggesting otherwise." Pessy snorted into the back of her palm, feigning a cough to muffle the sound. Ignoring that, Caspian continued.

"So, to answer your question, they're not mortal. They're stronger than a mortal would be."

This brought me back to the man I'd fought earlier tonight. "Are the royals from Sleotha of a special bloodline too?" Caspian's brows furrowed at the random direction I'd taken before he nodded.

"Yes, but they're not Neraids. They draw their strength from the land, not from water." *Huh.* So maybe that man was a royal from Sleotha. "Why do you ask?"

"No reason." I shrugged to play off my interest. He decided it wasn't worth further investigating and resumed his instructions.

"I'd advise you not to use your compulsion right away, or in public. When you use it on someone, I'd do it in private, one on one."

"Why?" The corners of Caspian's lips twitched upward.

"When you use your abilities, your eyes glow. Normally, they're green, but when you compel someone, they turn gold. The person wouldn't notice it in the moment, but someone looking from the outside would."

"*What?* How have I never known that?" I frowned at my parents.

"It was the one advantage we had over you," Isaias replied, making even Roara smile.

I grumbled under my breath, then turned back to Caspian. "What else do I need to know about Esteopia?"

"There are some creatures you should look out for when you're there. Ashrays look like horses, but when they're exposed to sunlight, they melt into puddles. Be careful if you decide to ride any horse like creatures while you're there. You probably won't if you bring Krystal, but just something to look out for. Phorcydes are gorgons that live in caves. They have sharp fangs and hair of venomous snakes. I've never seen one, but I'd stay clear of any caverns just in case. Kappas are intelligent water spirits. They're monkey-like creatures with saucer-shaped heads, long noses, and yellowish-green skin. If one ever attacks you, make sure you hit their head against something solid, and do it hard. Their heads are full of water, and when it's spilled out, they lose their powers."

I was taking mental notes as he spoke, cataloguing all the creatures and tucking them into a box in the back of my brain for safekeeping.

"Do sirens and mermaids exist?"

"Sirens, no. Mermaids, yes. Mermaids are wonderful creatures. It's a common misconception that mermaids can't walk on land. They can. Actually, do me a favour, would you? If you happen to meet the mermaid Solara, tell them I say hello." The tone of his voice changed subtly, softening when he said their name.

I wondered if they were close.

"Does the Esteopian army have any sort of powers? You know, like the Kylantian army's strength and speed?"

"The soldiers in the Esteopian army are also Neraids, but not as strong as the Elrods. The Elrods are of a royal bloodline, so their much more potent than a regular Neraid, but they're still stronger than a human."

"Interesting. Are they also—"

"Good Gods, do we have to sit here and listen to these two drone on for the rest of the night?" Lucius groaned.

Until this moment, I'd totally forgotten we were still in the throne room.

"Yes," Isaias replied, icy with contempt. "Or, at least *you* have to. Everyone else can go, if they'd like."

"Actually," Roara interrupted, patting her husband's hand, her silent way of telling him to cool off, "I think we should all stop for now. I can answer any more questions Tympany may have tomorrow, but it's been a long night. Everyone, go get some rest. We'll reconvene in the early morning."

She flicked her wrist, bidding the door to the throne room to open, a signal that the meeting was adjourned.

As we each rose from our chairs, Roara called out, "Lucius. Stay back," her expression now as arctic as her husband's threat had been. I took pleasure in knowing he would be reprimanded for strangling me, no longer feeling guilty about outing him to our parents.

Once we'd shuffled into the hall, Pessy and I lingered a moment, exchanging a look full of emotion. We would wait until we'd returned to my bedchamber to celebrate our triumph, but our smiles said everything we were thinking.

The uproar coming from the throne room broadcasted like a clap of thunder, quaking the whole palace. It quieted a moment, and then, Lucius appeared in the entryway, swearing under his breath.

His eyes lowered over me before he began marching towards where I stood, ochre eyes blazing with hatred. Pessy threw herself in front of me, fists raised in preparation for an attack. Jax blocked his path, setting a hand on Lucius's chest to shove him back.

"I wouldn't," he threatened.

Lucius peered around Jaxith and growled at me, "Thanks to *you,* I'm stuck in Kylantis until you return from Esteopia. You're such a little tattle tale." It was amazing he'd accused *me* of immaturity.

"It's not Tympany's fault," Nox interjected, coming to my defense. "You brought this on yourself."

"I didn't tattle on you purposefully, Lucius." I was grateful for my brothers' intervention, but didn't need them to fight my battles. "I actually planned to keep what happened tonight to myself, but *you're* the one who brought up me compelling you in the corridor without mentioning what provoked me to do it."

"I didn't provoke you earlier when you compelled Jaxith to steal nectar from the kitchen."

"Jax stole the nectar at his own volition," I insisted. "I didn't compel or inspire him to do it."

"I'm capable of making my own bad decisions," Jax asserted.

"Leave her alone," Calliope said, adding, "You're just jealous Mother chose Tympany to succeed her on the throne over you."

"Stay out of this, Callie," Lucius snarled. She backed away with her hands up, not wishing to enrage him further.

"First Hadestia, now Tympany…" Eira threw over her shoulder, "Must suck to always be second best, Luce."

Lucius turned on her, raising a hand saturated with sunshine to strike her. She squeezed her fingers into a taut fist and narrowed glacial eyes, drenching his hand in snow, which offset the light and immobilised his fingers.

He gasped, summoning a kindle of fire from the center of his palm to melt the snow from his skin.

"Bitch!" He started towards her again.

"All of you, knock it off!" Isaias thundered from the doorway of the throne room, having witnessed the whole fight. He managed to catch Lucius's wrist before he made it one more step towards Eira. "If you're going to act like children, then I'm going to treat you as such. Go to bed. *Now.*"

He released Lucius's arm, then marched towards his and Roara's quarters without giving us another look.

Lucius glared at Eira, spitting, "This isn't over. I'll get you."

"When Nekropolis freezes over," she sneered, the tips of her fingers flickering a white light as she wiggled them in a jeering wave.

After Lucius fled the hall and the crowd began to clear, Jax asked me, "Are you okay?"

"Am *I* okay? I'm not the one he just tried to attack." I turned to Eira. "You didn't have to do that."

"I know. I wanted to." She smiled impishly. "I'd do it again."

I didn't always see eye to eye with Eira, but in this moment, she was my new favourite sibling.

"Don't listen to a word he says," Benjen advised as we started strolling towards the subdivision of the palace he, Jaxith, Calliope and I shared. "He's always been a jealous bastard."

"It's a good thing Mother forbade him from leaving Kylantis until you return from Esteopia," Jax added. "You've been stuck up here for eons. Serves him right. It's *his* turn to be detained."

"Are you excited?" Callie grabbed my arm, shaking it. "You're finally getting to see the Realm! What you've always wanted!"

"I know," I murmured, fighting a yawn. I was so many different emotions at once that it was difficult to latch onto one and identify it as the predominant feeling. When we'd first left the throne room, I was brimming with joy, but after the quarrel between Lucius and Eira, I was utterly exhausted.

"So...Mother wants you to be the next Queen?" Jax's question woke me from my stupor.

I'd forgotten, in the throes of all the chaos, that I hadn't spoken about this with any of my siblings.

"That's what *she* wants. Not me. I told her, I'm not ready." Calliope nodded, seeming impressed.

"Good for you for standing your ground," Ben praised. "You shouldn't take the throne until you're absolutely certain it's what you want."

"I agree," Callie said, rubbing my shoulder. Something Eira said suddenly struck me.

"Was Hadestia supposed to take the throne after Mother, before she left for Nekropolis?" When Lucius griped earlier about always being the second choice, I hadn't understood where he'd gotten that from.

"That's what Mother intended." Jaxith explained, "Hadestia was supposed to devote her time to both Nekropolis and Kylantis equally, but she chose to live solely in Nekropolis. No one knows why, not even Mother. I always assumed Lucius was her top choice to take the throne after Hadestia, but I'm relieved to know she chose you instead. You're a way better person than he is." I had to laugh at that.

I said goodnight to my brothers and sister in the hall, heading with Pessy to my bedchamber.

Once the door was sealed shut, we both erupted.

"Holy shit!" she squealed, jumping up and down with elation. "We're leaving Kylantis! Together!"

"I know!" It still didn't feel real.

"I was *so* proud of you in there." Pessy began to undo the ties at the back of my bustier, relieving the pressure of the corset around my ribs. For the first time in hours, when I exhaled a breath, it didn't ache. "You handled Lucius like a *boss*, even though I know you were scared." The gown crashed down to my ankles. After Pessy helped me step out of it, I crossed the room to my dresser, climbing into a sheer, cream slip with thin straps, the dress spilling down to my mid-calf. I bunched the skirt in my hand, crawled into bed, then arranged the velvet grey covers over my bare legs.

"You want to stay in here with me tonight? Since we're both waking up early to leave?"

"I would," she replied, "but if tonight's my last night in Kylantis for a while, I want to spend it with my mum."

My heart warmed, then sunk with remorse. Pessy and Mergona were inseparable. I felt guilty for stealing Pess away from her mother, since we didn't know how long we'd be in Esteopia.

"Before you go, can we try to communicate through the bond?" We hadn't gotten a chance to try it out, with all that transpired and being called into an emergency council meeting.

"Oh, yes!" Pessy plopped down at the foot of the bed, squaring her shoulders so it was clear she meant business.

She closed her eyes, her forehead wrinkling with concentration. When the voice in my head reverberated, it wasn't my voice ringing back at me.

Tymp? Can you hear me?

Pessy's high-pitched cadence filled my brain. I shut my eyes, visualising my lips saying the words, "I can hear you, Pess."

"I heard you!" she yelped, clapping her hands and kicking her feet. "That's so cool!"

"It'll come in handy when we want to shit talk someone," I said, her adorable giggle saturating the room.

"Alright, missy. We have to wake up early tomorrow, so, as your *official* guardian, it's time to go to sleep now." She steered a firm finger in my face, then directed it towards my pillow. "Lie your pretty head down and go to sleep."

"Yes, ma'am." I curled around my pillow, watching Pessy from the corner of my eye head for the door. "Pess?"

"Yeah, Tymp?" She spun around to face me.

"Thank you. For what you said during the ritual." Her eyes softened.

"I hope it never comes to that."

"Me neither." She waved goodbye, then flicked the lights off and shut the door.

I rolled onto my back, staring up at the diaphanous grey canopy that rounded over my bed.

What a day.

From the argument with Roara over the painting, to the party itself, my fight with Lucius and then the encounter with that man in the corridor, I hadn't had a chance to process any of it, or the fact that I was now five-thousand-years-old. I couldn't believe I'd actually lived that long. I'd waited forever to reach this milestone, enduring the monotony of the palace as patiently as I could until it was my time to be considered a full-fledged Goddess. I'd watched, after they each turned five thousand, the change in how my siblings were treated and viewed, in both society and in the eyes of our parents. I saw how they were included more in decisions regarding the Realm, gifted additional responsibility and given the space to develop their powers.

Now that it was finally my turn, it felt surreal, like I still wasn't quite old enough to be awarded this freedom.

I thought about what Lucius said about my powers growing stronger. Was that because I'd reached the full age of adulthood for a God? I didn't feel any different physically than I had yesterday.

I found it strange how much weight age could carry, when at the end of the day, it was just a number. It didn't determine someone's capability or readiness for something, no matter how old that person may be. Lucius was a prime example of where age didn't always equal aptitude.

I pulled my comforter over my head and snuggled my pillow. In the dark, I let my lips form a smile, because I knew, when I opened my eyes to a new day, I was getting what I'd always wanted.

I was finally leaving Kylantis.

Chapter Four

I didn't sleep that night.

I tried, but I was too revved up. I spent half the night tossing and turning. Then, after determining that sleep would evade me, I crept out of my room and headed for the East Wing library, sinking into one of the velvet teal winged back chairs with a blanket draped over my legs. I started with a novel I found on mythic creatures in the Realm, flipping to the Esteopia chapter. I read about a lake monster named Jeka that lived in Lake Azrord, a gigantic green serpent with a white stomach and grey thorns sticking out of her spine. Then, in the section on the Argent Ocean, I read about the Hippocampi, sea-horse creatures with the upper body of a horse and the lower body of a fish, with iridescent, polychrome scales.

While the Ashray horses stood as a symbol for Esteopia's resilience and were depicted on the flag, the Hippocampi were how the Neraids travelled through the waters.

I learned through my reading that this was also how the Neraids gathered their food—they relied on the Hippocampi to help them locate the fish in the ocean, and on monsters like Jeka in the lakes. They grew their own grain in the village, but aside from fish, they had no access to meat. This was one of the things they traded with Sleotha for, Argent Ocean water for meat, as well as various other crops the Sleothians harvested in the fields.

It made me wonder—why would they destroy Sleotha's crops, if they too benefited from the agriculture?

Though I understood it from the standpoint of screwing over Sleotha, wouldn't it negatively impact Esteopia to not have those crops reaped? It was something I planned to ask the King and Queen myself.

After that, I moved on to a book about the ancestry of the Esteopian royal family. Caspian's explanation was confirmed in the text, but in more detail—the Elrods had been in power since the creation of the kingdom. Esteopia was named after the first Princess, whom the original King and Queen, Alden and Lavinia Elrod, had gifted the empire to once she reached the age of thirty. Similarly to Kylantis, Esteopia was a matriarchy, meaning the Queen had more sway than the King. When the current Queen and King wed, Demetrio took Seraphina's last name, not the other way around, like in archaic tradition.

I wasn't sure why, but reading that made me strangely certain I would like Seraphina when I met her.

There wasn't much written about Demetrio and Seraphina's children, which I found sort of bizarre, but I assumed they wouldn't be transcribed in history until one of them ascended the throne.

When dappled sunlight dribbled in through the gossamer fabric of the curtains, sprinkling onto the page of my text, I closed the book and made my way back to my bedchamber to get ready for the day ahead. As I got dressed, I thought about the Elrods, wondering if they were like the Sleothian royal I'd met the night before.

What if, because they were royals, I couldn't compel them?

It would dismantle the whole plan if I had no influence over them. These were thoughts I had to keep to myself, though. If I voiced any of them, Roara wouldn't let me near Esteopia.

I'd been careful in selecting my attire for the road. I chose a grey jumpsuit that had one shoulder, the other side sleeveless, with floor length chiffon draping down the side. It was formal enough, but I'd have no problem riding Krystal in it. I wrapped a leather belt around my waist and tucked my favourite blade into the sheath, the weapon made of gilt with my emblem of a heart and mind emblazoned on the grip.

I strapped a pair of black sandals to my feet, leaving my hair down for the time being, though once we got on the road and were a safe distance away from Kylantis and my mother, I'd tie it back.

Pessy was waiting for me in the hall when I emerged from my bedchamber. She was dressed in her official Kylantian uniform, the waist cape fitted around her curvy torso. There was a sword stashed in the holster at her side, and she was gripping the hilt like she half expected someone to round the corner and attack us at any moment.

"Look at you!" I exclaimed, making her twirl for me. "You're so official!"

"I know," she laughed, pretending to flip her hair over her shoulder, even though it was tightly woven back in an intricate bun. "You ready?"

I wasn't sure if she was referring to heading for the stables to retrieve our horses, or leaving Kylantis in general.

Regardless, the answer was, "Yes."

We headed down the spiral marble staircase, neither one of us saying a word, because we had nothing to say. The excitement yawned out between us, threading us together as we made our way outside. We were a five minute walk from the stables—we remained on the stone path, composed of circular pebble tiles that shimmered in direct sunlight. I took a moment to admire the landscape, a marriage of rainbow hues congregated in the clouds. The leaves of the trees, like all the trees in Kylantis, were painted the signature colours of the Gods, red, orange, yellow, blue, purple, silver, grey, and white, all except green. The trunks were gold-plated in honour of Roara. A massive barn blossomed on the hill amid the meadow flowers, the wood it was fashioned from painted gold like the tree bark that surrounded it.

Though the timbers were aged and the light that streamed in from the perforated roof illuminated the dust like ethereal confetti, the structure was one of the pillars of Kylantis. If the barn was absent from the picture, the landscape would be missing something integral. It just belonged there, a beacon in the sun.

Roara and Mergona were standing outside the stables when Pessy and I arrived.

"Are you ready?" Roara asked me. I sensed her wish for my answer to be no underneath her words.

"I am," I promised, meaning it.

She scrutinised me hard, then seemed to determine I was being honest before leading me and Pessy inside.

The reason the stables were so mammoth in size was because they housed every horse in Kylantis. The booths were split up by families, horses that belonged to the same owner kept in the same stalls. For the Pegasi of the Gods, each were contained in their own cubicles, away from the other Kylantian steeds. As we approached my Pegasus, Krystal sensed my presence and raised her head from the bowl of water she was kneeling in front of, her amber-green eyes that matched my own radiating excitement at the sight of me. Krystal resembled the shape and colour of an Andalusian horse. Her coat was considered grey, but she was more white with spots of grey lining her abdomen and down her legs, the dots taking a beat before picking back up around her neck. She was strongly built, compact, and elegant, with a thick, dark mane and tail. Pressed up against her sides were her white feather wings, which, when completely unfurled, were nearly a yard in length.

"Hi, girl," I greeted her, Krystal nuzzling my palm. "Our dream's coming true. We're finally getting out of here."

Krystal neighed with delight.

I looked over at Pess, who was greeting her horse, Belgian. Belgian was a Friesian, and she'd named him that because the type of horse was known to be Belgian black. He was powerfully muscled, with a full flowing mane and tail. His feathered feet were typical of a draft breed, but he was built like a lighter riding horse. Pessy and I found immense pleasure in the fact that Krystal and Belgian were obsessed with one another, and took it as a symbol of our bond transferring to them.

I was surprised to see how many Kylantians were in here, preparing their horses for the journey. I predicted Roara would allot several Kylantians to my protection detail, but I'd expected five, maybe ten at most. I counted a hundred in total, not including Pessy.

"Is a hundred really necessary?" I asked. "Shouldn't we be more inconspicuous?"

Roara lowered her eyes in daggers. "Yes, Tympany. A hundred is necessary." This wouldn't be up for discussion. "Mergona, bring Krystal out front for Tympany."

"Yes, Your Grace." Mergona opened the stable door, slipping inside to free Krystal from her halter.

While Mergona tended to Krystal, I strolled over to Pessy and Belgian. I reached up, stroking the backside of Belgian's long neck. He let out a purr that was really more akin to the sound a feline makes.

"He thinks he's a cat," Pessy said, laughing when he licked her cheek.

"He's definitely got the soul of a lion. Don't you, Bel?" He nodded his head in agreement, and I rewarded him with a scratch behind his ear.

From the corner of my eye, I spotted Harrison Rottweiler heading towards us. Harrison and Pessy trained in the Kylantian army together and had always been rivals. He was a know-it-all who couldn't stand not being in command and felt threatened by any woman more talented than him. He wasn't bonded to any of the Gods, but if he was going to be bonded to anyone, it would be Lucius—they were friendly, and similar in temperament. He'd never done anything to me personally, but he didn't need to for me to despise him. All I needed to know was that Pessy hated him.

That was reason enough for me.

"Hi, Pest," he greeted her with a nasty smile, blonde hair sticking up in strange places, as though he'd been rolling around in the grass. When she spotted him, Pessy reached for her sword.

"No. Absolutely not. Stay back before I cut your hand off, Rottwiener."

"That's no way to treat a *senior* Kylantian." I knew it was a sore spot for Pessy that Harrison had graduated and been inducted into the Kylantian army before her, but the only reason she wasn't initiated sooner was because they'd been waiting to bond her to me when I turned five thousand.

"The only thing senior about you is your massive head," she snarled. "And I think, now that I'm bonded to a *Goddess,* I outrank you."

His eyes darkened. "You've been a Kylantian for not even a full day. I was top of our class. Just because your mother is bonded to the Queen of the Gods doesn't mean you're special, *Pessoranda.*"

"Do you have to be the worst in every possible way?" She swatted at him as if he were a pesky insect. "Get the fuck out of my face, Harrison."

"I can't. You're stuck with me."

When she realised what he meant in saying that, without giving him, or me, another look, Pessy marched over to Mergona, who was struggling to get Krystal to leave the comfort of her stall.

"Mum, *please* tell me Harrison Rottweiler, evil incarnate, *isn't* coming with us to Esteopia."

"I'm sorry, my love," Mergona said distractedly, Krystal nearly trampling her to get to where I was. I relieved Mergona of the hassle, taking Krystal's reins and caressing her chin groove in an effort to calm her down. Once she was in my possession, she relaxed.

"I would rather stick a needle in my eye than travel with that bastard anywhere," Pessy griped.

"I'm sorry, Pess, but Roara specifically requested he join you. He's top of his division. He's coming." Pessy's eyes enlarged before she fluttered her lashes and protruded her bottom lip in an exaggerated pout, putting on her best, beseeching puppy dog look. "That's not going to work on me," her mother guaranteed. "And I wouldn't try it on Roara either." Pessy slumped, then quickly turned to me.

"Could you maybe…compel your mum?" She'd never asked me to do something like that before. I opened my mouth to respond, but Pessy cut me off, rushing, "Forget I said that. That was so selfish of me to ask you to do."

"It was," Mergona agreed, scowling at her with disapproval.

"We're still getting our wish of leaving Kylantis together," I reminded her. "Not even Harrison can ruin that."

Pessy smiled, squeezing my hand.

"You're right, Tymp. I'm being stupid. Letting Harrison Rottweiler steal my joy is beneath me."

She shook her head like she was ridding her brain of every bad thought, then straightened her posture.

I knew it was time when Roara flicked her wrist and opened the doors to the stables. I didn't have to mount Krystal like one would normally climb onto a horse. I didn't need the stirrups. Gripping her saddle for extra support, I jumped and lifted myself effortlessly onto her, situating in the middle of her back. The feathers of her wings tickled my calves through the material of my jumpsuit.

Roara, with no preamble, leapt onto Krystal and nestled herself behind me, wrapping her arms around my waist.

We began our trek to the gates, Pessy and Mergona leading the way on Belgian. We were besieged from all corners with Kylantians on their steeds, forming a shield around where Roara and I rode.

"How're you feeling?" she asked me, her chin grazing the back of my skull. "About leaving?"

The nerves had started to settle in, but I was afraid, if I told her, she'd convince me this was a bad idea.

"I'm excited," I answered, which was still true underneath the anxiety. I paused, then admitted, "I'm going to miss you."

"You can always come home," she promised, her voice hoarse. "Whenever you want, angel. If halfway through the ride, you decide this was a mistake, just turn back. We'll all be here waiting for you."

I didn't like the implication that everyone was expecting me to regret my decision and run home at the first sign of trouble, but I knew the sentiment was one of support, not doubt in my ability to handle what was being asked of me.

"I know," I whispered, and she squeezed my waist.

"I know it hasn't always seemed like it, but I'll support you in anything you decide to do. I'm proud of you for stepping up this way. It's scary, venturing out into the world, but I know you're ready. This is your time." She said the last part wistfully, like she wished it wasn't true.

As we passed the lower courtyard of the palace, the gilded gates to Kylantis came into view. The wrought-iron metal was shaped elaborately, fashioned of concentrated light. It was half in the direct line of the sun, and half shrouded in the shadow of the Geddesia Mountains. I touched my palm against the metal, not hot from the sunshine or cold from the shade. It was as if the metal was so weightless, it would disintegrate, as if the atoms themselves were going to choose to be free at any moment to form something new. Yet I knew it was just an illusion. If anyone tried to slice through the gold, they would be fried on impact. The gates looked fragile, but were impenetrable.

Waiting for us at the entrance was seven out of nine of my siblings. I wasn't offended that Lucius hadn't come to say goodbye. He was never the type to show support for something after first disapproving.

I dismounted Krystal, landing on my feet on the gravel, then waltzed into my father's opened arms.

"My sweet girl," he cooed, his voice gruff with tears. "Promise me you'll stay true to yourself. That you'll continue to lead with your heart, and know when to lean on your mind for guidance."

"I promise," I whimpered into his chest. "I love you, Father."

"I love you to Nekropolis and back, darling. Until my last drop." When he cupped the side of my face, I felt like my insides were crumbling. I was passed next to Caspian, who wrapped me in a surprisingly tight hug.

"Between you and me, you've always been my favourite sister," he whispered, and then I had to close my arms around his waist and squeeze with all my might. "I think what you're doing is badass. The idea of infiltrating Esteopia from the inside never would've crossed my mind. You deserve all the praise you get, Tymp."

"Casp." I was definitely going to cry.

"I'm not worried about you at all," Nox declared, twirling a strand of my hair around his finger.

"You've got this," Ben agreed, kissing my forehead.

"Just trust your gut," Luna advised, gripping me fierce, like she was worried I'd dissolve in the wind if she let go even a fraction of an inch.

"And don't let anyone who wrongs you live to see another day." Eira winked.

"Not that she ever would." Callie laughed before her face crumpled with tears. "My baby sister's all grown up!"

Last, but certainly not least, was Jaxith.

His garish blue eyes were submersed with so much pride and love that I was instantly teary eyed.

"I'm going to miss you so much," Jax told me, stroking his hand down the length of my hair. "You've grown into such a confident, beautiful Goddess. I'm honoured to call you my sister."

I swallowed the lump in my throat, squeezing his hand. "I'm even more proud to be the sister of the voice of reason."

His laughter was one of my favourite sounds in the whole universe. I'd miss hearing it every day.

After a moment, I asked him, "Have you been to Esteopia? What can you tell me about it?"

"I haven't been as frequently as Caspian, but I've visited a few times. I'll say this much…the Elrods…they can be very charming. Don't tell that fool you, though. Remember, you're going there in service of Sleotha. Don't lose sight of that, no matter how beautiful the waters are, or how nice the Elrods treat you, because they *will* treat you nice. Sleotha is the one who deserves our support."

"I won't forget," I promised, then reached up on my tiptoes to kiss his cheek. "Drink a lot of nectar for me while I'm gone."

He chuckled, "Always," then reluctantly let me go.

Roara was waiting by Krystal. She looked on the cusp of tossing me over her shoulder and confining me in one of the cells in the dungeon, but she reined in the urge and folded her arms neatly around me.

"Remember who you are, my angel. The Goddess of the Heart and Mind. You are a muse, the epitome of inspiration. Nothing can stand in your way. You are utterly magnificent."

Magnificent.

I jolted at the unexpected use of that word. This time, in the arms of my mother, I felt it.

I hoisted myself up onto Krystal, gathering her reins in one hand. It had been a while since we'd rode together, so I took a second to fondle the top of her head, refamiliarising myself with her mannerisms.

She started to lift her wings, but I clamped my feet down over them.

"We're not flying," I told her. Krystal grunted, looking disappointed, but bobbed her head in a nod.

Roara lingered a moment at our side, then patted my leg and made her way back over to where Isaias stood. He snaked an arm around her waist, kissing her hair.

"Are we ready, Your Grace?" An older Kylantian named Alsandair asked. It took me a moment to realise they were asking *me,* not my mother.

"Ready," I called back.

Alsandair and Harrison lead the fifty Kylantians at the front of the group through the gates, trotting towards the Geddesia Mountains. Pessy and Belgian clung to my side. Behind us, there was another group of fifty, safeguarding the back of the troop.

I looked over my shoulder at where my family stood, huddled together with their arms around each other. I was gripped with the strangest sensation of loss, though I knew I would see them again.

The question wasn't *if*—it was *when.*

Because I somehow knew, deep in my soul, that I wouldn't be returning to Kylantis for a long, long time.

I waved goodbye, then sucked in a deep, preparing breath before turning my back on them. I lightly tapped Krystal's flank with the sole of my shoe, beckoning her forward.

Then, we were off.

We followed the winding trail down the Geddesia Mountains amid a chorus of trees. The further down we got, the leaves started to turn from multi-coloured and iridescent, to the brightest of greens, forming a jocund tousled canopy above the alpine path. When you looked up, you could pinpoint the mountain peak amid the breadth of clouds, a celebration of greys, from sweet blue-slate, to silver-white. The air smelt of lichen and moss, reminding me of the stench of a pile of wet petals.

We rode in silence, but that was only because Pessy and I were communicating privately through the bond.

Just look at the way Harrison is riding, Pessy commented. *Even his posture screams douche.*

I laughed rather boisterously, which triggered Harrison to cease all movement and whirl around to check on us.

"Everything okay?" he asked me.

"Yup," I replied, while Pessy fought a smile. "We're just shooting the breeze." He squinted his eyes, then swivelled back around to face front, gently kicking his horse and renewing his stride.

His horse looks like it's about to buck him off, Pess continued, and she was kind of right. The stallion acted as if it had never learned how to smile, as if rage was the only expression it knew how to make.

You're terrible, I chided. Pessy just shrugged her shoulders, like she knew, but didn't care.

About an hour into the ride down the mountain, we stopped to eat. Alsandair passed out loafs of bread containing an assortment of meats and cooked vegetables, which Pessy and I shoved into our mouths at record's speed. Within ten minutes, we started back up again.

Passing through the highlands, it felt like, if the universe had a pulse, it rose through the mountains, traveling up to Kylantis, then back down to the Realm. It palpitated below our feet, thrumming through the air. The path spilled ahead in rugged excellence, the light playing over the stone as if it were the fingers of a pianist, skating over delicate keys. In a rare moment of achieved mindfulness, I felt absorbed and at one with the scenery.

Another two hours passed before we reached the bottom. The ground suddenly changed from solid rock to mushy soil, which threw Krystal off. She lifted up onto her hind legs, backing away from the unknown substance in fright.

"It's okay," I assured her, petting her mane tenderly until she felt comfortable testing the earth again.

Pess and Belgian were waiting on the wide dusty path a few feet away, with Harrison and the other Kylantians. I felt a tad bit embarrassed that *my* horse, the almighty Pegasus, was the only one who retreated in fear.

"Is this Sleotha?" I asked Alsandair, looking around. Trees of a sun-drenched caramel, yellow, and red hue, infused with earthy tones, adorned the rising hill and spread their great arms heavenward. The variation in colour marked the end of autumn, and the impending return of winter.

"The outskirts," he explained, adding, "It's technically the land between the two kingdoms, but Sleotha considers it theirs."

"How far is Sleotha from here?" Pessy asked.

"Fifteen minutes," answered a Kylantian named Theodora, her chocolate shaded steed snorting at the sky.

"How long is the ride to the Dream Forest?" I asked.

"It should take us fifteen to twenty minutes to get there, but it will take us longer to pass through. You'll see why."

We stayed on the dirt road, keeping close. The deciduous trees on the fringes of the path sent a calming perfume into the ether, enriching the soil. The November autumn breeze swirled around our heads, dragging my hair out of the bun I'd tied it into. I had to keep redoing it every five minutes so I could see where I was leading Krystal. I was grateful then that my mother had insisted I keep my hair long enough to tie back.

The tempo of the gusts of wind slowed as we got our first glimpse of the Dream Forest. From the opulent brown tint of the forest floor, to the sweetness of the blue-white sky above, the forest looked like a three dimensional fairyland. A billion verdant wands of pine seemed to wave at us when we approached, stretching to the heavens and scuffing the bottom of the clouds. There was a subtle shimmer in the ambiance that became discernible if you focused really hard on it, looking like a translucent sheet of tiny sequins. It smothered the woodland, screaming that this place was magical.

The forest was difficult to move through. Something about the air felt heavy, reminding me of the clutches of sleep. I kept fighting a yawn, and saw Pessy and several other Kylantians doing the same. I had a feeling, if we stopped for even a minute, we wouldn't be motivated to continue with our journey.

I lost track of the time, but knew we'd reached the end when I felt the lethargy melt away, restoring my energy.

"Dream Forest," I muttered, then said to Pessy, "Aptly named."

Now, I understood why Mergona suggested we leave early, so we could make it to Esteopia by nightfall.

Once we were literally out of the woods, we stopped again to eat a late lunch. I guzzled my water, looking over at Pessy, who was gnawing on an orange. I glanced at Alsandair just as he finished his sandwich.

"How much longer until we reach Esteopia?"

"It's about thirty more minutes from here," he replied. I stifled a groan. I wanted to be there already.

After the heaviness of the Dream Forest, those thirty minutes flew by. The sun had begun to lower in the sky, secreting a piercing light that made it difficult to see. In a lot of ways, it made sense why Lucius was the way he was—sunlight could be quite imposing in its intensity, which was a perfect counterpart to his personality.

When I finally caught sight of the gates to Esteopia, my mouth dropped open in awe. They were similar to ours in style, but were absolutely nothing like them. They weren't crafted of metal—the bars were cylinders of water.

I couldn't help myself.

I leaned over and tried to flick my finger through one of the streams the gates were made out of.

"Tympany, don't!" Harrison screamed, but it was too late.

A shrill alarm bell hollered out from my touch. I jumped away, pulling on Krystal's reins to tug her back.

"I tried to warn you," Harrison muttered. Pessy glared at him over her shoulder.

"How was she supposed to know that would happen?"

"Because I was about to tell her."

She rolled her eyes, then sent me a compassionate smile when she saw how mortified I looked.

In the distance, a throng of Esteopian soldiers were advancing, dressed in cumbersome, multi-layered blue armour, their heads hidden under metal, faceless helmets. They halted about a foot away from the gates, rows of ten extending for miles. One soldier stepped forward, the late afternoon sun glinting off the titanium.

"Who wishes to enter Esteopia?" the voice bellowed.

"You stand before the Goddess Tympany," Pessy announced in a strong voice, "Living symbol of the Heart and Mind, and Muse to all mortals and celestials."

I didn't need to see their faces to feel the collective shock.

"Goddess Tympany," the Esteopian repeated in a now slightly trembling voice. "Please, show yourself."

I hopped down from Krystal, holding up a hand for her to stay where she was. I stepped forward and heard, even from a few feet away, the gasps of the Esteopian army. I channelled my mother in my aligned posture, tipping my chin up the way she did when she addressed the public.

"I am here to see the King and Queen of Esteopia," I proclaimed, the Esteopian soldier stumbling back. **"Alert them of my arrival, and open the gates."**

Something strange happened.

I'd been speaking to the one soldier at the front who'd stepped forward, but after I'd finished speaking, the entire militia seems to erupt into a frenzy. All of them, in sync with one another, repeated my words back to me.

"Alert the Queen and King of Goddess Tympany's arrival, and open the gates." They kept chanting the sentence, over and over, as the soldier in the front moved off to the side and wrapped his hand around one of the water rods. A silvery light swam up the stream, traveling to every bar.

Then, the gates opened.

The crowd cleared a path for us before marching towards the palace, still repeating the words I'd spoken like a brainwashed choir.

"Whoa." Harrison breathed.

"That was weird," Pessy said, voicing my thoughts exactly. Had I compelled them without realising it?

"Were my eyes glowing when I said that?" I asked her as we began our stride to the palace, the army now several feet ahead of us.

"I couldn't see from where I was," she answered. "That was so weird." I thought about what Pessy said when she introduced me.

"Muse to all mortals and celestials?" That wasn't one of my official titles.

Pessy's lips curled into a mischievous smile before she shrugged. "I thought it sounded powerful."

Flanking either side of the gravel path were waters of the most lurid, limpid blue, the creatures existing below visible beneath the tideline. A rainbow trout with a pink stripe on its left side, black spots scattered throughout, and a layer of iridescence covering the whole physique, swam up to shore. It poked its tiny head out to say hello before flopping back under the surface. The waters flashed an almost white when the sun peppered over the waves, which rose and fell with rhythmic ease.

Something about the water called to me, made me itch to take a swim, the closest I've ever felt to being compelled myself.

The palace was spectacular. Painted a salmon pink hue, the structure was divided into five segments, the first one the shortest, the sections growing in size until it reached the third sector. There was an arch that connected the third and fourth units, and then, the final two, the fifth one at the end the same height as the first. The third section in the middle was the largest, grazing the heavens. The windows were made of an aqua streaked glass, and were opaque from the outside.

"Holy shit," Pessy exclaimed.

"It's so beautiful," I marvelled. I'd never seen anything like it.

Waiting at the threshold was who I assumed were the King and Queen of Esteopia, due to the pinkish gold crowns atop their heads, bejewelled with aqua blue gems that matched the palace behind them. Queen Seraphina was refined in her beauty, dressed in a metallic, light blue, off-the-shoulder gown, with a beaded trim, sleeves that reached her elbows, and a front left slit. Her dark, almost black hair was cut to her jawline and curled to perfection around her face, her cornflower blue eyes outlined by succulent lashes. Her husband was just as handsome, only sharper—chiselled jaw, hair that could pass as either dirty blonde or brunette, and eyes the colour of sapphires. He was dressed in colours that harmonised with the shade of his wife's gown, breeches that were cropped at the ankles and exposed shiny black loafers.

At Seraphina's other side stood a dark haired vixen who I determined must be her daughter, the Princess of Esteopia, Raevon. Her name felt appropriate seeing her in person, the colour of her long hair almost pitch black, with freckles dusted over her cheeks and cobalt eyes to match. She wore a dark navy gown with all-over embellishments, a daring V-neckline, and a stunning silhouette, the sequins adding a touch of sparkle.

When I looked past King Demetrio's shoulder, I noticed a man standing slightly behind him that could only be the Prince of Esteopia, Blekket Elrod. When he inclined forward and revealed his face, I gasped.

It was *him*—the man from the corridor.

Chapter Five

Tymp? You okay? Pessy communicated through the bond. I must've looked pale, or like I was about to hurl.

That's him, I told her. *The man from last night.* Pessy's eyes whisked over to me, nearly spilling out of their sockets.

I glanced back at Blekket, whose expression I summed up as smug. He was the only member of his family not dressed in some shade of blue, wearing the same black petticoat he had on the night before, though the vest underneath was black this time, not the grey he'd worn in my honour.

Those midnight blue eyes latched onto mine and snagged my next breath, then the one after it, assailing my senses.

Did his parents know he'd gone to Kylantis? Had they sent him there, the way mine sent me here?

Did they know my powers didn't work on their son?

If he'd told them what happened, or if somehow, his immunity ran in the family, then this plan would never work.

I was on the verge of hysteria.

As we dismounted our horses, all four of the Esteopian royals curtseyed. Blekket was the last to bend a knee, keeping my eye the whole time with a self-satisfied smirk.

"Goddess Tympany," Queen Seraphina greeted with wonder, as if she couldn't believe I was really there. "We are delighted to welcome you to the kingdom of Esteopia." I had to force my eyes away from her son in order to address her.

"It is an honour and privilege to visit your home," I told her in as clear a voice as I could muster under my angst. I meant that—while my reasons for being here were less than chivalrous, I was already in awe of Esteopia's beauty. I gave a permitting nod, and the four of them rose off the floor.

"I hope your journey here was stress-free." I nearly laughed. *It was*, I thought, *until I saw who your son is!*

"Passing through the Dream Forest was…interesting," I replied, "but we made it here unscathed."

"I'm glad to hear that." She spoke with true sincerity.

"This is Pessoranda Whitereaver," I presented, gesturing to Pess. "My bonded Kylantian."

"But you can call me Pessy," she said, scowling at me. She hated her first name.

"This is my husband, Demetrio," the Queen introduced, "my daughter, Raevon, and my son, Blekket."

I half expected Blekket to pronounce we'd already met, and was relieved when he didn't.

"It's lovely to meet you all." Harrison had taken notice of the inflammatory way Blekket was looking at me and moved to the front, so he was somewhat blocking me from the Prince's point of view.

"Harrison Rottweiler," he announced himself. "Senior member of the Kylantian army." Both Pessy and Alsandair rolled their eyes.

"Less of the senior, kid," Alsandair joshed, touching Harrison's shoulder and forcing him to shuffle back before introducing himself. "Alsandair Hargreave. *Actual* senior member." He patted the top of his salt and pepper hair for further emphasis.

I hadn't pegged Alsandair to be the boastful type. Pessy and I looked at each other at the same time, both smirking. When I glanced at Blekket, he too was smiling, but not over Alsandair's attempt to squander Harrison's ego.

"It's a pleasure to make your acquaintance," King Demetrio said, bowing respectfully a second time.

"It's an honour to be in the presence of a Goddess," Raevon added from her mother's side, her voice a deeper octave than the Queen's. I got the sense this formal attitude wasn't natural to her, that she wouldn't be so proper if I wasn't there.

When Blekket stepped forward, my heart lunged into my throat. He stunned me by plucking my hand from my side, raising it to his lips, and planting a tender kiss over my knuckles, never breaking eye contact.

"You are as *magnificent* in person as the stories told about you, Goddess Tympany." His husky accent coiled around that word the same way it did the night before when he first uttered it.

For a second, I forgot how to breathe.

"I'd like to know what these stories are," I heard myself say, but it didn't sound or feel like me talking.

I hadn't even felt my lips form the words.

"I promise, they're all complimentary." I narrowed my eyes, and his grin widened, taking up more than half of his face. He released my hand, Pessy's voice shouting in my head, *Holy shit, Tymp!*

"Let's not linger by the door anymore," Seraphina proposed, exchanging a look with her husband I didn't entirely understand, but I suspected was laced with surprise as their son's unabashed actions. "Please, come inside. You must be famished from the day's ride." I spun around, handing Harrison Krystal's reins.

"Take Krystal," I directed, wanting him to stay busy, so he'd keep away from Pessy and me. I would give him useless tasks the whole time we were in Esteopia, so Pessy wouldn't have to stare at his obnoxious face all day.

"Yes, Your Grace."

When he reached for her, Krystal balked, roaring with outrage. She stood up on her hind legs and started to unfurl her massive wings. The Elrods, and the Esteopian army behind us, staggered back in fright, having never seen a Pegasus in the flesh before. I reached out, rubbing her belly with one hand and compressing my other against the wing that had begun to expand, shoving it back against her side. I kept my hands in place on her waist until she finally settled down, retracting her wings.

"Maybe Alsandair should take her," Harrison suggested, which *really* pissed me off.

"I asked *you* to do it," I barked. "You don't get to claim to be a senior member of the Kylantian army, then run at the sight of a riled up Pegasus. Take Krystal *now*. I will not ask again."

Pessy looked like she could burst from pleasure. Harrison appeared as if he might pee himself at any moment.

"I sincerely apologise, Your Grace. I'll take her." He wouldn't look me in the eye when he collected the reins from me.

"Lev, please show Harrison here where we keep the horses," Seraphina ordered the Esteopian who'd been the spokesperson at the gates. "And make sure...Krystal, was it?" I nodded. "That's a lovely name. Make sure Krystal is kept in her own stall."

"Yes, my Queen," Lev replied, then gesticulated with his hand to the left of him. "Right this way."

Harrison followed Lev in the direction of the stables. Pessy handed Belgian to Theodora, and the rest of the Kylantians joined the fold. The only two who remained with me were Pessy and Alsandair.

"I've always loved that horse," Pessy muttered under her breath. I stifled a laugh as we followed the Elrods inside.

The interior of the palace was just as miraculous as the outside. The walls were white marble, reminiscent of home, with accents of the same salmon pink and aqua blue as the exterior of the castle. We strolled through the great hall, a rectangular room that was three times as long as it was wide, with four times as high of a ceiling. We entered through a screens passage that had windows on one of the long sides, with a minstrel's gallery above, where an Esteopian was playing a harp. At the other end of the hall was a dais, where a top table was situated. The private rooms lay beyond the dais at the end of the hall, and the kitchen was on the opposite side of the screens passage.

I stopped walking when I noticed a painting hanging on the wall outside the sitting room we were heading towards. A man and a woman stood in the back, with a young girl who had to be no older than sixteen seated in front of them. Both the couple's hands were placed on the younger woman's shoulders. The older woman wore a light blue, A-line layered gown, with glitter tulle and floral beading that was off-the-shoulder and had illusion three quarter sleeves. Her blonde hair was curled in loose waves down her chest, and her eyes matched the gown. The man beside her was rugged in his configuration, much like the current King and Prince, with sharp, well-defined lines and clear definition. His doublet jacket was teetering between blue and silver, his breeches hidden behind the chair the young girl was seated in. She wore a glamorous chiffon gown with sequins, embroidered and printed with floral motifs. It was designed with a grosgrain waistband, and had a strapless bodice with supportive boning, kicking out to a voluminous layered skirt that was floor-sweeping length, eclipsing her feet. Her dark hair was pulled away from her face, and her lips were painted a deep plum colour that complimented the gown's floral print.

Seraphina noticed I'd stopped to admire the painting, halting at the doorway.

"That's King Alden and Queen Lavinia, with Princess Esteopia," she told me, adding, "My ancestors."

"They're a beautiful family," I murmured to myself. Seraphina's smile was wistful.

"They were," she answered, wilting a little.

"What happened to them? Did they die of old age?" I hadn't come across that information in my readings.

"Alden and Lavinia died in the Battle of Cimnard, when Queen Jacinda had the Sleothian army demolish what used to be our capital," she explained. There was bitter animosity and resentment fuelling her words. "Princess Esteopia, after she was crowned Queen, had to rebuild the palace here in Acadia, which took years to complete. She ultimately died of an unknown illness. No one to this day knows what it was. She was only forty years old."

"That's so young," I remarked with a shake of my head. "Was Esteopia married before she died?"

"She was, to a man named Xavier, but the kingdom fell to her eldest daughter, Arabella, after she passed." I was brought back to what Caspian said about Blekket not wanting to be king. It didn't make sense he would be next in line and not his sister, since Esteopia was known as a matriarchy.

"Does the firstborn child of the King and Queen inherit the throne, regardless of their gender?"

"Yes. That's tradition." Her eyes swung to Blekket, who tensed, his mask of self-control fracturing slightly.

"How long have you been Queen for?" I changed the subject because I didn't want to make anyone uncomfortable—even someone who'd bested me the night before and was immune to my compulsion.

"I've been Queen since I was thirty. I'm fifty-nine now."

"You've been Queen for twenty-nine years?" She nodded.

"I succeeded my mother, Rosabella, after she passed. That was of old age. Nothing nefarious. She died in her sleep." I started to ask another question before I became aware of the fact that everyone had halted in the hall, waiting for me to finish probing before heading into the sitting room.

"I'm sorry," I exclaimed, feeling guilty for making everyone stand around while I asked questions I could've waited to voice until we were all seated. "I didn't mean to make everyone stop on my account."

"No need to apologise, Goddess Tympany," Demetrio assured. "We appreciate your interest in our history."

"You can just call me Tympany," I said.

His smile knocked the wind out of me in its glory. I could see where Blekket got his...*charm* from.

We entered the sitting room in pairs, Demetrio and Seraphina leading the group, Pessy at my side, and Blekket and Raevon trailing behind us. The room was furnished with comfortable, plush white chairs, outlined with gold frames. A fireplace sat in the corner, twinkling with an already ignited flame. The furniture had a simplicity and flare all at once, the chairs arranged around a large oval table made of glass. The curtains, made of ivory with touches of lace at the end, were a glorious fusion of pink, blue, white, and gold, bringing a welcome pop of colour to the room. They were pulled back, so the patio outside was on full display, the furniture out there all grey stone and cream cloth and dark brown wood.

I felt drawn to a wide armchair, which housed a silver pillow with an aqua blue flower pattern embroidered over the material, the tassels along the fringe a light grey. Pessy sat beside me, her head swinging from side to side as she took everything in.

Blekket plopped down in the empty chair on my left. Our arms nearly grazed due to how close the chairs were.

"Hey. That's *my* chair." Raevon loomed over him, sulking.

"But I just look so much better sitting in it." Blekket flashed those criminally white teeth, crossing his ankles on the glass table.

"Fiend," Raevon hissed, but there was no real heat to her words. I could tell the two of them were close.

"Please forgive my children for their lack of manners," Seraphina said, scowling at Raevon and Blekket.

"There's no need. I'm the same with my siblings." I explained, "We each have our favourite places in the palace we're possessive of. Mine is this beautiful courtyard in the East Wing. There have been times where I've chased my siblings out of the garden with a broom when I wanted it for myself."

"We nicknamed it Tympany's Province, since she pretty much lives there," Pessy told them, making Seraphina laugh.

"That sounds like something Rae would do," Blekket chuckled, his voice spreading goosebumps over my flesh. "I can't count on two hands the amount of times I've been literally kicked out of this chair. She would've booted me if you guys weren't here."

"It's true," Raevon agreed, tossing her hair over her shoulder with a sly smirk. I immediately liked her.

"Would you like something to drink, Tympany? Pessy?" It made me so happy that Seraphina included Pess, that she didn't just disregard her presence because she was a solider and not a God.

"Could I have a glass of water, please?" I'd finished my canteen in the Dream Forest and was parched.

"Pessy?"

"I'll take a glass too," Pess replied, adding, "Thank you, Seraphina."

"Of course. Alsandair?" Alsandair had placed himself in the corner of the room, hands folded in front.

"I'm good," he replied, his tone cool, but she wouldn't have noticed.

Seraphina placed her thumb and index finger into her mouth, pushing the underside of her tongue over the ends of her fingers before blowing. The strident whistle that released past her lips triggered an outburst of commotion before an Esteopian guard appeared in the doorway, his helmet removed to reveal unkempt curly red hair, resting like a nest of ginger twigs at the top of his head. Big blue eyes awaited his orders.

"Can you please retrieve six glasses and a pitcher of water from the kitchen, Lev?" Seraphina instructed.

"Of course, my Queen."

I found it noteworthy that Seraphina always said please when she requested something of her staff.

My mother hardly ever said please.

Lev disappeared, returning a minute later with a silver tray of six glasses and a large pitcher of water. He placed everything on the coffee table, then poured the water into each of the individual glasses before passing them out. I thanked him when he handed me mine, noticing Blekket from the corner of my eye studying my movements, stroking his index finger over his bottom lip.

I took a sip and audibly moaned. "This is the best water I've ever had," I declared, Seraphina beaming with pride.

"It comes from the Argent Ocean," Demetrio explained as I swallowed another refreshing sip. "It's the cleanest water in existence."

"I didn't think water could taste so good!" Pessy squealed. I downed my cup in two seconds.

Lev was at my side the moment the last drop trickled down my throat, offering to replenish for me.

"Please," I insisted, extending it towards him to refill.

"So, Tympany." Demetrio intertwined his fingers in his lap. "To what do we owe the honour of your visit?"

I took another long drag of water to prolong the moment as I gathered my thoughts. I had to carefully select my words and remove any trace of emotion from my dialect, so the Elrods wouldn't suspect that what I was saying was disingenuous.

"It's come to my attention that the tensions between Sleotha and Esteopia are growing more catastrophic," I began. Something about my choice of words caused Demetrio to flinch. "I've come here to offer my support, and help Esteopia win the war." All four of the Elrods mouths popped open in unison.

"Wow." Seraphina breathed. "I was not expecting that."

"That is incredibly generous of you, Tympany," Demetrio gushed. I flushed, feeling like a fraud for accepting his praise. "Having someone with your abilities back us will mean great things for our kingdom. Esteopia thanks you for your support."

"It's my pleasure," I murmured, again flooded with guilt for lying to them about my true intentions.

"I thought all the Gods favoured Sleotha," Blekket interjected, which caused my organs to flip over inside my body from panic.

How does he know that? I said to Pessy. *Did the bastard see something when he was in the palace?*

Don't freak out yet, she counselled, but she sounded anxious too. *Ask him why he thinks that.*

"What makes you say that?" I asked gently, working overtime to calm the tremors in my voice.

"It's a rumor the villagers started," Seraphina explained, glowering at her son. "Some of the peasants claimed, during the time of the plague, they prayed to the God of Kindness, but he never came. It was said, when the Sleothians did, he healed them over the Esteopians."

"That doesn't sound like Jaxith," I protested. He'd just the other day defended Esteopia when our siblings wanted to starve the kingdom.

"Also, when there was a weeklong monsoon several years back, we prayed to the God of Light and Sun, but he never responded," Blekket added, his tone sharp. I wondered if he was thinking about what he witnessed in the corridor. "The villages nearly drowned because your brother didn't do anything to stop it."

That sounded like Lucius.

I wanted to argue, to defend my family against these accusations, but the assumption the Gods favoured Sleotha was true. I couldn't deny that. It was the whole reason I was in Esteopia to begin with.

I realised then the key to being a good liar—you don't fully lie.

You mingle the lie with enough half-truths that, when you speak, you believe what you're saying.

"It's true," I admitted. Pessy's head whipped so quickly to me that I was worried it would roll off her neck. "The Gods have historically backed Sleotha. To be honest, I don't know why. I'm not sure there's even a reason. Most of my siblings still do, but I don't." Seraphina's brow arched in surprise. "I've spent the last five thousand years studying both kingdoms, and Esteopia has been painted as the villain for far too long. I'm not saying you're totally innocent, but no one is faultless in a war. I came to Esteopia at my own volition. No one made me come here. I wanted to help you because I believe your side merits being heard just as much as Sleotha's and deserves a fighting chance." I actively forced my fingers to remain smooth on my thighs.

Nice, Tymp, Pessy esteemed.

"We appreciate your honesty and support immensely, Tympany," Demetrio said, I think a little awed by my speech.

"In order for me to be most accommodating towards you, I will need all the information, both past and present plans, so I can lend my abilities to where they will be most constructive," I continued.

"That can be arranged," Seraphina replied. I breathed a sigh of relief. *So far, so good.* "We would love for you to stay here with us and explore our kingdom more, become familiar with the land."

"So would I." I was curious if the villages were as stunning as the castle grounds. I also needed to gain their trust more, as it would be suspicious of me to start poking around having only been here one day. "I did have a question for you about something." Seraphina waved a permitting hand. "I'm aware of how, last night, Esteopian soldiers invaded Sleotha and destroyed several Sleothian crops. I was a bit confused by that, since I know Esteopia relies heavily on those produces too."

"We didn't destroy any crops," Seraphina disputed. "They're too valuable to be destroyed. We took them."

"You *stole* them?" Pessy gasped.

"Not just the crops. Some of the livestock as well," Demetrio added.

"What prompted you to do that?" I didn't bother to hide my censure this time. I supposed taking them was better than obliterating them completely, but they still slaughtered civilians and left Sleotha with nothing right on the cusp of winter.

"I would've thought, as a Goddess, you'd be all knowing," Raevon interrupted.

While Seraphina looked horrified at her daughter's impertinence, the comment made me smile, for some reason.

"I've only just been included in these conversations. I've spent most of my life on the outside looking in, forming opinions of my own, but never being given the chance to voice them. This is my first time venturing out to the Realm, so I'm still learning things. There's always room to grow." Raevon's lips twisted with amusement at my tone.

"Oh, I completely forgot! Happy birthday," Seraphina cried, for the first time daring to reach over and squeeze my hand.

She reminds me so much of myself. I hope she's serious about helping us. We would be so lucky to have her support.

I gasped, my hand slipping out of hers. Those hadn't been my thoughts reverberating back at me—they'd been Seraphina's.

"Is everything okay?" she asked me, now looking concerned.

"Yes," I promised, glancing fleetingly at Pessy before clearing my throat. I'd never been able to read thoughts before. This would be immensely useful down the road.

Then, I realised—if I'd been able to read Seraphina's thoughts, then that must've meant Blekket's immunity to my compulsion didn't run in the family. I would have to test it later, but I was fairly certain this wouldn't be an issue. It was an encouraging discovery.

"To answer your previous question," Demetrio said, which took me a moment to remember, "a week ago, the Sleothian military invaded Esteopia and burned the city of Eveium to the ground."

"Burned?!" I was appalled. "How?"

"With their drogons."

"Those are real?!" Pessy cried, then screamed at me *I told you so!*

Drogons were gargantuan, serpent-like creatures with wings, barbed tails, venomous teeth, and the ability to breathe fire. I'd only heard about them through mythic legend, not as something tangible that existed down in the Realm. They were mine and Pessy's favourite tales, and Pess always insisted they were real, despite my cynicism.

For something as substantial as the drogon to attack Esteopia, I was surprised my family hadn't intervened sooner, or that they hadn't admitted this when I'd asked what prompted Esteopia to strike.

Did they really *not* know?

"They're very real," Demetrio guaranteed, "and are controlled by the Sleothian Queen, Jacinda."

"The drogon burnt all our harvests in the village, killing thousands of inhabitants." Seraphina's shoulders sank. "Some of those villagers were like family to us." Her voice dripped despondence and grief.

"I'm sorry for your loss," I said, Demetrio grabbing his wife's hand and grazing her knuckles with a sweet kiss. Now, it made sense why they'd stolen Sleotha's crops.

The only part I didn't approve of was them killing the Sleothians that got in their way—everything else, I understood.

"With your help, their deaths will not be in vain." I was grateful she couldn't read *my* thoughts. "Are you hungry, Tympany? I never offered you all dinner. Please, forgive my manners."

"That's alright. Um…yeah, I could eat." I glanced at Pessy, who nodded her head while rubbing her stomach.

Lev appeared at Seraphina's side, like clockwork. "Please bring us dinner in here tonight," she directed kindly.

"Yes, my Queen." He twirled around and stalked off to the kitchen.

When Lev returned, he carried over a variety of rolls, seasoned rice with different fish, egg, and vegetable options, shaped inside a thin sheet of seaweed. I'd always wanted to try sushi, and it did not disappoint.

"Holy shit," I blurted, then covered my mouth when I realised I'd cursed. "Forgive my loose tongue, but this is *so* good."

Seraphina's smile was soft. "You are forgiven, Your Excellence."

"What's in the one I'm eating?" I wanted to make a log of it, so when I returned home to Kylantis, I could have Ben make it for me.

"Yellowtail and avocado," she informed me. I repeated it back to myself, shoving another into my mouth.

"I have a question." Raevon raised her hand high in the air, waiting to be called on. It reminded me of myself in council meetings. After Seraphina granted her permission, Raevon asked, "Can you really compel people to do whatever you want?" I avoided the smirk that materialised over Blekket's face, which practically screamed *not everyone*, as I nodded. "Can you show us?" I paused, debating if that was a good idea or not.

After all, I'd been plotting to utilise my abilities *against* the Elrods, and I'd planned to do so discreetly.

Also, what if it didn't work?

But I still needed to test if my compulsion affected the other members of the royal family apart from Blekket, so I decided to try.

I leaned over, locking my eyes with Raevon, and ordered, **"Give me your sushi."** She handed it over without any hesitation.

"Whoa!" she shrieked, reminding me of Pessy when she clapped her hands. "That's so cool!"

Phew—it worked.

"I bet you use it all the time," she said.

I popped the sushi roll into my mouth, shrugging to be elusive, but the truth was, I tried to limit how much I used my gifts, and with who. It was an invasion of free will to force someone to do something, a power that had the potential of being utterly destructive if fallen into the wrong hands. I knew how addictive that power was, and how easy it would be to abuse it. When I summoned my compulsion forward, I had to clear my mind of any persistent emotions, because if I applied it in the heat of the moment, I could say something I didn't mean and wouldn't have the chance to take back.

"What about your other siblings? What can they do?"

"Raevon, don't badger her," Seraphina chided.

"What? It's not every day you get to meet a *Goddess*," Raevon pointed out, making me like her even more.

"It's okay," I assured Seraphina. I thought Raevon's interest was endearing. "Benjen can create any food he wants with his mind. He just snaps his fingers, and it appears." Raevon's cobalt eyes glistened with fascination. "Jaxith has the ability to heal the sick or injured. Calliope can make music out of anything. She can make something inanimate come to life with the swipe of her finger. Nox can bend the stars to his will and control when night appears, and Luna can do the same with the moon and moonlight. Caspian, as you know, can control any type of water. Eira and Lucius have similar powers, but flipped. She can summon snow and ice at her fingertips, and he can do the same with sunlight and fire."

I tried not to look at Blekket when I mentioned Lucius, but it was difficult considering his eyes were piercing into me.

"Wow," Raevon uttered in awe. "Not that your siblings' abilities aren't awesome, but I think yours is the coolest."

"You're just saying that cause she's right there," Blekket accused. Raevon wrinkled her nose at him.

"I kind of think snapping your fingers and having any food you want appear right in front of you is kind of cool, but I have to agree with you." I winked, Raevon's grin enormous and stunning.

"What about your sister, Hadestia?" Seraphina asked, amazed.

"I've never met her, but I guess her abilities are that she can control and interact with the dead."

"You've never met her?"

I had to look at Blekket when I answered, which strangely made my palms perspire and my heartrate spike.

"She lives in Nekropolis and never visits Kylantis." He bobbed his head in a nod, but the corner of his mouth quirked up, like he could sense how nervous he made me and found it entertaining.

"What about your parents?"

"My mother can do a variation of all our abilities, just not as potently, since they're not her specialties. My father is an extension of her powers, since he wasn't born a God, just created as one."

"So cool," Raevon repeated, shaking her head.

"Would you like some dessert?" Seraphina offered. I remembered Jaxith's warning to me about not getting swept up in the lavish attention. I already felt myself falling under the Elrods' spell. I needed space to refocus on the mission.

"Maybe tomorrow," I said, ignoring Pessy's pout. "It's been a long day of travel. I think we should get some rest."

"Yes, of course! You must be so exhausted. I'm sorry we monopolised so much of your time."

"Please, don't be. I've enjoyed it greatly." I hadn't expected to take such a liking to the Elrod family right away. It would make this plan a lot harder, but also make it easier to be in an unfamiliar place.

"I can have Lev show you to your bedchamber."

"Actually, Mum, I can do it. I'm going that way anyway." My head whirled to Blekket, who was failing to suppress a smile.

Oh no, I thought. I knew I would have to face him eventually, but I didn't think it'd be so soon.

"That would be wonderful. Thank you, darling." She cupped the side of his face, and his eyes shone with love.

"It was so lovely to meet you, Tympany," Demetrio said as we headed for the exit. "I look forward to speaking with you further and learning what you have planned to help us win the war against Sleotha."

"I look forward to speaking more with you, too." I hadn't acknowledged the second part of his statement, which didn't go unnoticed.

"We'll see you in the morning." Seraphina curled her arm around Demetrio, then beckoned to Raevon. "Come, Rae."

"Bye, Tympany! Bye, Pessy!" She waved at us, then followed after her parents.

"I like her," Pess said, dragging her eyes down the train of Raevon's gown rather heatedly.

"Keep it in your pants, Pessoranda," I teased, Pessy growling at me.

We swivelled around to face Blekket, who was leaning against the marble wall, his hands tucked into his pant pockets. He was the personification of haughtiness in that moment, from the way his chin was tipped up, to the mirthful smirk fiddling with his lips, occupying the majority of the bottom half of his face.

"Long time, no see," he mocked.

I immediately wanted to do what I'd threatened the night before and tear him limb from limb.

"You have a lot of nerve," I reproved, crossing my arms over my chest. "Do your parents know you snuck into Kylantis and tried to fight a Goddess?"

"If they did, I wouldn't have been allowed anywhere near you when you arrived." His eyes skimmed down the length of my jumpsuit. "I like what you're wearing. I far prefer this to the dress you had on yesterday. No offense to the designer."

"I don't care what you think," I snapped, that frustratingly beauty smile reaching new heights in its flawlessness and egotism.

"You should. You are—"

"If you call me magnificent one more time, I'm going to rip your tongue out of your mouth."

Pessy looked shocked. I wasn't usually the type to resort to violence, but something about his arrogance lit my blood on fire and blitzed every compassionate, tolerant instinct in its path.

"So violent," he said with a shake of his head. "And for the record, just so we're being accurate here with the details, I didn't *try* to fight a Goddess. If I remember correctly, I won the third round."

"You wanna go for four?" I stomped forward with my fist raised, but Pessy seized my wrist before I reached him.

"I'd *love* it, sweetheart," he replied, leaning in so I got a good waft of lilac when I breathed in.

"Why did you go to Kylantis?" He thought about it, then shrugged.

"I was curious. I've always wanted to go, but Esteopians aren't exactly welcome there. I would've added that to the list of reasons which prove the Gods favour Sleotha, but didn't want to upset my mother." I felt a tad guilty for it being common knowledge in Esteopia that they weren't welcome in Kylantis. I'd always hoped they were so far removed that they didn't know. "I heard a rumor Sleothians were allowed through the gates for celebrations and wanted to see for myself."

"Sorry to disappoint," I sneered.

"Who said my visit was a disappointment?" I jerked my head back in surprise, making that sinful smile grow. "I love catching you off guard, angel."

"*Don't* call me that." I pointed a stern finger at him. "Unless you want your head on a spike."

He raised his hands in surrender. "Message received." I dropped my finger when I believed he wouldn't try anything. "I apologise for not wishing you a happy birthday when we met, but I was a bit…distracted."

I ignored the implication of that as we started walking up a marble staircase with a gilded railing.

"Well, I accept late birthday gifts. Like not being an asshole."

"That's what you want? I thought most girls prefer jewellery."

"If you really think that, then you know nothing about *most girls*," Pessy interjected like the legend she was.

"Good point," Blekket mumbled, then turned to Pessy and said, "I think I'm gonna like you."

"I am not *most* girls," I added after he spun back around.

"No, you most certainly are not. You are—"

"Seriously, *don't*. I'm not kidding when I say I will tear out your tongue and compel you to eat it."

"Well, since your compulsion doesn't work on me, I think I'm safe." My mouth dropped open, then sealed shut. I'd hoped he wouldn't acknowledge that part of our first encounter, but self-discipline didn't fit with the elements of his personality I'd already seen. Still, I was stunned by how shameless he was to disclose that in front of Pessy.

"Are you this irritating with everyone? Or just me?"

"I think you *inspire* it in me," Blekket answered, chuckling when I rolled my eyes. He glanced at Pessy. "Is she always this easy to tick off?"

"Not usually. You're a rare case." She flashed me an impish smile in response to the glare I shot her.

Don't egg him on, I grumbled.

We have SO much to talk about later, Pessy squealed.

"I have a question for you." Blekket dropped those dazzling midnight eyes and handsome smile to examine my face.

"You've got me on the edge of my seat," he drawled. "Let's hear it."

"How did you disappear into thin air after jumping off the balcony?"

"Disappear into thin air?" he repeated, then snorted. "I'm flattered to know you looked for me."

"Yeah, to make sure you weren't stealing anything. Seriously, answer the question."

"I'm just *that* fast." He wiggled his eyebrows.

"No. *I'm* that fast."

"You're not the only one with superhuman speed."

I was about to ask what he meant, before I remembered—he wasn't the Sleothian royal I'd originally thought he was. He was a Neraid, his strength and speed fuelled by the waters of the Argent Ocean.

He wasn't fully human.

We turned the corner into a narrow hallway, the closer proximity causing my shoulder to scrape against Blekket's. I gasped when the contact singed my bare flesh, sending an electric shock buzzing through my veins and down to the tips of my toes, leaving behind a tingle that made me wish I could crawl out of my skin. I wasn't sure if Blekket felt it too, as his face hadn't reformed the way mine must've in shock, but I could've sworn I saw his arm twitch in acknowledgement of the current.

He stopped in front of a doorway that was blue with several gold pegs prodding out of it, the doorknob cast in the shape of a teardrop.

"This is you," he announced, then offered, "I could come in, give you the tour, if you want…"

"We're good," I insisted, narrowing my eyes. "You can go."

"So demanding," he muttered with feigned disapproval. "I'm right down the hall if you need anything."

"Can I request a room change?" He pretended to consider, stroking his chin in mock contemplation.

"Request denied," he decided, flaunting a captivating smile that was fully aware of its own beauty. "Goodnight, Pessy." He bowed respectfully to her, and she spread out the ends of her waist cape, curtseying back.

"Goodnight, Blekket." She was enjoying this way too much.

"Tympany." He nodded to me. "I look forward to round four." He then turned on his heel, stuffing his hands into his pockets, and sauntered with oozing confidence to his bedchamber.

After he'd closed the door to his room and was out of sight, I groaned, "You're going to have to watch me and make sure I don't kill that guy."

"Mhm." An odd smile developed on Pessy's face. "I'm not too worried about that. You like him."

"What!" I cringed. "No, I don't."

"I've never seen you react that strongly to anyone. You never let someone get under your skin."

"Unless they're my brother," I muttered, twisting the doorknob.

"That doesn't count," Pessy protested, making her way inside.

The chamber was exquisite. The duvet on the massive, queen-sized bed was the same shade as the translucent waters we'd passed on the way to the palace, made of sanctuary mink with a pattern that looked like rippling waves. There

85

was an assembled seating area, with a cream chaise, glass table, and a similar wide armchair to the one I'd sat inside of in the drawing room.

Next to the bed was a neatly arranged cot, packed with posh pillows and a matching comforter.

"There's a bed for me!" Pessy flung herself across the room, landing in the center of the fluffy pillows with a giggle.

"They thought of everything." I took a seat on the bed, my feet dangling due to the impressive height, and began removing my sandals. "So…what do you think of the Elrods?" I asked her, unwrapping the leather holster around my waist. I grabbed my blade from inside the sheath and hid it under the mattress.

"So far, I like them," she said, curling her arms around her knees. "What did you think about them claiming Sleotha attacked first?"

"I just don't understand why my parents wouldn't have mentioned that in the council meeting." I undid the clasp around my bun, shaking my hair free. It tumbled down my neck, just grazing my shoulders. "There's no way they don't know about the drogon burning that village. If it's true, I totally understand why Esteopia stole their crops."

"*If* it's true? You think they're not telling the truth?"

"I don't know. I just don't buy that my parents know nothing about the attack. I wonder why they've waited so long to intervene."

"Me too." Pessy unclasped her harness and shook off her shoulder armour, so all she had on was a bodysuit tucked into her leggings.

"Something happened back there, when I touched Seraphina's hand. I heard her thoughts. She was thinking about how I remind her a lot of herself, and that she hopes I'm serious about helping them win the war."

"You're kidding. You *heard* her thoughts?" I nodded. "Your powers must be growing, like what Lucius said. You've never been able to read thoughts before, or compel a whole mass of people at once."

"Yeah. That was really weird." Pessy drummed her fingertips along the length of one of her pillows.

"So, are we gonna talk about Blekket? Or…"

"I'd rather not."

"Oh, come on!" She rose up onto her knees. "You gotta give me *something!* At least tell me why you have such a problem with him calling you *magnificent.*" She parodied him in a derisive, falsetto voice, fanning herself. I picked up my pillow and chucked it at her.

It hit her with such force that she toppled off the edge of her cot and onto the marble floor with a loud *umph.*

"Bitch," she huffed, then hurled it back at me.

I lifted my hands just in time to protect my face. The pillow bounced off my palms, landing in front of me on the bed.

"Deflect all you want, but you know it's true. You like him." I didn't know what I felt for Blekket, but I knew, whichever way those feelings leaned, either end of the spectrum was intense.

"He...confuses me." I wouldn't say more on the matter.

One of the Kylantians must've brought in our luggage while we were dinning. All our clothing was already assembled in the drawers and hung up on hangers. We changed into our pyjamas, me into a black slip dress, and Pessy into one of her oversized tunics that once belonged to her father.

We crawled under our comforters after closing the ivory drapes, facing one another in our parallel beds.

"I'm really glad you came with me," I told her, and saw, even in the dark, her cheeks blush a rosy red.

"I wouldn't want to be anywhere you're not." She nuzzled her pillow and sighed. "I kind of like it here."

"Me too," I mumbled.

As I closed my eyes, I prayed my growing affinity for the Elrods and wonder with Esteopia wouldn't become a conflict of interest.

Chapter Six

I woke before Pessy.

I scampered across the floor as quietly as my feet would carry me, sliding open the door to the bathroom and creeping inside. The walls were white tile, and there was a marble vanity to the right, complete with two sinks that had gold faucets and several drawers beneath it, where the towels, soaps, and other toiletries were kept. A ridiculously large glass shower that could comfortably fit a whole family of six sat in the corner. The showerhead was silver, fashioned in the shape of a teardrop, and there was a hose and bracket attached. I stripped off my nightdress, stepped under the nozzle, and twisted the valve to warm, awaiting the waters I'd tasted from the Argent Ocean to douse me in their revitalising splendour.

The shower was everything the water promised it would be.

I tipped my face up under the torrent and let the flood of pressure drown me, relieving the tension in my shoulders and neck. The shampoo and conditioner were infused with the lilac I'd inhaled on Blekket. I wished I could've stayed there forever in the shower's cocoon, but the day awaited, so I reluctantly turned off the water and climbed out. I dried myself with one of their plush towels, the cotton soft and embracing and tender against my sensitive skin. It took me longer than it should've to actually leave the bathroom, as I kept being drawn to something new, like the polish of the vanity and how smooth it felt beneath my fingers, or how the knobs on the drawers were also in the shape of water droplets, which I was beginning to realise must be Esteopia's pictogram.

Everything about Esteopia was so inviting. It's beauty and eccentricity, the kindness of the people so far, embedded itself deep within my core, making it impossible to see the kingdom as anything other than glorious.

I was still mulling over the fact that Sleotha had actually attacked first, destroying Eveium and all its inhabitants. It didn't make sense to me why my parents would intervene when Esteopia stole from Sleotha, but did nothing when the drogon burnt all their harvests. It didn't matter that they favoured Sleotha—the Esteopians were still our people. If they really did demolish an entire village, then Sleotha deserved the same punishment we were infringing upon Esteopia.

Either Seraphina and Demetrio were lying about the drogon attack, or I would need to have a serious talk with my parents when I returned home about their morals.

When I finally pulled myself away from the bathroom and made my way back into the bedchamber, Pessy was awake.

"Wow. I slept great," she mused, stretching her arms up over her head and releasing a forceful yawn.

"I did too, actually." I usually couldn't get comfortable, but I'd been so wearied from the journey that I fell asleep almost instantly.

"What do you think we'll do today?" she asked as I put on an off-the-shoulder, sleeveless jumpsuit the colour of steel, made of soft chiffon that went down to the floor. If anyone questioned me on why I'd chosen to wear pants versus a gown, which was not customary of a Goddess to do in public, I'd blame it on the assumption we were most likely riding today; but I knew, in my heart, I'd chosen it because I just didn't want to be confined by a corset or skirt.

"I hope we get to do some exploring," I said, then tied my hair back in a low bun. I splayed my hands out over the material of the jumpsuit, which clung to my curves. I wasn't as tall as the other Gods, built more like a warrior than a dainty princess. All my sisters were statuesque and thin, whereas my arms had definition, my thighs were thicker, and my hips wider.

I liked the extra meat around my bones, the way my stomach rolled when I sat down, the indented streaks on the backs of my thighs and above my breasts. My appearance was never something I'd wasted time being insecure about. At the end of the day, none of it mattered as much as what existed on the inside.

Another reason I'd selected this jumpsuit was because it had pockets. After Pessy buttoned the back, I tucked my trusty blade into my right pocket, feeling the iron graze my thigh through the chiffon.

I waited for Pessy to finish her shower, which took a while for the same reasons mine did.

I heard her squeal from the other room, "This pressure is amazing! I'll never look at baths the same again!"

When she finally emerged fifteen minutes later, she looked like she'd been through a transformation.

Lev was waiting for us outside our bedchamber, clad in blue armour, his auburn curls the hue of cinnamon on full display at the top of his head. He held his helmet against his hip, his posture straight against the wall.

"Good morning, Goddess," he greeted me politely, bowing his head. "I hope you had a restful sleep."

"I did. Thank you, Lev. Did you sleep well?" He looked startled, as if no one had ever asked him that before.

"I did, yes. Thank you, Your Excellence."

"Just Tympany is fine." His cheeks flushed an endearing shade of red. I stifled a groan at the sight of Harrison beside him, wishing it was Alsandair. Pessy didn't bother hiding her displeasure.

"What a shame. I was in such a good mood this morning." She made a *tisk* noise with her tongue, shaking her head.

"If all it takes is my face to ruin your mood, then it doesn't sound like it was so sturdy to begin with."

"Ugh! You're the *worst*, Harrison. You're like one of those leeches that sucks the fun out of everything."

"Leeches suck blood, not fun," Harrison stated matter-of-factly.

"You would know," Pessy spat. Lev glanced at me, silently asking *are they always like this?*

When I nodded, his lips curved up in a tiny, amused smile.

We began making our way down the same marble staircase from yesterday. I trailed the tips of my fingers over the gilded railing absentmindedly, admiring the gentle glide of the silky platinum. We turned left into a narrow hallway, which forced us into a single file line, then entered the main dining hall as a group. The space bore resemblance to the sitting room we'd convened in the day before, same marble walls with accents of salmon pink and aqua blue, same grandiose ivory drapes that were pulled back to allow the sun to drizzle over the furniture. There was a long glass octangular table, nearly a yard long in length, and the chairs positioned around it were all painted gold. The dining hall neighboured the kitchen, so we were assaulted upon arrival by the most alluring array of smells, the different spices mingling together in perfect harmony.

The Elrods were all seated when we arrived.

Seraphina was at the head of the table, dressed in a blue, floral stitched gown, her pink crown nestled atop her head. Demetrio sat at her side, clad in navy, his crown resting beside his plate on the table. At Seraphina's other side was

Raevon, her gown composed of a dark blue floral pattern, which had a surplice neckline and sheer long sleeves with button cuffs. Her black hair was loose, cascading down her abdomen, nearly reaching her hipbone. Blekket flanked his father's right side, his white dress shirt tucked inside black breeches. The sleeves were rolled halfway up his arms, revealing a preview of his burly biceps, and his pants were stuffed into black boots.

He'd just popped a blueberry into his mouth when his mother announced our arrival.

"Good morning, everyone," she said enthusiastically, like she was thrilled to discover we were real and not some illusion she contrived in her head. I wondered if, overnight, she'd debated whether or not my visit had been nothing but a dream.

"Good morning," I said back, doing my best to avoid Blekket's vigilant eye. "I hope everyone slept well."

"We did," Demetrio answered for the table. "Thank you for asking."

"Of course." I started for the empty chair next to Raevon, but Pessy occupied it before I had a chance to.

Really, Pess? I thought.

You weren't fast enough, she replied.

I glowered at her. She shrugged with a self-satisfied smirk, flipping her blonde hair over her shoulder. I huffed, then grudgingly situated myself in the seat next to Blekket.

"Good morning, Tympany," he greeted drolly. I refrained from rolling my eyes in front of his parents.

"I hope you've settled in okay," Seraphina said, "and taken advantage of our facilities."

"We have. Everything is so lovely. The bathrooms are particularly delightful. It was nearly impossible to leave."

"My shower this morning was life affirming," Pessy added, which made Seraphina smile widely.

I surveyed the smorgasbord before us, none of the fruit appealing to me.

I turned to Lev and asked, "Are there any more sushi rolls?" His returning smile was incredibly sweet.

"Anything for you, Your—" He quickly corrected himself, "My apologies...*Tympany*."

After Lev scuttled off towards the kitchen, Blekket commented, "Sushi for breakfast?" wrinkling his nose.

"Is there some rule that states I can't have sushi for breakfast?" Seraphina and Demetrio were taken off guard by our informality with one another, glancing nervously at each other.

"No," he chuckled. "It's just kind of strange."

"Hey. Don't yuck my yum."

"That sounded dirtier than you meant it to." I did end up rolling my eyes, while Pessy laughed loudly.

Seraphina looked helpless, Raevon amused, and Demetrio a cross between mortified and intrigued.

Lev placed a plate of yellowtail and avocado sushi in front of me. I thanked him, then shoved the first roll into my mouth. It was just as good as the night before.

"So," Seraphina interrupted, I think worried her son would take things too far and insult me if she let us continue with our casual banter. "We've been discussing plans for the day, and Raevon and Blekket have offered to bring you both," she nodded to Pessy, "into the heart of Esteopia, introduce you to the land and our people." While the idea of seeing more of Esteopia and interacting with the villagers excited me, spending the day with Blekket made me nervous. "Then tonight, we will host a ball in your honour."

"You don't have to do that," I insisted. *Another party?* Two in the span of two days was just overkill.

"We'd already planned to have a party tonight, before you arrived, but now that you're here, we have an excuse to actually celebrate something." Her eyes flickered over to Blekket, who shifted uncomfortably in his chair, shoveling a strawberry around his plate with his fork to evade his mother's scowl. The silent exchange did not go unnoticed.

"We'd be happy to attend," Pessy said graciously, squinting her eyes at me. She loved any excuse to dress up and not have to play chaperone for an evening.

"We thought we'd take you guys to see more of Acadia," Raevon proposed, "and then, depending on the time, we'd take you to Lake Azrord."

"That sounds perfect." I was thrilled I might actually get to meet the lake monster named Jeka.

"We plan to ride to Acadia, so it's a good thing you wore pants," Blekket added, that irritatingly beautiful smirk emerging on the bottom half of his face. I couldn't tell if he was purposefully mocking me, or if he was unaware of the fact that everything he said sounded like he was being sarcastic.

"I look forward to seeing more of your beautiful home," I directed at Seraphina, whose smile looked as though it had been molded by sunshine.

After we finished our meal, we made our way through the great hall and out to the courtyard behind the palace. The garden was brighter than any green I'd ever seen, which I attributed to the waters that flowed through the kingdom, making everything more vibrant. The buttercups were a glossy gold, the grass the shade of every dreamer's meadow, the roots quenched, and the soil renewed. My fingers itched to touch everything we passed, but knowing, if I did, everyone would stop to wait for me, I kept my fingers interlocked in front to resist temptation.

We arrived at the stables, a colossal, robust wooden structure that impressively didn't tremble despite the strength of the wind. I shivered, rubbing my hands over my naked arms.

"Here." Suddenly, Blekket leaned over and draped a hefty cloak around my shoulders, buttoning the clasp underneath my chin. It was black, made of velvet with wool on the inside, spilling down to my sandaled feet and shrouding my clothing. "So you'll blend in," he said, by means of explanation. His fingers lingered on the fabric near my throat before flattening over my shoulders.

I should've moved him away. I should've shaken him off and demanded personal space, but the minute he touched me, when he cinched those midnight eyes with mine and I watched his lips part, all objections died in my mouth. I felt as I had when Lucius throttled me, minus the physical pain.

It was a different kind of strangled, one I had no experience with and didn't know how to put words to.

Even if I wanted to look away, I couldn't.

Blekket cleared his throat before shuffling back, releasing my cloak and scratching the back of his neck in a somewhat awkward gesture. Once he was no longer touching me, the spell broken, my breath hitched. He turned on his heel, heading off to find his horse.

Holy shit, Tymp, Pessy's voice rang in my head.

I glanced at her and found not just Pessy staring at me with their mouth dropped open—Seraphina, Demetrio, Raevon, Harrison, and Lev as well. I straightened my posture, pushing my shoulders back, and walked over to Krystal, doing my best to feign obliviousness to the way everyone was looking at me.

My sweet Pegasus, in her equine beauty, raised her head when she felt me near. Krystal spoke of her emotions with every micro-movement she made. As I read her, she read me, sensing my unease and cocking her head.

Her eyes searched for the bastard who must've offended me for my lips to have drooped in a frown.

"I'm good, Kry," I assured, stroking her. She didn't look entirely convinced, but nuzzled my palm despite her doubts.

When Pessy saw Harrison readying his horse, her eyes swung to me. *Please, tell him he can't join us*, she begged.

Blekket spotted him as well while leading a brilliant stallion over to where we were standing. The steed resembled the structure and colour of a Lipizzan horse, its white coat sleek, with short, strong, well-defined legs that had broad joints.

"We need to be inconspicuous in Acadia, or we'll be mauled by the villagers in the streets." He then suggested, "I think, if possible, we should limit how many guards accompany us."

Harrison rejected the idea.

"She doesn't leave here without at least five guards," he asserted, shooting daggers at Blekket.

"I think *I'll* be the decider of that," I proclaimed.

"We'll be totally safe in Acadia," Blekket swore, his tone softer then I'd heard it. "And we won't be far from the palace, if anything were to happen." Harrison ignored him and stepped between us, blocking Blekket's path to me.

"With all due respect, Your Grace, it's not safe for you to venture out there without your guards present. Your mother would have my head on a silver platter if I didn't insist."

"But—"

He had the *audacity* to cut me off, then took it a step further and declared, "I'm saying *no,* Tympany."

White hot rage charged through my bloodstream, building like deep water currents beneath my ribcage.

"With all due *respect,* Harrison, you're not in a position to tell me what I can or cannot do. My mother's not here, so you answer to *me.* Don't *ever* speak to me that way, not in private or in public. Got it?"

"Yes, Your Grace," he murmured timidly, retreating a step.

"I would rather not compel you, but if you continue to put up a fight, I will if I have to. You and the other guards are staying here. Only Pessy comes with us. Nod your head if you understand." It took him a moment to recover before he mustered the strength to bob his head in a nod. "Good. You may go now."

He practically sprinted with his tail between his legs to the palace, his face a bright, chagrinned red.

I fixed my cloak and swivelled around to face the Elrods and Pessy, who I'd never seen smile so big.

You're my hero, she gushed.

Blekket shook his head at me, the corner of his mouth tugged upward. "Magnificent." He breathed.

"You *really* don't want round four to be right now, when I'm already riled up. It wouldn't be a fair fight."

"Oh, I disagree." His eyes sparkled with mischief, whereas mine lifted to the heavens in an eye roll.

Raevon leaned over to Pessy and whispered, "What does round four mean?"

Pessy smiled, murmuring back, "I'll tell you later."

Blekket, Raevon, and Pessy were each given their own cloaks for the road, Raevon's a dark navy that matched her dress, Pessy's a pale grey, and Blekket's black, just like mine. Raevon mounted her steed, a multi-coloured Pinto with large patches of white amidst a sea of brown, the mane and tail the colour of cream.

"What's your horse named?" I asked Raevon as I climbed onto Krystal, gathering her reins in one hand. Raevon's lashes fluttered, her mouth agape from watching me ascend my horse with supernatural ease.

After she'd recovered, she answered, "Her name's Autumn, cause her spots kind of look like fall leaves."

"I like that. It's cute."

"Mine's named Clarence," Blekket interjected, then added, "Not that you asked," with a wink.

"Why'd you name him Clarence?" Pessy wondered.

"Because he really likes to shout CLARENCE at the top of his lungs," Raevon answered, making both of us laugh.

Blekket just shrugged. "I like to make an entrance."

Demetrio and Seraphina loitered at the entrance with Lev, waving goodbye to us. We began our journey into the heart of Acadia, Blekket leading the troop, Raevon and I riding in the middle, and Pessy at the rear.

Esteopia was utterly breathtaking.

It was as if the gift of the skies and the Argent Ocean wasn't water, but liquid magic, washing over the kingdom to show nature in her humble brilliance. The path we followed was framed by a riot of gold, pink, blue, and soft cream blooms, a vision deprived of rivals. With boughs of berries and a carpet of florae unfurling below our feet, the scenery was comparable to an autumnal banquet.

I started to pick one of the berries off a protruding branch, before Blekket advised, "I wouldn't do that if I were you."

"Why? Will something happen?" I didn't want a repeat of the gate.

"No. It's just not clean." I stared at him, then popped the berry into my mouth. The delectable juice exploded over my tongue, spilling down my throat. "You really don't like to be told what to do, do you?"

"I'm not used to it. You know, being a Goddess and all." I enjoyed the way his eyes widened at my bold words.

"Oh, so *that's* how it is?" he laughed. I shrugged, mocking him with my own version of a smug smirk.

Pessy scoffed, shaking her head at me disapprovingly.

Through the ride, we learned more about both Blekket and Raevon. Blekket was twenty-nine, almost thirty, and Raevon was twenty-three. I'd been right in assuming they were close, the barbs traded with one another laced with the kind of familiarity that was reminiscent of me and Jaxith. Raevon clearly looked up to her brother, and he obviously adored her. It was entertaining to see her put Blekket in his place, always bursting his bubble when his ego started to swell. Pessy and I fell into a rhythm with them quite easily.

They wanted to know everything about Kylantis, particularly Raevon, and what it was like growing up there.

"I can't believe you're five-thousand-years-old," Raevon marvelled. "You look like you're twenty-five."

"Time is different in Kylantis," I said. "It's slower."

"Do you always have to wear grey?" she asked me next in her sequence of rapid fire questions.

"When I'm in public. Not when I'm in private."

"That must suck," she mumbled. "Grey is such an unhappy colour. Why wouldn't you have gotten red?"

"Cause that was Jax's signature."

"But you're the Goddess of the Heart and Mind! Both of those things are red!"

"Wait. That's *such* a good point," Pessy exclaimed, making Raevon flush crimson.

"Why didn't your parents make your colour green?" Blekket inserted. "It's the only colour not belonging to any of the Gods, and wasn't your sister's colour already silver? They're basically the same."

"Silver and grey next to one another look totally different," I claimed, but I couldn't deny he had somewhat of a point.

"That's just semantics."

"You don't even know what that word means," Raevon accused, making Pessy laugh so hard she snorted.

"Fuck you, Rae," Blekket barked, but he was grinning when he flipped her off.

I couldn't stop my eyes from straying over to Blekket during the ride. With the mottled sun leaking over his face, his freckles were more detectible. They mostly circulated on the bridge of his nose, only a few spots expanding out onto his cheeks. Every time I glanced his way, he shifted his head to meet my inquisitive gaze, having already been watching me from the corner of his eye and waiting for me to look back at him.

Each time I was caught, my eyes darted to the plants, to Krystal, to Pessy or Raevon, anywhere but him.

But they always returned, like a moth drawn to a flame.

Blekket suddenly threw out a hand, halting us. "We're here," he announced, climbing down from Clarence and landing on his feet in the soil, his boots making a squishy sound in the earth.

"What do we do with our horses?" Pessy asked, tugging on Belgian's reins to steer him away from eating a plant.

"I can't exactly leave a Pegasus lying around." I caressed Krystal's wing.

"You think I want to leave this guy here to be taken?" Blekket scratched Clarence behind the ear, and he whickered with delight, stretching his neck for more. "We'll bring them with us and keep a close eye on them."

Clarence moseyed over to where Krystal was, sniffing her. Krystal, who usually recoiled when any horse other than Belgian got too close, inclined her head towards him and nuzzled her cheek against his.

"I think our horses like each other," Blekket announced, sounding pleased.

"Just the horses," I retorted, but there was no heat to my words, and he knew it. I turned to Raevon, asking, "I thought Ashrays melt into puddles in direct sunlight," suddenly realising we'd been under the glare of the sun all morning, and nothing had happened to either Autumn or Clarence.

"Someone's done her homework," Blekket prided. I ignored him.

"These aren't Ashrays. They're just regular horses. We only ride Ashrays when the weather's cloudy."

"Right. Of course." I now felt stupid for asking.

"Ashrays are a symbol of our kingdom's resilience," Blekket explained. When I turned my head, I found him hovering over me, only a few centimeters of distance between us. I nearly smacked my head into his chest from the close proximity. "Even when they fall, they always rise again."

"Until the last drop!" Raevon cheered, raising her fist in the air.

The mosaic stone path we walked on was wide in width, so the horses fit at our sides comfortably. I found it interesting that no one seemed to notice Krystal's mammoth size or feathered wings. She blended in seamlessly with the rest of the horses, which overjoyed her, as she was normally bombarded with attention wherever we went.

Acadia was much more lively than I anticipated. While we went undetected in the sea of Esteopians, our hoods up so no one would recognise who we were or that we were with the royals, everyone was so friendly. We were stopped several times by Esteopians offering water to our horses, everyone we passed waving hello or sparking conversation with us about mundane things, like the wonderful weather we were having, or to compliment us on our steeds. Both Raevon and Blekket were incredibly patient with each of the Esteopians who stopped us, speaking with a gentleness I wouldn't have thought possible from Blekket. I was in awe of all the timber huts, with blue canopies made of translucent cloth draped over the roofs to add texture and a pop of colour. All the houses mirrored one another, and I was impressed with the uniformity.

"Is this the upper class?" I asked Blekket, admiring the intricate, extravagant looking attire the Esteopians were wearing. Krystal and Clarence had glommed on to one another, so I was forced to walk next to him.

"Yes," he replied, nodding in greeting to a passing Esteopian who smiled at him. "They're all Neraids. In the other villages, like Frofsea and Palens, the residents are mortal."

"Were the residents of Eveium mortal?" He nodded, my heart sinking for all the innocent, lost lives. "The mortals are the ones who plant the harvests?"

"It's how they make a profit. They trade the grains with the Neraids for things like clothing and household appliances, stuff they otherwise wouldn't have easy access to. The relationship between the upper and lower class is very amiable. They're only considered lower class because they're not Neraids, but they're treated very well."

I was happy to hear that. "Do the homes of the mortals look like these?" All the cabins were so quaint and eclectic.

"Similar, but not quite as fancy." He cocked his head. "What do the homes of the Kylantians look like?"

"They're made of marble, same as the palace, just smaller." I'd only ever been inside Pessy's home, but I'd seen the other residences in her neighbourhood. All the houses were identical to each other.

When Blekket tipped his face up, the sunlight accentuated the birthmark on his left ear, the one shaped like a teardrop.

"Are teardrops the symbol of Esteopia?"

"What a random question," he chuckled, then answered, "The symbol of Esteopia is the Ashray horse. That's why they're on the flag. Teardrops are the emblem of the royals." His brows furrowed. "Why'd you ask?"

"I noticed you have a birthmark on your left ear in the shape of a teardrop." I unconsciously tugged on my earlobe when I said this. "Also, all the knobs in the palace are shaped like water droplets, including the showerhead."

"I'm flattered you've paid such close attention to my appearance," he teased. I was tempted to slap him.

"Don't flatter yourself. I'm a very observant person."

"I've gathered that." His eyes softened. "Rae has the same birthmark. So does my mother. It's recognition of our heritage. It lets others know we're royal."

I glanced over at Raevon, who was walking a few paces ahead with Pessy. When she threw her head back and laughed at something Pess said, I saw the tiny black teardrop on the back of her left ear, in the same spot as Blekket's.

"Your father doesn't have one?"

"He wasn't born royal. He just married into it." *Kind of like my father*, I thought to myself.

Raevon led us in the direction of a charming tavern with outside seating, so we wouldn't have to leave our horses unattended. I stole the spot next to Blekket on the bench, Raevon and Pessy sitting shoulder to shoulder across from us.

"Have you ever had ale before, Tympany?" Raevon asked.

"No," I admitted, embarrassed. I'd only ever tried nectar, which was so privileged. I really was quite sheltered in Kylantis.

"You'll like it," Raevon insisted, and I was so swept up in her enthusiasm that I believed her.

A server dressed head to toe in blue came to take our order. Blekket spoke for the group, ordering us four ales and four fried fish dishes.

"What does nectar taste like?" Raevon asked after the man left us, resting her cheek in her palm.

"It tastes like liquid gold," I described, not sure how else to explain it. "It's quite potent. I don't think a human could handle it."

"Let the humans be the judge of that," Blekket opposed, his unlawfully white teeth making their highly anticipated appearance in the form of a smile.

"Can you get drunk off it? You know...as a Goddess?" Raevon lowered her voice in case of eavesdroppers.

"It takes a lot more of it to make a God drunk then a human or Kylantian," Pessy answered for me. "If a human had one glass, they'd be down for the count for days."

"Now I *really* want to try some." Blekket sighed.

The server returned, setting four bottles of ale down on the table. I twisted the cap off mine and took a swig of the amber liquid. The alcohol was sweet, tasting full-bodied and kind of fruity.

"Well?" Raevon prompted.

"It's delicious," I declared, receiving three smiles from around the table. "What's it made of?"

"Yeast," Blekket answered, his mouth gleaming from the liquor.

I watched him lick his lips and gulped, dragging my eyes quickly away before he noticed me staring.

"What makes it taste fruity?" Pessy wondered.

"It's mixed with citrus," he continued. "Ale yeasts work at higher temperatures, and create a variety of flavour compounds called esters. Esters give beers their characteristic fruity flavours. Yeasts are categorised by their profile, which can be either clear, fruity, or peppery and spicy."

I didn't want to admit it, but I was impressed. "How do you know so much about this?"

His smile was all at once smug. "If I'm not charming the pants off of Goddesses, I'm drinking." He chugged his ale as if it were water for further proof of his dexterity.

"You haven't charmed the pants off of anyone," I pointed out.

"Not yet." He winked.

"Not *ever*."

"We'll see." I didn't know what to say to that, so I just shook my head and took another sip.

"Maybe in your next life, you'll own a distillery," Pessy mused, saving me with a topic change.

"Who says I'm waiting until my next life? Sign me up now!" He lifted his bottle, and she laughed, clinking her glass with his.

The server returned with our dishes—fried tilapia with a side of chips and a mixed salad of arugula and tomatoes.

"Thank you, kind sir," Blekket said graciously to the server as he set everything down.

"Wait a second…" The older man leaned back. "Is that Blekket Elrod under there? Take off that hood and let me see you, boy!"

Blekket slid the hood of his cloak off his head, standing to embrace the server with an enchanting laugh.

"Have you shrunk, Sanders?" He patted the top of the man's white hair. "Looks like you're about an inch shorter. You should really see someone about that."

"Fuck you, Blek." I was startled to hear a townsperson use such crude language with the crown. "I'm still taller than you, asshole."

"Not by much." Blekket sat back down on the wooden bench beside me, his shoulder grazing mine.

"Hey there, Rae." Sanders waved at Raevon, who grinned and waved back. "I almost didn't recognise you with that hair of yours."

"I know. It's grown so much since the last time we saw each other." She ran her fingers through the long strands.

"And who are these pretty ladies you're here traveling with?" He gestured to Pess and me.

I opened my mouth to introduce us, but Blekket answered first, "This is Angel and Pessy. They're friends visiting from the north."

Angel.

I had no control over the way my cheeks blistered at the usage of that nickname. The curl of his accent around the word made my stomach flip over, and an odd, sort of lightheaded feeling enveloped my head, shoving it underwater.

I didn't like feeling so off balance, or that the sensation was triggered by something Blekket said.

"Such beautiful companions," Sanders complimented, flashing us a charismatic smile that was infectious in its size and sincerity.

"The word I'd use is magnificent," Blekket corrected, seeking a rise out of me I did everything in my power not to grant him.

"Are you enjoying your stay with us?" Both Pessy and I nodded. "The Elrods are like family to me. I've known Blek and Rae since they were children."

"You practically raised me here in this bar," Blekket added. Now I understood where he'd learned so much about ale from.

"Ser and Dem are the ones who gave me this tavern. The Elrods are saints. You couldn't ask for a better family to wear the crown."

"Sand," Raevon squeaked, her eyes glittering with tears.

"We'll be lucky when this one decides to get over himself and take the throne." He clamped his hand over Blekket's shoulder, who flinched at the mention, gulping down a large draft of ale. "I hope you enjoy your meal. If you need anything more, just holler at me. Your food is on the house."

"Thank you, Sanders," I said, charmed by his generosity. After he'd sauntered off to the back of the pub, I faced Blekket. "Was that man mortal, or a Neraid?"

"Sanders is mortal. He's a sweetheart. Mum and Dad love him so much, they set him up with his own lodgings in Acadia, so he'd get all the privileges of the Neraids. He lives in the bar. There's a room in the back where he sleeps."

Wow.

The first real mortal I interacted with had been Esteopian...and so pleasant.

As I ate and listened to the playful banter between Pessy, Raevon, and Blekket, I thought about how there was no way this was all an act. My family made Esteopia sound like everyone was cold and non-approachable. I would've considered the possibility that the Elrods were putting on a show for my benefit, but none of these Esteopians knew who I was. They were kind to me because that's who they were intrinsically at their core, their welcoming nature driven not by selfish intent, but by purity of heart. Not to mention, everyone looked happy, well-treated, and proud to be Esteopian. These didn't seem like people who deserved to lose their homes, who deserved to lose their lives in some inane war over land. What I'd said to Seraphina and Demetrio the day before now suddenly rang true—they deserved a chance, for someone to fight for them.

Even if that someone wasn't me.

Blekket reached over in an attempt to pilfer a chip from my plate.

"Touch my plate, and you're looking at round four," I threatened, slapping his hand away.

"Yes, ma'am," he quipped, saluting me.

"Okay, can someone explain what round four means?" Raevon griped, looking on the verge of detonating.

"Do you want to tell her, or should I?" Blekket scowled at me, then shifted to face his little sister head on, releasing a huff in anticipation of whatever reaction he expected to elicit from her.

"Tympany and I have met before," he confessed. Raevon's cobalt eyes looked like they were about to trundle out her skull. "I met her two nights ago, when I snuck into the palace at Kylantis during her birthday celebration."

"*That's* where you went?!" she shouted, slamming a fist on the table. "To *Kylantis?* Why didn't I get to come?!"

"I was worried, if we both went, a Sleothian might recognise us and cause a commotion."

"But you knew I've always wanted to go!" Raevon pouted, slumping on the bench. Pessy reached out to rub her back, and Raevon leaned into Pessy's hand, seeming to relax under her touch.

I noted this with interest, hiding a smile behind my chip.

"I'm sorry, Rae." Blekket plucked her hand off the table to plant a conciliatory kiss on her knuckles.

She squeezed back to show he was forgiven.

"That still doesn't explain what round four means," she reminded him, after realising he never answered the question.

"Well," I said, continuing where he left off, "while he was there, your brother not-so-gallantly attacked me."

"Blek!" Raevon ripped her hand out of her brother's in outrage.

"*Hey.*" Blekket turned to me. "Let's get something straight. I didn't attack you. I'd never attack a woman, whether she's mortal, Neraid, Goddess, Sleothian, anyone. I asked you if you were alright when I saw you were hurt. If anything, *you* attacked *me.* I was just defending myself."

"Because you were poking your head somewhere you didn't belong," I argued, but he'd been right in saying me wording it that way made it sound like something far more debauched happened than what actually occurred. He hadn't hurt me, or done anything immoral, other than hold me down so I didn't tear him limb from limb.

"She's forgetting the best part," Blekket told Raevon, ignoring what I'd said about him snooping. "She tried to compel me to leave, but it didn't work." Raevon's jaw plummeted to the table.

"How is that even possible?" she gasped.

"I have no idea," I confessed, and maybe shouldn't have. It made me vulnerable that two of the Elrods now knew my abilities didn't affect one of their own. They could use that to their advantage later on, proof I wasn't as strong as I was advertised as being. But I had a strong premonition they wouldn't, that the kindness they'd extended to me wasn't a farce in order for me to support them. Maybe it was because I wanted to believe what I was seeing was real, because I enjoyed their company so much, but I had faith they wouldn't try to use anything I told them against me.

I didn't know why, or if it was logical, but I trusted Raevon and Blekket— and I would continue to trust them, unless they gave me a reason not to.

"Can you try it now, on Blek? I wanna see if it doesn't work." I was curious to know if perhaps, magically overnight, his immunity had vanished, so I turned to Blekket and locked eyes with him.

"Give me your last chip." He grinned.

"Nice try, sweetheart, but no."

"Whoa!" Raevon cried. "Now, do me!"

I shifted to Raevon. **"Give me your last chip."** She handed it over without a moment's hesitation, then stared down at her outstretched hand, in awe that it had succumbed without her permission.

"That's insane," Raevon spluttered, shaking her head.

"Thank you for the chip." I munched down, beaming.

When we finished our meal, it was already three in the afternoon. The party being held in my honour would commence at five, so we needed to head back to the palace to start getting ready for the evening.

I was sad to cut our day short, as I'd been enjoying myself immensely and had hoped we'd get to see Jeka in the flesh.

It would have to wait for another day.

On the way back down the pebbled road, Blekket took a detour to the left, leading us in the opposite direction of the palace. I was confused at first where he was taking us, but when I got my first glimpse of the village, I gasped, understanding why he'd felt it necessary to delay our trek home with one more stop.

The ground was glazed in a thick sheet of ash. Everything was charred and reeked like burning matches, the houses crumbled into ember, the tips of the leaves singed black, the air laced with the reside of smoke, difficult to breathe through. The destruction spanned out for miles, annihilating everything that once existed there. Krystal tried to step forward to get a closer look, but tramped on something that caused her to stumble back. When I peeked down, I saw it was someone's bone she'd knocked with her hoof.

"This was the town of Eveium," Blekket explained, the normally animated cadence of his voice replaced with a somber lilt. "Sanders was originally from here. His entire family perished in the drogon attack."

"Holy shit," Pessy muttered under her breath.

"How many lives were lost in total?" I asked.

"We never got an official list, but the population of Eveium was over forty thousand people."

"Oh, Gods." I couldn't wrap my brain around that many lives lost. It was a far greater sum than the number of casualties from Sleotha. "Will you be able to rebuild it?" I hoped the town wasn't irredeemable.

"Not the way it was," Raevon replied, frowning. "The village was spectacular. So much life and joy. It will never be that way again, no matter who inhabits it next or what it looks like. It will always be haunted by this."

"I thought it was important you saw it," Blekket directed at me. "See what you're fighting for."

See what you're fighting for.

Those words tasted of death and betrayal in my mouth, but when I repeated them one more time, there was also the tiniest bit of truth.

Chapter Seven

I laid the dress I'd selected for tonight out on the bed. It was a pleated, metallic gown with knots as shoulder straps, a plunging V neckline, and a cinched waist with an A-line silhouette, the floor-length hem spilling down to the ground like melted down silver. Pessy went with Raevon to her bedchamber to borrow a gown for the ball, since she didn't bring any with her from Kylantis.

She'd been gone for almost an hour.

As I got ready for the party, images of Eveium, burnt to a crisp, kept flashing before my eyes. I had to take a pause every time I started trembling with fury. I wasn't sure who I was angrier with—the Sleothians who'd unleashed the drogon and scorched an entire village of innocent mortals, or my family, who'd done nothing to stop them. Now that I knew Seraphina and Demetrio were telling the truth about the attack, it didn't make sense to me why my family hadn't intervened, why they only sprang into action when Esteopia fought back in defense of their lost citizens.

What the Esteopians did the night of my birthday wasn't innocuous, but they'd only done it as a direct response to what the Sleothians did first. It made me question what else Sleotha had done to terrorise Esteopia over the centuries, what else they'd destroyed and taken that my family was complicit in.

I brushed my hair with my fingers, working to disentangle the strands that were knotted together from being tied back in a bun all day. When that didn't work, I stripped off my jumpsuit and climbed into the shower, keeping it short despite the allure of the water. I focused on quickly shampooing and conditioning my hair, not lingering longer than necessary. I hopped out, tying a cotton robe around my body, then searched the drawers for something to dry my hair with, discovering several different contraptions meant for hair styling below the sink.

I first used a black, bulky blow-dryer, which impressively dried my hair in under five minutes. I'd just plugged in and was about to start curling my hair when Pessy entered the bathroom.

"No!" she shouted, holding out her hands in protest. "Let me do it! You'll mess up."

"Why do you have no faith in me?" I handed her the curling iron and took a seat on one of the gold stools.

"I have faith in you with other things, but when it comes to your appearance, it's best to leave it to the professionals."

"And that's supposed to be you?" She stuck her tongue out at me, lifting a cluster of my hair and winding it around the iron. I took a moment to admire the gown she'd borrowed from Raevon. It was a rich navy made of stretch satin, with off-the-shoulder short sleeves, a V neckline, ruched waist, and a column silhouette. The dark hue of the dress made her hair look even blonder. "You look stunning, Pess."

"Thank you." She flushed.

"Did Raevon curl your hair?" Her blush got even deeper as she nodded.

"She's so cool, Tymp." I felt her fingers glide through my hair, separating the curls. "With Callie, I never knew where I stood. You were right in saying she never took anything seriously. I feel like Raevon's different. She even let slip to me that her last relationship was with a woman."

"How did that come up in conversation?" Pessy laughed, then shrugged.

"The point is, she wanted to make it clear to me what her preference was, so there'd be no confusion. It meant a lot to me, cause most of the time, with girls, I can never tell the difference between someone flirting or just being friendly. I don't know…do you think it's one sided? Am I being ridiculous?"

"Absolutely not!" I cried. "You're not ridiculous at all. I like Raevon, and she's way more your speed than Callie. I also don't think it's one sided. I saw how she reacted when you touched her. I wouldn't give you false hope if it meant getting your heart broken. You know I just want you to be happy."

"I know that." She leaned down to kiss my cheek. "I want you to be happy too. And I like Blekket."

"That makes one of us." She set a hand on my shoulder and whirled me around so I could see her glare.

"*Don't* lie, Tympany. I saw the way you two were acting today. I know what it looks like when you don't like someone, and that was certainly *not* it." I knit my lips shut, mulling over that, as she finished curling the front strands of my hair. "Besides, if you somehow end up with Blekket, and I end up with Raevon, it would be like we're sisters."

"We already *are* sisters," I argued. "And don't link me and Blekket together like that. It would just complicate things."

"You mean more than they already are?" She tugged the chord of the curling iron out of the wall, coiling it around the rod. "And by the way, you saying it would complicate things isn't saying you're not interested."

Shit—she'd caught me there.

"Since when did you become such an eternal optimist?" I teased, deliberately trying to change the subject.

"I don't know. Something about the waters here." I laughed. "You're all done. I had to work with what I was given, but I think you look pretty decent, if I do say so myself."

"No one likes a bragger, Pessoranda." Pessy gagged at her full name, mimicking the motion of vomiting.

She did a flawless job with my hair, far better than I would've done left to my own devices. It fell in loose waves to my shoulders, framing my face like a coronet of burnished chestnut. She helped me into my dress, buttoning the back, as I admired her handiwork.

"You're right," I said, running my fingers through the curls. "You have vision."

"Good thing my best friend's a muse. Now, are you ready to attend another ball in your honour?"

"Please, don't remind me." I linked my arm with hers, and we made our way out into the hall.

Alsandair and Harrison were waiting for us by the entrance to our bedchamber. They were both dressed in their official Kylantian uniforms, the picture of solemnity. Harrison frowned at Pessy's dress.

"Where are you keeping your blade?" he asked her.

"Wouldn't you like to know," she hissed.

"I would, since it's imperative all of Tympany's guards be armed at all times, especially with the…*townsfolk* entering the palace, who will be made aware of who she is by the Queen and King."

"*Hey.*" When Harrison's eyes swerved over to me, the colour depleted from his face. "Don't talk about the townsfolk like that. There's *nothing* wrong with them. All you need to know is that Pessy is armed. Where that weapon's currently located is none of your business. Got it?"

I didn't think he could get any paler.

"Of course, Your Grace," he stuttered respectfully, once again unable to look me in the eye when he spoke. Harrison abruptly turned on his heel, darting off in the direction of the ballroom.

"That was vicious," a voice behind us said.

I twirled to pinpoint the interloper and had to clamp my mouth shut, stifling the gasp at the sight of him. Blekket looked dapper in a navy velvet petticoat and matching breeches, the vest underneath a radiant silver that matched the metallic of my dress. The white button down underneath was unbuttoned at the top, the collar spread out over his clavicles, somehow making him look more roguish and dangerous then the mischief in his eyes already did. He completely froze when we turned around, his jaw dropping as he appraised the combination of my dress and hair.

"Wow." He breathed, sounding awestricken. "You look—"

"Don't say what I think you're about to say. We've had such a good day. I'd hate for you to spoil it now."

The comment woke him from his trance.

"At least you're admitting you enjoyed my company today." He then smiled at Pessy. "You look gorgeous, Pess."

"Thank you, Blek." Pessy's face warmed to a rosy pink.

"Would calling you beautiful make you want to tear me limb from limb, or is it just the word *magnificent* that triggers you? Just trying to avoid losing an arm tonight." He clasped his bicep protectively.

"You can call me beautiful," I permitted, ignoring his end statement.

"In that case, you look absolutely beautiful, Tympany." I wished my blood didn't boil in my cheeks to make it apparent how flattered I was.

"I didn't sign off on absolutely." Blekket mocked me with an eye roll. "You don't look too bad yourself. I like the jacket."

"This old thing?" He lifted the hem of his petticoat. "Fished it out from the bottom of my closet last minute."

"You sure you didn't agonise over a mirror for hours, trying to pick out the best colour to match your vest?"

"I had to look my best for the guest of honour." He became aware of the fact we were lingering in the hallway and gesticulated with his hand for us to go first. "Shall we?"

We strolled down the staircase at a slow, even pace, Pessy's arm interlocked with mine. Alsandair flanked my other side, and Blekket trailed behind us. No one spoke while we floated down the hall, gliding as fluently as rivulets of water.

The air thrummed with angst regarding tonight's festivities, but each of us for different reasons.

I'm just curious...where are *you hiding a blade?* I asked Pessy through the privacy of the bond.

Same place you are. Sheathed to my thigh.

It was true. I didn't mention this to Harrison, but I was also armed and at the ready. My blade was stashed under my skirt, strapped to my thigh just in case I encountered any instance where I was alone and needed to protect myself. After my birthday, I'd never leave myself vulnerable again.

Like I'd have shown Harrison THAT, she continued. *Only in his wildest dreams would he get a chance to see all this.*

I let out a tiny giggle, which revealed to the men that we were communicating clandestinely.

"How does the bond work?" Blekket asked us. "You just think a thought, and the other one can hear it?"

"Sort of." I explained, "I visualise myself speaking the words, and then, I hear Pessy reply."

"Have you ever heard a thought you weren't supposed to?" he asked Pess.

"Not yet," she answered. "We're only two days into this thing."

"If you hear anything about me, let me know. I have a feeling she won't tell me to my face."

"You're right about that," I threw over my shoulder. Blekket squinted his eyes at me in an artificial scowl.

Seraphina, Demetrio, and Raevon were waiting for us outside the large gold door to the ballroom. Seraphina looked elegant in a dark navy, long sleeve gown, complemented with a wide scoop neckline, an embroidered-lace bodice with glittering appeal and tiny beads, and layers of tulle flowing from the waistline to the floor in a figure-flattering A-line cut. Demetrio was dressed similarly to his son, dashing in a black petticoat with navy trousers, a black, indigo, and silver silk scarf wrapped around his throat and tucked into his black vest. Raevon looked utterly stunning in a light blue gown with spaghetti straps, the tulle skirt highlighting feminine morbidezza and grace. Her dark hair was parted to the right, curled, and there was a silver clip that looked like branches pulling the hair on her left side away from her face and off her shoulder.

"You look amazing," I told her, Raevon's face turning as red as Pessy's had when Blekket complimented her.

"So do you," she replied bashfully.

"Rae told us you had a wonderful day together," Seraphina said.

"We did. Acadia is so spectacular. And we got a chance to meet Sanders, who was a delight."

Seraphina's eyes filled with affection. "Sanders is one of our favourite people ever! I'm so glad you got to meet him."

"Blekket also said he took you guys to see what's left of Eveium," Demetrio added, his voice gruff.

My shoulders sunk at the mention. "He did. It was heartbreaking, and infuriating to see."

"I feel strange saying I'm glad to know it enraged you, but I am. It should." He reminded me so much of my father in that moment, the intensity in which he spoke with. What set him apart from Isaias was the underlying ire seething under the surface of every word he uttered, even when the topic was something light. Demetrio always looked on the verge on popping his top and spilling rage out onto the floor, no matter the circumstance or people around him.

"Lev will introduce us," Seraphina explained, Lev appearing at her side. "First Raevon, then Blek, then Demetrio and me, and lastly, you. It's custom we enter in the proper order of authority."

It was strange to think of myself as outranking them in their own home, but I supposed it was true a God surpassed a Queen.

We arranged ourselves in the order of hierarchy against the wall, Pessy and I at the back of the line, Raevon at the front. I tried to be subtle about it, but my palms were perspiring at the prospect of being presented before a room of strangers. Being a Goddess didn't exempt me from getting anxious over a bunch of eyes being glued to me, or cure me of my aversion to the limelight.

Blekket must've sensed something, for he leaned in and whispered, "I always picture everyone naked. Helps with the nerves."

"How would that help me be *less* nervous?" His lips curled up in an arrogant smile.

"It doesn't, but that just did." He was right—my anxiety had left me in my moment of irritation.

"You...you're—"

"Amazing? Wonderful? Magnificent?"

"I was going to say impossible," I joked. Even Demetrio smiled at that.

Like I said, Pessy mused after Blekket shifted back to face front. *You like him.*

"Fuck off." Everyone spun around, staring at me with a compilation of horror and amusement.

I smothered my palm over my mouth. I hadn't meant to say that aloud.

"I'm *so* sorry," I spluttered, Pessy covering her face with her hand. "I didn't...I shouldn't..."

"Don't apologise, Tympany. I tell Demetrio to fuck off all the time." I took Seraphina's hand, giving it a giant squeeze. Even if that wasn't true, I appreciated her claiming it was.

When I touched Seraphina, I heard her think *Tympany is such a sweetheart. I didn't expect to love her this much. I hope she never leaves.* When I squeezed her hand a second time, she didn't know the reason why.

The doors to the ballroom unbolted.

Lev stepped through them first, clasping his wrist behind his back as he strode in with his chin tipped up.

"Presenting Her Royal Highness, Princess of Esteopia, Raevon Elrod." Raevon plastered on an award winning smile, squaring her shoulders before stepping forward. She was met with a cacophony of hollers and cheers from the throng inside. I imagined she was putting on quite a show to receive such approbation.

Next, Lev's voice rang out, "Presenting His Royal Highness, Prince and future King of Esteopia, Blekket Elrod."

Blekket flinched at the title of *future king*, then made his way in. While I couldn't see into the ballroom, I heard the outpour of love and applause assail him the moment he entered, louder than the upheaval had been for Raevon. I remembered what Sanders said about Blekket taking the throne.

It was evident, while Blekket didn't want the crown next, his kingdom embraced him as their future king.

"Presenting, His and Her Imperial Majesty, Queen and King of Esteopia, Seraphina and Demetrio Elrod."

Demetrio tangled his fingers with Seraphina's, beaming at his wife, then lead her inside to be welcomed by their subjects. The moment reminded me of Roara and Isaias, how they always needed to be touching one another to feel centered in a sea of faces. Thinking about my parents made me wistful and misty eyed.

Now, I was about to enter a room full of strangers with sweaty palms, and a lump in my throat.

"Presenting Her Excellence, the Almighty Tympany," Lev pronounced. "Goddess of the Heart and Mind, and Muse to all mortals and celestials, accompanied by her bonded Kylantian, Pessoranda Whitereaver."

"Ooo, I got a shoutout!" Pessy squealed. "This is so cool!"

"Don't let go of my arm." She knew how much I detested being stared at, especially by strangers.

"I've got you," she promised, squeezing my wrist.

We controlled our steps, so they were in union with one another as we entered the ballroom. All of Esteopia's elite, dressed in their most opulent, alluring gowns and garb, received us with a round of roaring applause. When I'd first walked into the room, I felt uneasy with all these eyes on me, but once I was in there, inundated with the ovation and worship, I was overwhelmed, humbled, and, in a way, awe-inspired. Pessy clung to my side, just as amazed by the pandemonium as I was.

We headed over to where Raevon and Blekket were standing, applauding us with the rest of the mass.

"That was quite an entrance," Blekket said, scorching my cheeks.

"I didn't mean it to be," I blurted. Both Blekket and Raevon's laughs in response were tender.

"They love you," Raevon assured me, wrapping her arm around mine. "You don't realise what you've represented for so many humans over the years. You're a symbol of inspiration and hope. In our times of distress, we've prayed to you, knowing you couldn't come down to greet us until you came of age, but hoping you would when you could. And you did. You chose *us* as your first visit to the Realm. You have no idea what that means to us. You answered our prayers without even realising there were any."

The lump in my throat was now painful. "Th...thank you, Raevon," I squeaked, not sure what else to say.

"Tympany, there's sushi over here," Seraphina called out to me. That was enough to dry my tears.

I remained by Queen Seraphina's side for the first hour of the evening, Seraphina showing me off and introducing me to various Neraids. There was

Orson and Devina, who Seraphina grew up with in Acadia and appointed as her advisors when she ascended the throne. I met Anastasia and Pierce next, members of the Esteopian army who were in the mob when I first arrived at the gates. Lilianna Durchville, a close friend to Raevon, almost spilled her wine all over me because she was so overwrought to get the chance to talk to me. Everyone I spoke to was daunted by me at first, but once they saw I wasn't this intimidating, unsociable presence, they eased into conversation and grew laxer with their language.

Just like the villagers I interacted with in Acadia while undercover, everyone was affable, warm, and honoured to welcome me into their home.

She then introduced me to Marisa, Lev's wife, who was also a solider in the army, as well as their four-year-old daughter, Charlene. Charly had the same unruly ginger curls as her father, and, upon meeting me, adorably asked if I was an angel, her large blue eyes twinkling with elation.

I knelt on the ground before her and replied, "I'm no angel, Charly. *You're* the angel."

She threw her arms around my neck despite her mother trying to haul her back. I squeezed her tiny waist, struggling to suppress tears.

After I'd made my first set of rounds, I needed a moment alone and found myself in the corner of the ballroom. I had a napkin full of sushi cupped in one hand, and a wine glass filled to the brim with champagne in the other, which tasted carbonated and of crystalline pearls. Alsandair and Harrison were across the way, guarding the entrance and surveying the crowd, along with the other Kylantians, who circumscribed the perimeter of the ballroom. Pessy had gone somewhere with Raevon at the start of the night. I hadn't seen either of them since I was whisked off with Seraphina.

Looking around, I was surprised by the uneven ratio of women to men here. The women outnumbered the men by a staggering amount. I wondered if that was because the main sovereign was a woman, or if it was for some other reason. When I glanced over at Blekket, I realised why.

He was in the same spot he'd been in when I'd first entered the ballroom, not having moved once all night, due to the horde of women encircling him. They were lined up out the door, fighting for a moment alone with him. The effervesce I was used to seeing from him was absent in his cold, hard stare, his stance rigid, not as open and fluid as normal. Seeing his obvious discomfort and annoyance, how his eyes kept swinging to his mother, it became clear to me what Seraphina meant this morning when she said me being there gave them something to actually celebrate, why Blekket cringed at the mention of this party—this ball had originally been intended for Blekket to meet potential suitors. At thirty, he was expected to wed, and then, to ascend the throne.

By the looks of how he shook these women off, both those things were clearly not priorities to him.

I heard the sound of throat clearing and willed my eyes away from Blekket. Demetrio stood beside me, his shadow looming over the sushi in my hands.

"Are you enjoying yourself?" he asked me. I was brought back to two nights prior when Lucius asked me the same thing. It made me on guard for whatever it was he wished to discuss with me.

"Yes," I replied, adding, "Your wife has been very accommodating."

"She's thrilled you're here. You're a dream come true for her." I cocked my head to the side.

"Am I not for you?" I was pleased to have caught him off guard.

"Of course, you are. It's just..." I'd been right to assume he hadn't come over here purely to be social. "I hope you're serious when you say you've come to assist us in this war. I was surprised by your honesty in admitting the Gods have historically favoured Sleotha. While I was grateful you didn't try to sugar-coat it, it disturbed me to hear we've had no divine support over the years, when we've prayed to your siblings and parents and never gotten a response. In recent years, there was a rumor that passed through the kingdom that the Gods were asleep, since we never heard from them. Of course, you showing up disabused us of that speculation. But if you're the only God who's truly ever backed us, then your support is even more monumental than you realise. It would be a shame for us to welcome you into our home, only for you to turn around and decide we're not worth a second look. We're putting the fate of our kingdom in your hands, and it's scary, to trust someone you don't know, even if they are a God. Sleotha has taken more from us than you even know, Tympany. It's *imperative* we win this war, and I hope you genuinely agree and are ready to help with that in whatever way we need you to."

I was astonished by how forward he'd been in disclosing his reservations about whether or not my motives were pure, when, in truth, they weren't. I was even more surprised that I was offended by his claims.

I set my sushi and champagne down on one of the passing server's trays, so I could intertwine my fingers in an attempt to control my rage.

"Have I given you any reason to doubt what I say?" I tried to dampen my ire, so I could say my piece thoughtfully. "I've come here to learn more about the discord between the two kingdoms and form opinions of my own that are separate from my family. I've chosen to side with Esteopia, but that doesn't necessarily mean I endorse everything Esteopia has done in this war." His brows raised in shock. "That also doesn't mean I will rescind my endorsement if you do something I disapprove of, but I won't sit idly by and stay silent if I disagree with something being done by either kingdom. Giving you my support doesn't mean I have to agree with everything you do, and vice versa. I'm here to offer my assistance, and that might mean me saying things you don't like or agree with. We need to learn to have our different opinions, and still be able to work together towards our mutual goal. That's one of the ways we will beat Sleotha."

"I do appreciate that perspective." I started to taste relief, before he asked, "What have we done that you've disapproved of?" sounding vexed at the thought of me condemning anything they'd done over Sleotha.

"With all due respect, while I agree that what Sleotha did to Eveium is horrendous, and you deserve retribution, I also cannot condone you invading Sleotha and murdering innocent lives in order to steal their crops and livestock. I understand what motivated you to do it, and my heart goes out to all those families and loved ones, but some of the lives you took that night were also innocents, just likes the ones lost in Eveium. Stooping to the level of the Sleothians will not win us this war."

"You do understand that, in war, there are always casualties? And I mean that respectfully, Your Excellence."

A frisson of annoyance ran through me when he called me *Your Excellence* with cynicism staining the title.

"Yes, I'm aware of that, *Your Majesty,* but your war is not with the villagers of Sleotha. It's with the crown. They do not represent the whole of Sleotha. If you are to win this war over land, they will be your people too. It's important to recognise that in your next attack, so no more innocent lives are lost."

"You said *your* war, and *your* next attack. Do you not plan on staying with us for long?" I opened my mouth, then closed it.

"I didn't say that." I'd been trying to be careful wording my answers. Demetrio was cunning, and remarkably perceptive. "I plan to stay here for as long as it takes to help you win this war, but it's still *your* war, not mine."

"And how do you suggest we do that?" He now sounded like he genuinely wanted to know.

"I still have to give it some thought." His lips formed the first earnest smile.

"I apologise for being so forceful with you, Tympany. I mean no disrespect. I am humbled and grateful for your presence here, and your support. I just want to make it clear...Esteopia is my life, my home, my everything. I will do whatever it takes to insure we have many more tomorrows as a kingdom, even if that includes going to war against your family who refuse to assist or respond to us. I just want you to understand what supporting us might entail, if you're serious about backing us."

"I do," I repeated through my teeth.

"Good. Then I'm glad we're in agreement over something." He smiled, but it didn't reach his eyes. "Enjoy the rest of your evening."

I was curious to see if the reaction I'd had to touching Seraphina would happen with Demetrio, wishing to read his true thoughts, so I set my hand over his forearm in a show of good faith to test it.

I don't trust her with my kingdom or my children. She's just like her miserable excuse for a father.

I gasped, ripping my hand away from him. "Tympany? Are you alright?"

"I'm fine," I choked out, disguising it as a cough. "Just clearing phlegm out of my throat. All good."

I squeezed my hands into fists to restrain from lunging at him.

He lingered a moment, gauging whether or not he believed me, before crossing the room and weaving an arm around his wife's waist, joining her conversation. I exhaled for the first time in minutes when he was gone.

My father?

Demetrio knew my father? *How?*

As far as I knew, since Roara transformed him into a God almost ten thousand years ago, Isaias never ventured down to the Realm. Demetrio would've had no way of encountering Isaias in this lifetime.

If they didn't meet, how did they know each other? And what could he possibly have against my father to call him something so cruel?

I became aware of the mellifluous sound drifting through the air, coming from the same harp player from the minstrel's gallery when we first arrived here. Esteopians were breaking off into pairs, traveling to the center of the ballroom to begin their waltz. I was brought back to the early days, when Roara insisted each of us master every form of dance. Jax and I were partnered together for those lessons, which mostly consisted of me tripping over his feet and injuring him somehow.

I wrapped my arms around myself, pretending my hands were Jaxith's, suddenly overcome with homesickness.

For just a moment, I let myself crumble—let myself question if I was equipped to handle this mission and all it demanded, question if maybe Demetrio was right, and I shouldn't put these kind people through the grief of offering my support, only to take it away when they needed it most.

I only gave myself a moment to wallow before I exhaled a deep breath and straightened my posture.

I opened my eyes to find Blekket advancing towards me.

"May I have this dance, Goddess Tympany?" he asked, proffering his hand with a mirthful smile.

"What? None of these other girls good enough for you?" I teased.

His blue eyes warmed like an ignited flame before he whispered, "I can only think of one."

I stopped breathing for a few seconds.

I didn't even feel my hand raise, but then, it was inside Blekket's, and he was leading me to the dancefloor.

He slithered an arm around my waist, folding his other hand around mine and drawing me close as we started to move. While everyone around us followed some orchestrated dance, we just swayed back and forth, adhering to no particular rhythm other than what felt right in the moment.

"That looked heavy," he said, and it took me a moment to figure out he was referring to my talk with his father. "Was my dad being a prick? He gets like that sometimes."

"It's okay," I assured him. "He's just…a little intense." Blekket snorted at *a little*. "He reminds me a lot of my dad, actually."

"Your dad's a prick too?" I lowered my eyes in a scowl.

"Careful. You're talking about the King of the Gods when you say that."

"Sorry. It's easy to forget you're actually a Goddess when I'm around you. You're so…casual."

"Is that supposed to be a compliment?"

"I'm always complimenting you, sweetheart. You should know that by now."

I shook my head at his naughty smirk.

"I have a question for you."

"One I might answer." His grin deepened. "Fire away."

I waited a moment for dramatic effect, then asked, "Why don't you want to take the throne? Your people seem to love you."

"So do yours," he shot back.

"Yeah, but we're not talking about me. We're talking about you." We glared each other down, daring the other to break first. Fortunately for me, it with Blekket.

"I see my parents every day. They spend all their time inside, plotting their next move in a war they're probably going to lose." It surprised me to hear him say that. "I don't want that to be my life. I don't want to be tied down to a throne where everyone expects me to prevail, even when I might not. I don't want to be responsible for people, only to fail them. That's too much pressure for one person."

"I can relate to that," I mumbled.

"I thought you might." His voice was smoky.

"Is that also why you don't want to be married?" He frowned.

"Did my mother tell you I said that?" Blekket rolled his eyes. "It's not that I don't want to be married *ever*. I just don't want to be married under the assumption that, when I do, I have to ascend the throne. It kind of takes the fun out of it, don't you think?" I nodded, empathising with that way of thinking.

"So you want to marry for love, not business?"

"Doesn't everyone? Isn't that the dream, that you meet someone, hit it off, and realise you're each other's missing piece? Why's it so insane to think maybe I want that too?" My heart softened to Blekket for the first time since we met. His eyes scanned the room. "None of these women see me. They see my crown. That's not what I want my wife to see when she looks at me." He then asked, "What do *you* see when you look at me, Tympany?"

The question caught me off guard, as did my response. "A man who doesn't want to be caged. Who loves his people, who deserves to be free to make his own choices and follow his heart."

Blekket's lashes fluttered, his mouth popping open. He recovered quickly before he leaned in closer, his lips grazing my ear at the same moment his hand flattened over the small of my back.

"Would *you* want to be married to someone like that?"

The direction this conversation had taken, as well as his proximity, made my stomach dip.

"There are worse people one could be married to," I muttered, not recognising the sound of my voice.

"Like who? Lucius?" I don't know why, but that made me cackle, far noisier than it should've. Blekket looked just as shocked as I was that the sound travelled past my lips. "You know, that's the first real smile I've gotten out of you since we met."

"Hey. I smile."

"Yeah? When?" I actually had to think about it.

"When I'm with Pessy. Or my other siblings, particularly with Jax."

"What about your parents?" He lightly squeezed my hand. I wasn't sure he even realised that he did.

"I believe I've given you the wrong impression of my parents. They're good people. They are. This past year...there's just been a lot of talk about the future."

"And that makes you sad?" He didn't say it critically—there was fascination, as well as genuine concern there.

"It did, when I thought I was being pressured into taking the throne." It was way too easy to be frank with Blekket. I needed to limit how much I told him, but I lost control of my filter when he looked at me like that. Like I was the only person in the room.

The one person in existence.

"What about now?" His scruff scraped along my cheek as we swayed. "Are you sad now?"

"What do you think?" His leaned away so our eyes could meet, his lips twisting into an odd shape.

"I don't think so, but you're difficult to read sometimes." He was the first person who'd ever accused me of that.

"My father used to say my heart is sprinkled across my sleeve, that he can always tell what I'm feeling from the way I move my hands."

"I guess I'll just have to get to know you better," Blekket declared, which sounded like a challenge.

"If you're so lucky." The corner of his mouth twitched with amusement.

"I should be out there, mingling," he said, but pulled me closer to prove he had no intention of doing so anytime soon.

"And yet, you're here with me."

"Funny how that worked out." My lips turned up at their own accord. "Another smile. I'm going to start keeping track." I deliberately pouted so he'd laugh. "Why do you think your compulsion doesn't work on me?"

It was a random direction to steer the conversation in, but I was grateful for the topic change.

"I have no idea," I admitted, not trying to hide my frustration.

"That bothers you, doesn't it?" I sighed, then nodded. "I kind of like that it bothers you. It means you won't easily forget me."

Without thinking, I blurted, "You're not someone *anyone* would forget, Blekket. Not easily, not ever."

His eyes had never looked more like a midnight sky. His pupils gleamed so brightly against the blue backcloth, they resembled lustrous stars. He cleared his throat before swapping his shock for a delighted smirk.

"You know something, Tympany? You're a total flirt."

"What!" I gasped. "No, I'm not!"

"Yeah, you are. I'd heard the Gods were flirts, but I didn't think that would apply to you."

"I am *not* a flirt," I repeated sharply, his smile increasing in both size and beauty. "*You're* the flirt. You should be ashamed of yourself."

"Trust me, I am." There was an inkling of seriousness in that statement despite the grin on his face.

"Stop doing that."

"Doing what?" He managed to bring me even closer against his chest.

I was acutely aware of how every part of our bodies from the shoulders down were now connected.

"You know exactly what you're doing."

"No, I don't. Please, enlighten me." This man was trouble personified, and I was in danger of drowning every time he flashed those alluring white teeth. It took all the strength I had to remain above water.

"Stop flirting with me, Blek."

"You first, angel." I rolled my eyes. "Does your head not hurt from all that eye rolling?"

"If you're so worried about my head," I said, "then don't do shit that makes me want to roll them."

I gave him my most impish, scathing smile.

"That's three." His hand slid a little farther down my waist, resting on my hip. It scorched me through the gown.

"If you don't want to be King, why not hand the throne over to Raevon? Does she not want it?"

"Rae would take it if it was the last possible resort, if she had no other choice. She'd do it for me, because she loves me, but I wouldn't ask that of her. She doesn't want to be Queen. I would never ask her to take the throne just because I don't want it. At least one of us deserves to be free."

"So, if not you, then who?"

"I have no idea. It's never been done before. My mother's still holding out hope I'll either change my mind or fall in love and want to be married so desperately that I'll end up on the throne through that union. Neither of those things are likely to happen." He sounded hopeful that this would be the case.

"What happens when you turn thirty?"

"Again, I don't know, but I've got until March before that happens. I'm just going to enjoy my life until then, and let that be tomorrow's problem."

"Sounds healthy."

"You know what? It is." Somehow, we'd ended up with my arms around his neck, and his entwined over my waist. He lifted a hand, sweeping a fallen curl off my face before tucking it behind my ear. I held my breath when he began tracing my earlobe. "I like your hair like this," he murmured. "Though I prefer it when it's all messy around your face, or tied back in a bun. When you're in pants instead of a fancy dress. When it's the *real* you, not the Goddess of the Heart and Mind, or Muse to all mortals and celestials. When you're just…Tympany. That's my favourite version of you, but I have a suspicion I'll meet more versions and like those just as much as the others."

I had no words.

No one had ever been able to render me speechless so many times in the span of two days, if ever.

Just as I'd felt at the stables, I was entombed by his eyes, but the experience was not negative. My breath was on fire, my chest tight, and my limbs felt feeble, like they were weightless and could dissolve into thin air at any moment. If my arms weren't around his neck, I probably would've collapsed.

"You can't say things like that to me," I stammered, beginning to fragment into a panic and not even sure why.

"Why not?" The sweet gentleness he spoke with made me feel like a disintegrated puddle.

"Because I don't know what to do with it."

His smile was more sensitive and sincere then I'd thought he was capable of producing.

"You don't have to do anything with it, or say anything at all, Tymp. All you have to do is listen. That's it."

Something about the way he called me *Tymp* turned my body into molten chocolate. It was far better than when he called me *angel* or *magnificent*, though secretly, I loved those nicknames too.

"Just listen?" I squeaked, on the verge of bursting into tears for no apparent reason.

"Just listen," he repeated. "Nothing else is expected of you. Not with me."

I understood then why I was so emotional—because everyone expected something from me. My parents expected me to eventually take the throne of Kylantis. My siblings expected me to infiltrate Esteopia and gather intel to help Sleotha win the war, regardless of whether they deserved to or not. Even his parents and sister expected me to potentially go to war with my own family in order to abet Esteopia.

Everyone expected something from me, but not Blekket. All I had to be with him was Tympany.

I'd never learned how to be *just* Tympany.

I didn't even know what that looked like.

Blekket raised his eyes to somewhere over my head. He grimaced, tightening his hold around me.

"My mother is summoning me away," he said, sagging a little. He then released my waist, much to my hidden disappointment, and bowed his head. "Thank you for the dance. I hope it won't be the last."

"We'll see," I joshed, lifting my skirt to curtsey back.

"Oh, I'll make sure of it." He winked before turning on his heel and stalking off to where his mother was waiting with her arms intertwined over her chest. I felt strangely empty the moment he was no longer at my side.

You so like him, I heard Pessy's voice in my head.

I whirled around to find her approaching me on the dancefloor, her cheeks glowing with palpable joy.

"Where have you been all night?" The bourgeoning smile on her face told me everything I needed to know. Something happened with Raevon. "Oh my Gods," I squealed, grabbing her wrist. "Tell me *everything*!"

"Not here," she muttered, flushing when she made eye contact with Seraphina.

"Let's go back to the room." I'd socialised with everyone I needed to. My presence was no longer necessary.

"Okay." Pessy took my hand, leading me to the door.

"We're going back to our room," I informed Alsandair and Harrison. "The Kylantians are dismissed for the evening."

"Thank you, Your Grace."

Alsandair stooped chivalrously before me, then nudged Harrison in the ribs when he was too slow to mimic his actions.

"Harrison trembles at the sight of you now," Pessy observed in the hallway. "I love it. You've drained that man of his dignity."

"It's not like he had any to begin with."

"True," she laughed, squeezing my arm. "And you thinking that is exactly why you're my best friend."

We changed out of our evening attire and into our night apparel. The gargantuan tunic Pessy had on looked like it was wearing her, trickling down to her mid-calf. She sat cross legged at the foot of my bed, her fingers knotted in her lap.

"She's *amazing*," Pessy gushed, her voice heady with feeling. "She's so funny and free spirited. She's not constrained by typical convention. She thinks for herself, which reminds me, in a lot of ways, of you."

"I was gonna say that reminds me a lot of *you*," I replied, making her blush. "Where did she take you?"

"To the courtyard at the back of the palace. We just sat there together, talking and looking up at the stars. It was magical."

"Did you kiss?" Her cheeks got even redder, which was answer enough. "Pess! Who made the first move?"

"Raevon did. If she hadn't, I never would've bucked up the courage. You know how nervous I get with this stuff."

"It's why you flirted with my sister for centuries and never acted on anything."

"*Not* what I meant," Pessy grumbled. She then sat up straighter and continued, waving her hands spastically as she spoke. "She doesn't see me as your bonded Kylantian. Not that I don't love and feel so honoured to be that, but back home, that's all anyone thought when they saw me, including your family. Even my mom started viewing me as just that, the closer we got to the ritual. Raevon just…sees me. Just Pessy."

It brought me back to what Blekket said. *When you're just…Tympany. That's my favourite version of you.*

"I understand," I muttered, scratching my forearm. "That's how I feel when I'm with Blekket. He doesn't expect anything from me. I'm not supposed to be this perfect Goddess with him. I can just be me…the good and the ugly. I've never had that before either."

When I looked up, Pessy's jaw had dropped. She was shocked I'd admitted any of that, instead of maintaining my feelings for Blekket were purely platonic or non-existent. But after that dance, after all those things he said, I could no longer deny that what I was beginning to feel for him expanded far greater than just amicable.

"Raevon said she's never seen her brother look at anyone the way he looks at you," Pessy informed me. Now, I was surely as red as she was. "She's already noticed a difference in him since he met you."

"It still doesn't change the fact that nothing can happen between us." Pessy cocked her head to the side.

"Why not?"

"Because I didn't come here to befriend the Elrods, Pess, or have a relationship with the Prince. I didn't come here to support Esteopia. I came here to essentially destroy them from the inside."

"Come on, Tymp. You can swear that crap to your parents and siblings, but deep down, you and I both know that's not why you offered to come here. You came here to live, to experience life and humanity away from them. And you and I both know, after seeing what they did to Eveium, assisting Sleotha in this war would be the wrong course of action." She stretched across the mattress and plucked my hand off the duvet, giving it a squeeze. "I know you, Tympany. Better than anyone. I saw your face when you saw the wreckage. You want to help Esteopia, for real."

"But I *can't*." I choked on a sob, Pessy apprehending a fallen tear with her knuckle. "My parents…"

"Don't think about what your parents want. You've spent your whole life doing that. Listen to what *you* want for a change. Follow your gut. It's never wrong."

She crawled off my bed, hopping onto her cot, and climbed under the comforter, snuggling her pillow. I tugged the duvet up to my chin, then rolled onto my back, staring up at the ceiling.

"Tymp?"

"Yeah, Pess?" When I glanced over, she was staring at me.

"It's okay to have opinions that differ from your family. To have feelings. It doesn't mean there's something wrong with you, or that you're any less of a God if you do. I'd hate to see you deprive yourself of something potentially wonderful because you think you can't, or you think you don't deserve it. There's nothing wrong with desiring something purely for yourself. You've earned the right to live your life. Don't waste it."

Chapter Eight

As we made our way to breakfast the next morning, I told Pessy what I'd heard in Demetrio's thoughts about Isaias.

"There's no way he's met your father," she said, twisting her blonde hair into a braid down her left shoulder. "He hasn't ventured down to the Realm in over ten thousand years."

"I know that. But why would he call him a miserable excuse?"

"I have no idea. He can be a little intense sometimes, but Isaias would never hurt a fly. I don't know what Demetrio could have against him."

It was true—my father was the least violent and vindictive person I knew. He made it a point to treat the Kylantians the same as he treated his children, for there to be no discrepancy in conduct despite the Gods being more superior. I learned to value equality and fairness through him, and from my mother, I learned to never let someone who's wronged or disrespected me do it a second time. I couldn't fathom what Demetrio thought Isaias had done to merit such a hateful reaction.

"Don't let it offend you, what he said about trusting you with his kingdom and his children. He doesn't know you. Once he gets a chance to, he'll see he has nothing to worry about."

Pessy kept speaking like I'd already made up my mind to no longer aid Sleotha. While I was enthralled by Esteopia and beginning to lean towards seriously backing them in this war, it wouldn't be so easy as to just change my mind last minute. I'd have to be methodical about it, have to consider what my family might do to Esteopia in retaliation if I were to pull out of the mission. If me deciding to support Esteopia wound up hurting these kind people, then it might've been safer for them if I continued with the original plan. But since admitting to myself that what I was starting to feel for Blekket went beyond the confines of friendship, I felt sick at the prospect of betraying him and his beloved kingdom.

I honestly had no idea what I was going to do. It felt like, with either choice, I'd be letting down someone I cared for.

When we entered the dining hall, the Elrods were already seated. Raevon, Seraphina, and Blekket were present, but Demetrio was nowhere to be seen. I wondered if he was hiding from me after our tense conversation, if he may have figured out I'd heard his nasty thoughts about my father.

Seraphina's jaw dropped when she took in what I was wearing. I had on a pair of Pessy's black leggings and a white loose long sleeve tunic, with aqua blue and grey gems along the V neckline. I'd found it hanging in the closet, assuming it must've belonged to either Seraphina or Raevon.

"Is something wrong?" I asked, glancing over at Blekket before I looked down at the shirt, checking for any stains.

"That was my mother's," she replied, her voice hoarse. "She used to wear it all the time. The room you're staying in was hers. I haven't had the heart to move it from the closet since she died."

"I can change, if you'd like." Seraphina waved her hand, rejecting the offer.

"There's no need. It looks better on you than it does on a hanger. She would be so honoured to see you wearing it."

I splayed my hand out over my heart, touched.

Pessy sat beside Raevon, and the two exchanged an endearing set of blushes. I noticed their fingers tangle together under the table and hid a smile beneath the curtain of my hair. I took a seat next to Blekket, where there was already a plate of yellowtail and avocado sushi waiting for me.

"Thank you, Lev." I beamed at the Esteopian, whose dimpled face was rosy.

"You know, if you keep eating sushi every day, you're eventually going to get sick of it," Blekket said.

"Then I'll just keep eating it until that happens." I popped one into my mouth, and he rolled his eyes playfully.

"What's on the agenda for the day?" Pessy asked, scooping a spoonful of potatoes onto her plate and digging in.

"We thought we'd take you to the Argent Ocean," Raevon answered. Pessy and I looked at each other from across the table, our eyes the size of saucers and our smiles even wider.

"Tympany's always wanted to see a dolphin in the flesh," Pessy told them, chewing her eggs ravenously.

"Caspian used to tell me the most amazing stories about them. How they're known for their kindness and thirst for life."

"He's right," Seraphina replied. I took a sip of water, instantly refreshed. "A dolphin plays as if they are happiness itself, a soulful soul born for pure enjoyment. I can see why you're so drawn to them."

"They sound magical." I then asked, "What other creatures, besides dolphins and the Hippocampi, live in the ocean?"

"Lots of random fish, sharks, whales, and the mermaids, of course." A lightbulb went off in my head.

"Have any of you heard of the mermaid named Solara?" I wasn't sure why, but all three of the Elrods smiled. Raevon ducked her head to the side and smothered a snort with the sleeve of her dress.

"Let me guess," Seraphina chuckled, radiating amusement. "Your brother mentioned Solara to you?"

"Why? Are they bad?" Blekket's grin was gargantuan.

"Solara and your brother are sort of known to be…romantically entangled," Seraphina disclosed. "The entirety of the kingdom is aware of their liaison, since, whenever he comes to visit, the grounds shake for days." I shuddered at the images that generated.

"I didn't peg you to be the prudish type, Tympany." Blekket leaned in close and whispered, "Don't you want to hear about the time they sent an earthquake through the town of Prisver and shattered a monument? Or the time—"

"Say no more," I begged, stuffing my fingers in my ears. "I get it." After a second, I turned to Seraphina and asked timidly, "How exactly would they…how do they…with Solara having…a tail?"

I fit my fingers together to further accentuate the point I was trying to make.

Blekket let out a vigorous cackle that vibrated through the castle and caused the cutlery to tremble.

"That may have been the cutest thing I've ever heard," he declared, my cheeks scorching with embarrassment.

"Mermaids can walk on land," Seraphina explained, shooting a glower at her son to get him to stop snickering. "They don't live solely in the sea, though they much prefer it. Solara is the ruler of the mermaid race. They reign over the Argent Ocean and work directly with your brother."

"Work," Blekket muttered under his breath. "I think they do a bit more than wo—"

"*Enough.*" Seraphina's glare was ice cold. Blekket bit his tongue, but he never lost that good-humoured grin.

"When they're on land, where do they live?" Pessy enquired.

I was grateful she furthered the conversation, allowing me a moment to recover from mortification.

"The village of Jopolis is directly beside the Argent Ocean. It belongs exclusively to the merfolk."

"And when they're underwater?"

"Floatsim is what the underwater dominion is called," Raevon answered, guzzling her juice.

"What's the merfolk's contribution to society?" I asked Seraphina.

"They help fisherman locate the fish in the marine, same as the Hippocampi. They also maintain the cleanliness of the ocean, filtering out any toxins that could spoil the waters or the fish."

"So, they're glorified cleaners?" She frowned.

"I wouldn't call them that, but I suppose, in a way, they are. They're integral to the conservation of our society. We wouldn't have access to clean water, or the fish, without their guidance and protection."

"I didn't mean that offensively," I swore. "I think heavy laborers are underrated in the amount of work they do to preserve a civilisation. They're the pillars in which we stand upon, and they deserve so much more credit for the blood, sweat, and tears they put into maintaining a thriving ecosystem."

"I completely agree, Tympany." Her eyes dazzled with admiration.

While I'd grown to like both Raevon and obviously Blekket, it was Seraphina who made me question whether or not I'd follow through with the original mission to dismantle Esteopia from the inside. She'd been so gracious towards me, since the moment I arrived here. I could sense there wasn't a selfish bone in her body, that her kindness was genuine and not self-serving in the interest of me helping her kingdom. I wanted to believe, if my family had the chance to get to know her and see her altruism in action, they would agree with me that Esteopia deserved a fighting chance.

I nibbled quietly on my sushi for the remainder of breakfast, contemplating whether or not I would have the courage to say any of this to my parents when the time arose.

❖❖❖

We rode our horses through the gaudy sun, which trickled down in woven strands, free and united, flowing into the day it revealed and solidified. Every tree encircling our heads was a unique masterpiece, each wand of grass and abundant blossom something inimitable and magical. We headed to the west, the opposite direction we went in yesterday, following a similar path composed of gleaming mosaic pebbles. While Pessy chatted away with the Elrods, asking more questions about the Argent Ocean and the merfolk, I spent the majority of the ride chewing on my bottom lip, trying to concentrate on remaining present in the moment and not fragmenting into hysteria over all the decisions I would soon have to make.

"You're being unusually quiet," Blekket said, shattering my trance.

"I'm usually quiet."

"Not with me." He tilted his head to the side. "You okay? Did last night wear you out?"

"Just have a lot on my mind," I answered, keeping it purposefully vague, but also not wishing to lie to him.

"Can I take some of that burden off your shoulders?" When I first met him, I'd thought Blekket was disdainful without the capability of empathy. I'd been horribly wrong to assume he had no heart.

"That's sweet of you to ask, but no. Thank you, though."

"I'm here if you change your mind." He pointed to the right of us. "You see the willow trees over there?" I shifted my head to follow his finger. These was a collection of deciduous trees lining the margin of the path. They had to each be thirty to eighty feet tall, with a twenty foot spread of graceful arching boughs. "The villagers believe the branches are magic. If you lift one in your hand, close your eyes, and make a wish, it'll come true."

"Do *you* believe that?" Blekket inclined forward, lifting a drooping bough and bringing it to his chest.

"I think it's important to believe in something. To have hope." He shut his eyes, hugging the branch close, then released a dramatic, hefty sigh before passing it to me. "Try it. Wish for something."

I took the branch from him, the leaves feeling supple and light, like they could crumble into powder between my fingers. I shut my eyes and made my wish.

I wish for clarity on what to do about Sleotha and Esteopia.

"What did you wish for?" he probed when I opened my eyes and released the branch, so it could re-join its friends.

"If I tell you, it won't come true."

"You'll have to let me know if it does. I'm dying to know what you wished for." When he winked, I realised why he'd started this conversation about the trees—I was no longer sulking in my thoughts.

Raevon tugged on Autumn's reins, forcing Krystal, Belgian, and Clarence to come to a halt on the path.

"We go by foot from here," she announced, jumping down from Autumn.

Standing perpendicular and with pride before us was a massive statue fashioned from rock, whittled down and stonewashed from years of heavy rains and scorching sun. In the front was the construction of a large ship, with stone fisherman positioned on the inside, peeking down at the sculpted waters below. Underneath the ship was a plethora of mermaids, the etched scales on their long, flowing tails sprinkled with glitter. There was a gigantic rectangular square the ship appeared to be growing out of, and then, at the top, stood a solid gold carving of my brother, Caspian.

He was clenching a trident in his right fist, raising it up over his head. Two golden Ashrays were situated at his sides.

I could only imagine how much Caspian's ego grew every time he saw this thing. The thought made me smile.

"Does that really look like your brother?" Raevon asked.

"He's a little shorter in person," I teased, "but otherwise, it's pretty accurate." They even captured the cleft in his chin.

"What're your brothers and sisters like?" We guided our horses past the statue and in the direction of the ocean.

"Jaxith is a sweetheart. He's my favourite brother, if not my favourite sibling. Caspian can be a little full of himself, but he's very intelligent, so he's sort of earned the right to be. Benjen is hysterical. You will always find him eating." I giggled at the overabundance of memories I'd collected over the years of Ben shovelling food into his mouth. "Nox is quiet. He's not as assertive as our other brothers. He sort of keeps to himself. Lucius is an asshole who thinks everything is entitled to him."

"No kidding," Blekket mumbled, then pretended to be admiring a willow tree when I glared at him.

"Calliope is wonderful. She's very spirited and bubbly. Eira is kind of a grump. That's the best way I can describe her. She's always mad about something. Luna is very independent. I've always admired her for her forward way of thinking. She marches to the beat of her own drum and doesn't care what anyone thinks of her."

"Kind of like you," Raevon complimented.

"I guess..." I never considered myself as having things in common with Luna. I'd always respected her for her individuality and tried to mirror her to the best of my ability, but it never felt natural the way it seemed to be with her.

"What about your parents?"

"Roara is the most confident person I've ever met. She oozes elegance. It can be very intimidating, even to me, her daughter. My father is far more gentle then her, but he can be quite intense when he wants to be."

"That kind of sounds like our parents, Blek." That surprised me—I would've thought it was the other way around.

"Yeah," he replied quietly. "It does."

"Do you spend a lot of time with all the Gods, or just Tympany?" Raevon asked Pessy directly.

"I practically grew up in the palace," she replied. "My mother is bonded to Roara, which is how Tymp and I met. My father, before he died, was going to be bonded to Isaias. They were best friends."

"I'm sorry about your father, Pess," Blekket consoled.

"Don't be. It was a long time ago." She said that, but I knew the loss still ached for her. It was why she refused to wear anything other than his shirts to bed, why she carried his sword around everywhere she went.

"How is a Kylantian chosen to be bonded to a God? And is every God bonded to someone?"

"Not every God is bonded to a Kylantian," Pessy answered. "It takes having a special kind of relationship with that God or Goddess to even be considered to be bonded to them. It's a huge honour, and a lifelong responsibility."

"A God or Goddess would never be bonded to someone they had no kinship towards, or someone they didn't trust," I clarified. "Out of all my siblings, only me and Luna are bonded to someone. None of my brothers are. Pessy is the only person I've been bonded to in five thousand years."

After they let that sink in, Raevon asked Pessy, "How old are you? You look like you're in your twenties."

"Three hundred," she responded, blushing. Raevon's forehead crinkled, as if she was trying to wrap her brain around how many years that was. At twenty-three, the idea of living that long must've been incomprehensible to her. Pessy wilted with shame, her eyes dropping to her shoes to avoid looking at Raevon.

Don't be embarrassed, I told her. *You have nothing to be ashamed of.*

What if she doesn't like me now that she knows I'm so much older than her? The voice in my head sounded like it was on the verge of tears.

If she stops liking you because of how old you are, then she's not the right one for you. It's her loss.

Pessy raised her lustrous blue eyes that were glassy with tears. *Thanks, Tymp. You're the best.*

"We're here!" Raevon clapped her hands. "Welcome to the Argent Ocean!"

As the seabed swapped the salty brine for oceanic air, we saw a marvelous, mammoth beach unfurl beneath our toes and stretch out to the oceanfront. The sand was the most gentle hue of gold, almost earthen and muted, the humble star of the scene before it crashed into the dazzling marine that stole the show in all its glory. The soft sky above seemed to glow even more lurid than before, smooth stone and kaleidoscopic clouds caressing the sea with reflected light. The lacy waves in steady rhythm echoed my rising heartbeat and pulse. A chilled breeze brought long awaited relief to my tense bones, whilst the birds squawked and arced overhead, frolicking upon swirling updrafts.

"Wow," was all I was able to say. I would've used the word *magnificent*, had it not been co-opted by Blekket.

"This is our favourite place in all of Esteopia," Raevon declared, beaming at her brother, who grinned back.

"If we're not in the palace, Rae and I are usually here," he confirmed.

"I can see why." It was beguiling in its splendour, rousing the same feeling I had when I sat in my garden back home.

Blekket tied Clarence's reins around one of the tree trunks bordering the sand. I lead Krystal over, Clarence whinnying in greeting to his new friend, and knotted her reins tightly around the same shaft.

"Stay here," I ordered, caressing her muzzle. She nodded, then leaned over to cuddle Clarence.

I slipped my sandals off my feet, leaving them in the sand near where the horses were. The grains squished between my toes, ticking the soles of my feet. I was surprised by how difficult it was to walk through the sand, that something so soft could be so dense. Blekket and Raevon were already at the shoreline when Pessy and I caught up. They were kneeling on the beach, skimming their fingers through the spume of the waves, the churned organic matter fizzing over their hands and feet.

I crouched down, dipping my fingers in the incoming wave as it washed up to shore and drenched my toes and ankles. It was chillier than I expected, making me gasp.

"It's so cold!" I shrieked, scampering back to the safety of the warm sand. While I wasn't a huge fan of hot temperatures either, I *despised* being cold. Blekket, Raevon, and Pessy just laughed at me.

"You'll get used to it," Raevon promised.

"Here." Blekket extended his hand for to me take. "Try it again."

I slipped my fingers through his, my skin covered in goosebumps that weren't triggered by the chill of the water.

He led me back towards the coast, keeping my hand despite me now being beside him. When the ocean exhaled and a surge of water lapped up onto shore, soaking my ankles once more, it was far less frigid then it had been before.

"Better?" he asked. I nodded.

Raevon stooped to one knee, pressing her hand into the damp sand. She shut her eyes and was silent for several seconds.

In the distance, the ocean rumbled and undulated, the air whipping more ferociously around the rippling waves. The water at our feet rose in level, thrashing against the pressure of the wind, as we caught our first glimpse of the almighty Hippocampus. The heraldic sea-horse had the head and neck of a stallion, the serpentine tail of a fish, and webbed paws replacing its front hooves. Its scales were variegated of the most garish colours, the fins dipped in gilt. The creature was breathtaking in its iridescence and modishness, gliding through the waves with such conviction and ease. They exuded authority. Standing before them felt like you were in the presence of royalty.

Raevon stood, reaching out to stroke the Hippocampus's snout. It nuzzled her palm, recognising her.

"This is Calypso," she introduced, Calypso licking her hand.

A second Hippocampus shattered through the surface of the water, even more colossal in size than Calypso.

"There are you, Lex." Blekket approached the creature. "I was wondering where you were." He grinned the most heart-wrenchingly beautiful smile I'd ever seen from him as he stared at her with wonder and veneration. "This is Alexandria. She's my girl. Aren't you, Lex?" The Hippocampus whickered with delight, stretching her neck and planting a wet, slobbery kiss on Blekket's cheek.

"Do these Hippocampi belong to you guys?" Pessy asked.

"They technically belong to the merfolk, since they live in Floatsim," Raevon answered, "but they also belong to the crown."

"How many Hippocampi are there?" I inquired.

"Hundreds. There's a Hippocampus for every merfolk. But these two are our personal favourites. They always come to see us when we visit."

I edged closer to Alexandria to get a better look at her. The Hippocampus flickered her eyes to my extended hand, as if deliberating whether or not she trusted me, then dipped her chin to the left and burrowed her face in my palm, closing her eyes. She was softer than her scales made her skin appear, almost like silk.

"She likes you, Tymp," Blekket said, in awe. "She never does that with anyone who isn't royal."

"She must know somehow you're a God," Raevon added. Now, I understood the feeling I got when I first saw them.

It was power recognising power.

Raevon, with impressive skill, grabbed a hold of Calypso and slid onto her back, settling in the center of Calypso's spine.

"Climb on with me, Pess," Raevon hollered, gesturing her over. Pessy's eyes illuminated with relief, grateful the age revelation hadn't spoiled Raevon's perception of her. She waded through the water, jumped onto Calypso, and twisted her arms around Raevon's waist when the Hippocampus nearly made her toppled over into the ocean.

"They're cute together," Blekket observed. He shifted to face me, wiggling his brows. "Now it's our turn."

I rolled my eyes. "In your dreams, Blekket Elrod."

Blekket motioned Alexandria forward. The Hippocampus sloped her long neck, allowing him to grip her mane and spring forward to climb onto her back. Once on, he offered me his hand. Though I didn't need it to crawl onto Alexandria, I took it anyway and let him tug me up onto her, giving him the illusion of being helpful. I swung my leg over her vertebrae, settling behind him, and wrapped my arms around his waist, as Pessy had done with Raevon. His body jolted at the contact, a shiver rumbling down his back that pulsated through my arms. I knew then that every time I'd been shocked when touching him, he'd experienced the same voltage as I had.

"Is this okay?" I asked him, not wishing to make him uncomfortable, if that's what I was doing.

"It's perfect," he replied, his hoarse voice making it sound like he meant that in more ways than one. He turned to Raevon. "We ready?"

"Ready!" she squealed.

"Let's do this." He lightly kicked Alexandria's side, and the Hippocampus took off in the direction of the horizon.

Blekket started off slow at first so that we (well, mostly me) could get used to the feeling of being on Alexandria's back. As we cantered further from the land, Alexandria picked up speed and went full power, zipping ahead. Blekket liked to ride fast, I learned—it was apparently easier to control than going slow, as the water just drags underneath you if you don't follow the proper pace of the current. We rocketed over the little speedbumps, the waves so big that water spewed everywhere, spraying over my hair and clothing. Blekket was soaked too, his black button down and breeches clinging to his brawny figure, but he didn't seem to care, and neither did I.

Raevon and Pessy were in front of us for the majority of the ride, but at a certain point, after we'd coordinated speeds and were riding at the same level, Calypso and Alexandria randomly decided to race each other.

They surprised us and leapt forward, competing against the wind for dominance of the sea.

The most important feeling I latched onto during that ride was freedom. Despite me clinging to Blekket for dear life, I felt completely unfettered. We were defying gravity, unstoppable against the rapid breeze and fierce salt waves. Nothing and no one could interrupt the absolute *fun* we were having. None of the problems that plagued me before mattered out here.

It was impossible to not be completely present with my surroundings and company.

I noticed a flash of grey below the waterline and tapped Blekket's shoulder to retrieve his attention.

"Is that what I think it is?" I asked, brimming with excitement. Blekket looked down to see what I was referring to, then grinned.

"Yup. It's a dolphin." *Finally!*

I bent down and trailed my fingers over the body of the mammal. It felt as lithe as it looked, its skin slippery, like it was slick with grease. The dolphin was a streak of cheerful silver amid the blue that was its home, slithering beneath our feet in the tranquil turquoise, air bubbles rising to the surface in their clustered way. It then shocked us by hurdling through the waves and leaping high into the sultry air.

Water droplets cascaded down the grey topside and white underbelly, bejewelled in the sunlight.

Its body curved, tail flopped, and then, it vaulted down with a hearty splash, dowsing us in ocean water before swimming away.

"Tympany! Did you see that?" Pessy screamed at me.

"That was *so* cool!" I shrieked.

Blekket whirled around to look at me. "You're so cute," he chuckled, his cheeks windswept and glowing.

I'm not sure what possessed me to do this, but I leaned my head down, pressing my cheek against Blekket's back, and hugged him a little harder around the waist, my thighs snuggling his. I was so overcome with glee and gratitude that it felt natural to embrace him this way, despite how intimate it actually was. When I first squeezed him, he tensed in surprise, but then, as he got more familiar with the sensation, his whole body seemed to relax, melting into my touch.

"Thank you," I whispered tearfully. I wasn't even sure what I was thanking him for.

"Tymp," I heard him moan.

Then, he set his hand over mine on his stomach, giving my fingers a light squeeze.

"How close is Floatsim from where we are now?" Pessy shouted over the roar of the wind.

Blekket cleared his throat, then answered, "We're hovering over it right now. Would you guys like to see it?"

That was an easy yes.

"Hold your breath," Raevon advised. Pessy and I sucked in lungfuls of air, our cheeks puffed out.

"You look like a blowfish," Blekket teased, and because I was holding my breath, I couldn't stick my tongue out at him.

When Blekket kicked Alexandria's side, she dove down under the waves. I squeezed Blekket tighter from fear of the tide dragging me away, my hair smacking my cheeks. When I opened my eyes, I would've gasped if I wasn't holding my breath. The city of Floatsim, in a lot of ways, resembled Acadia, except the palace and all the homes were made of stone, not wood or marble, and were adorned with polyzoan, not cloth. A diverse medley of fish swam between the dwellings.

I spotted two more dolphins near another large figurine of my brother, who was once again pictured with a trident. When I returned to Kylantis, I would ask Caspian why he was always depicted with one in statues when I'd never seen him hold one before in real life.

Through the moss and seaweed, I caught sight of my first mermaid swimming towards the palace. They wore gold sleeveless armour from the waist up that had the design of scales incised over the chest, their tail the colour of red wine. They moved through the current with such adroitness, at one with the water.

It was impossible not to be mesmerised.

When I looked over at Blekket and then Raevon, neither one of them was holding their breath. They too were at one with the ocean, breathing as naturally as they had when we were on land. It was the Neraid in them that bound them to the sea.

While I wanted to explore Floatsim more, get a closer look at the palace and speak to the mermaid, Pessy and I were running out of oxygen.

Blekket kicked Alexandria's side, and we travelled back up to the surface, where I could finally exhale.

"That might've been the coolest thing I've ever seen," Pessy declared, gasping for breath. Raevon leaned over, giving Pessy a quick kiss on the cheek before tucking a strand of damp hair behind her ear.

"You could breathe underwater," I marvelled.

"We were both born in Floatsim," Blekket explained, running his fingers through the soaked strands of his hair, shoving them off his forehead. "As was our mother and father, and their parents before them."

"Are you stronger when you're in the water?" Both of them nodded. "Could you live underwater forever, if you wanted?"

"I suppose," he answered, "but it would get to be a bit uncomfortable, I'd think, being wet all the time."

"A bit uncomfortable," Pessy repeated. "You make it sound like it's nothing."

"For us, it is," Raevon said, her cobalt eyes twinkling almost a pale periwinkle under the glare of the sun.

"It's kind of cool we can do something a Goddess can't," Blekket mused, grinning wickedly at my scowl. "If you didn't hold your breath down there, what do you think would've happened?"

"I'm not sure." I don't think I would've drowned, the way Pessy might've, but it definitely would've affected me somehow. "Caspian can breathe underwater. I've seen him do it for hours. I used to sit at the edge of our pool and time him. It was our favourite thing to do together, when I was young."

"I'd love to try and outsit a God." Blekket sighed.

"I doubt you'd win against the God of Water and Rain."

"You're severely underestimating my skills, sweetheart." I reached up and flicked him behind the ear. "Ow! What was that for?"

"You deserved it," I muttered, shrugging my shoulders.

"She's right. You kind of did," Raevon concurred.

"Both of you suck," he grumbled, rubbing the spot where I struck him. "The only person I like here is Pessy."

"Awe. Thanks, Blek." She flushed.

Blekket swung his head over to Raevon, his face spangled with a youthful enthusiasm that was infectious.

"Race back?" Raevon grinned with a nod.

"Oh, absolutely." They started gearing up their Hippocampi, Pessy and I clinging to them in preparation.

They lightly tapped Calypso and Alexandria before we galloped off to the races.

When we reached the shore, I spotted someone in the distance loitering by our horses. Reflex drove me to reach for my blade, which was tucked inside the pocket of my leggings, and leap over the beach to avoid the density of the sand. When my vision cleared and the face came into view, I saw it was just Lev, who wasn't alone.

Alsandair and Harrison were with him as well.

I landed right in front of them, tucking my blade back into my pocket once I knew we weren't in any peril.

"Do you always carry that around?" Blekket asked when he caught up to me, seeming surprised to learn I'd had a weapon on me this whole time.

141

"Just in case I'm alone and need to defend myself. You should keep that in mind." His lips arched into a spectacular smile.

"You're amazing." He breathed.

Pessy was at my side less than a minute later, a hand on the hilt of her sword. Lev's hands wouldn't stop trembling, his eyes enlarged to a worrisome degree. As I got a more thorough look at him, I noticed his armour was smeared with blood.

"Lev, what happened?" Raevon asked.

"Frofsea is under attack," he stammered. "The drogon are here."

Chapter Nine

"How many?" Blekket asked, his voice rough with horror.

"I'm not sure. I only saw one, but that doesn't mean there aren't more. There's no way to know for sure."

"Yes, there is," I interjected, everyone turning to look at me. "I can fly up there with Krystal and see how many drogon there are."

"That's a great idea, Tymp," Pessy prided.

"Everyone else should start heading to Frofsea," I instructed, Lev and Raevon nodding before they began mounting their horses. "I'll meet you there."

"What should we do, Your Grace?" I knew what Alsandair was really asking underneath the question.

Are the Kylantians really going to defend Esteopia, or pretend to?

"You *fight*," I demanded. "Until every last Sleothian intruder is either dead, or running back to Sleotha with their tails between their legs." He seemed stunned by the vigor of the order, but recovered quick and nodded.

I slipped my sandals back on and scurried over to Krystal, unraveling her reins from around the tree trunk. She cocked her head at my flagrant agitation, tensing in response. I spun around, pointing at Blekket.

"Come with me."

"Seriously?" he spluttered.

"I need someone to direct me to Frofsea." I'd never seen a face fracture with such a large smile before.

"Oh, fuck yeah!" he exclaimed with a clap. "I've always wanted to ride a Pegasus. Thanks, Tymp!" I flushed crimson, then glanced at Pessy, who was smirking at me.

You must REALLY like him, she mused. *You don't even let me ride Krystal.*

Shut up, I grumbled.

I mounted Krystal with ease, gathering her reins. Blekket placed his foot in the stirrup and climbed onto her rather sloppily due to her excessive height. I thought I'd have to convince her to tolerate Blekket's presence, but she was unruffled. He situated on her croup, then scooted forward to meet me in the middle. I felt two arms slither around my waist, his thighs snuggling against mine and his chest pressing up over my spine. Now, I regretted asking him to come with me instead of Raevon.

"Is this okay?" he asked me, not a trace of humour in his voice. I didn't trust myself not to tell him how strangely nostalgic and emotional his arms made me feel, how I wanted him to cuddle me closer and eliminate any persisting space between us, so I just nodded. "Lev, could you please take Clarence back to the palace?"

"Yes, Your Highness."

"I'll meet you there," Pessy said, adding, "Reach out if you need anything." *Good luck riding with Blekket.*

We watched Raevon, Pessy, Lev, Harrison, and Alsandair charge off down the road, disappearing into the shadows of the deciduous trees. I tugged on Krystal's reins to retrieve her attention, stroking her mane.

"You wanna go for a fly?" Krystal's amber eyes amplified with tentative excitement, as if she was afraid to believe I was serious. "Go on, Kry. Stretch your wings." Krystal vibrated, prolonging her neck while clenching her muscles in preparation for release. "Lift your legs," I alerted Blekket, who obeyed immediately, much to my surprise.

I felt Krystal's power pulse through her as her mammoth white feather wings unfurled to their full length, cruising the apex of the willow trees. Blekket's jaw dropped open, watching them expand with awe.

"Holy shit." He reached out, skimming the feathers with the tips of his fingers. "They're beautiful."

"I know," I said proudly. "Ready to go, Kry?" She bobbed her head in a nod. If she had thumbs, they would be flipped up.

Krystal flapped her wings, the wind submitting to her will. She leapt off her feet and launched us towards the clouds. Blekket squished my ribs, to the point where I choked on a gasp.

"Jeez, if you squeeze me any tighter, you're going to cut off my circulation." I got no response back.

I started to swivel around so I could check on him before he snapped, "Can you look where you're going, please?" his face drained of colour.

"Blekket...are you scared of heights?"

"No," he barked, but his eyes remained resolutely ahead, anywhere but at the ground below.

"Blek?"

"What, Tympany?" My lips twisted into a smile.

"I kind of need you to give me directions to Frofsea."

"Oh." He swallowed. "Follow the path we took to Eveium. It's the village right beside it."

"Thanks." I jerked Krystal's reins, steering her to the left.

I hadn't flown with Krystal in so long. I'd forgotten how freeing it was, the buoyancy of the clouds circulating below Krystal's hoofs, the gentle sway of the wind blowing my hair off my face, drying the ocean water from the short strands, the control that thrummed through my tissues from maneuvring a being of such magnitude.

While I imagined, if I looked back, I'd see Blekket pale as a ghost, I couldn't wipe the grin off my face.

I saw, whenever Krystal elevated her head, her lips warped up in just as wide of a smile as mine.

The only thing that could've splintered the high of flying was Blekket gasping, "Good Gods," at the first sight of Frofsea.

The village was on fire.

Or, at least it appeared that way from the clouds. Below us was an amalgamation of blue and red figures in the throes of battle, blue the armour of the Esteopians, and red the Sleothians. From this high up, the Sleothian army looked like nothing more than streaks of fire whizzing between the contours of blue, setting the earth aflame. I caught sight of the first drogon, which was planted in the soil and blitzing everything in its path. Its huge neck ran down from its head into a bulky body, the top covered in ample scales, with rows of small fan-like growths spilling down its spine. Its bottom was covered in more rounded flakes, coloured differently than the rest of its physique. The head, spine, and tail were pitch black, and the underbelly was red. Four slender limbs supported its body and allowed the drogon to stand potent and towering over the scared civilians of Frofsea. Each limb had five digits, all of which ended in jagged claws made of onyx.

Terrifying wings that surpassed Krystal's in length sprouted from its shoulders, just passing its shoulder blades. The wings were almost bat like, the inside texture membranous, like gauze.

It looked malleable, like it could break easily, but I knew they were sturdier then they appeared.

Small, sharp thorns lined the edges like spears.

There was a second drogon marching through the village, its long tail ending in a curved talon and covered in the same wide scales as its counterpart. We watched it open its giant mouth, slobbering fire over a chain of houses. I prayed those homes had already been evacuated, but had a suspicion they were not. Blekket flinched behind me, hugging my tighter.

"Look, Tymp." He pointed over my shoulder to where a third drogon was hovering in the air a few feet away from us, shrouded in the clouds. Enormous, fiery eyes sat high within the creature's thick green skull, scanning the combat below with a callous awareness that felt frighteningly human.

I searched the sea of soldiers below for Pessy, but couldn't locate her. I shut my eyes and reached out through the bond.

Pess, where are you?

It took a moment, but then, I heard her nearly shout in my head, *I'm near the black drogon.*

I located a patch of vacant terrain for us to land on and steered Krystal downward towards the crusade.

"Blekket, close your eyes," I warned.

I had no idea if he listened, but I felt his grip on my waist get stronger as we approached the ground.

He couldn't have been faster getting off Krystal once we disembarked, nearly collapsing onto the soil. An Esteopian was at his side within seconds, tossing him a sword.

"Thanks, Mal," Blekket said. Then, without another moment's hesitation, he sprinted into the heart of the battle.

I didn't dither, unearthing my blade from my pocket and dashing off to find Pessy. I was pleased to see gold mixed in with the blue, the Kylantians fighting alongside the Esteopians, just as I'd asked. I found Pessy shoved up against one of the huts, a Sleothian digging the hilt of his sword into her windpipe. I leapt off my feet, landing behind the solider, who wasn't fast enough to see me coming.

I gripped the hair at the nape of his neck and swiped my dagger across his throat, severing his head from his body. The rest of him crumpled to the ground at my feet. I kicked his bulk off me, then hurled the uncoupled skull to the side. Pessy watched it roll before looking back at me, her lips turned up at the corners.

"Took you long enough." She sighed.

"Where are Demetrio and Seraphina?"

"Seraphina's back at the castle. Demetrio's here somewhere. Lev said he wouldn't stay back."

"Good." I had a newfound respect for Demetrio after hearing that. If it were me, I wouldn't stay behind either.

"Let's go kick some ass," Pessy declared.

I grinned. "Let's."

Now that I was on land, I saw the armour the Sleothians wore didn't just look like it was on fire—it was *actually* on fire. The metal secreted a heat that scorched the skin of anyone who grazed it. I learned this from watching a Sleothian ruthlessly shove an Esteopian soldier's cheek against the titanium, melting the flesh on the right side of his face. The man passed out from the pain, and the Sleothian promptly put him out of his misery, amputating his skull from his neck before moving on to the next.

A Sleothian scampered towards me, sword raised in opposition. I ducked under his arm, seizing his calf, then wrenched it back so he landed on his behind in the soil. I pressed the heel of my sandal into his throat, thrusting my blade into his chest. His eyes fluttered shut, the sword slipping out of his hand. I noticed, on the hilt, was the same shape as the pictogram of the royals, only flipped, so now, the teardrop looked like a flame.

Fire against water.

I retrieved my blade from inside the man's chest, pinpointing Raevon in the middle of the combat. I watched her impressively disembowel a Sleothian solider before booting his now deceased body into a stack of logs, which had been transformed, by the drogon, into a bonfire. The flames ate up his gouged physique, converting bone to charred ash.

"That's my girl," Pessy muttered, then spun on her heel just as a Sleothian tried to accost her from behind, elbowing him in the throat.

I found Blekket battling a man twice his size with striking ease. He'd clearly mastered the art of discernment when it came to anticipating someone's movements, and was able to detect what the Sleothian would do before he did it. When the man tried to dip under Blekket's arm to come at him from behind, Blekket twirled around and kneed him in the stomach. He plunged his sword into

147

the man's spine when he doubled over in pain, the blade peeking out from the other side of his chest.

When he extracted the sword from the Sleothian's body, he rotated around and drove it into another man's skull, right between his eyes.

I had absolutely no experience with what attraction usually felt like, but I was well read and knowledgeable enough that I knew what emotion stormed through me at the sight of him battling the Sleothians.

Arousal.

Which was a useless emotion, I decided, since it would ultimately get me nowhere in this fight.

I observed a Sleothian charging at Blekket from behind, who was engaging another solider and didn't notice. I sprinted forward, catching the Sleothian by the back of his armour. It faintly scorched the tips of my fingers, but wouldn't burn me the way it would a mortal. I yanked him away from Blekket, chucking him into an already crumbling hut. The man crashed into the trodden wood, groaning in agony as I loomed over him.

"You're not human," the Sleothian accused.

He tried to strike me with his blade, but I caught his wrist before the knife-edge reached its target, crushing his bones in my grip. The man screamed, flexing his fingers and dropping his weapon into the dilapidated timber.

"No, I'm not," I replied, twirling my dagger in my hand. "You just tried to take a swipe at a Goddess."

The man blinked in shock, opening his mouth to respond, but I slit his throat before he had a chance to utter a single word in defense of himself.

I backed away from the Sleothian, turning around to find Blekket there, having watched the whole thing.

His lips rounded up into a breathtaking smile. "So magnificent." He breathed with reverence.

"Watch it, or it'll be you next."

"I genuinely believe that." He tipped his chin up. "Behind you."

I rotated, gripping the hilt of my dagger, and slid in the soil to circumvent the incoming blade aimed directly for my face. The Sleothian it belonged to let out an ear-splitting battle cry as she raced towards me, forehead crinkled with rage, flashing her razor sharp teeth. I sidestepped her, catching her wrist, and flipped her onto her back, where I shoved my foot into her abdomen and held her down before prodding my dagger into her chest. I sensed someone approaching and jabbed my elbow into the stomach of the Sleothian behind me, reaching up and grabbing a handful of their hair before throwing them over my shoulder. They landed in an inferno that once was an Esteopian home.

I spotted Harrison across the way, a Sleothian shoving him into the mud, throttling the life out of him.

I came up behind the solider, cupping him around the back of his neck, and pitched him into the conflagration, the flames engulfing his limbs and screams.

"Thank you," Harrison coughed, clutching his throat.

"You're welcome." I offered him my hand, and he rose to his feet, dusting the grime of the earth off his uniform.

A raucous roar above my head caused me to halt in place. The drogon that had been hovering in the clouds sloped towards the destruction, casting its daunting shadow over the Sleothians and Esteopians at war. Ferocious, blood red eyes blinked within the creature's scaled, hard skull, browsing the battle impassively. Two enormous horns sat atop its head, just above its thick, angular ears. Several large, fan-like skin and bone structures ran down the side of each of its jawlines. Its nose was flat and had two wide, rounded nostrils, with small horns extending out from its chin.

Several rows of pointed fangs leaked out from the side of its mouth, giving a preview of the venomous terror concealed inside.

The drogon landed in the soil, narrowing those petrifying eyes...over Blekket.

He stopped fighting, turning to stone under the drogon's glare. The Sleothian he'd been engaging seemed to understand the drogon's claim, handing him over and rushing off to find another Esteopian to terrorise.

"Blek, don't move!" Raevon shouted as she and Pessy joined me where I was standing a few feet away.

Blekket gritted his teeth, not breaking eye contact with the drogon, and hissed, "Yeah, cause I'm really thinking about *dancing* right now, Raevon."

I'd never felt such blinding horror before.

Seeing Blekket in a compromising position awoke a fear in me that was staggering, so excruciating in its intensity that it left me breathless. One wrong move, and the drogon would lunge.

The colossal creature hoisted its left wing in the air, then sprang forward, thrashing Blekket in the face and hurling him into one of the ravaged sheds.

Blekket sliced his arm on a protruding rod of lumber when he crashed, falling onto the ground with a raw groan that pierced my heart.

"Blek!" I screamed. I couldn't just stand there and do nothing. I stepped forward and shouted at the top of my lungs, "HEY! OVER HERE!" waving my arms in the air. I made enough of a commotion to attract the drogon's attention, shifting its focus away from Blekket and onto me.

"Tympany, no!" Blekket cried.

I cinched my eyes with the drogon's and ordered, **"Go home."** The drogon's black pupil, floating in the center of a raging sea of red fire, enlarged, then shrunk in response to my compulsion.

The creature stumbled back, then swung its body away from me, leaping up onto its feet and soaring towards the sky. In the distance, the other two drogon followed the lead of the first, flying away.

It wasn't just the drogon.

All the Sleothians suddenly stopped what they were doing, dropping their weapons and repeating my order.

"*Go home*," they thundered like a brainwashed chorus. None of the Esteopians or Kylantians knew what to do, freezing in place.

The Sleothians turned on their heels and began marching off in the direction of the gates. Their movements were synchronised, continuing to echo my words back at me. Once they had dissolved in the distance and their presence no longer roasted the air, everyone loosed a collective sigh of relief.

"Holy shit," I gasped. "I can't believe that worked."

"Thank *fuck* it worked," Blekket said, walking to me. I grabbed his arm and turned it over to inspect the cut he'd acquired from the wood.

"Does it hurt?" His smile was surprisingly tender.

"Don't worry about it." He bent down to the soil, pressing his hand into the loam. A single drop of water travelled up the length of his arm, smearing the wound in liquid, cleansing the scrape. When the water dispersed, there was no longer an injury there. He stood, flexing his arm. "Try it."

I knelt to the floor, mimicking what Blekket had just done. I felt a large droplet of water writhe up my arm, migrating to all corners of my body, sluicing my skin of any scrapes and blotches of blood I'd obtained through the battle. The sensation tingled, making me laugh.

"That's so cool!" I squealed. Blekket flashed me my favourite toothy grin of his, his teeth reflecting the sun.

"What does it feel like, Tymp?" Pessy asked.

"It kind of tickles. Try it!"

Pessy knelt in the soil, mirroring what Blekket and I did by splaying her fingers out in the mud.

"Whoa!" she yelped, giggling. "I wish we had that in Kylantis!"

Demetrio suddenly appeared, nudging his way through the swarm of Esteopians, his features wrought with panic.

"Rae! Blek! Is everyone okay?" Demetrio cradled Raevon's face, examining her to make sure she wasn't hurt.

"Yeah," Raevon replied, "Thanks to Tympany." Demetrio released her, swinging his head in my direction.

He frowned. "I don't understand."

"Tympany compelled the drogon and the entire army to leave. She saved Blek from being dinner."

"Hey," Blekket jested, "I could've taken him." Everyone stared at him like he'd grown an extra limb.

"No, Blekket. You *could not* have." Raevon enunciated each word.

Demetrio took a step towards me. "You saved my son?" he asked in a low voice, needing me to confirm it.

I nodded slowly.

He surprised me by wrapping his arms around me, squeezing me almost as tight as Blekket did when we flew on Krystal.

"Thank you, Tympany," he gushed in my ear, hoarse with appreciation, tears brewing in his eyes.

Through the contact, I heard him think, *Perhaps she's not the fraud I thought she was. She really is here to save us all.*

I lifted my arms and forced myself to embrace him back.

"What should we do next?" he asked when he let go. I was shocked Demetrio actually deferred to me.

"We should collect all the weapons the Sleothians dropped," I dictated. "They may come in handy at some point. Then, I guess…look for any survivors." I cringed at that along with everyone else.

It was pretty obvious, looking around at all the kindled fires and myriad bodies, there was most likely no one who subsisted the devastation, but we wouldn't know that unless we sifted through everything.

The earth was littered with corpses, gilded daggers, and silver swords. We started stockpiling the weapons, forming a heap of metal in the only bare patch of land we could find. An Esteopian named Augustus trailed behind, making a list of the fallen soldiers he identified amid the debris.

"How was riding Krystal?" Raevon asked Blekket, tossing a sword into the pile of armaments.

"It was…an experience," he replied, putting it mildly.

"Your brother was kind of a wuss," I said, and I'd never seen her smile wider. "He's afraid of heights."

"No, I'm not!" He pouted like a sullen toddler.

"He has been since he was a kid," Demetrio disproved, Blekket smothering his hand over his face to hide from the humiliating truth. "He used to refuse to come out on the deck and greet our subjects because he was terrified of balconies."

"I remember that!" Raevon exclaimed. "He always said he had growing pains and needed to stay inside."

"Both of you, shut up," Blekket hissed, his cheeks flushing an endearing shade of pink. He cleared his throat, aligning his posture with forced poise, then declared, "I bet Tympany has some irrational fears too."

"Nope," I answered with a shake of my head. "I'm all clean."

"Seriously?" Pessy snorted. "Are you really going to pretend you have no fears with me standing right here?"

"Pessoranda," I cautioned, but it was too late.

"She's afraid of spiders." Blekket's head whirled to face me, his earlier chagrin traded for stunning amusement.

"Spiders? Really, Tymp?"

"I don't like the feeling of something crawling all over me. Also, hating something doesn't mean you're afraid of it."

"That's not all," Pess continued. "She also hates it when someone comes up behind her and squeezes her hips."

"Pessy!" *Don't give away all my secrets!*

"I wouldn't like it if someone did that to me either." I sent Raevon an appreciative smile for being on my side.

"So you wouldn't like it if I did this…"

Before Blekket could even stretch out his hands, I snatched his wrist, flipping him onto his back. I straddled his waist, shoved my forearm into his throat, and leaned over him, gripping the hilt of my dagger in the other hand.

"*No.* I wouldn't," I snarled.

"Message received." He blinked up at me, the personification of arrogance. "I sure do love getting under your skin, angel. Which I literally am, at the moment, with you sitting on top of me."

I opened my mouth to respond, but then, I noticed the arm of the corpse lying to the right of us was gold, not blue.

It was a Kylantian.

I crawled off Blekket and rolled the body over, revealing the solider to be Theodora. Her throat had been gashed, and one of her hands was clutching her left rib, which was skewered by a stick of wood. I didn't know her as well as Alsandair and Harrison did, but knowing the Sleothians had taken one of my own, it stung, badly.

I covered her face with my hand, slid her eyes closed, and muttered, "With your last drop, you are free."

Something moved inside one of the mounds of trampled timber. There was a flicker of blue cloth, and then, the tiniest little hand skated its way through one of the chasms in the pile, elongating towards the sky.

"There's someone in there!" I shouted, hurrying over to where the hand was sticking out, waggling their fingers.

I shunted away the demolished lumber, tugging on the arm and pulling the Esteopian villager out from underneath the wreckage. It was a young girl who had to be no older than five, dressed in a long sleeve blue dress that toppled down to her bare feet, tattered and fraying at the bottom. Her blonde hair was tangled with wood scraps and brittle blood.

When she was on her feet, her knees gave out. She collapsed into my arms in the soil, gasping.

"What's your name, sweetheart?" I situated her head in the middle of my pressed together thighs.

"Cos...Cosmina," she coughed out, choking on smoke and sawdust. "Do you...do you know...where my...pa..."

Her airway clogged, hampering her ability to finish her question. She spat up an alarming amount of blood, which trickled down her chin and tarnished the collar of her dress. As I inspected her for further injuries, I found the source of the problem—a dowel of wood was sticking out of her stomach, ripping the cloth around it and percolating the area in warm, gushing blood.

"I think I'm going to be sick," I heard Harrison mutter from behind me. If my eyes were made of the drogon's fire, he would've been reduced to powder under my glare.

"Go back to the palace," I ordered.

I would not have someone retching behind me and terrifying this poor girl even more than she already was.

After Harrison obeyed the command and trudged off to the palace, I glanced up at Pessy, helpless.

Cosmina was slipping away, and fast.

What do I do? I asked her.

Pray to Jax, she proposed.

Yes! Of course!

Jaxith was the God of Kindness. He'd inherited our mother's ability to heal the sick and injured.

I closed my eyes, placing my hands on either side of Cosmina's face to keep her head from rolling into the mud. I reached out to Jaxith, envisioning his face in my thoughts. I let the memory of his presence deluge my senses, enveloping my taut shoulders and clenched muscles in his radiant glow.

Jax? Are you there? I need you.

Thunder rumbled, a flash of lightning reverberating through the clouds before they cleaved apart, revealing a powerful figure up ahead, encased in a garland of light. I recognised the black stallion with massive wings, which were tainted at the edges with black before bleeding into grey, as Bartholomew, Jaxith's Pegasus. The stallion landed with grace on the earth, Jaxith springing down from the horse and causing the ground to tremble with the force of his stomp. He was dressed in his signature colour, a red tunic over loose black slacks, with a gilded leather cord around his waist, carrying his blade. His long blonde hair poured down his neck, framing his jaw like a crown.

"Jax!" I cried with joy.

I passed Cosmina's head to Pessy before leaping off my feet and running to him, throwing my arms around his neck. I'd questioned whether or not he'd heed my call, since it was in direct correlation to what just occurred in Esteopia, but he'd put his predispositions aside and came to help me, regardless of his personal feelings.

154

"Hey, Tymp," he murmured as he embraced me back, stroking a hand down my spine. "I missed you."

"I missed you too," I squeaked.

He cupped my cheeks, inspecting my body for any injuries. "Are you okay? Are you hurt?"

"I'm fine. It's not me." I took his hand and led him over to where Pessy sat with Cosmina. Her skin had begun to deplete of colour, a perilous, sallow chill replacing her earlier warmth. "This little girl was injured in the attack. Can you heal her?"

Jaxith knelt in the soil beside Pessy, surveying the damage. Cosmina's breaths transmuted into wheezes, the life dwindling from her brown eyes at a rapid pace. He rose to his feet, his expression grim.

"Tympany...I can't." My rising pulse pounded viciously in my ears.

"Can't?" I accused, "Or *won't?*" His lips pinched together, his jaw clenching. He didn't need to answer the question.

His silence was deafening.

Cosmina didn't have the luxury of waiting for me to fragment into hysteria. I waved Pessy away, sinking to my knees, and settled her head in my lap, stroking her bedraggled, sodden with blood and sweat hair. She peeked up at me with large doe eyes that deserved so much more time to flicker, deserved so much more time to witness and learn and live and love. I swallowed the lump in my throat, summoning my compulsion forward.

"You're not going to feel any pain," I commanded in a trembling voice. **"You're going to think of something that makes you happy. Think of dolphins, and rainbows. Then close your eyes, and go to sleep."**

Cosmina's pupils reacted to my compulsion, broadening as they absorbed the order, then withdrawing in submission.

Her eyes closed, her hand going limp over her stomach. I glided her out of my lap and onto a bed of soil.

"With your last drop, you are free," I whispered, a tear dripping down my face and onto her cheek.

I rose to my feet and knuckled away my tears, sadness superseded by anger. I lunged at Jaxith with prodigious speed. I landed in front of him and detained him by his hair before he had a chance to react.

"How could you deny her help?!" I shrieked.

"Tympany—"

"She was just a child!"

I raised my fist, aiming for his jaw. Jaxith caught my balled up fingers in his hand before I made contact with his face, tugging me to his chest. He bound my wrists behind my back, so I couldn't strike at him again. I writhed in his iron hold, grunting in frustration.

"Can I speak to you in private, please?" he hissed through his teeth, trying, and failing, to rein in his temper.

I'd nearly forgotten we had an audience.

He shepherded me behind one of the burning sheds, so the Esteopians' view of us was hindered by the fire.

"What're you doing?" he reproached, releasing my wrists. "This wasn't part of the mission."

"What am *I* doing? What about *you,* Jaxith? You just let a little girl die because you couldn't get over your prejudices against Esteopia. I would've expected more from the God of Kindness."

"*Hey.* Watch it," he warned. "You know Esteopia isn't innocent. They attacked Sleotha the night of your birthday."

"Yeah, as a counter attack to their village being destroyed by the drogon! Why did no one mention *that* during the council meeting?" His lips knit together. "You don't actually know anything about what's going on down here. Or you do, and you simply don't care. Sleotha has destroyed more land and slaughtered far more people than Esteopia, yet the Gods support *them?* It makes no sense!"

"You have no idea what you're talking about, Tympany."

"Yeah? Tell me this, Jax. Did you let Esteopians die during the time of the plague, and only heal Sleothians?"

"What?" Jaxith stammered. "Who told you that?"

"Seraphina. Apparently, it's common knowledge in the kingdom." His reflex was to deny, but I sensed, through the tremor honing his words, how ashen his features had become, what he said next wasn't the truth.

"They're lying to you, Tympany. I swear. I would never do that."

"I just watched you refuse to heal one. I don't believe you." He crossed his arms over his chest, shaking his head at me.

"I told you to be careful with the Elrods," he said with disappointment. "They've clearly manipulated you. Maybe Lucius was right, and you're too sensitive. Mother and Father never should've sent you here."

156

"No one's manipulated me. I saw with my own eyes what Sleotha did to Eveium. I watched them obliterate the entire village of Frofsea with no remorse or care. I don't need to be coerced to form my own opinions that may differ from yours. Now, unless you're going to tell me why the Gods *actually* favour Sleotha over Esteopia, instead of the usual answer, 'They just do,' I think you should go."

His jaw crashed to the ground.

"Tympany…" He reached for me, but I stepped back. "You know this has nothing to do with you. It's not personal."

"It's *absolutely* personal, Jaxith." I was appalled that he'd say such a thing. "Theodora died in the attack on Frofsea. She was one of our own. You, and our entire family for that matter, allowed the Sleothians to wound people I care about. We are no longer on the same side. **Now, go home.**" He dawdled a moment, not because the compulsion didn't work, but because he'd lost the strength to move under his despondence.

"It didn't have to be this way," he muttered, then stalked off to where Bartholomew was waiting.

I watched him mount his Pegasus with slumped shoulders, soaring off to the Geddesia Mountains without looking back.

I headed over to meet the Elrods and Pessy, tears streaming down my face. I was strangled by that same sense of loss I'd felt when I left Kylantis, only now, more forceful. I grieved the brother I thought I knew, the one who valued honesty, who would've helped anyone regardless of who they were or where they came from.

I mourned the family I once thought was guiltless, as I made my way to the family I was now officially choosing to stand with.

Chapter Ten

No one spoke a word on the ride back to the palace.

Since Lev had taken Clarence back to the stables, Blekket rode with me on Krystal. His tight embrace around my waist was the only thing that stopped me from ejecting igneous rage over everyone around us.

I was a combustible combination of several different emotions at once—incensed, heartbroken, gripped by grief and loss, but somewhere, amidst the pain, there was also serenity. I'd finally made the choice to support Esteopia, despite what my family believed or wanted. There was peace in that decision. I was proud of myself for making the choice that best profited myself and the people I cared for, not allowing myself to succumb to what was expected of me by others.

Still, losing the illusion of who I thought my family was left a cavity in my chest where my trust in them had been.

I kept thinking about what Jaxith said: *Maybe Lucius was right, and you're too sensitive. Mother and Father never should've sent you here.* If I hadn't volunteered for this, I never would've seen the damage Sleotha had done to Esteopia. I never would've met the Elrods, or the Esteopian villagers, and seen what good people they are. I would've stayed up in my bubble in Kylantis and continued to blindly support a kingdom without actually knowing anything about it, or what they were doing.

I'd be just as complicit as my siblings and would've never realised the destruction I was causing to the world below me.

So, I was grateful this mission fell into my lap—because even though I was losing my family, I wouldn't be blissfully ignorant anymore. That felt like a necessary sacrifice.

Blekket must've sensed my inner turmoil, because he snuggled his thighs closer, resting his chin on my shoulder.

"You did the right thing, Tymp," he promised, speaking for the first time in what felt like hours.

"I know," I muttered. "That doesn't make it hurt less." He nodded before turning his face into my neck.

I could've swore I felt his lips graze my throat. The sensation was respite for my tortured soul.

From the battle with the Sleothians, to the confrontation with Jaxith, to using my compulsion on more people then I was used to in one go, I was utterly exhausted. I handed Krystal's reins to Lev with my eyes half open, smothering a yawn with my hand. I headed straight for my bedchamber, while Pessy went off somewhere with Raevon. I climbed under the duvet and passed out within seconds.

When I awoke sometime later in the evening, Pessy still hadn't returned. My stomach was twisting in knots, my intestines grumbling at me for having missed dinner. I crawled out of bed, slipping on a black silk robe, and tiptoed my way into the hall.

I was surprised to find Harrison squatting outside my door.

"Where's Pessy?" I asked, tying the sash around my waist to cover the sheer slip I wore underneath.

"I think she's with Raevon," he replied, then asked, "Can I help you with anything, Your Grace?"

"No, it's okay. I was just going to get something to eat from the kitchen."

"I'll join you." I internally groaned as he stood.

"You don't have to come with me."

"It's kind of my job." He really was a wiseacre.

"Okay, fine. Make yourself useful and light a match for the torch over there." I pointed at the unlit lantern resting in the metal holster on the wall. Harrison slipped inside my bedchamber, returning with a box of matches.

He quickly lit one, then tipped the flame over the candle, blowing it out once the torch was ignited.

"After you," he said with a wave of his hand, irradiating the hallway with the taper so I could see where I was going.

We scuttled down the staircase in complete silence, my arms swathed around my shoulders. The castle was dead asleep, eerily quiet, and there were no other candles sparked. I lead Harrison into the kitchen, directing him with my finger to remain by the door while I assembled something for myself to eat.

Roara had insisted all nine of us learn how to cook, that we never leave ourselves vulnerable in any regard, in case we were ever alone and needed to fend for ourselves. Although I didn't know how to properly make sushi, I'd eaten it enough times at this point to gather what the finished product was supposed to look like.

I grabbed from the fridge a container of sticky rice, a box with sheets of seaweed, an avocado from the counter, and a thing of yellowtail that was wrapped in paper, held together by a string of yarn. I started by dicing the fish into cubes, shoving the accumulated pile into the corner of the chopping board before peeling off the exocarp of the avocado. I sliced that into tiny blocks, and they joined the heap of yellowtail. I splayed out a long sheet of seaweed, then spread the prepared rice over the sheet, flattening it with the heel of my hand and flicking off the grains that stuck to my palm. After that, I trickled the yellowtail and avocado bits over the compressed rice, then began rolling the seaweed up. Some of the contents spilled out onto the cutting board.

I just popped those into my mouth, chewing the excess as I squeezed the roll together firmly, so nothing more would topple out. I grabbed a serrated knife and cut the roll up into pieces, twelve of them in total.

I scampered through the kitchen, searching for a plate, then situated the sushi on a ceramic dish.

I made sure none of the rolls were touching each other, only satisfied when they were all scattered.

"That was incredibly entertaining to watch," Harrison observed with a smile. I'd completely forgotten he was there.

"Are you hungry?" I offered him one.

"Actually, yeah. Kind of." He set the torch in the empty holster on the wall, ambling across the room to take the roll from me. "Thanks, Tympany."

"You're welcome." I raised my sushi. "Cheers."

"Cheers," he laughed, clinking his roll with mine before we both shoved them into our mouths. While it wasn't nearly as delicious as when Lev made it, I hadn't botched the whole thing, which was a relief. "This is pretty good."

"Thank you." I leaned my elbows on the hardwood table, digging into my meal.

I felt his eyes penetrate through the material of my robe, but ignored the unsettled chill that stormed through me in response to the unsolicited glances. I engulfed the rolls, feeling strangely on edge, like I had to rush back to my room.

"Thank you again, for saving my life," he said, after several minutes of us just standing there in silence.

"You don't have to thank me, Harrison. It was nothing."

"It was not nothing, Tympany. You saved me." He took a step closer and was now crowding over me.

Alarm sirens went off in my head. "What are you doing?" I stammered.

"Thanking you." He sauntered forward again despite me angling my body away from him.

"You already did that." I gripped the edge of my plate for support.

"Come on, Tympany. All those times you pick on me, I know what it really is. You like me."

"*Like* you?" I spluttered, nearing choking on the yellowtail and avocado. "What're you talking about?"

"You just shared your sushi with me."

"Yeah, to be nice!" I offered him part of my dinner, and he took that as a sign I *wanted* him?

"I always catch you and Pessy looking at me."

"Because Pessy hates your guts, and every time you come near us, I have to talk her down from chopping off your head."

"Because you like me." Was he being for real?

"Harrison, I don't even like you as a *person*, let alone in the way you're insinuating. Now *get out* of my way."

"So you'd rather the *Neraid* then me?" I somehow ended up against the wall. He planted his hands on either side of my head, effectively trapping me beneath him. While I could quite easily overpower him, fear skewered my survival instincts, weakening me in my moment of need.

"Harrison, I swear to the Gods, if you don't back up right now—"

"You'll what? Compel me again? We both know you won't do that." He raised a hand, tracing it down my cheek. I jerked back in disgust. "Deep down, Tympany, you know the truth. You talk a big game, but when the going gets rough, you're more bark than bite."

"Harrison—"

"You won't compel me," he repeated, more to himself then me, as he slipped his fingers into my hair and leaned in.

I set my hands on his shoulders and plunged my knee into his groin, then punched him in the face. He staggered, stumbling onto the marble floor, and clutched his nose, which was now gushing blood.

I marched over to him and grabbed a handful of his shirt, lifting him off his feet in the air above me.

"You want to do something *really* useful?" I hissed. **"Light yourself on fire, Harrison."**

I let go of his shirt, and he crumbled to the ground like a discarded, crinkled sheet of paper. I watched him stand, spin around, and wordlessly stride over to where the torch sat in the holster, sliding it out by the handle.

After realising I'd inadvertently activated my compulsion, when I'd only intended to scorn him, I lurched forward, waving my hands spastically to try to prevent what was about to transpire.

"Wait, stop. I didn't mean..." He raised the torch over his head, slanting it towards his hair. "Harrison, **NO!"**

It was too late.

The flames surged down from the crown of his head to the tips of his toes, incinerating every limb, tendon, sinew, and bone. The smoke restricted his oxygen flow, his soft tissues contracting, which caused the skin to tear and his fat and muscles to shrink. As his skin scorched and melted away, his muscles dried up and withered, his internal organs reaching a boiling point before erupting, spewing guts all over me and the walls. I lifted my arms to cover my face, then ran to find a bucket. I found one in the cupboard and filled it with water in the sink before dumping it over the kindled fire, the flames reducing until they dissipated completely. Then, all I was left with was his carbonised body.

He didn't even scream.

Fire rained down on him, and he didn't even scream.

The only sound echoing through the scullery was my piercing sob. I dropped the bucket, threading my fingers in my hair. I crashed to my knees before the charred bits of him, horrified by what I'd done, gasping for breath that was unattainable. I felt disgusting, never wishing more for a zipper to be appended to the back of my head, one I could pull down and use to crawl out of my skin.

In all my five thousand years of existence, I'd never killed someone—until today. I'd never used my abilities so selfishly, or without separating myself from emotion, so I wouldn't utter something I didn't mean.

Something I couldn't retract.

What Harrison did was wrong, but he didn't deserve to die. He had a family back in Kylantis, who were waiting for him to return home when the mission concluded. He had a little sister named Yasmine who idolised him. He had a loving grandmother, a close friend of my mother's. Evaline was a kind soul, who would always bring us tea and biscuits when we were training. They didn't deserve to suffer.

They didn't deserve to have to accept his death just because it was at the hands of a Goddess.

You never realise the power of words until you can't take them back.

I heard footsteps in the hall, which intensified in volume the closer they got to the kitchen, before Blekket appeared in the doorway. He had on the same black button down and breeches he'd worn earlier, despite them being blotted with grime and gore from the battle. He must've been too wearied to change before bed.

I idly wondered if that was *his* blood staining the clothes, or someone else's.

His brows furrowed as he poked his head into the room, searching angrily for whatever sound awoke him.

"Tympany?" Horror replaced annoyance. He rushed forward and fell to his knees before me, shouting, "Tympany! Are you okay? What happened?"

"I…I…" I could barely breathe, let alone speak. Blekket hitched my hair behind my ears so it wouldn't glom onto my sticky cheeks, but otherwise was careful not to touch me, undertaking how much I was shaking. "Harrison tried to…tried to kiss me? I don't…I don't even…he tried to, and I…I freaked out, and I…" I peeked over at the residue on the floor. "I compelled him to light himself on fire." Blekket's eyes enlarged, flickering around the room to find the mess I was referring to.

When he located it, his mouth opened, then closed, repeating this several times.

"I can't…I can't believe…I killed him…I killed him…" I was crying so violently that I gagged on a sob.

Blekket's hands hovered near me, waiting until I granted him permission. When I nodded, reaching for him, he lifted me into his lap and wrapped his strong, comforting arms around me.

I sagged against him as I wailed.

"It's okay, Tympany," he cooed, stroking his hand down the length of my hair, tucking my head underneath his chin. I was surprised to find no revulsion in his voice, which I felt I deserved.

"No, it's not," I wept. "It's not. I'm a terrible person."

"No, you're not, Tymp. You're not. Harrison was touching you without your consent. *He's* the terrible one. Not you."

"I killed him, Blek! I killed him!" I buried my face in his chest, slobbering all over his shirt.

"I'm sorry, Tympany," he groaned into my hair, holding me even tighter. "Fuck. I'm so sorry."

"I didn't mean to," I mewled, which felt important to say. "I didn't mean to. I didn't mean to compel him. I don't know what happened."

"I know, Tymp. I know you didn't mean to. I know."

"I don't...I'm sorry. I'm sorry." I kept repeating that over and over, to Harrison, to Blekket, to the universe.

Words that were meaningless after the ones I'd just uttered.

Several minutes elapsed of me bawling hysterically before my breaths started to regulate, and I was able to lean back. I looked down at my hands, at the metaphorical blood that took shape as Harrison's ashes, staining my fingers and caked in my nails.

"I...I have his...his ashes...all...all over...me..." My entire body was trembling from adrenaline and shock.

"Let's get you cleaned up. Okay?" He swiped his thumbs through the streaks of tears on my cheeks. "Let's clean you up."

Blekket proffered his hands, and I took them, letting him tug me to my feet. I didn't feel sturdy enough yet to support myself on my own, so I curled my arms around his waist and nuzzled my cheek against his chest, silently asking for his help. He took half my weight from me by slithering an arm around my torso and tugging me close, allowing me to lean on him as we started for the hallway.

"Wait," I exclaimed. We stopped walking. "We can't just leave his body." Blekket looked over his shoulder at the kitchen.

"Lev can clean it tomorrow." The thought of sweet Lev seeing what I'd done tasted nasty.

"Lev shouldn't have to do it. It should be me." Roara instilled in me young that it was my responsibility to clean my own messes, that I should never transfer the burden to someone else when I was capable of doing it myself.

I started back towards the kitchen, but Blekket grabbed my hand before I made it two steps.

"Tympany, no. It doesn't have to be you. I'll let Lev know in the morning what happened, and he can get one of the cleaners to do it. It shouldn't be you." He laced his fingers through mine, squeezing.

It took another minute of convincing for me to feel even the tiniest bit comfortable leaving the wreckage behind.

Then, Blekket escorted me up the stairs.

When we passed my bedchamber on the way to his, I wondered if Pessy had returned and questioned where I'd went. If that were the case, I thought, she would've reached out through the bond.

She was still with Raevon.

Blekket's room looked a lot like mine, except it didn't. His bedsheets were a darker blue, the same colour as his eyes. The canopy draping down was composed of delicate gossamer that reflected the mottled moonlight onto the duvet in tiny silver spots, like polka dots. He left me by the bed and crossed the room to his dresser, pulling open one of the drawers and sifting through the folded clothing for a clean shirt. I made a mental note of the leather journal on the bedside table, the iron dagger sleeping beside it, and how his shoes were strewn across the floor, some of his shirts flung in random places.

The black petticoat he wore the night we met was hanging on the outside of the closet, like a souvenir.

When Blekket returned to me, he had a long sleeve black tunic in his hand.

"Do you want a shower to wash off all this...stuff?" He said the last word apologetically. I nodded. "Here." He handed me the shirt. "For when you get out. I can have the maids wash your robe and dress tomorrow."

"Thank you, Blek." I took the shirt from him sheepishly, feeling unworthy of his kindness. I started for the bathroom, but I was still trembling so much that I barely made it a step without tripping over my feet. I swivelled around, my cheeks blistering, and asked, "Could you...help me?"

I'd never seen someone look so paralysed and invigorated at the same time. "Are you...sure?" His voice was hoarse.

"I'm...shaking too much," I explained, flushing deeper.

"Hold on." He went back to his dresser and opened the same drawer, retrieving another long sleeve tunic, this one navy blue with a scoop neck. He passed it to me. "You can wear one in the shower, and one to bed."

"I feel bad taking two shirts from you." His eyes twinkled, like daybreak rupturing through the stupor of night.

"Tympany, it's okay. I'll have them both washed tomorrow." He scratched the back of his neck, shifting on the balls of his feet. "Um…let me know when you're dressed, and I'll come into the bathroom."

"Okay." I dithered a moment, not because I regretted asking for his help, but because I didn't want to leave his side.

I pulled myself together and scuttled into the bathroom, sliding the door shut. I stripped off my robe and nightdress, slipping on the black tunic. It was enormous and trickled down to my knees, shrouding the majority of my thighs and my whole backside. Bruises coated my calves and arms from the battle at Frofsea, as well as a few lingering welts the Argent Ocean water hadn't completely healed.

Those would vanish by tomorrow.

"I'm ready," I called out to Blekket, listening to his fast paced footsteps before he glided the door open.

His jaw dropped to the floor. When he swallowed, it looked like it was hard for him to do so.

"You really are magnificent, Tympany." There was no trace of humor in that statement.

I usually balked at anyone attempting to compliment me, but with Blekket, I let the praise wash over me, not rejecting the warmth that ensued.

"Thanks," I answered in a quiet voice.

I stepped into the shower, Blekket following behind me. He leaned over, twisting the valve to warm.

An inundation of water doused my hair, face, and back, the now damp shirt clinging to my physique. I tipped my face up to the torrent, closing my eyes for a much-needed moment of tranquility under the alleviating downpour. When I opened them, Blekket was squirting shampoo into his palm.

"Turn around, please." I complied, angling my head back as he began to massage the lather into my hair.

"Hmm…" I let out an involuntary sigh.

"How does this feel?" he asked softly, kneading my scalp with his fingernails, leaving no section of my head neglected.

"Amazing," I confessed, and felt him smile rather than saw it.

"You have the most incredible hair," he murmured to himself absentmindedly, rinsing out the suds.

"Thank you. I grow it myself." He snickered at my little joke, and I felt ten feet tall.

He spurted the conditioner into his palm, rubbing his hands together, then glided his fingers back into my hair.

"I never liked Harrison," Blekket admitted while working the moisturiser in, the tips of his fingers trailing over my shoulder blades as he folded the ends into the rest of my hair, mixing it all together at the top of my head. "I sure won't be crying over his death, and I know Pessy won't be either."

"What I did was still bad," I mumbled.

"Do you want me to tell you that? You already know it was. Why would I further torture you?"

"Because I deserve it."

His fingers stilled in my hair before settling on my shoulders. He spun me around, so I was forced to look at him.

He then said urgently, "I don't *ever* want to hear you say that again. You don't, Tympany. What *he* was doing was wrong. You defended yourself. There's nothing wrong with that."

"But I—"

"So you compelled a man to light himself on fire. I'm not saying it was the best solution, or that it's something to be proud of, but you were scared and didn't know what else to do." He cradled the side of my face, running his thumb down my cheek. Unlike when Harrison did it, Blekket's touch seeped deep under my skin, distributing warmth through my bloodstream. "You can't punish yourself forever, Tymp. This doesn't make you a bad person. You want to know how I know that?"

"How?" I squeaked.

"Because when your brother, the God of Kindness, refused to heal that girl, you eased her suffering. When you saw me in danger with that drogon, you put yourself between it and me despite the risk. You fought today, killed humans, for a kingdom that's not even your home. *That's* how I know."

Tears pricked the corners of my eyes. Blekket leaned over and turned off the water. He strode out of the shower, retrieving a white towel that was draped over the dark wood bath linen rack.

He opened it for me.

I scurried out to meet him, then leaned back, allowing him to encase me in the supple cotton.

I was thrilled when he didn't remove his arms from around me.

"You're a good person, Tympany," he promised, his lips grazing my earlobe. His warm breath initiated another upwelling of shudders, which pulsated through my body and into his limbs he held me with. "If you ever have a moment where you doubt that, come find me, and I'll remind you." I turned in his embrace, twisting my arms around his stomach.

"Thank you, Blekket," I whispered, squeezing my eyes shut. "For being there. For helping me get clean. For everything."

"Oh, Tympany," he moaned, burying his face in my damp hair. "I'm so sorry this happened to you."

I wouldn't say it was okay—but I would no longer declare I deserved to be punished for it either.

"I can walk you back to your room, if you'd like," he offered, making me hug him even tighter.

I strangely missed him, yet he was still right here, in my arms.

"Pessy's with Raevon. I don't want to be alone tonight." I hid my blush in his shirt. "Can I stay with you?"

"Absolutely." I felt his lips in my hair, and I think he kissed the crown of my head. "I can sleep on the floor."

"You don't have to sleep on the floor." I glowered at him for suggesting such a thing. "I think we can share the bed and it not be an issue."

"You're giving me way too much credit, angel, especially with you in my shirt." He tucked my hair behind my ear while what he said sank in. "But I promise to behave myself if you do."

I narrowed my eyes. "I *always* behave myself."

"No, you really don't." He chuckled at my pout. "I'll leave you alone to get dressed." He released me, much to my hidden disappointment. I could've sworn I saw him frown before he turned on his heel and shut the door.

After I quickly undressed, folding the damp shirt on the vanity, I slipped on the navy tunic, which fell to my knees just as the first one had. I then met Blekket in his bedchamber. It felt natural to weave my fingers through the slots between his, to squeeze his hand, letting him lead me towards the bed. He lifted the duvet for me, and I thanked him shyly as I crawled under the covers, tugging them up to my chin. Blekket climbed in after me, keeping three feet of distance between us.

We were facing each other on opposite sides.

"Why were you in the kitchen to begin with?" he wondered aloud randomly, like he'd been pondering it for a while and was waiting to ask.

"I woke up starving. Harrison was camped outside my room, on guard. He came with me so I could get something to eat."

"What'd you make yourself?" His hand inched closer to mine on the mattress.

"Yellowtail and avocado, though it wasn't nearly as good as when Lev makes it."

"I would've loved to see you try to make that for yourself," he laughed, ducking away from the swing of my hand.

"I offered some of it to Harrison, which was a mistake. I guess he took that as me coming on to him...I don't know."

"That bastard," Blekket growled. "If he wasn't already dead, I'd kill him myself for laying a hand on you."

I was stunned by the fervor of that declaration, and knew, without a shadow of a doubt, he meant it.

"He's gone now," I reassured, in an effort to assuage his mounting exasperation and my own lingering distress. "He can no longer bother me, or anyone else. Pessy will probably rejoice, or be bitter she didn't get to off him herself." He cackled at that, the sound reminiscent of the chime of bells. With his index finger, he outlined the bumps of my knuckles on the back of my hand, which was flat on the bed. "Blek?" I whispered.

"Yeah, Tymp?"

"Who was the first person you ever killed?"

His movements ceased. In the moonlight, I watched an array of goosebumps pimple his flesh.

"I was nineteen," he murmured, turning my hand over and tracing the lines on my palm. "Sleotha attempted to invade Acadia. No drogon, just soldiers. We won that battle. Anyway, I was minding my business, walking through the castle grounds, and stumbled upon a Sleothian solider trying to break into the palace."

"Were you scared?"

"Not really. I'd been training with the Esteopian army since I was fourteen. My father said it was imperative we knew how to defend ourselves, in case we were ever alone and in peril."

"Same as my mother," I muttered.

"Right. Exactly. So, the man was twice my size and quite obese, which I thought was kind of strange, since he was a solider. I looked at him and asked, with my big mouth, 'Shouldn't you be in much better shape?'" I giggled into my pillow, Blekket's face illuminating with a dazzling smile. "That's a great sound." He sighed.

I stopped. "What is?"

"Your laugh. You don't laugh enough." I hoped he couldn't see my cheeks flush in the darkness. "Well, that comment *really* set him off," Blekket continued. "The solider lunged at me, but I used his weight against him and stole his dagger. I slit his throat before he even realised I had it."

"How did it feel?" His lips knit together as he thought it over.

"It felt...sort of empowering, that I'd managed to slay a man twice my size. But it also felt wrong. Like I was playing God. I mean, yes, he was attempting to break into my home, but he had a home too, you know? I deprived him of the chance to return to his family. I think about that a lot, with every Sleothian I've killed. My perception of them being evil might not be who they are at their core. They're supporting their cause, defending their home, just like I'm doing. Am I really any better than them?" He stared down at our hands. "I don't know if that makes any sense."

"No, it does. Completely." I laced my fingers with his. "When I watched Harrison burn, I thought about his grandmother and sister. What he did to me was wrong, but they don't deserve to suffer now because of it."

"That's not your fault, Tymp."

"It is. I took his life away. Even though I was provoked to do it, he can't go home to them now. I did that. I'm going to have to live with that for the rest of my life, and for me, that's forever." He got quiet for a moment, his fingers stirring between mine.

"Does the idea of living forever scare you?"

"A little," I answered honestly. "I appreciate the way humans value life and the limited time they have. I envy that a bit. My siblings and I, we take life for granted sometimes, since it's guaranteed to always be there. The years just sort of blend into each other. Time is different in Kylantis. Every day is the same."

"That sounds boring," he muttered.

"It is. Extremely. I was growing so restless up there. That's one of the reasons I came down here. I needed...more."

"Do you feel like you've found that here? More?" His voice was kitten soft.

"*So* much more. Esteopia is just magical. The creatures, the waters...it's all so fantastic. And the people...you're all so kind and grateful for life. You guys have opened my eyes to so much, made me see the world and my family and these kingdoms in a completely new way. I can't thank you enough for that. I needed to be disillusioned. To question what was told to me. To wake up. So, thank you."

Blekket reached across the mattress, skimming the tips of his fingers down the side of my face. I angled my cheek into his palm, nuzzling him without even realising I'd made the choice to do so.

"You're extraordinary, Tympany." He sounded awestruck. "And I don't mean because you're a Goddess. Because of who you are, at your core. You are utterly extraordinary."

There were so many things I wanted to do in that moment—burst into tears, snuggle up against him, possibly even lean over and kiss him...but I felt rooted to my spot on the bed under the intensity of his eyes, feeling bizarrely buoyant with his hand on my cheek, stroking my face with such tenderness. With every caress of his fingers over my skin, my head was dunked further underwater.

"We should go to sleep," Blekket announced.

"Um...yeah, we should." I cleared my throat, shuffling back, but he tugged my hand, pulling on my arm before I could move any further away from him. "I thought we were behaving," I stuttered, and watched his lips whorl into a gorgeous, impish smile in the moonlight.

"We are," he swore. "I just wanted you a little closer."

"That sounds dangerous." He cackled up at the ceiling, wriggling until he was lying on his back.

"Goodnight, Tympany." He sighed.

"Goodnight, Blekket." I rolled onto my side, my hand still ensnared in his when my eyes fluttered shut.

Chapter Eleven

I woke up from the best sleep of my life to Blekket's head resting on my chest.

At some point in the night, I must've crawled across the bed onto his side, or, he tugged on my hand in his sleep and dragged me over there. My leg was inserted between his, and one of his limbs was curled around my waist. One of my arms was looped around his shoulders, my fingers twisted in the hair at the nape of his neck, and my other hand was under his shirt, pressed against his lower back. I peeked down, admiring how his long lashes fanned out over his cheeks, casting a delicate shadow over his faint freckles, how young and carefree he looked in slumber. Quiet, adorable snores discharged past his lips when they parted, bringing a small smile to my face.

While I was a bit overheated, I didn't want to disturb him, or the peacefulness that first encompassed me when I awoke. However, I made the mistake of stilling when I was trying not to rouse him.

Blekket's eyes flashed open, his head raising quickly to scan the bed for any trespassers. When he discovered nothing there, he turned back to me, his lips curling up in a languid, beautiful smile.

"Good morning," he murmured in a husky, sonorous voice, lowering his chin over my sternum.

"Morning." When I squirmed beneath him, he suddenly realised he was on top of me.

"Gods, I'm so sorry," he exclaimed, scooting back in the bed. "I didn't mean to climb on you like that."

"Don't be." I didn't want to tell him I'd woken up with a grin on my face, seeing how we were entwined together, but I also didn't want him to think he took advantage or made me uncomfortable in any way.

"Did you sleep okay?" He tucked a loose strand of my hair behind my ear.

"Pretty good, despite all your snoring." His forehead crinkled with annoyance, his hand falling to his side.

"I *do not* snore."

"Yes, you do."

"Well, you talk in your sleep. Did you know that?" I did. Pessy and Jax both teased me about it hundreds of times.

"What was I saying?" I cringed before I even knew the answer.

"Nothing embarrassing, or intelligible. You said a few times, 'underwater', which I thought was cute."

Underwater...huh.

I was grateful I hadn't said anything more lucid—or, if I had, that Blekket didn't disclose it.

"What else?" His smile amplified.

"You said 'magnificent' once. I especially liked that." My blood had never felt fierier underneath the skin of my cheeks.

"You're lying," I accused.

"I would never!"

"You said you didn't snore. That was a lie. You said you weren't afraid of heights. That was a lie."

"You should know by now I would *never* lie if it had something to do with you, Tympany." I didn't think my blush could get any deeper. "I've never seen you so red. Are you feeling feverish? Should I get you a damp washcloth?"

"Shut up!" I shouted, picking up my pillow and smacking him with it. I sometimes underestimated my own godly strength, for Blekket, upon impact with the pillow, trundled off the bed and bumped his nose into the floorboard. "Blek!" I dove across the mattress, peeking down. "Are you okay?"

He jumped up, grabbed his pillow and leapt onto the bed, swatting me with very little force.

I squealed, blocking the impact with my forearms.

"Is that the best you can do?" I goaded, reaching for my pillow and walloping him across the face.

"Fuck, Tympany!" He cupped where I socked him. I ceased all movements, worried I'd hurt him again.

"Shit, Blek, I'm sorry. I—"

He struck me across the face with his pillow, managing to catch me off guard and knock me over the side of the bed.

"Got you!" he cheered, shaking his fist in the air with triumph. "I may not be able to outsit a God, but I can out-pillow one!"

"You're gonna pay for that!" I shrieked.

I stayed on my feet, so Blekket didn't have an opening to whack me off the bed again, and stalked around the periphery of the mattress. Blekket remained in the center, the security of several cushions around him, both of us waiting in anticipation of the other one's actions, shrouding our faces with our pillows just in case the other decided to strike. The moment I lunged, Blekket lurched forward, snatching me by the hips, and flipped me onto my back beneath him. He loomed over me after filching the pillow from between my fingers, chucking it over his shoulder.

"I win round four," he declared, his hands on either side of my head in a push up position.

"I think we're way passed round four by now," I said breathlessly.

"What number would you say we're on? Ten?" His lips were hovering over mine.

If I stretched my neck and tipped my head up even a fraction of an inch, our mouths would meet.

"You really are so beautiful, Tympany," he whispered. My breath hitched. My hand, at its own accord, curled around the back of his neck, fully prepared to yank him down and close the distance between us once and for all.

Suddenly, the door to his bedchamber opened.

"Hey, Blek. Could I bo—" Raevon screamed when she saw us, covering her eyes with her hand and backing up against the wall. I screeched, rolling out from under Blekket to cloak my bare legs under the duvet.

"Raevon!" Blekket snapped, blocking her view of me with his body. "Knock, would you?"

"I'm *so* sorry," she exclaimed, her fingers still smothered over her eyes. "I came in here to borrow some shampoo. I ran out of mine."

"Yeah, you can take it. Be quick." She scurried into the bathroom, ducking her head to evade looking at us. I could only imagine what she believed happened between her brother and me.

As she scampered back in, she repeated, "Sorry, again," then quickly shut the door behind her.

We both breathed a sigh of relief when she was gone.

"I should probably go," I murmured, crawling off the bed. I hurried across the floor, retrieving my robe and nightdress from the night before, as well as the tunic I'd worn in the shower.

"Tympany—"

"Bye, Blek," I threw over my shoulder, rushing out.

I dashed down the hall as fast as my feet could carry me, so no one would stumble upon me in just Blekket's shirt.

When I locked the door to my bedchamber and turned around, I found Pessy mid pacing back and forth.

When she saw me, her features softened.

"Where were you? I was about to reach out through the bond. I was so worried." I set the clothing down in the laundry basket by the dresser, Pessy following me with her eyes. I made a mental note to ask Lev later how they wash clothing in Esteopia, so I could do it myself. "Are you okay?" she asked me, palpably concerned.

"Um..." *Was I?*

No.

That was the truth, but I didn't want to accept it, didn't want to let that soak in, because I was afraid, once it did, I'd never recover.

The last twenty-four hours—the last ten minutes—crashed over me all at once like a tidal wave, as if the ceiling had collapsed onto my head. My knees gave out. I crumbled to the ground, sobbing hysterically.

"Tymp!" Pessy fell to the floor beside me, wrapping her arms around me. "Tympany, what happened?"

Somehow, I managed to calm myself down long enough to profess to her, "Harrison's dead."

"What? How do you know that?"

"Because I killed him." Pessy's jaw dropped so far down, I feared it would dislocate. "He tried to...kiss me...I told him to back up, and he...I didn't know what to do, Pess," I cried, dissolving into tears. "I was so scared. I didn't know what to do...so I compelled him to light himself on fire."

"Holy shit!" Her unbridled reaction calmed me down a little.

"Blek found me after. He comforted me. That was all that happened. He just...held me." I didn't mention the shower. It felt like overkill. That memory was so sacred, and I wanted to keep it for myself. "I woke up in his arms. It was the best sleep I've ever had. We were about to kiss before Raevon walked in on us. I think she thought we..." I shuddered. "I just got so...embarrassed. It was all so much. I've never been attracted to someone before. I've never even kissed someone, let alone slept in the same bed as them, and I just…I feel…I don't even know…"

"Oh, Tymp." Pessy swept my hair off my face. "I'm so sorry. I'm so sorry this happened to you. I'm so sorry I wasn't there. I should've been there."

Suddenly, her face crumpled, and she began to weep, clutching her gut in horror as she backed away from me. In all the three hundred years I'd known her, I had never seen Pessy cry before. It was staggering enough to dry my own tears.

"You shouldn't have been alone with him. I should've been there. Oh Gods, I'm so sorry, Tympany. I'm the worst guardian ever. I don't deserve to be bonded to you."

"Pess!" I smudged away the pools of tears collecting on her cheeks with my thumbs. "Pessy, please, don't say that. You did nothing wrong."

"My job is to protect you, Tympany. My job is to always be there for you. While you were alone with him, I was with…with *Raevon*." She uttered Raevon's name like it was dirty, burying her face in her hands, wracked with violent sobs. "You're more than just my bonded. You're my best friend. You're my whole life. I should've been there. I should've been there. I'll never forgive myself."

"Stop. Listen to me." I seized her hands, pulling them away from her face, so she could see me. "You did nothing wrong. I'm not mad at you, but I will be if you try to blame yourself for this. Stop." Her gorgeous blue eyes were still glazed over with tears, but she seemed to absorb what I was saying. "This isn't your fault. It's not my fault either. Well, I don't entirely believe that, but I'm going to keep repeating it to myself until I do. He's gone now. What's done is done."

Pessy nodded, wiping snot on the back of her hand.

She was silent for a moment, then whispered, "You really compelled him to light himself on fire?"

"I didn't mean to. I didn't even realise what I was doing. I was so mad, Pess. The words just…came out."

"Gods, I'm so sorry, Tymp. I can't even imagine what you were feeling." She laced her fingers with mine, squeezing. She sniffled, then asked, "What did it look like? To see him…burn?"

"It was really strange. He didn't even scream, I think because of my compulsion. His organs exploded, and he didn't even scream."

"Shit. That's dark."

"I know." I sagged with regret.

"Can I say something that is totally inappropriate and makes me a horrible person for even thinking?" I had an inkling where she was going with this and figured we could both use a laugh, so I nodded. "I'm kind of jealous you beat me to it." I burst into gales of laughter, Pessy joining me shortly after.

"I told Blekket you would say that," I giggled.

"Gods, I've wanted to chop off that bastard's head, rip out his tongue, push him off a cliff, so many fucking times over the years. I really wish I could've been there to see Harrison Rottweiler *finally* get what he deserved. It would've been a sight for sore eyes."

"You're right. That does make you a horrible person." I stooped in time to dodge the swing of her hand before it collided with my head.

"Hey. I'm not the one who compelled someone to light themselves on fire."

"No, you're just the one who's jealous she didn't get to do it herself. Cause that makes it so much better."

"Fuck you," she snickered, flipping me off.

When our laughter died down, we both had to sit in our self-reproach, but at least we had each other to keep us company while we drowned.

After sitting in silence for several minutes, Pessy erupted, "You and Blek almost kissed?!" as if she'd totally glossed over that part of what I said before, and it was only now sinking in.

"I know."

"Who initiated it? Before Raevon came in."

"Me...kind of."

"Tymp!"

"I know. I *know*. And then I basically ran away after Raevon left. He probably thinks I'm insane."

"No. He probably thinks you got scared after last night and is blaming himself, thinking he did something to make you uncomfortable." That was more likely accurate. "Are you going to try to kiss him again? You really should. You're perfect for each other."

"Pess!"

"What? You know it's true." She clambered off the floor, reaching for my hands to wrench me up with her.

177

"Right now, all I'm thinking about is getting something to eat and making sure Lev hasn't cleaned up Harrison's remains before I get a chance to."

"Wait, you left his body there?" Pessy squealed, "This I *have* to see! I want to save his ashes as a keepsake!"

"Pessoranda Whitereaver!" I shouted, but had a massive grin on my face as I watched her skip to get dressed.

We headed to the kitchen, checking to see if Lev got around to cleaning up Harrison's ashes.

Unfortunately, he had.

The scullery was spotless when we arrived.

"Dammit," Pessy muttered under her breath, slumping with disappointment. "I really wanted to dance over his remains."

"Pess! You can't speak of the dead like that."

"I can, if the person I'm speaking of was as awful as Harrison. He deserves to rot in Nekropolis for what he did to you. I hope Hadestia is giving him hell." I pinched my lips at her disapprovingly.

She just shrugged.

Even if he was dreadful and annoying, he still deserved to live. He'd now never have the chance to grow, to be better. I would feel that way for the rest of my life.

Pessy and I decided to avoid the Elrods for as long as we could and have breakfast just the two of us. We collected enough food for the morning and afternoon, gathering everything in a wicker basket we found in the cupboard, and retrieved a cream white blanket with blue tassels from the closet in our bedchamber. We strode through the palace, arms linked, to the garden at the back, where we draped the picnic blanket over the freshly sheared grass and splayed the assortment of foods out over the towel. I gathered the train of my dress and squatted to the floor, curling my legs to the side as I got comfortable on the blanket. I had on a grey gown, made of lightweight fabric draped into a surplice bodice, atop a banded waistline. The cascading skirt fell to a maxi hem with a sultry side slit, giving my limbs room to breathe.

"It's so nice out." Pessy sighed, popping a strawberry into her mouth. The weather was warm and lovely, the sky unsullied of clouds, though the air did feel a bit muggy due to the persistent smoke wafting in from Frofsea.

Which then made me wonder—Caspian should've given Esteopia rain following the devastation from yesterday. By denying them precipitation, he left the soot loitering in the ether for anyone to inhale and choke on. Was that done on purpose, to prolong the Esteopians' suffering?

When the sun dribbled down my arm, I thought of Lucius. Was he deliberately making the sunlight scalding? Had Jax told my family about me changing sides, and they were already taking it out on the Esteopians through the climate?

I hoped not. I could do a lot for Esteopia, but I had no control when it came to the weather.

We made it the whole day without being spotted or summoned, lounging in the glare of the sun for hours and reminiscing on times back in Kylantis. We laughed at the memory of when Pessy and I snuck into Lucius's bedchamber while he was down in the Realm and squirted sunblock over his mattress, so when he returned to Kylantis and flung himself onto the bed, his spine was coated in a thick layer of lotion. Pessy reminded me of when I was first learning to ride Krystal, and I accidentally got my ankle caught in her stirrup. When she trotted off, she dragged me along the ground for miles.

"I think I may have peed myself," Pessy giggled. I hurled my loaf of bread, and she swooped out of the way before it hit her.

"Hi, guys." We looked up to find Raevon approaching us. She had on a dusty blue gown with a pleated design, the plunging neckline and thin straps embellished with tiny diamonds, the skirt made out of fine, soft sheer mesh. Her long black hair was twisted into a braid down her back, so the delicate glide of her jawline was on full display. She plopped down next to Pessy, who sort of angled herself away from Raevon, much to my astonishment. Raevon didn't even notice.

"Hi, Rae." I passed her a bread roll.

"Thanks." She ripped at the loaf, stuffing it into her mouth, then angled her face towards the sunlight. "It's hot today."

"I know," I mumbled, wincing at the thought of Lucius having something to do with this, hoping it was just residue from the fires and not a meditative divine response. "Where's...your brother?"

179

"Don't know. I went to the dining hall for breakfast and again for lunch, but no one was there." She smirked. "Why? Already want seconds?"

"Raevon!" Pessy cried, slapping her arm and glowering at her.

"I'm just joking," Raevon insisted, raising her hands in defense. "You know I'm only kidding, Tymp."

"I know that." I scowled at Pessy, not sure why she was acting this way. "And nothing happened between me and your brother, by the way."

"So you just happened to be sleeping in the same bed?" Raevon arched a brow in suspicion.

"He found me last night after an…altercation with Harrison." Pessy flinched, shrouding her frown behind a curtain of her hair. "He helped me clean up and just…held me. It was very innocent."

"Blekket and the word *innocent* have never been used in the same sentence *ever*," Raevon laughed, "but I'm pleased to hear he was a perfect gentleman. I knew he had it in him somewhere."

I tensed at the implications of that, what sordid past she was hinting at him having.

"Has Blekket been with…a lot of people?" Raevon's eyes enlarged when she realised how what she said landed for me.

"No! No, he hasn't. I didn't mean…shit, I shouldn't be talking about this. But trust me, in that regard, you have nothing to worry about." She plucked my hand off the blanket to give it a light squeeze.

I raised my eyes and located Blekket across the way, strolling down the path in the direction of the palace. He'd changed into a white dress shirt, which was tucked into navy breeches, his sleeves rolled to his elbows. The sun trickled over the short strands of his hair that were shoved off his forehead, accentuating the natural blonde highlights that existed between the exterior of brown.

My lips formed a smile at the sight of him. I nearly lifted a hand to beckon him over, until I saw he wasn't alone.

A woman walked beside him, a beautiful one at that. Long blonde hair the colour of straw surged down her chest in iridescent waves, finishing off mid sternum. Her dress was a royal blue, rendered in rich emerald satin with a plunging neckline, ruched waist, and a full skirt that flowed out into a sweeping train. She was talking rather garrulously, waving her hands as she spoke. Blekket was politely listening, clasping his wrist behind his back and bobbing his head in a nod. He didn't treat her with the same disdain as he had the women from the ball, so I assumed they must be acquaintances, but there was a sense of removal in how his body was facing forward, not sloped towards her. I tasted the tiniest bit of relief, seeing how he was only half engaging her, unlike how her torso was twisted so she was pressed up against his side, her breasts close to his bicep.

And then...she curled her arm around his.

A similar rage to the one I felt last night with Harrison brewed beneath my skin, but it was laced with something far more potent and dangerous, an emotion I had no experience with and didn't know how to control.

"I think she's jealous," Raevon whispered to Pessy. I wondered what my face must've looked like for her to gauge that so quickly.

"I think you're right," Pessy murmured back.

"Hey." I swivelled around. "I don't like this whole 'teaming up against Tympany' thing. Stick to being a cute couple, and leave my non-existent love life alone."

"Got it, boss." Pessy saluted me.

"If it makes you feel any better, I like you *way* more than Emilia," Raevon said. "She's kind of a dud."

I wouldn't admit it, but that did make me feel slightly better. "Are they...together?"

"Gods no," Raevon asserted, and I did sigh with relief then. "She wants to be, but he's not interested in her like that."

"She wants to be?"

Whatever reassurance I'd been savouring died on my tongue. It's not like I had any claim over Blekket, but hearing that made me want to march right over there, rip her from his side, and tear her limb from limb. Jealousy, I decided, was far more treacherous than anger.

"Careful there, Tymp. You don't want to light anyone else on fire." Pessy's lips knit shut when she saw how little that amused me.

"Wait...what?" Raevon turned to Pessy. "What're you talking about?"

"I don't mean this to be rude," I said, "but can you guys please leave me alone?" If Pessy was going to tell Raevon about what happened with Harrison, I'd rather not bear witness to the horror that would most likely occupy her face when she heard what I'd done.

"Okay." Pessy and Raevon started gathering some of the food into the wicker basket, so I wouldn't have to worry over it. Pess set her hand on my shoulder. "Reach out if you need anything."

I'm sorry, she expressed through the bond. *That was so insensitive of me. I shouldn't make jokes about that.*

It's okay, I assured her, giving the hand she had on my shoulder a pat.

I didn't see Pessy or Raevon leave. I was too busy scowling at where Emilia and Blekket had stopped walking a few feet away from me. They were just standing now, flaunting their conversation in my face. Her arm was still linked with his.

I didn't fully understand why seeing Blekket and Emilia together hurt so much, but it was a kind of pain I'd never undergone before, one that felt bigger than me, like the blustery flames that assailed Frofsea and left nothing intact.

Somehow, without my permission, Blekket Elrod stole a piece of my heart I'd never meant to leave exposed for him to take. That made me feel like I was drowning, like I'd never breathe again.

Emilia reached up on her tiptoes to wrap her arms around his neck. I sucked in a breath and held it. Blekket didn't reciprocate, sort of fidgeting awkwardly in her arms, which was a comfort.

He did give her hand a squeeze when she pulled back, and that stung.

He loitered by the stone wall adorned with vines, watching her walk away. He stuffed his hands in his pockets while frowning at her shadow. He turned to leave, but then, he spotted me on the grass.

It did not go unnoticed how his eyes illuminated at the sight of me, the opposite reaction he'd had to Emilia.

"Hey," he said in greeting. "I was looking for you all morning." I hoped my warm chest wasn't reflected in my cheeks.

"I needed to tell Pessy what happened," I explained, Blekket situating on the blanket with me and kicking off his shoes.

"I'm sure she's distraught, hates you, and will miss him terribly." I narrowed my eyes at the sarcasm.

"Actually, I was right. She was jealous she didn't get to do it herself." Blekket cackled up at the sky.

"I've always liked that girl."

"Me too." I tried to bite my tongue, but I couldn't help myself and blurted, "Who was that girl?"

"Her?" He pointed with his thumb towards where he and Emilia were just standing. "Emilia Danbridge. She's a close family friend."

"She looked like more than a friend," I muttered bitterly. He cocked his head to the side, the corner of his mouth lifting.

"Are you jealous, Tympany?"

"What? No, of course not." I shook my hair out of my face and straightened my posture, like that would make me more convincing.

"Emilia's been in my life since we were babies. We grew up together. There was once a time where she and I were…more, but that was years ago." I clenched my muscles so I wouldn't flinch.

"So you *were* with her? Emilia?"

"A long, long time ago, when we were sixteen."

"How long were you together for?"

"We were together, if you could even say we were together, for nine months." To me, nine months was nothing in the grand scheme of eternity, but to a human, that was a much longer amount of time.

"Did you love her?" I felt kind of bad for badgering him, but I needed to know, for my own peace of mind.

"No. I've…I've never been in love." His cheeks were deluged in an attractive rush of pink.

"But she loved you?"

"Her version of love is sinking her claws into someone and saying no one else can have them, even after they're no longer hers. I wouldn't call that love." He started scooting closer to me on the blanket before he set his hand over mine. "What type are *you,* Tympany?" I flexed my fingers under his, gulping.

"I….I wouldn't know."

"You haven't…?" I shook my head. "Never?"

"I've never even had a first kiss." It sounded so pathetic out loud. "I know, it's weird."

"No, it's not."

"I'm five-thousand-years-old and have never been kissed. It's a little weird, Blekket."

"It's not weird. Not at all." He was surprisingly tender in his insistence.

"I never even thought it was an option for me," I continued. "Up in Kylantis, no one ever looked at me that way. They only saw me as a Goddess they were created to protect, not as anything more. Over the years, I sort of just accepted I would never have that and made my peace with it."

"That sounds miserable," he whispered, curling his fingers around mine and flipping my hand over, dousing my palm in sunlight. "Miserable, and lonely."

When he said it, I realised how right he was. Back in Kylantis, I never would've labelled myself as either of those things, since I was constantly surrounded by people I trusted and loved, but I always carried the feeling I was missing something.

He was right—when I thought about it through that lens, it *was* miserable, and lonely.

I existed for five thousand years as half a person.

That's no way to live.

"I missed out on so much," I muttered in disbelief, my fingers weaving through the slots between his.

"You don't have to miss out anymore," he said gently, giving my hand a squeeze.

"What? Are you volunteering?" *HOLY SHIT.*

I couldn't believe I'd just said that. His eyes widened to the size of saucers, his mouth tumbling open.

"I'm sorry," I sputtered, ripping my hand out of his. "I....I shouldn't have said that. I'm sorry."

"Tympany." I started for the palace, but Blekket leapt to his feet and caught my arm before I made it to the exit. "Tymp, wait."

When he spun me around, we were nose to nose.

The close proximity, the pungent scent of lilac drifting off his skin and tongue, made me gasp. I felt every point of pressure humming out from the fingers of his that were enfolded around my forearm, pimpling my flesh in goosebumps. The invisible current that reared its head every time we touched towed us closer together, so the only point of contact we didn't possess was the distance between our mouths.

There was a pause, his midnight blue eyes silently asking. I could feel his desire charging through him, intensifying his body temperature, but knew, without a shadow of a doubt, he wouldn't do anything unless I said so. I let out a tiny whimper, mouthing the word *yes*. That was all he could handle.

"Fuck," he moaned, then moved.

He slithered an arm around my waist, hauling me to his chest, and lifted me off my feet. I set my hands on his shoulders to balance myself, clenching the material of his shirt between my fingers, which felt damp from either the broiling sun, or the potency of his desire.

I didn't have another moment to think about what I was doing, or question what it would mean or change.

Before I'd taken my next breath, his lips came down over mine.

Chapter Twelve

Kissing him for the first time felt like waking up from a long, restful sleep to unearth the sun.

While I'd never done this before, instinct told me to tangle my fingers in his hair, to press my hips up against his when he came closer, to tug the short brown strands when his teeth grazed my lower lip.

It told me to open my mouth at the appropriate moment, when his tongue implored to enter, then stroke mine along the length of his as they battled for dominance of the shared space we'd created.

I'd never done this before, but in the weirdest way, it felt like I had, like we'd been doing this forever.

Blekket was incredibly tender. Whatever raged inside him was beautifully regulated in the soft pace he set the kiss, in the gentle way he held my face, as if it were fragile and made of glass. I found it sort of humorous how he was treating me like *I* was breakable, when I was the one who had to be careful of the force I used when pulling at his hair, so I didn't accidentally sever his head from his neck.

Far too soon, he broke the kiss, leaning back with a hefty pant that let me know he was just as affected as I was.

"Whoa." I breathed, once I'd regained the ability *to* breathe. "That was…"

"Magnificent," he echoed, and it was the first time he said that where it was actually accurate.

"Blek," I whimpered, reaching for him again. The small taste of him wasn't enough to quench my craving.

I needed more.

"Oh, Tympany," he groaned, meeting me in the middle.

His head slanted down, capturing my lips once more. Somehow, I ended up crashing against the wall.

Instinct drove the way once more, ordering me to lift my leg through the slit in my dress and curl it around his torso. It told me to arch my back, so I could feel every delicious inch of him against me, the buttons of his dress shirt scuffing me through the thin material of my dress. I felt another emotion I'd never experienced before—unabashed desire—flood its way through my system, the muscles below my navel clenching as a warm pulse throbbed between my legs, where he rubbed me through his breeches. I suddenly wished there was no cloth between us, that I could truly feel every inch of him, that I could melt our skin together, so we'd be one instead of two separate beings.

"Good Gods," he groaned into my throat when he found my blade sheathed to my bare thigh. He pulled on my knee, bringing my leg even tighter around him. "I definitely approve of this dress."

I wanted to reply something snarky about not caring what he thought, but my words blended into a moan after his teeth caught my earlobe between them.

"Blek," I whined, not recognising the sound of my voice. "Come back. Please."

"*That* is an amazing sound," he praised, licking his way up my throat. "I need to hear it again."

I stretched my neck, giving him unfettered access to all of me.

His lips climbed back to mine, our teeth clashing. His hands, which had started in my hair and skated down to my waist, glided around my hips to cup my behind, pushing me even closer, which I didn't think was possible. When I gasped into his mouth, Blekket stopped for a moment, moving his hands away.

"Is this okay?" he asked.

"Yes," I assured, gripping his wrists on a brave impulse and sliding his hands back down to my backside.

"Tym." He sighed before our lips recoupled.

I flicked my tongue over his, nearly ripping a handful of hair out of his scalp when he squeezed my ass.

I'd never felt more free. I was finally liberated from the fear I would be considered less of a God for wanting something purely for myself, that there was something wrong with me because I'd spent so long not truly living. If this was the high of humanity, then I would never come back down.

I was so absorbed in the taste of him that I didn't notice a flash of gold marching towards us.

Then, Blekket was ripped away from me.

I was rudely dropped back down from the clouds, where Alsandair raised his fist over his head, ready to pummel the life out of the Prince of Esteopia.

"Stop!" I screamed. **"Don't touch him!"** Alsandair's hand fell to his side immediately in submission.

"He wasn't hurting you?" he asked me.

"No! Let him go this instant!" Alsandair glanced at Blekket, then back at me before he finally released him.

"Thanks for that," Blekket grumbled, smoothing the wrinkles in his shirt.

"What's going on here?" Demetrio demanded, appearing at the threshold of the courtyard.

He set his hands on his son's shoulders and steered him away from Alsandair, stepping in front of him protectively.

"I found the Prince on top of the Goddess. I was concerned he was...hurting her, but that appears to not be the case." There was wonder and bemusement lacing the edges of Alsandair's explanation.

"He wasn't doing anything wrong," I snapped, scowling at Alsandair. "Not that it's anyone's business besides Blekket's and mine, but we were only kissing. It was entirely consensual, and I'd like to get back to it, if everyone could just get over themselves and back off."

When I realised what I'd said, I gasped. I couldn't believe I'd uttered those words, particularly in front of the King.

Blekket's lips curled up in a mirthful, proud smile, while Demetrio looked like he'd swallowed his own tongue.

"Can I please have a moment alone with my son, Tympany? Then...you can...have him back." I imagined it expunged a lot of energy for Demetrio to choke that out keeping a straight face.

"Of course," I stuttered.

I gathered the train of my skirt and scampered off towards the palace, avoiding Blekket's wide eyes begging me not to leave him alone with his father. When I turned the corner, Pessy was standing there with her eyes virtually spilling out of their sockets.

She clearly watched the whole thing.

"You have a lot of expla—" I covered her mouth with my hand, pressing us up against the wall.

"Quiet," I hissed, then peeped my head over to eavesdrop on Blekket and Demetrio's conversation.

"What were you thinking?" Demetrio reprimanded. Blekket drove the toe of his loafer into the lawn, digging a hole in the soil.

"I was thinking I wanted to kiss her, so I did."

"Now is *not* the time for sarcasm, Blekket."

"I'm not being sarcastic. I'm serious. I wanted to kiss her, so I did. I've wanted to kiss her since the second I laid eyes on her, but I've held myself back. Regardless, it's none of your business. The only person who is allowed to be concerned with what I do and how I spend my time is Tympany."

"Is it *absolutely* my business, if this attraction of yours affects our kingdom," Demetrio roared.

"Tympany's not going to retract her support from Esteopia because of me."

"I'm not worried about Tympany retracting her support. I'm worried about *you*." He sighed heavily, crossing his arms over his chest. "She's a *Goddess,* son. There's no way this ends well."

"You don't know that," Blekket objected, his hands balling into fists. "I don't know what this is, or what it will be, but what I do know is, when I'm around her…I feel the most free I ever have in my whole life. It might be her presence inspiring it in me, but I've never felt more myself with anyone. She understands me. She calls me out on my shit. She makes me look at the world a different way. She's everything I've ever wanted and never knew I needed. She's not a Goddess to me. She's just Tympany."

My heart melted into a puddle in my chest.

It wasn't an insult for him to say that about me. It was the highest form of flattery I could receive.

He didn't want me because of *what* I was—he wanted me because of *who* I was.

"What about Emilia?" I flinched at the mention of that girl. If Blekket had been keeping a handle on his temper before, he lost control of it now.

"What *about* Emilia?" he bellowed. "Emilia and I are not together. We haven't been since we were sixteen. You and Mum expect me to marry her. That's not what I want. She's completely irrelevant in this conversation." *Wait a second. Seraphina and Demetrio want Blekket to marry Emilia?* I wasn't expecting to hear that.

"Well, would you marry Tympany? You have to marry someone."

"I don't *have* to do anything." Blekket rolled his eyes. "Why can't I just be with her and be happy?"

"Because you are heir to this kingdom, and you must be married when you turn thirty and ascend the throne in March."

"I don't want the fucking throne!" he screamed, a cathartic release for him. "If taking the throne is your one justification for why I can't be with Tymp, then fucking forget it. It has no validity."

"Son—"

"I only just kissed her, for fuck's sake. I'm not thinking about marriage right now, but even if I *was,* I wouldn't ask her to marry me because I'd become king after. It would be because I love her and want to be with her."

Hearing him utter the words *I love her*, even though that's not what he was actually saying, knocked the wind out of me. If I wasn't holding Pessy, I would've toppled over.

"But none of that is happening right now. You and Mum are rushing this. You're both in good health. You can stay on the throne for a little while more. This doesn't have to happen right now."

"We've talked about this, Blek. If we give you more time, like you've asked, you're never going to be ready to ascend the throne. The longer we put it off, the less you're going to want it."

"I'm *never* going to want it. Get that through your head now. If I ever take the throne, it'll be against my will."

"I know you think that, but you could change your mind." This conversation felt all too familiar to me.

"I won't! Thirty years, I haven't changed my mind. Why would I all of a sudden change it now?"

"Because your kingdom *needs* you, Blek. They're scared, and they need you."

"I'm still here for them. I'm not going anywhere. I will continue to fight for them, *with* them, at all costs. I'm just not ready to lead them into a war we're probably going to lose. And I'm *especially* not ready to let Tympany go because you and Mum want me to marry someone I don't love, just so I can ascend the throne. With everything happening in the world right now, with what happened in Eveium and Frofsea, I've come to really understand that tomorrow isn't promised. I just want to be happy, while I still can be. *She* makes me happy. Don't you want that for me? Don't you want me to be happy?"

Demetrio's lips knit shut, which was honestly worse than if he'd just flat out said *no*. Seeing the hurt flicker in Blekket's eyes stung, as if Demetrio had distanced himself from me and not his son.

"I see," he murmured, taking a step away from his father.

"Blek..." Demetrio reached for him, but Blekket moved out of his range.

"I think you've made your stance perfectly clear." He cleared his throat of all traces of vulnerability, so when he spoke, he sounded impassive and detached. "Now it's my turn. I'm not leaving Tympany. You can't make me. And if that means I don't ascend your precious throne in March, then make your peace with it now."

The Elrod men gaped at each other like they didn't recognise who they saw staring back. It broke my heart that I had something to do with this strain, but I also knew this tension existed long before I showed up. Blekket didn't deserve to be pressured into taking the throne if he didn't want it, just like I hadn't when Roara tried to do the same with me. Demetrio shouldn't expect his son to trade his happiness away because of an archaic tradition. Neither of those things were fair.

"I originally came out here to call you into a meeting to discuss the kingdom. We're convening in the dining hall."

"Okay." Blekket squared his shoulders. "I'll meet you in there." Demetrio lingered a moment, just shaking his head.

"You would've made a great king."

"Sorry I'm such a disappointment," Blekket sneered, but there was no heat in his words.

Only desolate ice.

I waited until Demetrio wandered off in the direction of the dining hall before I removed my hand from Pessy's mouth.

"Whoa," she uttered once my hand was gone. "That was intense."

"You can come out now, Tymp," Blekket shouted, fiddling with the sleeves of his shirt. "I know you're still here." Pessy and I exchanged a look, then inched our way out from behind the wall.

"Are you okay?" I asked, reaching for him in unison with him reaching for me.

He buried his face in my throat, clinging to me. It felt natural to wrap my arms around him and stroke the hair at the nape of his neck, something my father used to do for me when I had nightmares.

"I am now," he muttered, kissing my shoulder. Pessy looked like she was about to explode from ecstasy.

"I'm sorry," I whispered, feeling guilty for that whole exchange.

"Don't be. This has been an issue since long before you came here." He ran a hand down my spine. "I'm just tired of being told what to do. Tired of having things expected of me that I don't want."

"I know the feeling." He moved back, sweeping a strand of hair out of my eye and hitching it behind my ear.

"I know you do," he said, then leaned in and brushed his lips over mine in a kiss so soft and earth-shatteringly gentle, I felt like my ribs were liquifying from the warmth that ensued.

I totally forgot Pessy was there, until she coughed loudly, "Ahem," and waved a hand. "Still standing here."

"Don't pretend like you're not bursting at the seams right now, thrilled this is happening," I snarled at her for interrupting.

"Oh, I absolutely am. And later, I want a front row seat. But we have a meeting we have to get to."

Honestly, thank the Gods Pessy was there, because Blekket and I totally would've missed the meeting if she hadn't reminded us.

We walked to the dining hall with Pessy between us, because she rightfully didn't trust us not to grab each other and sneak off. Seraphina, Demetrio, and Raevon were already seated when we arrived, with Lev at the Queen's side, and Alsandair in the corner of the room, refusing to look me in the eye. Pessy stole the spot next to Demetrio so Blekket didn't have to sit next to his father, which I knew he appreciated.

Blekket pulled out my chair for me, in part to be chivalrous, but also to piss off his father, to remind him of the choice he'd made between the throne and me. Demetrio shifted uncomfortably, narrowing his eyes over me in daggers. I wondered what I'd hear in his thoughts if I touched him right now.

Under the table, Blekket wove his fingers through mine, resting our intertwined hands on his knee.

Raevon peeked down, noting our embrace. Her lips rounded up before she nudged me with her elbow.

"Alright," Seraphina announced, completely oblivious to the friction in the room around her. "We're here to discuss the next best course of action against

Sleotha. All ideas will be heard, and debated. Who would like to go first?" Of course, Demetrio's hand shot up.

"Obviously, us stealing their livestock and crops didn't damage them for long enough. We need to hit them where it hurts, like how they keep hitting us. Khidayle is where they keep the drogon. We should bomb it."

"You guys have bombs?" Pessy stammered.

"We have tons of nuclear weapons," he replied, her eyes glittering with intrigue. "We've restrained from using any of them because our one advantage right now is that Sleotha has no idea we have it, but after two drogon attacks in the span of two weeks, I think our hand is being forced here. We must fight, as they say, fire with fire."

"Are there any civilians in Khidayle?" I asked, but Demetrio kept talking as if I hadn't said anything.

"If we manage to kill even one of their drogon, it would severely—"

"Tympany was speaking, Father," Blekket interjected, his words honed by enough belligerence that it finally caught his mother's attention. "Unless you don't respect the authority of a *Goddess,* you should be quiet when she is talking." I squeezed his hand under the table, both to thank him, and to get him to simmer down.

"I sincerely apologise," Demetrio said disingenuously. "Please, Your Excellence, finish what you were saying." I nodded with appreciation, then continued.

"All I was going to say was, if there are civilians who live in Khidayle, I don't think bombing them is the right solution. I think, if possible, we should limit the amount of causalities."

"After they took nearly ten thousand lives from us yesterday, you want to worry about *their* numbers?" Demetrio hissed.

"I'm not saying they should be left alone. Obviously, if killing more Sleothians is the only way to get a strong message across, then that's what we'll do, but it should be a last resort. Not all of the Sleothians are monsters who deserve to be slaughtered."

"I agree," Raevon piped up, giving my other hand a small squeeze.

"Let it also be stated that Sleotha is now aware we have Tympany with us, and that she can control the drogon." Blekket stroked his thumb over the veins on the back of my hand. "They now know, if they send the drogon here again, Tympany can compel them to leave, as well as their army. That gives us an advantage we didn't have before. They won't send anyone here again until they come up with a new strategy. We have some time now while they recuperate. There's no rush." He repeated the same words he spoke in the garden, looking directly at his father.

"We have time, but we shouldn't waste it," Demetrio spat, glaring at his son.

"Tympany? What would your nonviolent approach look like?" Seraphina asked in spite of her husband's scowl.

"I've been giving this a lot of thought since I got here, and especially after yesterday. This war is over the land, and the only bit of land in the entire Realm no one has officially claimed is the outskirts."

"You mean the patch of land below the Geddesia Mountains?" I nodded. "That technically belongs to Sleotha."

"Yes, but they haven't built anything on it. It's only technically theirs because it's closer to them than it is to us. If we were to rebuild one of the villages we lost in the outskirts, it would block Sleotha's direct line of passage to the Gods." With my free hand, I tucked a strand of my hair that dribbled over my eye behind my ear. "I've lived in Kylantis my whole life. Sleotha heavily depends on having such easy access to the Gods. They have a representative climb the mountain every time they need something from us, whether it be more rain, more crops, or even the smallest of needs. If we rob them of that easy access, it will severely damage their civilisation."

"Huh," Seraphina mumbled, sitting back in her chair.

"Wouldn't your family be upset with us for building right below them on land they didn't sanction?" Raevon asked.

"You leave that up to me," I replied. "I can manage my family."

"Can you?" I turned my eyes over to Demetrio, surprised by his brazen disrespect, especially in front of his wife. "It just seemed like, with your brother yesterday, your family may be your weak spot."

"Demetrio," Seraphina gasped.

"I don't *have* a weak spot," I snapped, Blekket squeezing my hand. "I made it very clear to my brother yesterday where I stand in this war. As long as the other Gods support Sleotha, we are no longer on the same side. I believe that's one of the reasons we're having such…scalding sun today, which I apologise for."

"Please, don't," Seraphina assured me.

"My family is aware of which side I've chosen. I can deal with whatever issues arise from that choice, but it's *my* choice, one I don't regret making." Especially with the way Blekket was caressing my knuckles.

"I'd rather not start a war with the Gods, on top of Sleotha," Demetrio argued.

"With all due respect, *Your Majesty*, you're already *at* war with the Gods. They support Sleotha. They will do anything to help Sleotha." *Including send me here to gather intel.* I left that part out. "This is the best way to strike at both the Gods, *and* the Sleothians who depend on them."

"I think this idea could work," Seraphina said, "but I have my reservations. Like my husband said, I don't think causalities are preventable, especially if we start building on what the Sleothians consider to be their land."

"We'll have all the Kylantians and Esteopian soldiers protecting the outskirts while we're constructing."

"But if all the soldiers are protecting the outskirts, who is defending Esteopia?" It was the first thing Demetrio said I couldn't deny had merit.

"What about the merfolk?" Raevon suggested. "They're trained fighters. Plus, they're connected to the water, like the Neraids are."

"We could arrange to have a certain amount of merfolk in every village," I proposed, piggybacking off Raevon's point, "so no town is unprotected."

"You'll have to speak to Solara about that," Seraphina advised. "I don't think they'll be on board with dispensing a number of merfolk to the villages."

"But if it's in service of Esteopia, they *have* to be okay with it. No?" I looked over at Blekket.

"I don't see why not, but Solara can be…difficult." When he smirked, I knew he was thinking about Caspian.

"Let *me* deal with Solara," I challenged, Blekket's smile growing.

"If anyone can, it would be you, Your Excellence." His midnight blue eyes blazed with desire, warming my cheeks.

"It would be a more tactical approach to weaken Sleotha's power through their connection to the Gods," Seraphina considered, stroking her index finger over her bottom lip. "And I agree with Tympany that lessening the amount of Sleothians we kill will be beneficial for all in the long run."

"It's also incredibly dangerous," Demetrio opposed.

"But is it more dangerous then dropping a bunch of bombs on their drogon? I'd think that would be more hazardous, and violent, than us building on land they've never officially claimed as theirs."

"I agree with Tympany," Blekket declared.

"Of course you do." Demetrio actually rolled his eyes.

"Demetrio!" Seraphina scolded in horror. I had a feeling the Queen and King would be having words when this meeting was over.

"Yes, *of course* I do, because the plan is brilliant, as is she." Blekket threaded his fingers through mine even tighter.

"Thank you, Blek," I whispered shyly.

"I say, we put it to a vote," Seraphina decided. "All those in favour of rebuilding Eveium and Frofsea in the outskirts, raise your hand." Me, Blekket, Pessy, Raevon, and Seraphina all raised our hands.

Even Lev lifted a finger, flashing me a dimpled smile when I beamed at him.

Demetrio fidgeted under his wife, daughter, and son's beseeching gazes. I'd told him accepting my help meant hearing and conceding to things he wouldn't always agree with, and with majority rules, it looked like this was one of those times.

"Different perspectives, Demetrio," I reminded him, forcing my shoulders not to cave in under his glower.

"*Fine.*" He reluctantly raised his hand.

"So we're all in agreement," Seraphina said with a pleased nod. "Wonderful. Now, who wants dinner?"

Chapter Thirteen

I dreamt that night I was a mermaid.

My tail was painted all the colours of the rainbow, my scales comprised of silk, embedded with lustrous diamonds. The gold armour I wore on my chest felt weightless, like it wasn't even there, as I glided through the waves, following the pull of the current. My arms swayed behind me as if they were wisps of seaweed, my hair spiraling around me. I passed a dolphin on my way to the palace, and it nuzzled up against my arm, smothering my skin in its slick wonder before sashaying away.

I passed the statue of Caspian, who seemed to approve of my new form.

When I looked up, I saw Blekket standing at the foot of the palace in Floatsim, dressed in the same petticoat and vest he'd been wearing the night we met. His smile dazzled and barraged my senses. He outstretched his hand for me to take.

"Tymp?" Blekket said, but the Blekket in my dream hadn't moved his lips. He was still grinning, imploring me to join him. The voice came from outside my slumber, rudely splintering the illusion.

"Hmm?" I groaned, and heard laughter in my ear behind my closed eyes.

"Wake up, angel."

"No. I'm not ready." His chuckle grew louder.

"Not even for me?" When he got no response, I heard him sigh. "Alright. I guess I've got to break out the big guns." Then, I felt him peck the corner of my mouth.

My heart fluttered awake.

My head shifted, lips seeking his at their own accord, disintegrating the last cobwebs of sleep. I discovered Blekket looming over me when my vision was no longer bleary from inertia.

"There. Much better." I glowered at him through half open eyes. "Jeez. You are not a morning person."

"There's no way it's morning right now. It's not even light outside."

"Five in the morning is still morning, Tympany. You're just used to waking up at ten every day, when the sun's already out."

Blekket's hair flopped over his brows, his eyes sprightlier under the luminosity of the moon.

His good mood was infectious.

"Why're you waking me at five in the morning?" I asked, reaching up to swipe the fallen strands of hair off his forehead. The tips of my fingers skimmed the faint freckles on the apples of his cheeks. He took a seat on the bed beside me, prompting himself up on his elbow.

"While I was thoroughly enjoying my front row seat to your sleep talk, there's something I want to show you."

"Oh, Gods. What was I saying now?" He curled a strand of my hair around his finger, an amused smile toying with his full, sinfully tempting lips. Now that I'd gotten a taste of them, every time I caught a whiff of the lilac on his tongue, I wanted more.

"You were trying to say Floatsim, I think, but you kept slurring it, so it sounded more like Fart-sim." He snorted, then shielded his face with his hands when I tried to smack him. "You said my name once, which I won't lie, made me ridiculously happy." I flushed to my roots. "My favourite was when you squealed really loudly, 'Dolphin'!" His eyes warmed. "That was particularly cute."

"How long have you been sitting here, creepily watching me sleep?" I snatched his hand, fiddling with his long fingers.

"I've been here ten minutes at most. I would've woken you up sooner, but I was sort of captivated."

"That's sweet…I think." I frowned.

"I'm surprised Pessy sleeps so soundly with you blabbering all night. You're quite loud." I shifted over to look at Pess, who was curled up on her side, swathed around her pillow, passed out, her blonde hair rioting around her face and comforter.

"Yeah. She's a heavy sleeper." I wondered why she was here and not with Raevon.

"Get dressed, please. We're leaving the palace. I want to get to our destination before the sun is up."

He crawled off the bed, pulling my duvet back, and proffered his hand, helping me glide off the mattress. Excitement thrummed in my veins as I scampered to my dresser, sifting through my different clothing options for something nice to wear. I selected a dark green jumpsuit, conscious when I chose it that Blekket liked me in pants. The jumpsuit featured a delicately shirred one shoulder bodice, complete with an asymmetrical, three-quarter length bell sleeve, and wide pant legs made of crepe fabric, the textile from the waist up a darker shade of green then the pants.

Blekket graciously turned around while I got dressed, facing the window. I wound my hair back into a tight bun, tucking the shorter strands behind my ears, then slipped on my sandals, inserting my blade into my right pocket.

"Okay. You can turn around now." He spun so fast, I worried he would get a headache from the rapid movement.

"Damn," he spluttered, trailing the tips of his fingers down my side to sample the feel of the material. "I don't think I've ever seen you wear green."

"I own other colours besides grey. I just don't usually get the luxury of wearing them unless I'm in private."

"Do you ever wear red? Or pink?"

"Red, maybe once in my life. Pink, *never*." His lips twitched.

"Would you wear pink for me?"

"I think you're overvaluing your influence over me." Blekket laughed, then leaned in close, causing my breath to hitch.

"Green's my favourite colour," he muttered in my ear, kissing the skin below it. The light sweep of his lips on my neck triggered a forceful shudder, drenching me head to toe in goosebumps.

"Duly noted." I felt him smile into my throat as I wrapped my arms around him.

"You're so beautiful, Tympany." His lips grazed my chin. "I'm extraordinarily unworthy of you."

"Don't say that." I would reject that statement every time he uttered it. Besides, if either one of us was unworthy, it was definitely me, the person who'd come to his home and befriended him under false pretenses. "You are incredibly beautiful, and I don't just mean outwardly. I mean here." I set my hand on his breast, over where his heart pattered riotously beneath my fingers through the thin cloth of his black tunic.

"Do you not think I'm beautiful outwardly too?" I rolled my eyes and removed my hand from his chest.

"You just had to ruin it."

I scuttled over to Pessy, kneeling by the cot where her head was. She was leaking drool from the corner of her mouth, slavering all over the pillowcase.

Pess? I reached out through the bond.

Pessy sprung out of bed and dove down to the ground to retrieve her sword. She sat upright with the hilt clasped between both hands, her eyes half open as she swiped the weapon through the air, almost severing my head from my neck.

"Whoa, Pess! It's okay," I assured her, palms up. "I'm going somewhere with Blek and just didn't want to leave without you knowing."

"But you're okay? You're not hurt?" I shook my head, and she exhaled with relief, dropping the sword. "Go, have fun," she grumbled, shooing me with her hand. "Next time, leave a note, would you?"

She then tugged her duvet over her head, curled up around her pillow, and went right back to sleep.

"I guess that means she's fine with us going?" Blekket chuckled.

"That's the best you'll get from Pessy this early in the morning," I said, following him out the door.

"What're Pessy's parents like?" he asked as we made our way down the staircase and out to the courtyard in the back, strolling hand in hand. I glanced at the wall and flushed, knowing I'd never look at it again without remembering how Blekket had been pressed up between the juncture of my thighs, how his hands cradled my ass when his lips took long, dizzying sips from mine.

"Pessy's mother, Mergona, has been bonded to my mother for over four thousand years. That's the longest any Kylantian has ever lived. Their typical lifespan is up to one thousand years, if they're lucky."

"Has she lived that long because she's bonded to the Queen?" I nodded. "Do all bonded Kylantians live forever?"

"Yes. After the ritual, their lifelines are linked to the God they're bonded to. Mergona hasn't aged since the bonding ritual."

"Was she the first person to ever be bonded to a God?"

"Yes. They've been inseparable since they met, like Pess and me. Roara created the whole concept of bonding because she didn't want to lose her best friend. Mergona's incredibly wise, strong, and nurturing. She adores Pess, and has always treated me like another daughter. She's the best fighter in all of Kylantis. She's viewed as royalty."

"What was Pessy's father like?" It always ached a little, even now, to talk about Zion. I'd spent so much time with Pessy's family over the years, and viewed him as a second father of sorts.

"Zion was the most incredibly warm person you'd ever know. He had the ability to make you feel hugged without even touching you. He was so handsome. Pessy gets her good looks and kind blue eyes from him. His smile set the world on fire." I sighed. "Pessy worshipped him. We all did. He was supposed to be bonded to my father before he died. His death affected us all deeply. It still does." Blekket squeezed my hand, raising it to his lips to tease my knuckles with a tender kiss.

"How did he die, if you don't mind me asking?"

"He had a nocturnal seizure and died in his sleep." I'll never forget the morning I woke to Mergona barging through the front door of the palace. She was screaming, dragging Zion's body through the great hall.

She begged Roara and Jaxith to heal him. Both tried, but he was already gone by the time they made it to the palace. Pessy had been fast asleep and missed the whole thing.

I knew that plagued her every time she took a breath he would never be able to inhale again.

"His death hardened her. You wouldn't be able to tell looking at Pessy, because she's always so bubbly and spirited, but you'd notice the difference if you knew her before, when he was alive. Her mother is her mentor, but her father was her best friend. All the Kylantians, to this day, calls her Zion's mini-me. I think it bothers her, though she'd never admit it. I loved Zion, but Pessy's always been edgier than he was. I don't think it's fair how she gets linked back to him. She's her own person."

"Kind of like how all the villagers always compare you to your mother?" I jerked my head back in surprise.

"What do you mean?"

"Part of the myth of the Goddess Tympany is that you're Roara's clone. The legends say the Goddess of the Heart and Mind is a replica of the Queen, and that's why she's the one to watch amongst the Gods when it comes to the race of who will succeed her on the throne."

"I never knew that," I mumbled, grimacing.

I didn't like the thought of being equated to Roara, of anyone thinking of me as a facsimile of her. Though Roara would probably be flattered to hear that, I took it as an insult. We were polar opposites when it came to what actually mattered, proven in the fact I was down here in Esteopia, helping our people, while she remained up in her safety bubble, turning her back on them. I shuddered, cuddling closer under Blekket's arm when he draped it around my shoulders.

"I didn't mean to upset you," he said, squeezing me.

"You didn't. I just don't want to be compared to my mother anymore. I'm nothing like her, or any of my siblings."

"Well, once the historians record our triumph in claiming the outskirts and how big a part you played in it, no one will dare say you're like your family again." He bent down to kiss the crown of my head.

"I like the sound of that." I tipped my chin up to look at him. "Do you really think it's a good idea? Or did you just say that to piss off your father?"

"I think it's a great idea. I wouldn't have said that if I didn't mean it, no matter how infuriated I was with my dad or how badly I wanted to piss him off. Us rebuilding Eveium and Frofsea in the outskirts will prevent Sleotha from having a direct line of passage to the Gods, which will hurt them in the long run far more than damaging a village they can eventually repair."

"But do you think we can really do it? Rebuild the two villages we lost?"

"I think it won't be easy. There will be speedbumps along the way we'll have to manage, but I think, if we're successful, it'll mean great things for Esteopia." I couldn't help but be swept up in his enthusiasm.

Approaching the stables, Blekket's hand slid down my spine to my lower back, hovering over my backside. I unconsciously leaned in to his touch, brushing my hand against his thigh.

"Will your mother try to rebuild some semblance of a village where Eveium and Frofsea once were, or leave them the way they are now?"

"I'm not sure what she has planned for that," he answered. "If it were up to me, I'd leave the wreckage. I wouldn't try to rebuild over the bones of our lost villagers. It would feel wrong. I'd leave it as remembrance of what once existed there, a reminder of what we're fighting for. I much prefer the idea of rebuilding homes on land that wasn't once an established village than try to recapture a town that will always be tainted by destruction. I wouldn't want to live in a place that's haunted."

"Neither would I." I watched Blekket greet Clarence, kissing the top of his muzzle. "I know you don't want to take the throne, and I totally respect that, but your father's right. You would make a great king."

"You'd make a great queen," he fired back, narrowing his eyes.

"I guess the Realm will forever be deprived of our sovereign skills." Blekket chuckled as I climbed onto Krystal.

It was difficult to see where we were going in the dark, but as the sun began to fracture through the dusk, the apices of the trees reflecting the incandescence of dawn, the golden leaves parted to reveal a dazzling brook. White water wove flowed threads within the torrent, amid rocks capped in verdant moss. Behind it, arching over the massive creek like a sunshade, was a dynamic waterfall, which brought its own music and lacy white to the travelling stream.

The cascade was a lively blue-green, singing a steady song amongst the gold and red leaves crowning it.

There was a power and luster in the tranquility, a sense of stillness even with the roar of the water.

Peace personified.

"Welcome to Lake Azrord, Tympany," Blekket announced with a gleaming smile.

Lake Azrord!

"Is Jeka really here?" I asked, unable to mask my excitement. When Blekket nodded, I squealed so loudly that Krystal balked in surprise.

"I didn't realise you were such a fan of Jeka," he laughed, jumping down from Clarence to tie his reins around a tree trunk.

"I wouldn't call myself a fan, per say…but I've wanted to see her since we got here. Unless, of course, Jeka isn't friendly."

"Not usually, but she is with me. I tend to have that effect on people." He winked at me, his smile oozing palpable arrogance.

"You had the opposite effect on me when we met."

"I'm only doing something wrong if I'm not effecting you at all, sweetheart." He slithered his arms around my waist from behind, then rested his chin on my shoulder. "You want me to summon her?"

I bobbed my head in an eager nod.

Blekket stuck his fingers in his mouth, like his mother did the first day we arrived in Esteopia, and whistled stridently. The ground rumbled in response. Blekket gripped my waist tighter, I think so *he* wouldn't fall over. Then, fragmenting through the unstable surface of the lake, came a long, skinny, ginormous green serpent, its stomach painted white with grey thorns sticking out of its spine.

Jeka's eyes were beady and small in her face, but surprisingly expressive, even from so far away.

"Blekket," she purred. I gasped when she actually spoke. "Why're you waking me from my ssssslumber?"

"I asked him the same thing," I muttered.

"This is the Goddess Tympany," Blekket introduced me. "She *really* wanted to meet you."

"Goddesssssss Tympany?" Jeka stammered, those tiny black eyes broadening as far as they could go. She sloped her head down in her version of a bow. "It'ssssss an honour to make your acquaintanccccce."

"The honour is mine," I replied. "You are every bit as magical as the stories told about you."

I could've sworn I saw Jeka flush.

"Ssssssame asssss you," she praised. "Though I don't know what you're doing here with Blekket."

"Hey!" he shouted, while I cackled. "She could do a lot worse."

"She could alsssssso do a lot better."

"Alright, now I regret bringing her here. Come on, Tympany." Blekket grabbed my hand, but I tugged on his arm, hauling him back.

"I don't want to leave yet. Can't we explore a little?" I widened my eyes, fluttering my lashes, and plastered on an exaggerated pout.

"Oh, come on. That's not fair."

"What am I doing?" I asked innocently, noticing Jeka's lips curl up into an amused smile.

"You know exactly what you're doing."

"Please, enlighten me." I threw his words from the ball back at him.

"It'ssssss about time sssssssssomeone put you in your placccccce, Blekket," Jeka said approvingly.

"If it was anyone else, you wouldn't be saying that," he accused her.

"I promisssssssse you, I would." Jeka's tail floated behind her through the rivulet, a flicker of green amidst a sea of blue. "You know I teassssssse becaussssssse I care. Who elsssssse will pop that big head of yoursssss?"

"Now that I'm here, you're relieved of the job," I promised.

"I'm finally free." Blekket raised his eyes to the heavens, as if entreating it for answers on how to get us to stop. "I'll leave you two to your morning delight. Tympany…" She bowed once more, "Ssssssso lovely to meet you."

"Same. I'm sure we'll meet again soon."

"Pleasssse do come back. I'd love to sssssssee you again." She turned to Blekket. "Bye, Blek."

"Yeah, yeah," he grumbled petulantly, waving his hand. Her smile lost its humor and became all at once sincere.

"I'm happy you've finally found ssssssssomeone truly worthy of all that you are. You desssserve it."

His eyes softened. "Maybe one day you'll find the same, Jek, if you stop scaring everyone away."

"Why do I need sssssssomeone? I'm perfectly content with my own company." She winked at me, then dove below the waves and slithered down the current, the sun bouncing off the scales on her spine.

"I *love* her," I gushed to Blekket.

"Figured you would. You two have a lot in common."

"Because we both put you in your place? You could stand to be knocked down a few pegs."

"I was going to say because you're both fiercely independent, but now, I take it back. I think *your* head is the one that needs to be deflated, not mine."

"Agree to disagree," I determined with a shrug.

He glanced over at the water, then wiggled his brows at me mischievously. "Want to go for a swim?"

"Now?" I looked down at my jumpsuit. "I don't want to get my clothing wet."

"Then don't. You can wear this." He grappled the hem of his tunic and pulled it over his head.

At the first glimpse of Blekket's shirtless chest, my jaw dropped so fast, I thought it might disjoint from its socket. Burnished skin glistened as if it were glazed in a sheet of glitter, chiselled with the same punctilious attention to detail as each of the Gods had been crafted with. He looked more like an angel then a Neraid or mortal. His skin coerced the light towards it, as if every follicle was comprised of magnets, swathing him in an aura of brilliance that encompassed him like a halo.

In all my five thousand years, I'd never been so viscerally mesmerised, never saw something so breathtaking where I felt like, if I tried to speak, I would choke on my words. I was once more suffocated by his beauty, stunned by how I even had the capacity to be rendered speechless by something as simple as his chest.

"Tympany? Are you still there?" He was smirking, the bastard.

"Mhm," I managed to spit out after a minute of just staring with my mouth open, then finally came back to life and took the shirt from him. "You just love giving me shirts of yours to ruin."

"Or I just love seeing you *in* my shirts." He winked.

Blekket turned, facing the water so I could have privacy shimmying out of my jumpsuit and climbing into his shirt.

When he turned around, he whistled through his teeth. "Now that's a sight for sore eyes," he commended.

I just rolled my eyes playfully.

He seized my hand, weaving his fingers through the slots between mine. It awoke a thrill in me I didn't know was asleep before him.

"Ready?" he asked, his midnight eyes blazing with a childish glow. I nodded. "One…two…three!"

We broke out into a sprint, never untangling our fingers from each other, and sprinted to the water, leaping off our feet at the same time and hurdling under the waves. Our fingers split apart due to the vigor of the current, but we found each other soon after. Blekket gripped my waist, dragging me through the water until I was flush against him. I folded my arms and legs around his neck and torso as he pushed off the ocean floor from the tips of his toes. He waded through the tide and launched us back towards the surface, where we splintered through the waves and were assaulted by a gale of morning wind that felt even cooler against our damp faces.

"How do you feel?" he asked with the most beautiful smile.

"I feel…" It was hard to describe. There was something about the motion of it, of swimming, that felt so effortless and freeing, the saline water washing over my skin and dripping through my hair. It felt like here, in the waves, I wasn't the Goddess of the Heart and Mind. I didn't have a million things to worry about. I was just Tympany.

Just Tympany, with a man I was already beginning to fall in love with.

"I feel alive," I ultimately answered, a lump forming, digging against the walls of my throat. When I exhaled, it felt like the first time in my whole life where I actually breathed, as if I never had before.

"Oh, Tymp," he cried, then leaned in and kissed me.

I clung to Blekket as the pull of the water jerked us from left to right, hooking my ankles around his waist and twisting my fingers in his hair. Every time we kissed, I felt the strangest sense of urgency for there to be no space between him and I, wracked with frustration that we were perpetually hindered by the barrier of cloth and skin. His tongue stroked mine, and when he caught my lower lip between his teeth, I felt a rush of heat and irrepressible pleasure dribble through me. It prompted my legs to tighten around his midriff, granting my wish of bringing me even closer.

I scraped my fingernails down his back, and he hissed into my mouth. He cupped my backside in both hands and began rocking me against him, so I felt every inch of him between my thighs, pulsing.

"Tympany," he mumbled against my lips, then pulled back so he could look at me.

"What?" Worry reared it's not-so-rational head, convincing me something was wrong, that he wasn't as at peace with me as I was with him. That fear was unfounded in the way his entire body melted around me, how he rested his forehead against mine, closed his eyes, and moaned.

"I've never felt this before," he whispered, the wall around my heart rupturing at the crack in his voice.

"Neither have I," I admitted, and felt no shame saying, "I want you, Blek. All of you. Every single part of you."

"Sweetheart," he groaned into my throat. "You have me. You've had me since the second I laid eyes on you. Since the second I heard you speak. You've ruined me for anyone else. I'm yours, Tympany. I am all yours."

He buried his face in my shoulder and just held me amongst the mounting waves, held me as if I were a life raft keeping him afloat. He gripped me as though his life depended on it, like, if he were to loosen his clutch even a fraction of an inch, he'd drown, not just physically in the lake, but psychologically in his mind. I wrapped myself around him, arms, limbs, mooring my soul to his. My muscles and heart latched on, screaming in protest at the suggestion I would eventually have to let go.

I understood now why I'd said the word *underwater* in my sleep—because falling in love with Blekket felt like my head was being shoved under the waves, rammed further and further down, liquid swarming in my lungs with no chance of breathing the same ever again. And while that thought was scary, the lack of control which came with free falling, I was more terrified of the moment that fear would leave me, when his warmth no longer encased me, and the safety net of his affection was gone.

I wasn't sure what was more frightening—having and potentially losing him, or never truly having him at all.

"There's something I need to tell you," I blurted. Blekket leaned back, so he could look me in the eye when I spoke. He tucked my damp hair behind my ear with his free hand, while the other held me up against him. If we were going to seriously be with one another, then he needed to know about my original intentions for coming here. Even if it forever changed the way he saw me, he deserved to know the truth. He deserved to have all the information before he made the choice of whether or not he wanted me. "When I first came here to Esteopia...it wasn't to help you guys."

Blekket's brows furrowed. "What do you mean?" I closed my eyes and took a deep, preparing breath.

"My family sent me here to gather intel, find out your plans, and feed that information to Sleotha, so they would have the advantage in the war."

When I opened my eyes, Blekket's lips were knit shut, and he was startlingly quiet. I choked on a sob waiting for him to say something. Even him shouting at me would've been better than absolute silence, but that's what I got, and what I deserved. I deserved to have to sit in my self-reproach, to let the repugnance of what I'd just confessed wash over me. I deserved to let it really sink in how wrong I'd been to agree to do this in the first place, agree to befriend these people, only to abandon them when they needed me most. Even before I knew them, before I knew their kind hearts, it was still callous that I'd planned to offer assistance and play the part of divine support, only to take it away in their lowest moment—and it had been *my* idea in the first place. I was disgusted with myself and expected Blekket to be too.

After several minutes, he finally spoke again.

"Why are you telling me this?" I was surprised by the lack of rage I heard in those few words.

"Because I realised, after meeting you guys, how wrong they are, about Sleotha and all of it. I've come to care so much about you, your family, and Esteopia. *You* deserve to win this war. I mean that, and I mean it now when I say I will do whatever it takes to help you win it. I promise you, Blekket."

"I know that." His fingers elevated through the water, tracing my cheek. "I know, Tymp. I believe you."

I breathed a sigh of relief.

"You didn't have to tell me that. It wouldn't have made any difference, since you've now chosen to help us, but you told me anyway. You have no idea how much I appreciate you taking the risk of me hating you because you felt I deserved to know the truth." He trailed a series of heart-wrenchingly gentle kisses up the slope of my neck. "You really are so magnificent," he whispered in my ear.

"I'm so sorry," I squeaked, a tear escaping from the corner of my eye.

"Don't be." He kissed the teardrop away. "You didn't follow through with it. You have nothing to apologise for, not to me, not to your family, not to anyone. You're allowed to change your mind, to think for yourself. It doesn't make you a bad person. I know that's what you're thinking right now, and you're not. I will keep reminding you of that. You're not a bad person, Tympany."

"How did you know I was thinking that?" He smirked.

"Your dad was right in saying he can always tell what you're feeling in the way you move your hands. Whenever you start thinking self-deprecating thoughts, you pick at your hangnails."

"I didn't know I did that," I mumbled, frowning at my fingers. Blekket kissed my cheek, and I squeezed his waist with my legs.

"You want to know something else I noticed?" He leaned in closer. "I know when you're thinking about me because you start trailing your fingers along whatever you're touching really slowly…kind of like this."

His fingers, underneath the water, began traveling leisurely up the length of my thigh, producing a surge of goosebumps in their path uphill. I sighed, stretching my neck. I scrubbed my nails over his shoulders as he deposited a row of searing kisses down my throat, nipping and sucking at the skin. I don't know what possessed me to do this, but I unhooked my ankles from around his waist and clenched my toes over his butt cheeks through his breeches. His mouth was on my chin when I did this, and his gasp against my skin sent his warm breath and a vehement shudder down my spine.

"Fuck, Tympany," he groaned. "You've really never done this before? Because you're freakishly good at it."

"I'm good at everything."

"Like I said. It's *your* head that needs to be deflated, not mine." I beamed. "Can I try something? If you don't like it, just tell me, and I'll stop." I nodded my head. "I need to hear you say yes, Tymp. I will never do anything unless I hear you tell me you want me to in words. I promise you that, now and forever."

"Yes," I replied, touched by the sentiment. "I want you to."

"Thank you." The hand he had on my thigh slid even further up, crawling under his tunic and flattening over my bare stomach. I gasped, my hips jerking forward and colliding with his. He jolted in response. "How does that feel?" he asked, his voice rougher than normal.

"Really...good." He grinned.

"Your skin feels like silk." His fingers slewed up my belly, grazing my navel with his thumb. "You have an outie."

"A...what?" I panted, his hand gliding over my ribs.

"Your belly button. Every Neraid has an innie. It's cute." The tips of his fingers brushed my underboob. I tensed. "Is this okay?" I couldn't begin to articulate how *okay* this felt. I bobbed my head in a nod. "I need to hear you say it, angel."

"More," was all that came out.

"I guess that works too," he chuckled, and if I wasn't so drunk on the feeling of his hand on me, I would've slapped him.

His fingers slid up, grazing the swell of my breast. Instinct ordered me to arch my back, thrusting my breast into his palm, which fit perfectly in his long fingers. He skimmed the pad of his thumb over the pebbled peak of my nipple, and a guttural moan, a sound I'd never once emitted before, escaped past my lips.

"*That* is a beautiful sound," he declared. "My new favourite."

"I need you closer." I threaded my fingers in his hair and dragged his mouth back to mine.

"Tympany," he moaned, kneading my breast underneath the shirt as his tongue dove through the opening between my lips.

"Blek," I whimpered at the plethora of competing sensations—the massage of my breast, his other hand hoisting me up higher around his waist, his tongue twirling along the length of mine. Delicious, tantalising heat fulminated inside me and collected between my legs, where he sat comfortably underwater, coaxing me with the grind of his hips to lose myself to the tempo he was setting.

His nails abraded the inside of my thigh in conjuncture with his other thumb brushing over my nipple again, rubbing it in a slow, aching circle under the shirt. I cried out, my legs crushing his waist even tighter.

"Do you want me to stop?" he asked into my mouth, the answer an easy shake of my head. "I need you to—"

"Keep going," I nearly screeched.

His laughter blowing across my neck added a whole new dimension to the onslaught of pleasure.

I felt a burn I'd never experienced before rage through my bloodstream, blazing in a circular, downward motion in sync with the movement of his thumb. Everything south of me clamped in preparation of letting go. The scrape of his teeth on my neck was the last thing I could take before my eyes pinched shut, I kicked my head back, and I completely unravelled in his arms.

He buried his face between my breasts, hugging me to him, and caressed my back with a tenderness that brought the lump in my throat closer to the brink of bursting.

"Are you okay?" he asked me. I was grateful for the water droplets on my face dripping down from my soaked hair, concealing the tears toppling over from the corners of my eyes.

"Better than okay," I whispered, pouring all my gratitude into our kiss. "Thank you." I wasn't sure why that made him laugh.

"You are so welcome," he chuckled, kissing my damp hair. His hands returned to my hips. "You have an amazing body."

"Eira used to call me Thunder Thighs when we were younger, because they jiggle when I walk."

"That's horrible." Blekket skimmed his hand up my leg, squeezing my thigh. "I love your legs."

"I love your freckles." I swept my index finger down the bridge of his nose. "Raevon has freckles too, but neither of your parents do."

"They come from my grandmother on my mum's side. You would've loved Rosabella. She always made fun of me for being pompous. She used to say my head was bigger than my body could balance, and if I wasn't careful, it would roll off my neck."

"I like that. I'm going to steal it." I cradled his cheeks, tracing my thumbs over the faint freckles. He angled his face into my palm, closed his eyes, and sighed. "Can I try something?" He nodded. "I need to hear you say yes, Blek."

"Yes, Tympany." He breathed huskily, his voice a seductive whisper. "Do whatever you want with me."

I smoothed my hands out over his shoulders, the backdrop of his light skin making my brown fingers glow, then skated my palms down his chest, fondling every hard sinew of muscle. His chest rose and fell with regulated breaths, picking up speed when I lightly grazed his skin with my nails. His breath hitched, the flesh beneath my fingers inundated with a feverish flush, like his blood was boiling.

"Tell me what you're thinking," he demanded softly.

"I'm thinking, you're perfect," I muttered without a single iota of shame.

"I am *not* perfect, Tympany." He gave my hips a squeeze of defiance.

"You're pretty damn close, Blekket Elrod."

"If I said that to you, you would hit me." I laughed at that.

"You're probably right." I felt two fingers curl around my chin, and then, my head was gently tipped back.

His midnight blue eyes were scorching. "Tymp?"

"Yes, Blek?"

"Make me a promise. No matter what happens, we will always have this. When things get tough, and they *will* get tough, we can always come together and be nothing other than Tympany and Blekket with each other. Promise me we will always have each other to fall back on."

My heart crumbled into a million different shards, with no chance of ever recuperating from the blow.

What he said before suddenly rang true for me as well—he'd completely ruined me for anyone else.

I was his.

"I promise," I swore with my whole being.

"Thank you," he whispered before his lips came down over mine with gratitude.

Chapter Fourteen

"Where have you guys been all morning?" Raevon asked when Blekket and I entered the dining hall together. It was just her and Pessy in there, sitting across from one another instead of beside. Seraphina and Demetrio were nowhere to be found.

"And why are you soaking wet?" Pessy added, smirking before she popped a blueberry into her mouth.

"I took her to Lake Azrord," Blekket told them as we sat down, Pessy perking up at the familiar name.

"Did you meet Jeka, Tymp?" I nodded.

"She's *amazing*. She's feisty, and she has no problem bursting Blekket's ego." Pessy laughed, while Blekket frowned.

"Wait, she talks? That's so cool! I want to meet her."

"We'll go back together," I promised, scooping some honeydew onto my plate.

"I'm just curious. How much about Esteopia did you research before you came here?" Blekket's fingers found mine under the table.

"Why? Worried I know all your secrets?" I wiggled my brows, like he did sometimes, and he narrowed his eyes over my curled up lips. "Caspian told me most of it, about the history of your family and some of the creatures to look out for. He told me about Ashrays, the Hippocampi, and about Phorcydes and Kappas." I wasn't sure why, but Blekket and Raevon both groaned when I said that.

"Phorcydes don't actually exist," Raevon said matter-of-factly. "That's a myth started by Sleotha to keep their inhabitants away from us. They tell their children Phorcydes are attracted to Sleothian little boys and girls, and will eat anyone who isn't Esteopian. It's insulting."

"I didn't mean any offense," I swore, feeling guilty for souring her mood.

Blekket lifted my hand to his lips, grazing my knuckles with a sweet kiss. "It's okay. We're just really sensitive to any lies Sleotha tells about us. I'm surprised your brother told you about them. He surely knows they don't exist."

"He said he's never seen one before. Just to look out for any caverns just in case." Raevon was still moping, but now, I suspected it had nothing to do with the mention of the Phorcydes, seeing as her grimace intensified every time her eyes strayed over to Pessy.

"What about Kappas?" Pessy asked, pointedly evading Raevon's frown. "Do they exist?"

"Yes, but they're harmless. Your brother probably said they're vicious creatures, and they can be, but only when provoked. They're the protectors of the merfolk, and they're very defensive of their people. I don't think that equates to them being evil if they're just trying to protect what's theirs."

"Neither do I." I stroked my thumb over Blekket's knuckles. "Where are Seraphina and Demetrio?"

"Mum's making preparations for our trip today," Raevon replied. We planned to voyage to the outskirts and begin mapping out a floor plan for the settlement. "I'm not sure where Dad is. Probably sulking."

"He usually sulks when he doesn't get his way," Blekket confirmed. I felt him start tracing the pattern of a script T along the interior of my wrist. When I looked over, he was innocently gnawing on a strawberry.

"Have either of you been to Sleotha?" I asked the Elrods.

"A long, long time ago." Blekket swiped his thumb over my pulse. "Rae wouldn't remember it. She was two. I was nine."

"What's it like?"

"I don't totally remember…the images that come up are from a little kid's lens, so I imagine everything I thought was so gigantic wouldn't be quite so enormous now. But it was very…red. Everything there is fuelled by fire. The gates are composed of flames. The castle is made of stone, surrounded by a moat of lava."

"What would she need a moat for?"

"To keep intruders out, I guess. Queen Jacinda rarely leaves the palace, but when she does, she never goes anywhere without the Fiery Folk."

"Fiery Folk?" I repeated.

"That's the technical term for what the Sleothian army is. They're not totally human, like the Neraids. They're humanoid beings made out of fire. They're born in the ember, like how we're born in the sea."

"Is *that* why their armour singed your skin when you touched it? Because their flesh is formed from fire?"

"Yes. Their body temperatures heat the metal." I'd wondered how they kept the steel so hot during the battle. That made so much more sense than them dipping their armour in fire before they ventured to Esteopia.

"Caspian said the Sleothians draw their strength from the land. Did he really mean fire?"

"They draw strength from the countryside too, having the luxury of all those fields to grow their crops, but their power comes from fire. Not the land."

"Is that where the drogon came from?"

"You know, I'm not sure about the drogon's speciation." Blekket looked adorable when he pouted. "Legends claim the drogon didn't show up until Queen Jacinda took control of Sleotha, after her parents, the original Queen and King, perished. She's a pretty elusive figure, Jacinda. She's never seen outside the palace, and she's been on the throne longer than anyone here in Esteopia."

"Wait," Pessy interrupted. "Jacinda is the daughter of the *original* Queen and King? She's been Queen all this time? How old would that make her?"

"Too old to be human," Blekket replied. "The Sleothians believe Jacinda is a descendant of the Gods, and that's how she's lived so long."

"That's impossible," I protested, affronted by the suggestion she was somehow a progeny of my family.

"You'll like this." He squeezed my hand. "The rumor is, Queen Sleotha had an affair with the God of Light and Sun, and Jacinda is actually his daughter. They believe that's how the Fiery Folk were first created."

"*Lucius?*" The idea of Lucius procreating was terrifying, and appalling. "If Lucius had a daughter who was somehow immortal, my mother would've demanded she be raised as a Goddess in Kylantis."

"Unless your mother didn't know," Pessy countered.

"I find it hard to believe Lucius would have a daughter and *not* tell my mother. She would've been in seventh heaven to have a grandchild. Lucius would automatically become her favourite by association, which is his dream. Not to mention, Lucius would want to raise any daughter of his up in Kylantis, away from all the war and destruction. I wholeheartedly regret the idea she's part God."

"Believe what you want," Blekket said with a shrug, "but regardless, Jacinda is definitely not human."

That sent a chill down my spine.

The idea of our adversary outlasting a normal human lifecycle and subsisting on the throne for so many years was a disturbing thought.

If she was immortal, *and* she controlled the drogon, then did we really stand any chance against her?

The more I thought about it, the more Jacinda being a half-God seemed possible. If she was somehow immortal without being related to the Gods, wouldn't my family take that as a crime against nature and destroy her? Why else would they allow her to live so long?

Unless she really *was* Lucius's daughter, and somehow, Roara knew that.

Maybe that's why the Gods favour Sleotha.

"I kind of think Queen Jacinda's dead," Blekket declared, ripping me away from my potential epiphany.

"You think she's *dead*? Why?"

"Because she hasn't been seen in years. I think she's dead, and the Fiery Folk are hiding it from the Sleothians."

"That's stupid," Raevon refuted. "If she's dead, then who's on the throne? And who controls the drogon? Way more likely she's part God then *dead*."

"It's only a theory," Blekket mumbled in defense of himself. "I just think it's strange she's never seen outside her palace. She never goes down to the villages. She always sends a proxy to do her bidding. Mum and Dad are never *not* interacting with their people. She could very well just be a recluse, but I think it's all really fishy. Maybe they want the world to *think* she's immortal. Maybe it's the illusion of her perseverance they want the Sleothians to believe in."

"Again, stupid." Blekket glowered at his little sister.

"You're no fun," he grumbled.

"I have another question." I realised I was raising my hand and put it down. "Sorry. Force of habit."

"Don't apologise, Tymp." Blekket kissed the back of my hand. "What's your question?"

"Why is Paramore the capital of Sleotha and not Khidayle, if that's where they keep the drogon?"

"Because it would make them vulnerable to have both the crown and the drogon in the same place. Or, at least that's why *I* think they're kept separate. I honestly have no idea." I smiled at that.

"Wow. Something Blekket Elrod doesn't know? That's a first." He feigned annoyance, but I knew he was struggling to repress a smile.

"So. You two finally…" Raevon flicked her finger between Blekket and me, but before either of us could respond, Seraphina arrived.

"Good morning, everyone," she announced when she entered the room. She strode to the head of the table, sinking down in her chair. "Tympany, you look stunning in green." I looked down at my jumpsuit, having completely forgotten what I was wearing, then flushed with embarrassment.

"Thank you," I replied, squirming.

"You know, green is Blek's favourite colour." Blekket ducked behind the bowl of fruit, his cheeks swamped with heat as well.

"I know that *now*," I mumbled, smirking at him.

"You are all set for your trip to the outskirts today," Seraphina told us, shoveling scrambled eggs onto her plate. "Lev, Augustus, and another Esteopian named Olivette, will accompany you, as well as Alsandair and five other Kylantians, whose names I'm blanking on, at the moment."

"Oh. You won't be joining us?" I was a bit disappointed. I'd been itching to spend more time with the Queen now that I'd made the choice to support Esteopia, and since things between me and her son had turned romantic. Seraphina shook her head.

"I'm needed here. I'm going to ride to Frofsea and see if there's anything we can salvage from the village."

"Do you think you'll find anything?" Pessy asked.

"Doubtful, but maybe there are some kitchen appliances and clothes that weren't burned in the fires, something we could use in the new settlement to honour the old one."

"I think that's a wise plan, Mum," Blekket said.

"Thank you, darling." She beamed at him.

"Where's Dad?" Raevon wondered. "Will he be coming with us?" I noticed Blekket cross his index and middle fingers under the table.

"Dad's joining me today." Blekket breathed a sigh of relief, smoothing his hand over his knee. "You guys don't have to wait for me," Seraphina insisted.

"If you're all finished eating, you can head out. The Dream Forest will slow you down, and you should aim to make it back here by nightfall."

"You sure you don't want company?" Raevon sounded uncertain.

"Nonsense. You should go." We dawdled a moment more, then stood and began gathering our things.

"Tympany? Can I talk to you for a moment?" Raevon asked when we shuffled into the hall.

"Of course." I glanced at Blekket and Pessy, who both nodded, picking up on the fact we wished to be alone. They headed in the direction of the stables, shoulder to shoulder.

When they were a safe distance away, I linked my arm with Raevon's, commencing our trek outside.

"What's up?"

"I wanted to talk to you about Pessy." She tried to disguise a tremble in her voice as a cough. "I really like her. I don't think I've ever felt this strongly about someone before. She's beautiful and smart and way out of my league, and I still can't believe she's even interested in someone like me."

"Don't sell yourself short, Rae. You're a catch." An endearing blush bombarded her face in colour.

"Anyway, things were going so well, but ever since the battle, Pessy seems...colder. I don't know what I did wrong, and I don't know how to fix it." Raevon pouted, her lashes fluttering as she strained to fight off tears. My heart shattered for her.

"It's not you," I promised. "Pessy is someone who has always taken pride in being a guardian. She's fiercely protective of the people she loves. She's mad at herself for not being there when Harrison attacked me. She's not mad at *you*."

"Oh," Raevon said, seeming surprised with herself for not considering this outlook. "What do you suggest I do? Should I say something to her?"

"I think you just keep being you and doing what you're doing. This might sound harsh, but Pessy needs to get over it. She can't punish herself through you. It's not fair to either one of you."

"Could you...maybe say that to her? I wouldn't want to put you in the middle—"

"I'd be happy to." I hated the idea of Pessy hurting Raevon to maltreat herself for something she wasn't to blame for.

"Thanks, Tymp. And I'm really happy for you and Blek. I've never seen him look at anyone the way he looks at you. All I've ever wanted was for him to be happy, for him to stand up for himself and demand the things he wants, instead of always surrendering to our parents' needs. I've hated seeing how miserable he's been the last few months, with his impending birthday and everything coupled with that. Seeing him with you…it's wonderful. I think you're really good for him."

"I think he's good for me too," I confessed, her cobalt eyes radiating such a splendid, mesmeric delight.

I wished I could bottle it up and save it for whenever I needed a reminder that wholesomeness existed.

Entering the stables, I unravelled my arm from Raevon's and made a beeline for where Pessy was standing with Belgian.

"Hey," she said when she noticed me approaching, stroking his muzzle. "What was that about?"

"Don't punish yourself through Raevon. Let yourself be happy, Pess. You deserve it."

Her mouth opened in shock. "I don't—"

"Yes, you do. I've noticed it for the past two days. You've been icing her out, and you need to stop. If you're not interested, that's one thing, but I know you are. Raevon didn't do anything wrong that night, and neither did you. Stop. Punishing. Yourself." I set my hands on her shoulders and squeezed with each word.

Her eyes glazed over with tears, her bottom lip quivering. "I was supposed to be there, Tymp. I should've been there."

"But you weren't. You can't change that now, and giving Raevon the cold shoulder isn't going to make you feel any better. You're only going to end up feeling worse, which is exactly why you're doing it. You weren't there then, but you are now. That's what matters. Raevon's here, and she wants you. You told me to stop depriving myself of joy, and now it's your turn. **Stop punishing yourself.**"

When I watched her pupils dilate and shrink, I realised I'd accidentally compelled her, like I had with Harrison. It was disconcerting that this kept happening, that I was losing control of such a potent ability. I needed to be more careful with what I said, and who I said it to.

I pulled my hands away and stepped back, terrified of inadvertently compelling her further.

"How was Lake Azrord with Blekket?" she asked tauntingly.

I mounted myself onto Krystal, giving her a scratch behind the ear when she stretched her neck in greeting.

"It was amazing." I think Pessy was surprised I didn't tell her to shut up and actually answered the question.

"What did you guys do? Besides talk with a freaking *sea monster!* We *have* to go back there together, so I can meet her."

"You would *love* her, Pess." I verified that Blekket wasn't in earshot, then told her, "We swam in the lake. We kissed, and then he...he touched me."

"Tymp!" I'd never seen her eyes so wide. "Wait, what constitutes *touching* in your book? I know this is all new for you, so *my* version of touching might not be the same as yours."

"I'm pretty sure it is." I flushed to my roots. "I was wearing his shirt in the water, so I wouldn't get my jumpsuit wet."

"Was he wearing pants?"

"Yes, of course! Why wouldn't he be?"

"I don't know. I mean, if he already lost his shirt..." She ducked at the swing of my hand, shielding her face with a giggle. "Tell me more."

"Well...I mean..." I didn't understand why this was so hard for me to admit. It was Pessy here, who'd already disclosed to me all the excruciating details of every single one of her sexual encounters in the last three hundred years. We weren't impervious to being brutally honest with each other. "He touched me under the shirt."

"How did it feel?"

"Good. *Really* good." If it was possible, my blood got hotter beneath my cheeks.

"Did he touch you down..." She pointed between her thighs, boosting her eyebrows with a smirk.

"No!" I was now completely mortified.

"Don't be embarrassed! Even if he did, that's perfectly natural."

"I know." I still frowned.

"Don't be embarrassed about any of it, Tymp. Seriously. You have nothing to be ashamed of."

"I know that." And I did. "It was more than just touching, Pess. We were…connected. I told him the truth about the original plan, about why we really came here, and he didn't judge me for it. He was so understanding, even though I didn't deserve it. I told him I wanted him, and he told me I've ruined him for anyone else."

"Tymp!" She splayed her fingers out over her heart, her eyes glistening. "My baby girl's all grown up!"

"Alright, let's not make a big deal out of this."

"Um, it's a *huge* deal!" She grabbed my wrist. "Do you have any idea how long I've waited for this moment? *Centuries,* Tympany. *Centuries.*"

"What have you waited centuries for?" Blekket sidled up to us on Clarence. The stippled sunlight casted an alluring beam of light over his coiffed brown hair, sprinkling flecks of gilt onto the short strands.

Pessy released Belgian's straps and began clapping for Blekket, disregarding the glower of horror I shot her.

"A round of applause for the man who finally broke Tympany out of her shell. Three cheers for Blekket Elrod!"

"I'm never telling you anything ever again," I hissed.

"Hey. Let the woman give credit where credit is due." Blekket shooed me with his hand, then regathered Clarence's reins and bowed his head. "Thanks, Pess. I'll gladly accept the praise."

"Gods, I hate you both."

"You know you love us," Pessy disputed, tossing her blonde hair over her shoulder. She then lightly kicked Belgian's flank, scampering off towards where Raevon was. Bel nuzzled up against Autumn's side, alerting Raevon that Pessy was near.

I watched Pessy lean over, stealing a quick kiss from Raevon, whose face illuminated like a cloudless dawn.

"Hey," Blekket cooed when we were alone. "How's my girl doing?" My heart did somersaults when he called me that.

"Pretty good. You?"

"I didn't like being so far away from you. I knew you needed your moment with Pessy, but I wanted to ride next to you. Does that make me a total sap?"

"We love saps. With the right amount of tender, love, and care, they grow into thriving trees."

He paused, then burst out laughing.

"You're so cute," he gushed, making me beam. Blekket tipped his chin over to where Pessy and Raevon were giggling, which I had the strangest inclination was about me. "They seem better."

"Yeah. Pessy was punishing herself through Raevon for not being there when Harrison attacked me. I told her to stop blaming herself and just be happy."

"Good advice. Are you gonna take it?" I cocked my head.

"What do you think I'm blaming myself for?"

"This scalding sun, as you put it so eloquently yesterday." He flipped his hand over, saturating his palm in a downpour of sunlight. "If this is Lucius's doing, it's not your fault, Tympany." It shocked me, how well he already had me figured out.

"Are you really not worried about how my family might retaliate against Esteopia for me turning my back on the original mission?"

"No, I'm not, because we have the strongest of the Gods right here." He ran a hand down the back of my hair, which I'd released from the confines of an elastic. It was now surging down, tickling my shoulders.

"I can't control the weather, Blek."

"No, you can't. It's the one area you're lacking in." He smirked when my mouth popped open.

"How dare you," I gasped, swatting his hand away.

"I told you your ego needed to be deflated."

"My ego is not the enlarged one, Mr I'll-Gladly-Accept-The-Praise." He chuckled, his arm falling to his side.

"If someone gives me praise, you know I'm going to accept it."

"In the most self-effacing manner, of course."

"Yes. I'm the king of modesty." I rolled my eyes. "Would you have me any other way, angel?"

The answer was no—I wanted him exactly as he was, arrogant, facetious, and magnificent.

That didn't mean I'd tell him, though.

"I could maybe do without the overinflated self-image," I teased. "I rather enjoy your head on your neck. I don't want it to roll away."

"I regret telling you about that saying. My grandmother is turning over in her grave." I cackled so loud that we attracted the attention of our entire riding party, who stared at me as if I'd grown an extra arm.

The sun trickled down between the pines as we reached the Dream Forest, the light streaking through the boughs in both brilliant and shadowy beams. Upon the forest floor, woven with the ancient tree roots, came the rays of sequins filtered by the bouquet of foliage above, softened, verdant, and freshly aromatic. The lethargy of the forest seeped its way deep into my bones, triggering a forceful yawn that left me somnolent in its wake.

Krystal decelerated her pace, so she was slow trotting in time with Clarence, whose eyes were drooping shut.

"Hey," Blekket said, jostling Clarence gently. "Don't close your eyes, bud. We've got to keep going."

Clarence bobbed his head, but he was really nodding off.

"I've never been to the Dream Forest before," Raevon stammered through a drowsy sigh. "Not that I remember, anyway."

"Who thought to put this here in their construction of the Realm?" Pessy sounded exasperated, struggling to keep her head up.

"Good question." I smothered another yawn with my hand.

Was it my mother? Was this her way of trying to confine the Esteopians to their corner of the Realm?

I would have to ask her when I returned to Kylantis.

Which made me wonder...*would* I return to Kylantis? Could I, after everything I'd learned, on top of the relationship forging between me and Blekket?

Would I even be welcomed back there by my family?

This would need further consideration...but not now. It wasn't an issue I'd need to deliberate over for a long time, at least not until we finished erecting the new settlement in the outskirts.

And even then, I couldn't imagine, at this point in time, leaving Esteopia, leaving Blekket or Raevon. I wondered how Pessy would feel if she never got to see her mother again.

Two hours later, we finally escaped the clutches of the Dream Forest and arrived in the outskirts. The caramelised tips of the gold and scarlet leaves reflected the buoyant mood of our party. We dismounted our steeds, leading them off to the side, so we could have an unobstructed view of the space. Lev retrieved a silver contraption from his satchel, which turned out to be a large tape measurer. He started from the entrance of the Dream Forest, unspooling the sterling tape with the help of Augustus, Olivette, Alsandair, and the other Kylantians who travelled with us.

Blekket, Raevon, Pessy and I stood off to the side with the horses, waiting for them to complete their measurement of the distance. When they returned, Lev's dimpled face was dewy with sweat.

"How many miles?" Blekket enquired.

"Three," Lev replied, "which would be one thousand..." he paused a moment, calculating in his head, "nine hundred and twenty acres."

"That's more than enough space for a village," Raevon cheered.

"Are the gates to Sleotha at the end of the road?" I asked Lev. He nodded. "Okay. We definitely need to keep some distance from the gates, so we make sure we aren't building on anything that is actually their land. I think we should begin and end the village fifty feet away from the Sleothian gates and the Dream Forest, so the fog from the forest doesn't affect any of the townspeople."

"Good point," Raevon muttered, glaring back at the woodland.

"Should we line the houses by the edge of the path?" Pessy crossed over to the other side of the wide dirt road, swiping her hand down the line that stretched for miles. "Or spread them out?"

"I feel like lining them up makes the most sense, so there's space in the center for people to stroll." Blekket turned to me. "What do you think?"

"I don't think the houses should be so close to the trees. It'll look strange." I gestured for the measuring tape. After Lev tossed it to me, I tugged at the spool, measuring six feet of distance from the edge of the road. "If we start the houses here, they won't bump into the trees behind them."

"That's a great idea, Tymp," Blekket praised.

While Pessy dug her sword into the dirt, marking the starting point for future reference, Olivette and Augustus were taking notes for Seraphina.

"Do we leave the opening to the Geddesia Mountains as is?" Raevon asked. I'd nearly forgotten we were at the foot of the mountains.

I peeked over at where the earth bled into rock, migrating up to where Kylantis sat in the clouds. It was strange to think about how close I was to my family right now, how little interest I had in seeing or speaking to them ever again, when the last time I'd been here, I was still under their spell, ready to do their bidding.

I'd finally woken up.

"We can't block it completely. We should rope it off or something, but always have guards positioned there. We can allocate some of the Kylantians who came with us to guarding the entrance, so when any Kylantians come down the mountain in service of the Gods, they'll be more inclined to be receptive when they see some of their own."

"See?" Blekket draped an arm around my shoulders. "I told you we're with the best of the Gods." I rested my cheek on his chest, squeezing his waist appreciatively.

We trekked on foot, leading our horses back to the Dream Forest. We then used the measuring tape to compute fifty feet of distance between the starting point of our settlement and the forest itself.

Raevon rummaged through Lev's satchel, retrieving a large Esteopian flag made of blue nylon, the image of an Ashray horse emblazoned over it. She moseyed over to where I was standing and handed it to me.

"You should do the honours," she said. I peeked up at Blekket, whose grin couldn't have been more dazzling.

I took it from her and found our marker, sucking in a deep breath. I relished the taste of autumn on my tongue, how the thick breeze blustered my hair off my face, savouring the act in its entirety.

This was the moment where I became my own person. Once I placed that flag in the earth, I would no longer just be the Goddess of the Heart and Mind, Muse to all mortals and celestials.

I would be the protector of Esteopia, dedicating my life to the well-being and safety of its inhabitants.

They would never be neglected by the Gods again.

With a roar of exhilaration around me and my family hovering above, I plunged the flag of Esteopia into the soil.

Chapter Fifteen

Two months had passed since we first visited the outskirts. Raevon, Pessy, Blekket and I went back every single day, scoping out the land and further defining the plans for the settlement. I never knew how much time and preparation goes into building one house, let alone hundreds. It's one of those things you take for granted, where you never consider the hard labour that went into it, because once you have it, it's already done. After we finalised the plans, we'd first have to prepare the construction site and pour foundation; then, complete rough framing, rough plumbing, electrical work, install insulation, complete drywall and interior fixtures, then begin exterior finishes.

Then, after finishing the interior trim, we would need to install hard surface flooring, countertops, bathroom fixtures, mirrors, shower doors, and then, we'd finish exterior landscaping before doing a final walk-through.

We would have to repeat this for each of the hundreds of houses we planned to erect for the many residents to come.

We needed hands—and a lot of them.

While we advanced the plan for the layout of the new town, Seraphina and Demetrio ventured out to the villages, asking their people for help in developing furniture, textiles, and appliances for the homes. In the village of Driland, which neighboured where Eveium and Frofsea once were, a seamstress named Susannah Fraisure volunteered to make duvets, blankets, pillows, and pillowcases for the new inhabitants. In Blythe, the Wilson family, a large dynasty of woodworkers, began preparing furniture for the new homes, while in Prisver, manufacturers produced household items, such as refrigerators, air conditioning units, heaters, ovens, microwaves, and more.

All the Esteopians we spoke to were thrilled to lend their services and unique talents to the construction of the settlement. It seemed like everyone was excited about the prospect of expanding the land, and we had many volunteers who wished to live in the new village once we finished constructing.

With the Esteopian army and the Kylantians working together on the actual hard labour of constructing the homes, our numbers were two thousand, five hundred and thirty. That would be plenty, but if all the soldiers were in the outskirts helping with the formation, there would be no one guarding Esteopia. Before we began constructing, we decided to make the trip to Jopolis and speak to Solara about assigning the merfolk as protection detail for the citizens of Esteopia, while we built the new village with the army.

I had to admit, I was very curious about Solara, considering they'd been romantically entangled—as Seraphina put it—with my brother for centuries. I figured anyone who Caspian opened his heart to had to be dependable, given the fact my brother hardly ever displayed real emotion, and hoped Solara would be amendable to this plan.

Blekket, however, doubted they would be.

"You're such a pessimist," I accused him the morning we were set to journey to Jopolis. I watched him clamber into his dress shirt, rolling the sleeves up to his elbows. For the past eight weeks, I'd been sleeping with Blekket in his bedchamber every night. We never went further than just kissing and holding one another, but when I wasn't in his presence, I felt incomplete, like an integral part of me was missing.

"I'm not a pessimist," he claimed. "I'm a realist."

"Realism is the slayer of hope."

"Not always."

"It is when the person is using logic to kill someone else's faith." He chuckled, then leaned forward, positioning his hands on either side of me on the bed. I was lying down on my back, prompted up by my elbows. I lifted one hand, running my fingers down his cheek.

"I'm just trying to prepare you," Blekket explained. "I've met Solara. They're only interested in what benefits the merfolk. Appointing their people to protecting the citizens of Esteopia is not a priority to them."

"Well, it should be. Esteopia is their home too." He smirked, skimming my bottom lip with his thumb.

"I admire your passion, angel, and I think Solara will too. I just don't want you to get your hopes up, in case they get stubborn and say no. There's a very good chance they won't agree to this."

"What will we do if they don't?" We wanted the soldiers to be the construction workers because they knew how to fight, in case we encountered any Sleothian attacks while building. We didn't want to risk a single villager's life.

"Then we won't use the entire army. We'll have less numbers, but it won't be the end of the world. We'll make it work, Tymp." He kissed me over the frown lines crinkling my forehead. "When you worry, a little V forms between your brows. It's cute." His lips trickled down from my temple to my cheek, then captured my pout, which instantly transformed into a smile under his kiss.

I headed back to my bedchamber and changed out of Blekket's oversized tunic for the day ahead. I chose a long sleeve jumpsuit I'd borrowed from Raevon, made of dusty blue crepe fabric with a printed floral pattern. It had a surplice bodice, waist tie, and side slant pockets. I left my hair down, the waves framing my face and spilling down to the tips of my shoulders, then stashed my blade in the pocket of my jumpsuit, slipping on my sandals. Pessy was nowhere to be found, but I knew she'd be there when I made it to the stables.

On my way through the courtyard, I ran into Emilia, who was walking in the opposite direction.

We nearly crashed into one another.

"Emilia," I spluttered, folding a hand over my pounding heart. "Sorry. You scared me." I didn't understand why her eyes were so large, until I realised: we'd never actually met, and I'd just referred to her by name.

"Goddess Tympany," Emilia stammered, bowing before me. "It's an honour to make your acquaintance."

"You as well," I forced out in an effort to be polite. "What brings you to the palace this morning?"

Better not be Blekket, or we're going to have a serious problem, I seethed under the question.

"I came to have tea with the King and Queen." *What? Why is she having tea with Seraphina and Demetrio?* "Seraphina has always treated me like another daughter. Hopefully soon, there will be a marriage proposal, so that will become official."

"Marriage proposal?" My fingers collapsed into fists at my sides. "Yeah, *that's* not going to happen." Emilia tilted her head, her brows hoisting up in surprise.

"I beg your pardon?" she said somewhat sharply, then took a step back at whatever she saw flare up in my eyes. This delusion of hers would no longer be nurtured, not if I had anything to say about it.

Let's nip this in the bud and wash our hands of her once and for all.

My eyes locked with hers before I asserted, "**You are *not* marrying Blekket. Go home, and find yourself a suitor who is actually in your league.**"

Her pupils dilated in response to the compulsion, then contracted in submission. Without saying another word, she turned on her heel and stalked off towards the exit, fingers interlocked in front of her.

When she was finally gone, I flipped my hair over my shoulder with a huff before spinning around.

I gasped, finding Blekket there.

He was leaning against the wall, his arms crossed over his chest, lips turned up with amusement.

"I'm not proud of that," I promised.

"I am," he declared, strolling over to wrap his arms around my waist. "That was ruthless."

"You like it when I'm ruthless."

"Yes, I do." I grinned into his kiss.

"Why was she here having tea with your parents?" I skated my hands down from his hair to his biceps.

"I haven't had a chance yet to tell them about us."

"Even though your dad already knows?" Blekket snorted.

"Seeing us kiss one time doesn't mean he knows we're *together,* Tymp. He doesn't know I've done it again, many, many times..." His mouth hovered over mine, teasing me with its close proximity.

"Yes, you have." I inclined forward, pecking his lips.

"I'll tell them now, if you want."

"I do. I don't want any more suitors coming into the palace."

"Yes, ma'am," he quipped. "Just don't be surprised if my mother starts talking marriage with you."

"It'll be a necessary sacrifice," I laughed.

Blekket left me to go find his parents. On my way to the stables, I kept staring down at my hands, wracked with shame for compelling Emilia in another emotionally charged moment, like what I'd done with Harrison. While this time, it had been more calculated then when I'd thoughtlessly ordered him to light himself on fire, that was almost worse, because I'd purposefully used my abilities in the heat of my rage for selfish intent. I thought about what I'd said that morning, about realism being the slayer of hope. Blekket was right—you

229

sometimes need realism to be the bearer of bad news, to keep you in line from spiraling.

Isaias used to say I was the perfect balance between logic and feeling, that I was the master of knowing when to favour one over the other. I needed to get back in touch with the logical side of myself and stop letting emotion take the reins.

While Emilia, a beautiful woman, would find another suitor and go on to eventually be fine after what I'd compelled her to do, Harrison was a reminder I wouldn't always be so lucky.

When Pessy saw me, she knew immediately something was off.

"What happened?" she demanded, a hand on the hilt of her sword. Raevon was standing beside her, twisting Autumn's reins around her wrist.

"I did a bad thing." Pessy's shoulders tensed.

"You didn't compel anyone to light themselves on fire again, did you?" I squinted my eyes in a scowl.

"No...but I did compel Emilia to leave Blekket alone and find someone who's actually in her league."

Pessy and Raevon exchanged a look, then both burst out laughing.

"It's not funny," I grumbled, frowning at them. "What I did was wrong. I shouldn't have used my powers on her because I was jealous."

"Hey, it's okay," Raevon assured me, stroking my back supportively. "No one's rational all the time."

"Rae's right," Pessy agreed. "Except most people, when they're not being rational, don't compel someone to get a life."

"Fuck you, Pess," I snapped, flipping her off while Raevon cackled.

"I take it Tympany told you all about her little confrontation with Emilia," Blekket said as he entered the stables. He set his hands on my shoulders from behind before slithering his arms around them, resting his chin on the top of my head.

"Doesn't sound like it was so little," Pessy teased, then mouthed *sorry* when I glowered at her.

"Don't be embarrassed, angel. If I could've compelled Harrison to not be such a dick, I would've."

He bent down to kiss the corner of my mouth.

"But you weren't jealous of Harrison," I fired back, watching him climb up onto Clarence and situate his feet in the stirrups.

"And you have no reason to be jealous of Emilia." After I'd mounted Krystal, he reached out, tracing my cheek with his thumb. "I meant it when I said you've ruined me for anyone else, Tympany. No one could ever hold a candle to you." My heart felt like it was liquifying in my chest.

"Same," I whispered, then turned my head to kiss the center of his palm.

"We ready to go?" Raevon asked from the front of the group, Pessy on Belgian cemented to her side.

"Tymp?" I loved how he always deferred to me.

"Ready," I announced, tapping Krystal with the sole of my shoe to get her to start trotting.

Jopolis was a perfect replica of Floatsim, only transplanted on land.

The homes were comprised of stone, unlike the wooden houses from the other villages, the rock refined and immaculate. Everything looked damp, as if glossed with water or lubricant, but when you actually touched it, it felt dry and warm from the roasting sun. Solara's home was modelled the same as the palace in Floatsim, only much more diminutive in size, though still large juxtaposed with the houses around it. Guarding the entrance to the dwelling was a medium-sized monkey-like creature with a saucer-shaped head, long nose, and yellowish-green skin. It had an iron trident gripped in its small fist that was nearly the same size as the creature itself.

When the Kappa saw us approaching on our horses, it flipped into fight mode, hurling the trident through the air—aimed directly at me.

"Tymp!" Pessy screamed.

I tracked the velocity in which the spear was soaring at and caught the stem of it in my hand, before it made contact with my face.

"Whoa," Raevon muttered, lashes fluttering at the same fast pace as a hummingbird's wings. "That was so cool."

"Magnificent," Blekket concurred.

"Do you always throw your weapon before knowing who your target is?" I asked the Kappa.

I hopped down from Krystal, twirling the trident in my hand before handing it back.

"Usually," the creature replied without a trace of regret. "Not everyone's so quick with their reflexes."

"Unfortunate for them." The Kappa's gaudy blue eyes trailed down my body, sizing me up.

"You must be the Goddess," it decided.

"My, whatever gave me away?" The creature's lips tugged up.

"My name is Sterling," the Kappa announced just as Blekket, Pessy, and Raevon joined us by the threshold. "I'm one of Their Majesty's personal guards." He bowed respectfully before me. "It's an honour to make your acquaintance, Your Excellence."

"I think it's a little too late to be civil now," I teased, gesturing for Sterling to stand upright.

He let out a laugh before straightening his posture. "I like you. You're different from your siblings."

"I take that as a compliment."

"You should." Sterling surveyed the four of us. "I see you've brought the Prince and Princess with you. And who's this?" He tipped his chin towards Pessy.

"This is Pessoranda Whitereaver," I introduced, gesturing to Pess. "My bonded Kylantian."

"Ah." He nodded to her in greeting. "It's good you're a small group. Solara hates a lot of people in their space, especially when they're on land."

"Solara was made aware we were coming, right?" Blekket asked.

"I only just started my shift, but I believe Marple reminded them of your visit this morning." Sterling held up a hand when Raevon started to step forward, then turned and knocked on the door. "Solara?" he called out loudly. "The Prince, Princess, and Goddess Tympany are here to see you."

It took a second, and then, we heard Solara shout, "Let them in!"

Sterling turned back to us, gesticulating into the house. "Right this way," he said, beaming at me as I passed him.

The reflective light of day seeped in through the glass windows, painting the walls in a million warm hues of grey, each as magical and iridescent as the others. The furniture was all dark wood and blue velvet, from the plush couches to the wide arm chairs, the coffee table in the sitting area made of glass, much like the drawing room back at the palace in Acadia. There was a beautiful, detailed painting of the Argent Ocean on the wall, protected by a pane of glass and a black wooden frame. Standing in the center of the room was Solara in all their glory, dressed in a loose, black jumpsuit with a slash neck, three-quarter length sleeves, a drawstring waist, and a wide pant leg, their dark hair cropped close to their scalp. When their chocolate brown eyes were doused in sunlight, they converted to a rich, buttery caramel that expressed a surprising amount of sincerity.

I was expecting Solara to be cold, from what Blekket told me about them, but my first impression of the ruler of the merfolk was anything but when they crossed the room and opened their arms to hug me.

"Goddess Tympany," they said in greeting, wrapping me in a tight embrace. My eyes flicked over to Blekket, who looked surprised as well. "I feel like I already know so much about you from your brother." The mention of Caspian threw me off guard, but also softened me.

"If you heard about me from my brother, then I worry what he might have told you."

They laughed, then released me. "Only good things. He speaks very highly of you."

"You as well." Solara blushed. "We have much to discuss."

"Yes, it seems we do. Please, follow me into the dining room. You must be hungry from your travels."

"Thank you," Raevon said, a hand on her growling stomach.

While everyone began traipsing after Solara, my eyes vacillated around the foyer, landing on a specific arm chair. At first, I wasn't sure what drew me to it, but then, I noticed a flash of movement behind the backrest that stopped me in my tracks.

"Casp?!" I gasped.

The group came to an abrupt halt in the hallway, turning around and rushing back over to where I stood.

A blonde head poked out, Caspian's cerulean blue eyes abnormally shy.

"Oh. Hey, Tymp." His hands shrouded his manhood as he stepped out from behind the chair.

He was butt naked.

My jaw had never dropped further to the ground.

Pessy's hand flew up to her agape mouth. Raevon hid behind a cloud of Pessy's hair, trying to be respectful, while Blekket looked like he might burst from pleasure at my shocked expression.

When I regained the ability to breathe, I choked out, "Solara, could you please fetch some clothing for my brother?"

"Of course." The mermaid glared at Caspian, then dashed into the other room, returning with a maroon velvet robe that had a gold yarn sash at the waist. Caspian ducked behind the arm chair, reappearing completely cloaked.

"What're you doing here?" I demanded.

"I came to check on the ocean. Among...other things." I'd never seen my older brother look so bashful. It was almost humanising. He glanced over at Pessy, and his face lit up. "Hey, Pess!"

"Hey, Casp." She raised her hand in a wave, struggling to suppress a laugh. "How's it hanging?"

Blekket snorted.

I swivelled around to silence him with a harsh stare. "Make one joke, and I will cut out your tongue."

"You wouldn't if it means I can't kiss you," he replied, and now it was Caspian's turn to look shell-shocked.

"You can still kiss without a tongue," I pointed out.

"It wouldn't be the same, and you know it." Caspian's head oscillated between Blekket and me in disbelief. Solara stood in the entrance of the foyer helplessly.

"Shall we take this into the dining room?" they proposed again, I think bothered by us dawdling near the door.

"Caspian? Will you be joining us?" I asked tersely.

"I was going to try to sneak out of here undetected...but since that didn't work, I guess I'll join you guys."

"Wonderful." Solara then marched down the hall, tired of waiting for us.

"So...what's new with you, Tymp?" Caspian asked on our way to the dining room, nudging me with his elbow before gathering his long blonde hair into a ponytail.

"Don't try to be all sweet now," I hissed. "I can't believe you came to Esteopia and didn't come see me first."

"You would've been my second visit."

"I wouldn't have even crossed your mind, Casp. Don't be ridiculous."

"That's not true. You know you're my favourite sister." I shook my head at him, immune to his charms. "But seriously, you look good, Tymp. I know it hasn't been that long since we last saw each other, but you look...happy."

I flushed. "I *feel* happy."

"I'm really glad to hear that." His eyes swung over to Blekket before he muttered, "I can see why…"

"Shut up," I grumbled, shoving his head.

I took a seat between Caspian and Blekket at the long mahogany table in the dining room, Solara at the helm, with Raevon and Pessy across from us. Blekket's hand gravitated towards mine under the table. I rested our interwoven fingers on my thigh. Caspian looked down, taking note, and smirked at me with a knowing smile I would slap off his face when we were alone.

"Sterling," Solara called, grasping the arms of their chair. The Kappa appeared in the doorway with his fingers clasped in front. "Can you retrieve some sushi for our guests, please?"

"Yes, Your Majesty," he replied, scuttling off.

"Have you had a chance to try sushi yet, Tympany?" Blekket chuckled under his breath before I could answer.

"It's all she's eaten since she got here," he replied, ignoring my glare.

"I'm surprised you eat sushi," I said, pretending as if Blekket hadn't spoken. "Considering…what you are."

"I don't eat sushi that has fish in it," the mermaid quickly debunked at the same time Sterling returned with a tray of plates, which had various different types of vegetable rolls. I thanked Sterling when he set a dish in front of me, then stretched across the table and placed a few plain avocado rolls onto my plate, popping one into my mouth.

"Can I ask a question quickly, before we get down to business?" Solara nodded, permitting me to speak. "How do you walk on land? And how often do you split your time between Floatsim and Jopolis?"

"I spend the majority of my time in Floatsim. I much prefer the water to the land, as do all mermaids. I come on land when I need to conduct meetings, particularly with the crown. To answer your other question, as long as I stay dry, I keep my legs. When I'm wet, they transform into my tail."

"Have you ever accidentally spilled water on yourself?" Pessy wondered. The corners of Solara's mouth quirked up.

"Every mermaid has at least once." I smiled at the image that formed in my head. "So," the merfolk ruler said, folding their fingers together on the table. "What would you like to discuss with me today?" Everyone shifted to face me, awaiting the explanation.

I wasn't used to being the spokesperson. I fidgeted uncomfortably under all these expectant eyes, then cleared my throat.

Before anyone said anything, I stared at Caspian and compelled, **"Nothing we say leaves this room."**

I didn't want to risk him blabbing to our family about our plans, then have them run to Sleotha to intercept.

"I've always wanted to see that in person," Solara marvelled, while Caspian frowned at them.

"See what?" He wasn't even aware anything had happened.

Blekket saved me from being outed by Solara and explained, "We've decided to rebuild the villages of Eveium and Frofsea in the outskirts, which would directly block Sleotha's path to the Gods."

"Hm. Interesting idea," Solara commented, drumming their fingers on the polished surface of the table.

"You can't obstruct the opening to the Geddesia Mountains," Caspian objected.

"We don't plan to," I assured. "We're going to rope off the entrance to the mountains and build around it, so we don't impose on the path to Kylantis. We will also have fifty feet of space between the new settlement and the Sleothian gates, so we don't infringe on anything that's actually their land."

"Good." He nodded with approval, not that we needed it.

"Where do the merfolk factor into this idea of yours?" Solara asked.

"We plan to have the Esteopian army, and the Kylantians who travelled with Tympany and Pessy, build the homes in the outskirts," Blekket continued. "In case there are any attacks during the construction, we'd like the soldiers to complete the manual labour, so we don't risk any of the residents' lives, and so we're heavily protected. This would mean though that Esteopia wouldn't be safeguarded by the army while we construct the village. We were hoping you could arrange to have some of the merfolk protecting the villagers and the palace in the meantime, while the army focuses on building the new settlement."

"What would the backup plan be if I were to say no to this?" I winced, squeezing Blekket's hand.

"We would have half the amount of people working on the settlement, which means it would take longer to build. It wouldn't be the end of the world, but we're hoping to finish the construction as quickly as possible to avoid any Sleothian interference."

Solara was quiet for several moments, considering. "How many mermaids are you thinking you might need?" My faith was restored, pouring light into the hollows of doubt.

"Rough estimate…five hundred."

"That's far too many," they protested, robbing me of my embryonic hope. "Are you insane?"

"That's not even half your numbers," Blekket argued. I squeezed his hand again, this time to get him to cool off.

"I don't mean this to be rude, Your Highness, but the merfolk's primary concern isn't the welfare of the villagers. It's the maintenance of the ocean and lakes. You're asking for almost half the merfolk to abandon their duties, when their abilities are much more advantageous in the water, not on land."

"What about one hundred?" I suggested as a counter offer. "Twenty can be placed by the palace to protect the King and Queen, and the other eighty can be dispersed through the villages. We don't need much, but we need enough to secure Esteopia's safety while we focus on the construction of the new settlement." Solara still looked unsure. "I know you say the villagers aren't a priority for you, but Esteopia is your home, too. You live here the same as them. By building this village, we are diminishing Sleotha's power in their close connection to the Gods, which will hopefully aid us in conquering the entirety of the Realm. If we were to lose this war over the land, you would be stuck with the Sleothians who don't value the conservation of the ocean the same way the Esteopians do. If you look at it through that lens, then it should be a priority for you to protect these people."

Caspian stared at me like he didn't recognise the woman sitting beside him, while Solara's lips warped into a smile.

"I like her, Casp," they said, touching Caspian's hand flirtatiously on the table. "She's like a mini you."

"She's way smarter than me," Caspian contested, making me blush to my roots.

"I agree with that." Caspian gave Solara a heated look I'd rather not have seen. "I appreciate this different perspective, Tympany. I will grant you two hundred merfolk, but in exchange, I want a favour."

"Anything," Blekket agreed.

"You misunderstand. I want to save a favour for the future, something I can cash in at any date, at any time."

"That seems fair," Raevon answered, glancing around the table to confirm with the rest of us.

"I will also reserve the right to retract those two hundred, should we need the merfolk back in the waters, for any reason."

"Again, that's understandable." Blekket stroked my knuckles with his thumb.

"Then you can have your interim army." I wanted to leap onto the table and rejoice. I hadn't expected this meeting to go so smoothly, or for Solara to be so cooperative. I was grateful for Caspian's presence tempering the merfolk ruler.

"Thank you for being so accommodating," Pessy acknowledged softly.

"Don't thank me. Thank her." Solara tipped their chin in my direction. "You're very persuasive, Tympany."

"It must be the muse in me." The mermaid kicked their head back and chortled.

"Yes. It all makes sense now." They looked around the table. "Is that all you wanted to discuss with me?"

"That's all," Blekket said.

"Then I wish you the best of luck in the creation of this new settlement. I look forward to visiting when it's finished." Solara eyed Caspian with barefaced yearning.

That was our cue to leave.

As we rose from the table, Caspian requested, "Tymp? Can I have a moment alone with you, before you go?" I looked at Pessy, then Blekket, nodding to let them know it was okay to go ahead without me.

They followed Solara into the hall, closing the door to the dining room.

"I wanted to tell you how proud I am of you. I think what you're doing is amazing, and so brave."

I was not expecting that. "You think it's amazing?" He nodded. "Wait. You support Esteopia?"

"Of course I do. I support anyone who's connected to the ocean and who actually cares about its maintenance. You were right in saying, if Sleotha wins this war and gains control of the marines, they're going to pollute the waters. They've done a bang-up job with the few lakes they do have." He shook his head with disappointment.

"Does our family know you support Esteopia?"

"Mother does. She's fine with it, as long as I don't actively do anything that would impair Sleotha, like what you're doing. The reason I supported you coming here was because I knew, out of all our siblings, you'd see the good in them and support their cause. Though I didn't think you'd see it quite so intimately…"

"This coming from the guy I found butt naked when we first came in here," I snarled, which made him chuckle.

"Hey, I'm not judging. I'm a firm believer in a little rebellious behaviour every now and then."

"I'm not being rebellious." Calling what I was doing rebellious made it sound childish.

"I heard about what happened with Jax. You should've seen Mother's face. It was priceless." He set a hand on my shoulder and sighed. "You could do a lot worse than Blekket Elrod. Just remember *he's* the lucky one, not you. Make him work every day for the honour of being with you. If he slacks off for even a second, pray for me, and I'll come give him a piece of my mind."

I laughed, "I'll remember that," then patted his hand.

It was strange getting advice from my brother regarding a romantic relationship—it was a moment I never thought I'd have. I was thankful to still have one family member on my side, even if it was surprisingly Caspian and not Jaxith.

While I had him here, I asked, "Is it true Lucius had an affair with the original Queen of Sleotha, and Jacinda is his daughter?"

"Lucius having a *daughter?*" Caspian burst out laughing. "That's the most frightening thing I've ever heard."

"I know, but when I heard the rumor, I wondered if that's why the Gods favour Sleotha. It otherwise doesn't make sense why they do."

"I can debunk that myth right now. Jacinda is not Lucius's daughter. She is the child of Sleotha and King Rafferty, through and through."

"Then how has she lived so long?"

"I heard somewhere her lifespan is tied to the drogon, but I have no idea if that's true. I've never bothered to ask."

My brows pulled together. "You've never bothered to ask?"

"You've always been the more curious one. I stick to what I know. Water. I don't bother myself with the innerworkings of the Realm, and honestly, I just don't care." I found that hard to believe, but didn't press him further.

"Well, if it's not because Jacinda is a descendent of the Gods, then why does our mother insist we back Sleotha?"

Caspian got all at once serious.

"That's a conversation you should have with Mother and Father. It's not my story to tell you."

"What's that supposed to mean?"

"It means, it's not my story to tell, Tympany. And don't even think about trying to compel it out of me."

"I wasn't." I actually was, but I wouldn't admit that. "I just…I don't know if I'll ever have the chance to ask them."

"What do you mean?" I stared down at my intertwined fingers. "Tymp? What do you mean?"

"I don't think I can return to Kylantis, Casp." I raised my head to look at him. "I can't face Mother and Father. Not after everything I've seen here, everything I'm doing. These people have become like my family. I can't turn my back on them. I can't."

Caspian was silent for a while. After a minute, he asked, "Do you love him? Blekket?"

"I don't know what love's supposed to feel like, but what I feel for him…" When I thought about it, it made a lump form in my throat, my chest tightened to the point of almost bursting, and the corners of my eyes stung. "I've never felt anything like it before. How do you know you love someone?"

"I think you just know. I know, that's not helpful, but I think it's knowing you're connected to that person, that you can be totally yourself with them, and there's no fear of judgement. When that person becomes your safety net, when you're able to look at them and know exactly what they're thinking, when you're in tune with their emotions and mannerisms, that's when you know. When you can come together and just be, and it doesn't feel forced. It's not the perfect moments. It's the messy ones in between you're willing to stay through. *That's* love."

I thought about what Blekket said at Lake Azrord.

We can always come together and be nothing other than Tympany and Blekket with each other.

"Do you love Solara?"

"I do." His eyes twinkled with devotion.

"Have you ever considered…staying in Esteopia? To be with them?"

"To be honest, no, I haven't. I always know I'm coming back, so it's never a permanent goodbye, but Solara understands I can't turn my back on Sleotha either. And I'd never ask Sol to come to Kylantis with me. It doesn't mean I don't love them, but I have responsibilities, just like they do." He cupped the side of my face. "You really have grown into such a beautiful, intelligent, strong woman. I'm so proud of you. Whatever you decide to do, I have no doubt you're going to be just fine."

"I wish you could stay," I whispered, Caspian tugging on my hand and wrapping his arms around me.

"Me too. But I'm always here, Tymp. If you need anything, anything at all, just pray for me, and I'll come." He kissed the crown of my head, releasing me. "You should head back to your friends."

"Okay. Have fun with Solara." I cringed after I said that.

"Trust me. I will." I shuddered, then began making my way to the exit. "Tympany?"

"Yeah?" I rotated around, my fingers clasping the doorknob.

"Sleotha are our people too. Remember that. While you've been here, there are still lost Sleothians praying to you for inspiration. Don't forget about them. They need you just as much, if not more."

Chapter Sixteen

On the day we were set to begin building the settlement in the outskirts, we had our first bout of rain since I'd been in Esteopia—Caspian's parting gift, after months of consistently scorching sun.

Raevon and Pessy questioned if we should put off the start of the construction, but I told them it would be fine. The plan for the crew day one would be to level the site, put up wooden forms to serve as a template for the foundation, and start digging the holes and trenches, all things we would be able to achieve despite the inclement weather. We couldn't let a little thing like a drizzle deter us from our plans any longer than absolutely necessary.

If the lightning became an issue, or if anyone felt unsafe, we would return to Esteopia at once.

I half listened to the talk around me over breakfast, shoving fruit into my mouth without really tasting it.

While it poured outside, it rained inside me too.

I hadn't stopped thinking about Caspian's last words to me since we left Jopolis. What he'd said about the villagers of Sleotha had felt like a rude awakening from the wonderful dream that was Esteopia. The thought of there being Sleothians praying to me, that I hadn't even felt their call because I'd been so wrapped up in helping Esteopia, felt like someone plunged a dagger in my chest and twisted the blade in circles. I hated the idea of any mortals feeling abandoned by me, like how my siblings and parents abandoned the Esteopians. I tried to change my perspective and focus on how winning this war against the crown of Sleotha would benefit those lost villagers in the long run, once they were under new leadership. I threw myself into the arrangements for the settlement to distract from the guilt I felt over how what we were doing would harm those who were still considered my people, who were as innocent in this war as the Esteopians were in Eveium and Frofsea. Despite my best efforts, nothing seemed to lessen these new qualms.

"Tymp? You okay?" Blekket's voice shattered through my miasma of despair.

"Mhm," I said quietly, his hand finding mine under the table. We were trying to be chaste in front of Seraphina and Demetrio, though neither the King nor Queen had stopped looking at us since we sat down. Now that Blekket told them about our relationship, they analysed every interaction between us, every graze of a hand or barb passed. They memorised each modification in our faces in reaction to something the other said, or how we responded when someone else mentioned the other by name.

I didn't like being so closely dissected. I knew it bothered Blekket too, but it was a price we could afford to pay.

Blekket clearly wasn't convinced. "Do you think we should hold off until the rain dies down?"

"No. The longer we wait, the more likely Sleotha will figure out what we're planning and try to stop us. We've waited long enough. It has to be today."

"Okay. Then we'll stick to the original plan." His eyes asked the questions his mouth refused to voice in front of our company.

They said *do you want to go somewhere private to talk?*

It warmed me from head to toe, bringing me back to what Caspian said about knowing you love someone.

When that person becomes your safety net, when you're able to look at them and know exactly what they're thinking, when you're in tune with their emotions and mannerisms, that's when you know.

I mouthed to him, "Later," and he nodded, giving my hand a squeeze that sent a pulse of adoration up my arm, exploding in my head. It screamed *you don't deserve this man.*

A truth I couldn't handle in my current state.

Before we left to meet the armies who were already at the outskirts, Seraphina asked to speak with me in private. Blekket was disinclined to leave me alone with her, but reluctantly handed me over and left with Pessy and Raevon for the stables. I followed Seraphina into the sitting room we'd sat in the day we first arrived, hunkering down in the same arm chair across from her.

"He's very protective of you," Seraphina observed, interlocking her fingers in her lap. I couldn't distinguish from her facial expression if this pleased or perturbed her.

I wasn't sure what to say, so I just shifted in my chair, crossed my ankles, and cleared my throat.

"What was it you wished to speak with me about?"

"I just wanted to check in with you and see how you were feeling," she explained. "You seemed off this morning, and I wanted to make sure you were okay."

"Oh." I'd been expecting to be on the defense. It took me a second to switch out of fight mode. "Um…I feel…"

I didn't entirely understand why that made me burst into tears. Maybe because it'd been years since my mother asked me a question like that, if ever, and it meant so much to me that she'd noticed my mind wasn't fully present. Maybe because I'd been trying to suppress my emotions so I wouldn't lose control of them, and her saying that made me feel seen in the midst of my shame. Maybe because I felt I didn't deserve her kindness, or her sympathy.

"I feel guilty," I admitted. Seraphina reached behind her to retrieve a napkin for me to wipe my tears with. "I've loved being here with you guys, and there's truly nowhere else I'd rather be…but I forgot there are innocent people in Sleotha, who are praying to me for inspiration and guidance. I feel guilty for turning my back on them."

"But you haven't, Tympany." She smudged my tears with her knuckle. "What you're doing, helping us win this war, *is* helping them. Those innocent people deserve to be under leadership who will care for them and communicate with them, who won't leave them out to dry and hide away in their palace, never to be seen or heard from again. They deserve to not live in fear. Our first step in claiming the entirety of the Realm is conquering the outskirts. Once we've achieved that, after Sleotha's power is weakened without that easy access to the Gods, we will be able to strike at the crown in a way that's more effective with their walls down, and will harm less innocent civilians. You haven't forgotten about anyone, and the fact you care so much, the fact you feel remorse, shows what good a person you are. It's easy to look at Sleotha as a whole as evil. I catch myself doing it sometimes too, but it's so important to remember they're not. They're not *all* bad. No one's perfect. The minute we start thinking we're better than them is the moment we become worse. We have to acknowledge we're cut from the same cloth, in order for us not to repeat their mistakes."

"Thank you for saying that." I sniffled. "It means a lot."

"Anytime, Tympany." I blew my nose into the napkin, feeling absurd for bawling my eyes out in front of the Queen over her enemies.

"You probably think I'm insane." She chortled, tucking a strand of my hair behind my ear.

"Not insane," she refuted. "I think you're a kind, intelligent, strong, beautiful woman. I couldn't imagine someone better for Blek."

"You don't mind...us being together?" I'd assumed both Seraphina and Demetrio were against me being with Blekket, since I already knew how Demetrio felt.

"Of course not! Oh, I'm *thrilled* you're with my son. If I had to pick anyone to succeed me on the throne, never in my wildest dreams did I think it would be someone as incredible, and formidable, as you!" I flinched, lowering the napkin to my lap.

Her approval of me with Blekket was contingent on me succeeding her on the throne, something I didn't intend to do. I needed to disabuse her of this notion before it caused problems down the road.

"Seraphina...I mean no disrespect in saying this, but my interest in your son, our relationship, has nothing to do with the crown or the kingdom. We just...want to be together. We've had no talks of marriage at this time, and I don't imagine we will. That's not what Blekket wants."

"That's nonsense. Blekket wants to be married. He just doesn't want to be married under the presumption that, when he does, he has to take the throne, but he wants to be married. I can't imagine him being with you and not wanting to make your relationship legitimate." She sighed, shaking her head. "A relationship can be enjoyable, Tympany, but it has to be going somewhere. Where do you see this going?"

"I'm trying not to think too far into the future, because if I start doing that, I think about how I'm going to live forever, and Blekket isn't. Then, I think about living an eternity without him, and I feel like I'm dying. I have to remain in the present moment, or I'll trip over the future and get stuck there. I care so much about your son. I've never felt this way before. Right now, being with him the way we have been, taking it one day at a time, it's enough. I know this isn't what you want to hear, but you can't force Blek to take the throne, and I certainly won't let anyone try to force him through me."

"I'm trying not to." I could hear the strain it took for her not to bark this at me. "Believe me, Tympany, I'm trying to be understanding of his wishes, but there are certain customs we're expected to follow as the royals. I'm having a hard time wrapping my head around him breaking those traditions, and what it would mean for the kingdom if he doesn't take the throne in March. The law states the eldest child of the crown shall ascend the throne at the age of thirty. I endured the same when I became Queen. It didn't matter whether I was ready for it or not. That was the custom, so I accepted my fate, regardless of my personal feelings. Blekket has known this was expected of him his whole life. He's had thirty years to prepare for it, yet he's acting like he found this out yesterday."

"Just because he's had the time doesn't mean he's used it to actually prepare for what it means to be King. Turning thirty doesn't guarantee he'll be magically ready to ascend the throne. I'm five-thousand-years-old, and I wasn't ready to become Queen when my mother asked me. Age doesn't equal readiness." This had been the source of the tension between Roara and me.

"Your mother wanted you to take the throne of Kylantis?" I realised then I'd never actually disclosed that to her—the only person who knew, outside of my family and Pessy, was Blekket.

"She did. She's wanted that for the last year, and I said no. I wasn't ready, just like Blekket isn't. I'm sure, if he has no other choice, he will step up and be an amazing king, but he deserves that choice." I took a deep breath. "I'm going to be honest with you, Seraphina, because I respect you greatly. I've been tempted several times in this conversation to compel you to stop pressuring Blek to take the throne, but I've held myself back from doing so because you deserve your autonomy. So does Blekket. If he's going to get there, it has to be on his terms. I don't need to tell you any of this, because he's your son and you, of course, know him better, but what I've gathered of Blekket is that he's, in a lot of ways, just like me. If someone tries to force me to do something, a switch goes off in my brain that shuts down the rest of my body from functioning. Which is kind of ironic, given my abilities." I laughed at that, and even Seraphina cracked a smile. "If I'm going to do something, it has to be because I come to that decision on my own."

"Blekket's definitely the same. He's always been like that, since he was a young boy. Stubborn as a doorknob."

I smirked. "We have that in common."

"Though I imagine you were a lot less destructive." That made me giggle. "Let me ask you this. In a hypothetical universe, if Blekket were to ask you to marry him and be his Queen…would you say yes?"

To indulge Seraphina, I really gave it thought. Being a queen was never something I aspired to. It was why I declined the offer when my mother presented it to me. I didn't view myself as a leader, not the way Lucius had always taken it upon himself to be. I was far more comfortable blending into the background, leaving the big decisions to who I considered the professionals to be, but that was mostly because I was the youngest and always felt like no one ever took me seriously in Kylantis.

Here in Esteopia, I'd stepped up. I'd taken control on more than one occasion, and it hadn't felt frightening. It felt natural, like what I was supposed to do.

But I wasn't sure if that was because I was meant to be their leader, or if that confidence came from not having the pressure of being the main sovereign.

"Marriage isn't something I ever thought I'd have," I told her truthfully. "I never once considered even falling in love with anyone. I'd sort of just accepted that, as a Goddess, that wasn't in the cards for me. So I don't really know how I feel about it. But I do know, at this moment in time, I can't imagine being without Blekket. What that means down the road is a conversation for him and me later, but I can't see myself leaving him. I don't know if that's what you wanted to hear—"

"It is," she insisted. "It is. Look, at the end of the day, all I want is for both my children to find happiness. You make him happy. He's made that abundantly clear. As Queen, I have to worry about the kingdom, but as his mother…nothing makes me happier than seeing the way he lights up every time you walk into a room. I don't know what it means, or where it's going, but as long as you keep that smile on his face, and he does the same for you, I will find a way to be supportive, because you're right. Blekket is not the type of person who responds well to being pressured. He never has, and I have to learn to let go a little. It's just hard to change the pattern of a lifetime."

"I completely understand that." Seraphina would get along swimmingly with Roara, if Roara could get over herself long enough to meet her. "I'm sorry if I overstepped with anything I said. I didn't mean to preach to you about your son, or act like I know him better."

"You didn't," she assured me, reaching for my hand.

I took it to show there were no hard feelings, but also because I was curious to hear her thoughts.

They will get married and ascend the throne together. I'm certain of it. Esteopia will be lucky to have them when they do.

I slipped my hand out of hers.

"I hope everything goes according to plan today," Seraphina said, walking me to the door.

"Me too." I surprised her, and myself, by leaping forward to hug her. "Thank you for trusting me with your people…and your family. I haven't always deserved your acceptance, but I will work every day to protect your kingdom and earn the right to be with your son."

"You've already earned it," she swore, embracing me back. "But I appreciate the gesture, Tympany."

Seraphina cupped the side of my face. *She will be an amazing daughter-in-law and Queen,* she thought to herself.

I headed to the stables, my arms snaked around my shoulders, contemplating the potential of marrying Blekket one day. I didn't feel fear, per say, at the thought of it, but something coiled around my throat that made me feel garroted, an outlandish amalgamation of joy and sadness. What I'd said to Seraphina was the truth—I couldn't imagine not being with Blekket, but no matter how happy he made me or how committed we were to one another, something that would always hang over us would be time.

As a Goddess, now that I'd reached the full age of adulthood, I would no longer age. Blekket didn't have the luxury of an eternity like I did. Was it even worth it to be married if I could have a forever, and he couldn't? Or was the gift of a smaller infinity that much more precious?

I knew nothing about love or relationships. What I knew came from what I'd read, but reading someone else's account of something wasn't the same as experience. This was the kind of thing you needed to undergo to actually comprehend, something I never thought to prepare myself for because I'd always assumed it would never happen for me. Now that it had, I was way out of my depth.

When I reached the stables, an immediate smile latched onto my face, seeing Blekket, Pessy, Raevon, Lev, and Alsandair waiting for me. Blekket was double fisting both Clarence and Krystal's reins, beaming.

"I took the liberty of procuring Krystal for you, because I'm *such* a good boyfriend." He winked.

"Careful. Your head's about to roll off your neck." I accepted her reins from him, then reached up on my tiptoes to give him a kiss on the cheek.

"What did my mother want to speak to you about?" Raevon asked. I mounted Krystal, stroking her mane, and relished her hum of appreciation.

"She just wanted to check in and see how I was feeling." It wasn't totally a lie—just a lie of omission.

"You okay?" Blekket probed, having sensed earlier that my mood was off.

"I think so." I took his proffered hand and squeezed. He didn't seem fully convinced, but we were still in public, so he wouldn't press. After he released my hand, my eyes flicked over to Pessy.

What did she really *want to talk about?* Pessy asked through the bond.

She wanted to talk about Blekket and marriage and the crown. It kind of freaked me out a little. I'm just not sure what kind of future we can have together, and it made me really sad.

Don't think like that, Tympany, she ordered, the group trotting off in the direction of the gates.

Haven't you thought about it? Now that we're bonded, you're going to live forever too. You'll outlive Raevon. I wanted to know I wasn't the only one beleaguered by the threat of time. I saw her shift uncomfortably on Belgian, her shoulders stiffening.

I've tried very hard not *to think about that.* Her voice in my head sounded gruff. *I've also tried hard not to think about the possibility of never seeing my mother again, if we end up staying in Esteopia. These are things that will drown me if I give them the power to. People like us, who've lived as long as we have, need to take it one day at a time, or else we can't function. We get so deep into our heads that there's no way out. Don't think so far into the future where you can't appreciate the present, Tymp. That's no way to live.*

A lump appeared, digging at the walls of my throat, threatening to shoot out in the form of a mewl.

I love you, Pessoranda Whitereaver, I gushed, wishing I could lean over and squish her in a gargantuan hug. The horses hindered us. *I'm sorry if I don't say that enough.*

She turned her head back to smile at me. *You don't always need to say it. I know.*

We arrived at the outskirts an hour later.

The army had begun construction at the crack of dawn, and were well on their way when we absconded the Dream Forest. We'd divided the two thousand, five hundred and thirty Esteopians and Kylantians by one hundred, so there were roughly twenty five people working on each house at a time. Twelve would work during the day, and the other twelve or thirteen would take the night shift, so we were building at all hours. This would be optimal in getting us to finish the construction as quickly as possible, before Sleotha became aware of what we were doing fifty feet away from them.

We arranged for Lev and Alsandair to oversee the soldiers when Blekket, Pessy, Raevon and I weren't able to be there.

I thought I'd have to convince or compel Alsandair to cooperate with the Esteopians, but he'd struck a friendship with Lev and never once questioned me on my sincerity towards helping Esteopia. He'd come to understand that I'd switched sides, and his allegiance was with me, so long as he was still in Esteopia.

I imagined this would change, should he ever decide to return to Kylantis, but I appreciated having him as my second next to Pessy, while he was still here.

Everything looked like it was going reasonably well despite the rain. They'd been digging for hours, and some of the pits were already seven feet deep underground, while others were only at four or five feet. We'd determined they should dig ten feet deep for each of the houses, allowing us to have plenty of foundation above the grade line to create a good slope, so water could drain away from the foundation after the concrete was poured.

"This is so cool," Raevon admired, looking around at the clusters of soldiers hard at work.

I had to agree with her, but for different reasons.

What delighted me was watching the Kylantians and Esteopians compose the new settlement together, and that this was happening right beneath the Geddesia Mountains, where the Gods were tucked away with their prejudices, oblivious to their people working in harmony with their enemies. It was the biggest, proudest *fuck you* to my family.

"What's the estimate, you think, of how long all this will take?" I asked Lev as we began strolling down the path between the different work sites.

"If we're quick," he replied, "I'd say three weeks."

"But that's only *if* we don't encounter any obstacles from our not-so-friendly neighbours," Blekket reminded matter-of-factly.

"I'd say we could pray to the Goddess of the Heart and Mind for inspiration, but she's already here." Lev winked at me.

"I'm sticking with optimism," I declared, beaming back at him. "In fact, I'm *so* optimistic that I'll bet we're finished in *two* weeks. How about *that*?" I got right in Blekket's face, who just shook his head at me.

"That sounds like denial," he muttered.

"That sounds like pessimism," I hissed. He squinted his eyes in a scowl at my conceited smirk.

"Idealist."

"Worrywart."

"Worrywart? What's a worrywart?"

"A person who tends to dwell unduly on difficulty or troubles. Otherwise known as Blekket Elrod."

While Raevon giggled ahead of us, Blekket argued, "If I don't voice these things, none of you will acknowledge the very real risks. You'll just live in the fantasy without consulting the harsh reality. Someone has to be the voice of reason." I remembered a time when I thought the voice of reason was Jaxith— before he irrationally refused to heal a five-year-old girl because she was Esteopian.

"In no world is Blekket Shamus Elrod the voice of reason," Raevon objected, rolling her eyes.

"You really do have quite the overinflated ego," I agreed. "How does your neck handle all that weight without crumbling?"

"That's what Nana used to say!" Raevon tossed her head back and cackled up at the storm clouds.

A large dollop of rain dropped into her open mouth unexpectedly. She nearly choked on it in surprise.

"Wait..." I faced Blekket, my lips losing the battle against a smile. "Your middle name is *Shamus?*"

"It was my grandfather's name," he explained, flushing adorably.

"What's your middle name?" I asked Raevon.

"Audrey," she replied, then added, "*Way* better then *Shamus,*" making both Pessy and me laugh.

"Can all the women in my life please stop badgering me?" Blekket griped. "I'm trying to have a good day today."

"*I* haven't said anything," Pessy mumbled.

"And that's why you're my favourite, Pess."

He gave her hand an affectionate squeeze that made both Raevon and me scoff under our breaths.

"Do you have a middle name, Pess?" Raevon rested her cheek on Pessy's shoulder.

Pessy kissed Raevon's hair, then answered, "It's Halynn." I stopped in my tracks, everyone turning around to look at me.

"Pessoranda Whitereaver," I gasped. Pessy's face illuminated with a smile, as she knew where this was going. "I've known you three hundred years, and I didn't know your middle name is *Halynn?* What in the world—"

I wasn't looking where I was going, and suddenly, the earth vanished beneath my feet. I released Krystal's reins so I didn't drag her down with me, then plummeted into one of the ten foot pits.

I plopped right into the damp soil, which sullied the lovely light blue, almost white jumpsuit I'd borrowed from Raevon.

"Tymp!" A series of heads poked out from the perimeter of the hole, peering down into the chasm.

"Are you okay?" Raevon shouted.

"I'm fine," I grumbled, swatting off a splotch of mud from my arm. "Move out of the way."

All the heads retreated, making space for me.

I leapt off my feet, soaring along the current of the wind, and landed in front of the group. I lifted a strand of my hair that was soggy and now jumbled with mire. I tried to tug at it, but I only made the knot worse.

The sound of someone laughing caused me to raise my head. Pessy had a hand smothered over her mouth, trying to keep the noise from releasing again. It managed to leak past her lips in the form of another boisterous snort.

I bent down to the ground, scooping some mud from the edge of the pit, then chucked it at her.

"Hey!" she screamed, lifting her arms to protect her face, but she wasn't fast enough. The mud splattered over her cheek, dripping down to her collarbone. Raevon burst out laughing, which prompted Pessy to crouch to the soil, fist out a pellet of sludge, and hurl it right into her girlfriend's hair.

"Pess!" Raevon shrieked, dashing for her.

When my eyes swung over to Blekket, in the time it took me watching Pessy and Raevon begin flinging mud at one another, he'd already obtained a handful of dank dirt, squishing it between his fingers.

"Blek," I warned, backing away. "Don't even think about it."

"Bet you wish you could compel me now, huh, angel?"

"BLEKKET—"

He heaved the thing of mud at me, but I ducked my head just in time. It ended up hitting Lev instead.

"Lev! I'm *so* sorry," Blekket exclaimed, his face swamped with horror. "That was meant for Tympany."

Lev said absolutely nothing.

He just bent down to the ground, excavated some damp soil from the side of the hole, and threw it at the Prince.

"Yes, Lev!" I gave him a high five.

While my back was turned, I felt something cold, soft, damp, and sticky spatter against my spine.

I rotated just as Blekket crashed into me, smearing mud over the back and front of my jumpsuit. His hand skimmed my backside before dragging his fingers down my leg, all the way to the bottom of the material at my ankle. His other hand, which was also plastered in mud, flattened over my stomach, leaving a large imprint of his fingers on the fabric. I grabbed a hold of his wrist, flipping him onto his back, then crawled on top of him, daubing mud all over his face, hair, and clothes.

"Tympany, stop!" he screamed through a strangled laugh, his fingers clenching the earth in desperation.

"I won that round," I announced breathlessly. Blekket's hands freed the dirt, gliding to my hips.

"Sweetheart, I win every round just by looking at you."

He rolled us so I was beneath him, then slanted his head and captured my lips in a victorious kiss.

"Why are you all...dirty?" Demetrio asked us when we entered the palace. The entire crew turned their heads to glare at me.

"Blame Tympany," Raevon grumbled, grimacing at how I'd tarnished the jumpsuit she let me borrow.

"Actually, blame Pessy," I fired back. "She had to laugh at me when I fell into one of the pits."

"Because it was funny," she maintained. "If it wasn't me, it would've been Blekket."

"Absolutely true," he concurred, the two grinning wickedly at each other. They were a match constructed of nightmares.

"Can you all please clean up before dinner?" Seraphina begged. "I'd rather not have you dripping mud onto the furniture."

"Of course, Mother." Blekket leaned down, trying to kiss her cheek, but she jerked back just in time.

"Oh, no you don't." She scurried away from him. "You're not getting me all dirty too. Go take a shower."

She turned on her heel, scuttling off in the direction of the dining hall, with Demetrio following shortly after.

"Let's go get clean," Pessy said, reaching for Raevon's hand.

I had to will my eyes away at the zealous look that passed between them, my cheeks flaming.

"I'm gonna go shower," I told Blekket, who bobbed his head in a nod, scratching the back of his neck.

"Yeah, me too," he mumbled, but neither one of us left for our bedchambers, just loitering in the hall.

I'm not sure what possessed me, but then, I proposed, "Want to join me?"

Blekket's eyes nearly toppled out of his skull, not quite believing what I'd just said. I couldn't believe it either, but once the words were out, I couldn't deny how badly I wanted them to come true.

"Uh…yeah," he blurted, his unbridled reaction making me smile. "Are you sure?" I nodded, then went a step further and offered him my hand. With no further preamble, he laced his fingers with mine and lead me to his bedchamber.

He left me by the vanity in the bathroom to shut the door, then spun around to face me. He lingered there, not hesitantly, but to give me space, in case I changed my mind. I appreciated it so much it made me teary eyed, ridding me of any anxiety lurking beneath the surface of my smile.

"Could you…?" I pointed to the buttons on the back of the jumpsuit.

"It's a difficult task, but a challenge I'm up for facing." I rolled my eyes as he sauntered over to me.

"You're impossible." I felt his fingers start unclasping the buttons down my spine, relieving the burden around my ribs that the form fitting jumpsuit compressed. He finished off the row right above my behind, the tips of his fingers sliding up the length of my arm to my shoulder.

"You like that I'm impossible," he whispered, skating the strap down my arm at an erotic, slow pace.

He then bent to plant a kiss on my bicep.

"Debatable," I mumbled, angling my neck to the side, so I could give him full access to my throat.

"Hmm…you smell so good." He kissed me on a spot below my ear that sent a shudder down my spine.

"I smell like mud."

"No. Your hair smells like lilac."

"Then I smell exactly like you." His lips ascended down my cheek, stealing a quick kiss from mine.

"Cute." His fingers trembled a little before he asked, "May I…" fiddling with the other strap. I nodded. "With words, angel."

"Yes," I replied, bracing myself.

I wasn't ashamed of my body. I'd never been insecure about how I looked, no matter how many jabs Eira used to take at me about my thunder thighs and thick arms, or how many times Roara tried to dissuade me from eating a pastry I shoved in my mouth just to spite her. Nothing could change that, not even when I decided to cut my hair short and Lucius told me I looked like a man.

Something Callie and Luna taught me was that the most gorgeous of people were the ones who were content in themselves. That aplomb emanated outward and coloured them in a kind of beauty that couldn't be replicated. I spent my whole life not caring what anyone thought about my appearance and was always happier for it.

The only reason I was even remotely insecure now was because no one had ever seen me like *this* before, not just physically naked, but emotionally. And this wasn't just anyone.

It was Blekket.

Still, I held my head up high, my chin tipped upward with self-assurance, as Blekket slithered my jumpsuit down my body, crouching to the floor at my ankles where the material pooled.

I stepped out of it and felt his eyes blaze over my skin, trickling up my physique in conjuncture with him standing.

The air whistled through his teeth.

"Tympany," he moaned, turning me around to face him. He just stared at me and shook his head, at a loss for words, it seemed. "There's no fucking way you're real, standing in *my* bathroom right now, looking this perfect. No fucking way. I have to be dreaming." I wasn't sure what I was supposed to say to that.

"You're awake," I promised.

"You are so fucking beautiful, Tymp." He cupped my cheek. "So beautiful, it's almost physically painful."

"Well, don't say that. Now I feel bad." His lips twitched into an indulgent smile, his thumb skimming my bottom lip.

"You have nothing to feel bad about. Seriously. You should go everywhere naked." He quickly amended, "Actually, I take that back. I don't want anyone else to *ever* see you like this. No one but me."

"No one but you," I agreed, reaching up on my tiptoes to kiss him. I didn't wait for him to undress.

I headed for the shower, knowing he'd join me when he was done. I was worried, if I watched him get naked too, I would lose my resolve, and all this would become too real and too much for me to bear. I wanted to enjoy this, before it caught up to me.

I switched the nob to hot and let the water saturate me, scrubbing away the filth from the outskirts that was incrusted in my hair and caked in my nails. I felt him enter the shower before I saw him. I tried controlling my reaction, but it was difficult—he was just glorious, so much so that he dazzled my eyes. He was all muscle with not an inch of flabby skin, broad shoulders and wiry legs. I'd seen him shirtless before, but the combination of that with his bare behind, strong limbs, and impressive length, was so captivating that it took my breath away. It was my turn to wonder if I was dreaming.

I just couldn't believe my luck.

"My eyes are up here," Blekket teased. I hadn't realised I'd been staring with my mouth open, drooling like a fool.

"S...sorry..."

"Don't apologise. I stare at you all the time."

He finally approached me, reaching over my head for one of the two bottles sitting in the caddy attached to the wall.

"You do?" I wasn't sure whether to feel flattered, or mortified. He grinned, squirting some shampoo into his palm.

"I can't help myself. You're beautiful, and you're mine." He shrugged like this was obvious, then gestured with his other hand for me to turn. I complied, spinning so my back was to his front, then shut my eyes.

I felt his fingers in my hair, massaging the lather in. I tilted my head further back into his expert hands.

"Hmm…"

"How does this feel?" he asked, kneading my scalp with his nails, leaning down to kiss the top of my head.

"*So* good," I purred.

"Good. You deserve to be pampered." I wasn't sure I agreed with that, but I didn't want to disturb the moment with any negativity.

He leaned down, lapping up water droplets from my shoulder with his tongue, all the way up to my hairline.

"Beautiful." He breathed.

I rested the back of my head on his collarbone and closed my eyes, basking in his tender, thorough ministration.

I'd never felt so cherished.

"I could stay here forever," Blekket whispered, echoing my thoughts exactly. He encased me in his arms, resting his chin on my shoulder, then turned his face into my neck and kissed the same spot on my throat several times.

Something came over me in that moment, something I'd never felt before. I was swamped with the need to feel his hands on me, craving his kiss and touch to the point of carnal pain, because it was *then* that I knew.

I loved him.

I'd fallen completely in love with Blekket Shamus Elrod.

I grabbed his wrist, while he still had his face buried in my neck. I spread his long fingers out over my stomach, covering his hand with my own, and began gliding it down my abdomen, every muscle clenching in anticipation. Blekket realised what I was doing and suddenly turned to stone.

"Wait." He stopped the trajectory of his hand, resting it over my hipbone. His eyes burned with longing, but he was reining it in, for *me*. It only made me want him more. "Are you sure? I need to hear you say it, Tympany."

"I'm sure," I whispered, dragging precious air into my lungs. He laid a series of kisses up, from my chin to the corner of my mouth.

"Promise me, if it becomes too much, you'll tell me to stop. I need you to promise me."

"I promise. Please, Blek," I found myself imploring, feeling no shame in doing so. His eyes softened, and he let out a passionate groan that spoke volumes as to what he'd been suppressing.

"Oh, sweetheart," he moaned, then continued sliding his hand down.

I took hold of his forearm, following his movements so nothing would be a surprise. His fingers skimmed my pelvic bone, and my breath hitched when he cupped me fully. My other hand, the one not gripping him for dear life, extended behind me, skating into the hair at the nape of his neck, holding on.

His thumb brushed against my clit. My hips bucked forward as I gasped. "Is this okay?" Blekket asked.

His voice was throttled when he spoke.

I had no doubt, if I said no, he would stop immediately, despite what he clearly wanted himself.

Knowing this made me want it even more. "Yes," I stuttered, my blood boiling. "Please, continue."

He began stroking my clit very gently with his thumb, rubbing in circles. He traced my throat with open mouthed kisses, grazing my jawline with his teeth. With his other hand, he splayed his fingers out over my belly, his thumb and pinkie stretching the span of each of my hipbones.

I moaned embarrassingly loud, the sound drowned out mostly by the pounding of the showerhead, and pulled at his hair to bring him closer.

"Fuck," I gasped into his mouth when he nipped at my lower lip.

"Do you want me to stop?" It meant more to me than I could say that he kept asking, kept checking to see if the answer had changed.

"Don't stop," I begged, reaching up on my tiptoes to find his lips again. He groaned into my mouth at the same moment he slid his index finger inside me.

"Fuck, Tymp." He sighed, sullying my face in sweet kisses. There wasn't room for me to think about anything but him, for any part of me to feel anything other than complete and utter bliss.

"Blek," I whimpered, throwing my head back against his shoulder.

"You are motherfucking perfection, Tympany." He pumped his finger in and out of me, all while persecuting my clit with his thumb.

"Blek," I gasped again, almost in warning. My legs began to tremble from the strain of remaining upright. "Blekket, I'm...I'm gonna..." Words failed me when he took my earlobe between his teeth.

"It's okay, sweetheart. I've got you. Let go. It's okay." Right on cue, I did, vigorously.

The sensation was so overpowering that I felt like I might collapse. I clung to him, his name rolling off my tongue over and over as he pressed the heel of his hand against my clitoris to prolong the sensation, trailing kisses down my throat.

"Tymp," he moaned, embracing me tighter, helping me ride out my orgasm. When it had officially passed, I relaxed in his arms, both exhausted and never more placated. "How was that?" he asked me, sounding nervous. I raised my head with what little energy I possessed, giving him a sated smile.

"Amazing," I replied, meaning it.

"*You're* amazing," he responded, giving me a playful nip on my chin.

I whirled around so I was facing him, my eyes trailing down the length of his outstanding, chiselled body.

"I want to touch you," I blurted. Blekket choked on his next breath.

"I'm all yours," he said with an arrogant curl of his lips, unfurling his hands for further emphasis.

I started at his shoulders, exploring the dip beneath his collarbones, then the delineation of his pecks. Blekket was so still the whole time I investigated that, if I didn't feel his chest rising and falling, I would've assumed he'd stopped breathing.

My fingers itched for more, my nails scraping over rock hard flesh, creeping their way downward.

I paused, then looked back up at him. "What should I do?" Blekket kissed me between my brows.

"Whatever feels right," he answered. "Literally anything you do will be good, Tymp. Literally anything."

With that assurance in mind, I followed my urge and wrapped my hand around the base of his cock.

"Oh, fuck," he cried out, jerking. I immediately let go.

"Sorry. Was that too tight?"

"*Don't* apologise," he stammered. "That wasn't a bad reaction. Please, do *exactly* that again."

Instinct took the reins and told me to stroke him from the base up, to not grip my fingers too tightly around him as I eased up and down his length. He groaned, his hands gliding down my waist and folding over my behind. He gripped my butt cheeks, as if squeezing them would curb the unruly sensations rioting inside him.

"How am I doing?" I asked.

He spluttered out a shaky laugh. "Perfect, sweetheart. Your fingers feel incredible."

"Would you say…magnificent?" I flicked my tongue up the stretch of his neck, giving him a taste of his own medicine by nibbling on his earlobe.

"Fuck, Tymp. I'm not going to last long if you keep doing that."

He started thrusting his hips forward, matching the rhythm of my hand while resting his forehead against mine. My other hand travelled up his strapping chest, my fingers fisting in the hair at his nape. I tugged, forcing his eyes to open and meet mine.

I hadn't expected to feel anything myself while doing this, but there was a power here I hadn't anticipated to find, that dripped through my body like warm, liquified chocolate, seeping under my bones and fashioning itself a permanent lodging in my chest. Every fluctuation in my movements, even the slightest of changes, elicited a different sound, each one that escaped his lips stoking a fire deep in my belly that roasted my blood. The way he looked at me was the most tormenting part, his midnight blue eyes drugged with desire, making me feel and want to do a million things at once.

"Tympany," he gasped out, his body shuddering. I wasn't sure if it was a good response, or a bad one.

"Do you want me to stop?"

"NO," he practically screamed, and that made me giggle. "Fuck, Tymp. With the sound of your laugh and the way your fingers feel like fucking silk around me, you're going to unman me."

Wetness gathered at his tip. Instinct told me to lift my thumb and swirl my finger around the top.

"That's it. I'm done," he growled, spasming in my hand.

We crashed against the wall, me below him, as he slammed a hand on the tile and screamed a garbled version of my name, burying his face in a cloud of my hair until the feeling subsided.

"How does it feel...for a man? I've always wondered." I didn't understand why that made him start hysterically laughing.

"Oh, sweetheart," he chuckled, curling his arms around my waist and nuzzling my cheek. "You really are so magnificent."

"That word is ruined for me now," I said, making us both laugh. Blekket leaned back to tip my chin up, eyes filled with awe.

"You've really never done that before?" I shook my head.

"Did I do it okay?"

"You did it *perfectly,* Tymp." He kissed the bridge of my nose, then asked in the most innocuous voice, "Will you stay with me?"

I wasn't sure if he meant for the night, or for forever. Either way, the answer was the same.

"Yes."

Chapter Seventeen

In the end, I'd gambled correctly—the soldiers worked day and night to complete the construction of the entire village in two weeks, a fact I rubbed in Blekket's face with overwhelming vanity.

"And you tell me *my* ego is inflated," he grumbled, after I danced around him victoriously.

It wasn't without a few speed bumps, which Blekket made sure to remind me when I'd been rejoicing. We had some hiccups when it came to installing the plumbing for a few of the houses, as well as with the insulation. Demetrio and Blekket kept butting heads over whether to pick fiberglass or cellulose, though that was mostly because they were already tense with each other and neither one of them wanted to admit that the other could be right. We went with cellulose, per Lev's advisement, which ended up being the best option, despite Demetrio's griping.

Other than that, the construction went seamlessly…a bit *too* seamlessly.

We didn't encounter any Sleothian interference, which was not a comforting thought to any of us. With the amount of noise we made during the formation of the town, there was no way Sleotha, or the Gods for that matter, didn't know what we were doing fifty feet away from them, which meant, if they were planning to strike, it would be when we were finished. We had four hundred Kylantian and Esteopian guards positioned at the settlement day and night, anticipating an attack, and planned to have the entire army on standby the day we moved the residents in.

We would never leave the town unprotected.

Seraphina decided to throw a massive party to celebrate the new village. It took some convincing, but she finally agreed to host the celebration on the beach of the Argent Ocean, rather than the palace, so we could invite any of the townsfolk who wished to attend that weren't just the elite Neraids. Sanders agreed to supply ale for the partygoers, and even the merfolk contributed by setting up ornamentations amongst the willow trees to make the beach feel more intimate.

On the day of the party, Blekket and I were lounging in bed. We had an hour before we were expected to be on the beach, but neither one of us had the strength to peel ourselves away from the mattress—or each other.

"You know what people are calling the settlement?" Blekket's fingers trailed leisurely up my leg, begetting goosebumps. My breathing turned laboured with the upward trajectory of his touch.

"What?" I sighed when he slid between my legs.

"Tympany's Province." He inclined down, planting a kiss on my collarbone.

"Let me guess. Pessy started that?" I arched my back and moaned when he nipped at the skin of my throat.

"She's nothing if not consistent." He breathed against my shoulder, his lips not neglecting a single patch of flesh as they made their way down my body. My breath was on fire, and my breasts felt heavy, throbbing from the weight of desire. He moved the cloth of the oversized tunic I had on away, unearthing one breast, then released a satisfied hum. "I do not deserve this."

"Stop saying that," I tried to object, but then he took the aching tip of my nipple between his teeth, and all words were massacred by the vigor of my moan. I gripped at the sheets, my hips lifting up to grind against his.

"You like that?" he asked, his warm breath tickling me.

"Mhm." I felt his lips form a smile around my breast, which added a whole new dimension of pleasure. "Blek," I panted out, raising a hand to thread my fingers in his hair, pushing his body flush against mine.

"Do you want me to continue?" I let out a guttural moan. "While that is a wonderful sound, it's not a yes."

"Yes, you dipshit," I sneered, almost ripping out a handful of his hair from frustration. He chuckled, midnight eyes alight with humor and yearning.

"Dipshit. That's a new one. I think I prefer that to worrywart."

"You're both." I groaned at the feel on his teeth grazing my belly, working his way downward in synchronisation with the parting of my thighs on the mattress.

"If you don't like this, just tell me to stop, and I'll stop. Okay?"

"Okay." The sight of him licking his lips nearly unravelled me.

"You are so sweet, Tympany," he murmured before leaning in and kissing up the interior of my right thigh. I flopped back onto the bed, unable to continue watching the course he was descending down. I let out a raucous moan at the first swipe of his tongue at the juncture of my thighs.

"Blekket," I gasped, smothering my mouth with my hand so I wouldn't scream embarrassingly loud.

"Gods, you taste so fucking good," he groaned, then kissed me in a way that should've been considered illegal, clamping down on the bundle of nerves.

My chest felt like it was being ravaged by a rampant inferno. My blood switched from being on simmer to a boiling point with each lap of his tongue, every scrape of his nails along the inside of my thighs, every puff of warm breath I felt against my skin when I whimpered, and it made him groan.

"Is this okay?" he asked.

"I swear to the Gods, if you stop right now, Blekket Elrod, I will never speak to you again."

"Okay. Yeesh, woman." The smile on top of his tongue in me was almost too much to bear.

"Don't stop, Blek." I thrusted my hips up unashamedly to meet what he was doing, spreading my legs even further.

"You are a beautiful combination of a dream and a nightmare, sweetheart, but I wouldn't have you any other way."

At the slightest trace of his teeth, the tension that had been mounting with every movement, lick, and uttered romantic word suddenly shattered. I bit down on my palm to repress the deafening scream that threatened to shoot out past my lips and quake the whole palace, my orgasm undulating through me. I unwound on the mattress as he eased up the length of my body, looming over me before leaning down to capture my lips in a gentle, besotted kiss. I was half present, half still hurled up into the clouds, when he dropped his cheek onto my chest and curled his arms around my waist.

"Will you *please* be mine?" he whispered, then raised his head to look at me.

"I'm yours," I promised, tracing the freckles on his nose with the pad of my index finger. "Are you mine?"

"I will never live a second of my life where I am anything but completely yours, Tympany," he pledged, leaving a trail of searing kisses from my cheek to my chin.

I was on the cusp of telling him I loved him, but before I had a chance to, we heard a knock on the door.

"I'm not coming in," Raevon assured from the hall, "but Mum is going to have an aneurism if you two don't start getting ready." Blekket buried his head between my breasts and grunted.

"Can we please run away together, so we don't have to deal with this shit anymore?"

"Sorry. You know I can't leave Pessy behind." I pecked his cheek, then crawled out of bed.

I selected for tonight a sage green, strapless tulle gown with a pleated neckline and floral accents across the bodice, the skirt draping tulle on a long, A-line silhouette. I twisted my hair back into a braid that finished off at the end of my neck, then lifted the skirt of my dress to sheath my dagger to my thigh, slipping on my sandals. It was hard to describe the change I saw in the girl reflected back at me in the mirror, but she was unrecognisable. Her brown skin glowed. Her lips were a little more swollen and pink than usual. Her amber eyes shimmered, and there was an organic ease to the way her shoulders were squared, not an iota of falsehood in the confidence she wore like a crown.

She was a queen, someone who commanded respect with nothing but a simple tilt of her head.

Blekket was waiting for me in the hallway, looking dapper in a navy blue, velvet petticoat and matching breeches, a black button down beneath the jacket. His loafers were spotless, bouncing the florescent light off the leather.

"Wow," he spluttered when he saw me. "Tymp. You look—"

"*Don't* say it."

His lips twisted into an exquisitely wicked smile. "It's way too easy to push your buttons, angel."

"Careful. That neck of yours doesn't look all that sturdy." I grabbed his ears and swung his head from side to side for further emphasis. He laughed, then reached for my hand, weaving his fingers through the slots between mine.

"You're too good for me," he declared with a shake of his head.

"Stop it." I pulled on his arm to get him to stop walking. "Seriously, Blek. Why do you keep saying that? It's not true."

"It is true, sweetheart." He traced the line of my jaw with his index finger. "You deserve someone who's as strong as you are. Who's as capable, as *good* as you. Someone who isn't a coward, abandoning his people because he's scared."

"You're not a coward, Blek." I cradled the side of his face, and he angled his cheek into my palm, closing his eyes with a moan. "You're not a coward for wanting things for your life that differ from what others expect of you. You're not deserting anyone. If you were to leave Esteopia in the middle of this war, I would call you a coward, but you're still here, still fighting for your home, even if you don't want to rule it. It doesn't mean you love your people any less for you to admit you don't feel ready to take the throne. It doesn't mean you don't deserve happiness. It just makes you human."

I reached up on my tiptoes to kiss him. He crashed into me, backing us up against the wall, his hips pinning me down. He cupped my chin, tipping it back, and plunged his tongue between my lips, his free hand slipping under the skirt of my dress to curl my leg around his waist. My fingers fisted in his hair, my other hand splaying across his back.

"Tymp," Blekket hissed when he found my dagger sheathed to my thigh. "You're fucking killing me."

"Sorry," I blurted, making him laugh.

"Gods, I want you," he groaned, his teeth grazing my earlobe before he lips lithered down my throat, heading to where my breasts were almost spilling out of my dress. I gripped the hair at the nape of his neck and arched my back, so our chests rubbed against one another. I stretched my neck to give him more access, and he took every inch I offered him, venerating me with his tongue.

"Blek," I moaned, gathering the hem of his jacket in my hand, tilting my hips up. "I need you closer."

"Um." The sound of throat clearing splintered the trance.

Lev was standing a few feet away, looking like he'd accidentally swallowed his own tongue. He clasped his hands in front, trying to appear professional under his embarrassment. I shoved Blekket off me, wiping my mouth with the back of my hand, and fixed my dress so I looked presentable.

"Sorry to…interrupt, but Queen Seraphina sent me to find out what was taking you both so long. Everyone else is already at the party."

"Tell her we're leaving now and will be there soon," Blekket replied, stepping in front of me to shield my indecent state from Lev.

"Of course, Your Highness." He nodded, then dashed off down the hall. I didn't know a face could blush so violently.

"Poor Lev." I sighed, frowning at his shadow.

"Poor *Lev?*" Blekket said. "Poor *me.* I'm about to walk into a party with the entire kingdom, my sister, and my *parents,* and my pants are now very uncomfortable."

"I don't feel the least bit sorry for you." I blew him an air kiss before scuttling down the hall towards the courtyard.

"You should," he shouted, then rushed to follow in my wake.

We arrived at the party thirty minutes later.

The trees were festooned with dazzling bulbs of light that reflected the setting sun, tables positioned off to the side of the sand with plates of sushi, drinks, and other various dishes. Almost the entire kingdom showed up to the celebration, the beach teeming with townsfolk, dressed in their nicest blue garb. Raevon and Pessy were huddled together close to the water, both looking radiant. Pessy had borrowed a dress from Raevon—a teal blue, velvet, floral embroidered cocktail dress, with spaghetti straps, a sweetheart neckline, pleated skirt, and an asymmetric hem. Her blonde hair was curled, tumbling down her chest in waves. Raevon wore a light blue sleeveless gown with fixed shoulder straps, a scoop neck, and an A-line skirt with a sequin fringe trim, offset with a front slit and covered all over with sequined mesh. Her black, long hair was blow-dried straight, framing her sharp jawline like the hood of a cloak. Raevon was tucking Pessy's hair behind her ear, and Pessy was gazing at Raevon as if she were paradise personified.

"You guys are so stunning together," I said in greeting, accepting a glass of champagne from one of the servers.

"Look who decided to show up," Pessy teased, making me grimace.

I couldn't begin to fathom what Raevon must've told her she heard inside Blekket's bedroom.

"You look beautiful, Tymp." Raevon then raised her eyes to her brother. "You...not so much."

"How dare you," he gasped, feigning offense.

"I think your ego will survive the blow." Blekket pounded a fist against his chest and doubled back, pretending to be wounded. She just flipped him the middle finger.

"Tympany! Blek! There you are." Seraphina and Demetrio advanced towards us, hand in hand. Seraphina was dressed in a royal blue gown with thin straps and a soft, cowl neckline, the bodice fitted and moving into a sleek column skirt with a full length hem. Her hair was tied back in a tight bun, her cornflower blue gaze accentuated by the hue of her gown. Demetrio wore all black apart from the tunic he had on underneath his coat, which was a rich sapphire that matched the colour of his eyes.

"Sorry we took so long," I said, evading Blekket's smirk.

"No need to apologise. You're here now." She kissed her son on the cheek.

"I wanted to say something, with everyone here." We all braced ourselves, just in case whatever Demetrio said was negative. "I had my reservations about this plan of yours, Tympany, but I wanted to pride you all on the work you've put into this settlement the past few months. It's incredibly impressive and deserves to be commended."

"Thank you, Dad." Blekket twisted an arm pointedly around my waist. "We appreciate that."

"I look forward to seeing your hard work in person tomorrow." The Queen and King were going to travel with us to the outskirts and assist moving in all the residents. It would be their first time seeing the village.

"Me too," Seraphina added, taking my hand. *Tympany and Blek look so good together*, she thought.

"We can't wait for you to see it," I responded, squeezing her hand back.

"Are you guys hungry? There's lots of sushi, Tympany." I opened my mouth to reply, but Blekket cut me off.

"I had some dessert before we left," he announced to the group. I didn't even want to know how red I was.

"Why would you eat before you came here?" Seraphina asked critically.

"It was too good to pass up."

Pessy caught on to the insinuation from the way my face blazed, looking like she was about to burst.

Why would he say that in front of his mother? she mused.

Because he's a masochist who's asking to get stabbed. She bit her lip to keep herself from laughing.

"Go get some sushi, and enjoy yourselves. You've all earned it." Seraphina curled her arm around Demetrio, leading him towards the horde of Esteopians. Raevon tugged on Pessy's hand, and the two went off in the direction of the food.

"I'm going to murder you in your sleep," I hissed at Blekket once everyone was a safe distance away.

"No, you won't. Who else will put up with your night babbling?"

"Pessy doesn't seem to mind."

"I know you're trying to make me jealous, angel, but that image only made my pants tighter."

I rolled my eyes. "I hate you."

"You don't hate me. You love me." My lashes fluttered, my mouth popping open.

I was so close to answering *yes, I do*, when we were interrupted.

"Was wondering when you'd bother to make an appearance," Sanders joked, patting Blekket forcefully on the back.

"You know me," he replied with a haughty grin. "Always one to make an entrance."

"And you sure made one, with this beauty on your arm." Sanders bent down and pecked me on the cheek very quickly. Blekket tightened his arm around my waist, dragging me closer when Sanders pulled away. He didn't even notice. "Hello, Tympany. Or should I say, Angel."

"Hi, Sanders. It's nice to officially meet you."

"I suppose I understand why you kept your identity a secret when we first met, but I'm honoured to know I served the Goddess of the Heart and Mind."

I laughed, "Trust me, the honour was all mine."

"I hope I get the chance to serve you many, many more times."

"You will. Your fried fish is one of my favourite things I've ever eaten."

"That's the highest of compliments I could be paid, coming from someone who's tasted the finest cuisines in Kylantis."

"And none nearly as good as yours." Sanders beamed with pride.

"I have to say, I didn't know what to expect meeting a Goddess, but you are as radiant on the inside as you are on the outside, Tympany." He lifted my hand, planting a kiss on my knuckles.

"Such a charmer," I said with mock disapproval. He chuckled, shrugging his shoulders bashfully.

"Alright, Sanders. Go find your wife." Blekket shooed him away from me.

"Why? Worried I might swoop in on your girl?" Sanders snickered, while Blekket's lips wilted in a frown.

"I'm sure Ceanna will find that hilarious. Let me go get her and tell her all about it."

"Alright, alright, I see your point. I'm leaving. Tympany." He bowed his head respectfully. "Always a pleasure."

"Same here." I gathered the skirt of my dress, curtseying.

"Debbie downer," Sanders spat at Blekket, making me giggle as he careened away.

Blekket turned to me and squinted his eyes. "Remember what I said about you being a flirt?"

I scowled. "I wasn't flirting with Sanders."

"Sure sounded like it." I couldn't tell if he was joking or not.

"I didn't peg you as the jealous type, Blek."

"Yeah, well, I wasn't, until I met you." His hands slid down my waist, resting on my hips before he leaned in to kiss my temple. "I'm going to get us something to eat. I assume you want sushi."

"You assumed correctly." I went to place a kiss on his jaw, but he quickly jerked his head back.

"Tympany! We're in public!"

"Oh, so it's okay for you to lewdly tease me about how I *taste* in front of your parents, but not okay for me to kiss you on the cheek?"

"I can't help it. You're the finest dessert I've ever consumed. I can't wait to have it again." I was about to argue, but he leaned in, stole a quick kiss, then turned on his heel and stalked off, calling out over his shoulder, "I win that round!"

I just shook my head at him, struggling to suppress a smile.

I found myself enticed by the water. I crouched down to the soft sand and pressed my hand against the damp beach, shutting my eyes. I felt the ground vibrate through the tips of my fingers before Alexandria appeared, parting the waves. She galloped over to where I stood at the water's edge.

"Hi, Lex," I greeted her, trailing my fingers over her variegated scales. She released a neigh that was more akin to a purr, slanting her cheek into my palm.

"She's not usually so friendly," I heard a voice behind me marvel. Solara was dressed in a purple one shoulder jumpsuit, with a draped panel at the front and a wide leg. They remained on the dry part of land, dodging the water when it lapped onto shore.

"I wasn't sure if you were coming," I said, my hand slipping off Alexandria. Once I was no longer touching her, the Hippocampus dove back beneath the waves, slithering off towards the horizon.

"I wanted to celebrate all your hard work, as well as us getting our merfolk back in the ocean."

"That's what you *really* wanted to celebrate." Solara's lips twitched up.

"I had high hopes for meeting you, Tympany, from what your brother's said, but you exceeded all expectations."

"So did you." I took a step closer, scratching my nail against my champagne glass. "How long have you and Caspian been…together?"

Their smile expanded. "Since before you were born," Solara answered, which startled me.

"You're over five thousand years old?"

"I'm the ruler of the merfolk, the first of my kind. Your brother created me to protect the seas."

"He *created* you?" They nodded.

"I'd never know the world without Caspian. He's literally given me life. I owe everything to him."

The mermaid spoke with such a tender fondness that even I felt swept up in the passion they clearly shared.

"Does it bother you he still supports Sleotha? That he doesn't stay here with you?"

"Of course not. I understand his obligations, and he understands mine. We'd never ask one another to give anything up. I also know, if I ever need him for anything, he will drop whatever it is he's doing to be here for me. That's all I need to know. The rest of the particulars aren't nearly as important."

When Solara set a hand on my shoulder, I heard in their thoughts, *I feel for her. She has no idea what it means to be a God.* They withdrew their hand when I winced.

"Are you okay?"

"Yes," I stammered. "I'm fine. Just a bit warm."

Their eyes assessed whether or not to believe me, but eventually decided it wasn't worth the hassle of pestering.

"Have a good evening, Tympany."

"You too." I watched them walk away, disintegrating into the sea of Esteopians flocking the beach.

I felt a tap on my shoulder and spun around, expecting it to be Blekket. I was surprised and disappointed to find Demetrio there instead.

"I meant what I said earlier," he swore in earnest. "I think what you've done in the outskirts is impressive. You should be very proud."

"Thank you, Demetrio. I appreciate that." I was hoping that would be all, but he lingered, so I knew he wasn't done.

"I know you and I haven't always seen eye to eye since you got here—"

"That's an understatement," I blurted. He knit his lips, narrowing his eyes. "Sorry. Please, continue."

"I've seen how you've embraced Esteopia since staying with us. You fought for us at Frofsea. You saved Blekket's life from the drogon. You convinced Solara to deploy the merfolk as protection detail for the kingdom, while the army constructed the village. You visited the outskirts every day to survey the progress. I was skeptical of you when you arrived because I was worried your support wasn't genuine, and for that, I sincerely apologise, Tympany. You have kept every promise you made to us, and I truly couldn't imagine a better person to be with my son."

I'm not sure what possessed me to be brutally honest with him, but I felt swayed by his apology to confess, "When I came to Esteopia, I did not originally come here with good intentions. My mother sent me to gather intel on your plans for the war, then have me feed that information back to Sleotha, so they would have the advantage. But after I met you and your family, after I saw Esteopia for its beauty and kindness, after I saw what happened in Eveium and experienced the destruction in Frofsea, I decided my allegiance lay with Esteopia. I have fallen completely in love with your kingdom, your people...and your son. I promise, I will do everything in my power to help you win this war, if it's the last thing I do."

Demetrio looked like he had absolutely no idea what to do with this information, but also like he was seeing the sun for the first time.

"Thank you for your candor, Tympany," he choked out, reverence in his eyes. "You are truly nothing like your family."

This reminded me of what I heard in his thoughts the night of the ball, what he'd said about my father.

"There's something I've been meaning to ask you, but we've never had a moment alone, so I haven't had the chance." Demetrio waved his hand, granting me permission. "Have you met my father?"

"Your father?" he repeated. "No. Why do you ask?"

"If you haven't met him, then why do you hate him?"

"Who told you I hate your father?" The one advantage I had over everyone was that no one knew I could read minds.

I couldn't disclose that now, so I answered, "Call it intuition," and shrugged.

Demetrio tapped the side of his glass, tracing the mouth of it with his index finger as he considered his answer carefully.

"No, I haven't met your father, so I can't speak from personal experience, but stories have been told about him for generations."

"What bad word could someone say about him?" Isaias was a sweetheart compared to my stern mother.

"What I heard from *my* father was, before your mother found and married your father, before you and your siblings were born, she used to rule the two kingdoms equally. She treated Sleotha and Esteopia the same, and had no favourites. It was only after she met Isaias and made him King that she turned her back on Esteopia, teaching her children to despise us as well. Isaias is the reason the Gods favour Sleotha."

Now it was *my* turn to be speechless. "Do you know why he turned her against Esteopia?"

Demetrio shook his head.

"It was never divulged, but knowing he's responsible for all those years of neglect is enough to make me loathe him." He cocked his head. "You really don't know any of this, do you?"

"No," I mumbled, clutching the stem of my glass so tautly that I nearly shattered it. "If that's true, then I'm sorry."

"You don't need to apologise for your father's actions, Tympany. They do not reflect who you are."

"Thank you, but I still feel like I should. If I don't, then no one will." Demetrio's eyes softened before he set a hand on my shoulder. *Ser's right,* he thought. *She's going to make a wonderful Queen.*

I watched Demetrio trek through the thick sand, enfolding his arms around his wife's waist from behind, joining her conversation.

I thought about what Caspian said when I asked him why the Gods favoured Sleotha. He'd said it wasn't his story to tell, which meant he knew the answer and just didn't want to tell me. He knew Isaias was what caused the rift between Esteopia and the Gods, which probably meant my other siblings knew as well.

Why did everyone have all the answers but me?

"Hey," Blekket cooed, circling one arm around me before presenting a plate of yellowtail and avocado rolls.

"Thank you," I squealed, popping one into my mouth.

"What were you and my dad discussing?" He tried to pilfer a sushi from my plate, but I swatted his hand away. "Seriously? I got them for you, and you won't let me have one? I haven't eaten all day."

"You should've thought of that when you got me a plate and not yourself." His jaw dropped to the floor, his expression so adorable that I ended up sharing my plate with him anyway. "And, to answer your question, he wanted to apologise for being so hard on me since I got here. It was actually…very sweet."

"I'm happy to hear he apologised to you," Blekket spoke through chews. "Dad's been a real dipshit since you arrived."

"He's not a dipshit. He's a concerned father and king. *You're* the dipshit." Blekket glowered at me while I munched happily on my sushi.

"There's something I want to show you," he said, all at once serious. He took the now empty plate from me, setting it down on one of the passing server's trays, and proffered his hand. "Will you come with me?" Saying yes was the easiest decision I'd ever made.

I slipped my hand into his and allowed him to bring me over to where Krystal was tied to one of the tree trunks.

"You sure you can handle this?" I teased, mounting Krystal with ease, then offered Blekket my hand to pull him up.

He was too proud to accept it and situated his foot in her stirrup, hoisting himself up onto her croup all on his own. He twined his arms around my waist and snuggled his thighs against mine, his lips grazing my temple.

"I can handle *anything*, sweetheart. You should know that by now."

I inclined down so I was near Krystal's ear, pretending to ask her, "Is the extra weight of his head too much for you? Should I buck him off?"

"I hate you," Blekket laughed.

"No, you don't." I shifted back to look at him.

His eyes scorched with adoration. "You're right. I don't." He leaned in close and kissed my brow ridge.

"Where are we going?" I asked, gathering Krystal's reins.

"Tympany's Province." He rested his chin on my shoulder, then kissed the spot below my ear that sent a shudder down my spine every time he tended to it. Krystal unfurled her massive wings and took off.

The clouds formed a perfect line-up amongst the sea of blue beneath us, as if they were boats safely moored in a celestial harbour. They were tinted with a rosy glow from the setting sun, releasing fissures of bright light that painted our faces in pink streaks. Adrenaline mingled with the wind and pumped through my veins, igniting every part of my body that was connected to Blekket's through the precious contact we shared. Flying had always been my safe haven from my troubles.

Now, it was in the arms of this magnificent Neraid who'd stolen my heart.

Soaring through the clouds, we got a bird's eye view of the village we'd spent months designing and managed to build in two weeks. It was modelled similarly to Acadia, the houses composed of the same wood and garlanded in blue cloth on the roofs, but what made it stand out were the flags we had positioned at every house. It was Blekket's idea, which was unanimously supported.

Those flags, proudly displaying the symbol of Esteopia's resilience, were the biggest middle finger we could give to the Gods and Sleotha, who would be forced to stare at them waving in the wind for all of eternity.

We landed at the bottom of the Geddesia Mountains. Blekket slipped off Krystal's back and landed roughly on the ground. I burst out laughing, leaping down to help him up. He stood, then wiped the dirt off his pants.

"I didn't laugh at you when you fell," he grumbled.

"You would've, if Pessy hadn't done it first." I set my hands on my hips. "So. What did you want to show me?"

"This." He gesticulated with his hand towards the house that sat directly across from the mountains. It was slightly bigger than the others around it, and the flag sticking out of the roof was larger than its neighbours.

"You wanted to show me one of the houses?"

"Not just any house." He snaked his arms around my shoulders from behind. "I wanted to show you *our* house." My neck cracked from the speed in which I spun around.

"*Our* house?" He nodded slowly, his expression as warm as a kindled flame. "You...you built me a house?"

"Correction. I built *us* a house." I was completely out of words.

"How…how did I not…know?"

"I had Lev keep it a secret." He laced his fingers through mine and began leading me over to it.

I was in such shock that he had no problem towing me inside.

The interior was just as quaint and picturesque as the exterior. The furniture resembled the palace, all plush blue velvet couches and armchairs, marble counters and a gorgeous light fixture above the dining room table that looked like bubbles. The bathroom was stocked with both a shower and a bath basin, the knobs carved in the shape of silver teardrops. My favourite room had to be the bedroom, which possessed the same gossamer canopy above the bed as the one in my bedchamber, the duvet a garish blue and textured like rivulets of water, with a side table beside it made of maple.

"This is incredible," I whispered to myself, in awe. He'd taken everything I loved about the palace and duplicated it.

"You like it?" He sounded nervous.

"Of course I like it! It's beautiful!" I turned to face him. "Where are Raevon and Pessy going to live?"

"The house right next door," he replied. "I'm going to show it to them tomorrow. They have no idea."

My lips decided to join him in the movement and widened into probably the biggest smile I'd ever had on my face.

"I can't believe you did this," I marvelled, looking around.

"I wanted us to have a place of our own. Somewhere we could come together and just be us, without any drama or stress." He reached for my hand, tugging me closer. "You've become my safe place to land, Tymp, and I thought, the only way I could repay you, would be to give you one in return."

"Blek," I moaned, stretching up on my tiptoes to embrace him around the neck. "This is the nicest thing anyone has ever done for me. I love it more than words can express. Thank you so much."

"Oh, sweetheart," he groaned into my throat, hugging me back. "You don't realise how much you've given me since we met. Before I found you, I was so lost. It was getting closer to my birthday, and I felt all this pressure from my parents and everyone around me to be someone I wasn't. Then, you came into my life, with your big ego—"

"Hey!" I leaned back to glare at him.

"And your beautiful heart," he continued, cupping my face, "and you gave me permission to be myself. For the first time in what felt like forever, I didn't have to pretend with someone. You let me be me, even if you tease me for it."

"You're easy to tease," I said, tracing my thumbs over the faint freckles dusted on his cheeks.

"You've made me happier than I ever thought I could be, by being nothing but purely yourself since the moment we met. I cherish you, Tympany, and I will spend the rest of my life making it up to you for all you've given me."

My eyes glazed over with tears, which Blekket was kind enough to bend down and apprehend for me with his lips. If I wasn't already irrevocably anchored to him, that would've sealed the deal.

"So? Will you live here with me?"

The hope outlining his question deteriorated the last bit of the wall that surrounded my heart.

"Yes, of course I will, you worrywart," I exclaimed, making him laugh into my mouth when we kissed.

"Thank the Gods," he chuckled. "It would've been kind of awkward if you said no. What would I have done with the house?"

"Given it to Lev, or Sanders."

"Sanders has a nice pub in Acadia he shares with his loving wife. He doesn't get my beautiful home with my beautiful girl."

"The girl wouldn't come with the house," I pointed out.

"Damn right she wouldn't," he growled, giving my hips a possessive squeeze. "You're stuck with me, Tympany. I hope you've come to terms with what that means. I'm never letting you get away."

"Good." I cuddled closer. "This is the only place I want to be."

Chapter Eighteen

"He built you a HOUSE?!" Pessy's scream reverberated off the walls, causing the chandelier to tremble.

"Be louder," I joked. "I don't think our parents heard you all the way up in Kylantis."

"He built you a *house*," she repeated. I worried her lashes would get caught in her eye sockets at the rapidity they were fluttering at.

"Not just me. You and Raevon too."

"WHAT?!" I flinched at the sound, covering my ears.

"I shouldn't have told you that. Blek wanted to surprise you guys with it today. Don't tell Raevon, please."

"I won't, I promise." Pessy's jaw refused to pick up off the floor. "Wow. A house. For us? That's *so* sweet of him."

"I know." I sighed, climbing into the lime green jumpsuit I'd selected for today, with spaghetti straps, a wrap neckline over the chest, and a matching sash around the waist. I twisted my hair back in a tight bun, clean off my face, and tucked my dagger into the belt, slipping my feet into my sandals.

"You know what this means, right?" I shook my head. "He loves you. Blekket Elrod, the future *King* of Esteopia, is totally in love with you. You have the Prince wrapped around your finger!" I just shook my head at her with a shit-eating smile. "It also means we're never going back to Kylantis." I couldn't tell from her tone if that saddened her or not.

I knew how I felt about it—Kylantis never felt like my home, not the way Esteopia or Blekket did.

"Does that make you sad?" I asked her.

"I'm not sure. Nothing makes me happier than being with Raevon, and home wouldn't be home without you. It's just…my mum…"

"I know." I plucked her hand off her knee, intertwining our fingers. "Blekket built our houses right across from the Geddesia Mountains. You can climb up the mountain whenever you want and go see her."

"Damn. He really thought of everything, huh?" She glided her sword into the holster at her waist, tracing her thumb over the hilt, where there was an engraved Z in honour of her father. "I wonder what Dad would think of all this."

"He'd be so proud of you, and would embrace Raevon with open arms."

"He'd *love* Raevon. They'd be best friends." She opened the door, gesturing for me to go first. "I saw you and Demetrio talking at the party."

"He came to apologise for being so hard on me. It was actually very genuine. I also finally asked him about his connection to my father."

"What did he say?"

"Demetrio's never met him, but he was told my father is the reason the Gods favour Sleotha. He said my mother used to rule the kingdoms equally, but stopped answering Esteopia's prayers after she met my father and made him her king."

"That doesn't sound like Isaias at all." I'd been struggling with the same thought. My father was the one who instilled in me my values of justice, who taught me to never talk down to someone who was in a subordinate position, to always lead with kindness. I couldn't fathom what he had against Esteopia to persuade my mother to turn her back on them for so many centuries.

"Do you think he was lying?" I asked her.

"No, not lying, but he doesn't know your father personally, so how can he judge? A story could be just that, a *story*."

"I know, but it otherwise makes no sense why Roara flipped against Esteopia. The only person who could convince her to turn her back on her own people would be my father. I just don't understand why."

"Maybe someday, you can ask them."

"Maybe," I murmured. That would have to be in the distant future, after we won the war against Sleotha.

I couldn't face my family until we were victorious.

Seraphina, Demetrio, Raevon and Blekket were seated when we entered the dining hall. It was the first time I arrived where, when Demetrio welcomed me, there wasn't an ounce of disinclination in his smile.

"Hi, beautiful," Blekket greeted, seizing my hand under the table. I wondered if his parents' smiles would falter when they discovered his plan to move out of the palace and make his permanent residence with me in Tympany's Province. "You okay? You're pulling at your fingers, which usually means you're nervous about something."

Nothing was more validating as to why I loved him then how well he'd mastered my facial expressions, or how quickly he noticed a change in the way I moved my hands.

"I'm feeling a little anxious and not entirely sure why," I admitted to the table. I'd woken up that morning unsettled. While yesterday had been jam-packed with jubilation, today felt arduous, like I should be on guard. I hadn't been able to shake the taste of unease off my tongue since I got out of bed.

"It's a big day," he said understandingly. "We're moving the residents into their homes. I think everyone's a bit on edge."

"How do we plan on doing this safely?" I turned to Lev. My main concern was the quiet we'd heard from Sleotha suddenly rupturing in a brutal attack on the innocent citizens.

"We have a thousand soldiers already stationed at Tympany's Province," Lev answered. "We're moving the families in by groups of three, and for each family, there will be ten guards escorting them through the Dream Forest."

"Okay. Good." That made me feel a little better, but my heartrate refused to regulate in spite of the reassurance.

"It's going to be okay, Tymp," Blekket promised me. "Even if we do encounter the Sleothians, the entire army will be present. *And,* most importantly, we have *you.* We're guaranteed a win."

He kissed my knuckles, the treasurable contact sizzling up my arm, pooling low in my belly.

"And you call *me* a worrywart," he mumbled, killing my libido and causing my eyes to narrow in a scowl.

"I guess we're perfect for each other, then." I wasn't prepared for how his smile would knock the wind out of me.

"Yes, we are," he concurred, his voice kitten soft.

"How long has it been since you left Esteopia?" I asked Seraphina, scooping some honeydew onto my plate.

"Gods, how long has it been, darling?" She deferred to Demetrio.

"Twenty-one years, maybe more," he replied, scratching his head as he tried to compute the numbers.

"How many times have you been to Sleotha?"

"Three. Once when I was a child, with my mother, once when I was first crowned Queen, and once with Blek and Rae, when Blek was nine and Raevon was two. All those times were for business meetings to discuss trade, never having to do with the war itself."

"So you've met Jacinda?" Seraphina shook her head.

"You haven't met her?" Pessy gasped.

"She always sends a proxy to speak on her behalf."

"Don't you think that's strange?" Why would the Queen summon them if not to speak in person?

"It's incredibly strange, and what's also strange is she *never* comes here. She always expects us to travel to her, then never bothers to show her face." Seraphina made a scornful *tsk* noise with her tongue. "It's disgusting if you ask me."

"The peak of entitlement," Demetrio agreed.

"Do you know anything about what the quality of life is like for the Sleothians in the villages?" I wondered. "Do you know if they feel deserted by the Queen, since they never see her?"

"What I've heard is, the Fiery Folk make sure the Sleothians never lose faith in Jacinda and keep her presence alive in the villages. The Sleothians worship Jacinda like a God. I can't necessarily speak on their quality of life, since I don't live there myself, but I can't imagine it's good when there's no transparency with your ruler and you pray to the Gods for everything, rather than try to fix problems yourself. Their dependence on the Gods is telling to me about the way their government treats them."

"We've learned to be very self-sufficient here," Demetrio added. "We know the Gods, besides you and Caspian, aren't going to listen to our prayers, so if there's an issue that arises, we must deal with it ourselves."

"It's a healthier way to live," I remarked, "but you shouldn't have ever felt like you couldn't depend on the Gods."

"I agree with you on that, but it is what it is." Seraphina shrugged like this was nothing, but how she'd just come to accept this as a norm angered me. There should never have been an imbalance to yield to.

It didn't matter if it was my mother's fault, or my father's—both were to blame for letting the rift go on as long as it had.

"Well, once we win this war and claim the land of Sleotha, I will ensure the Gods never ignore you again," I swore, curling the hand that wasn't inside Blekket's into a fist on the table.

"I'll hold you to it," Seraphina quipped, winking at me.

"Let's make a toast." Demetrio lifted his glass of juice, gesturing for all of us to do the same. "Here's to the success of Tympany's Province. May it thrive and prosper for many years to come."

"Until its last drop," we all said in unison.

"And cheers to the Goddess herself," Seraphina added, raising her glass to me, "for coming up with the idea to claim the outskirts in the first place."

"To the Elrods, and to Esteopia," I hailed, clinking my glass with Blekket's before taking a long sip of the crisp Argent Ocean water.

Blekket draped his arm around my shoulders as we headed to the stables to collect our horses. Seraphina and Demetrio lead the way, with Pessy and Raevon behind us. When I turned around, I caught Raevon nuzzling her face into Pessy's neck, while Pessy threw her head back and laughed. There was nothing I adored more than seeing Pessy happy, than seeing someone embrace my best friend for everything she was, someone to worship her for her quirks and strength and huge capacity for love. I'd spent so many years watching Pessy pine after Calliope, and even though she insisted it was never serious and she wouldn't act on those sentiments, I knew it weighed on her to not have those feelings reciprocated fully.

I worried for centuries about the loss of Zion crippling her ability to let someone in, knowing there was a possibility of losing them someday. I was inspired by Pessy's motivation to live in the present, to not let thoughts of the future plague the happiness she'd found with Raevon.

I would endeavor to mirror that attitude with Blekket, even if it sucked up all my brain power to do so.

"They look really good together," Blekket said, stroking his thumb along the nape of my neck. "I've never seen Raevon smile like that."

"Has Raevon been with a lot of people?" This would be a conversation I'd never repeat to Pessy, but I was curious.

"No. She was with one girl for a bit, Danielle, but she was a real piece of work. She treated Raevon like shit. Rae's so full of life, and she was so dimmed by Dani. She was so in love with the idea of love that she tolerated a lot of shit she shouldn't have for way longer than she should've. She should never have diminished herself to make Dani feel superior." He looked back at where the girls were huddled together. "It makes me so fucking happy to see someone love her the way she deserves, who sees her light and isn't intimidated by it. I'm honestly in awe of Raevon. I always have been. She's a way better person than I could ever be, and she deserves this more than anyone." It warmed my heart, the ardor he spoke with when talking about his little sister. "What about Pess? Has she been with a lot of people?"

"Um...define *a lot* of people..." I felt disloyal talking about Pessy's romantic history, especially considering she was way more experienced, given her age. "No girl Pessy's ever been with has ever been serious, or even constitutes a real relationship. Losing her father really shook her, and she closed herself off from feeling. She had a crush on my older sister for a while, but I think she latched onto Callie because she knew it was unattainable, and that was safer than putting herself in a position where it might actually work out. It thrills me to see her with Raevon. I think she's needed to feel seen for a long time as someone separate from the Goddess of the Heart and Mind. I'm so happy she finally found someone who looks at her and doesn't see me."

"And what about you? What do *you* need?" His lips grazed my temple.

"To feel like my own person. To stand on my own and not be afraid I'm doing something wrong because it's the opposite of what I was told to think. To feel like more than just a Goddess." I flushed. "I don't know if that makes sense."

"It does. Completely." He kissed the crown of my head.

"What do *you* need, Blek?" I tucked my hand in the back pocket of his breeches, laying my head on his chest.

"This." He buried his nose in my hair. "I need a lifetime of *this*."

"We can arrange that." I twisted my arms around his waist, meeting him in the middle when he bent down to kiss me.

We mounted our steeds and began our trek to Tympany's Province, Lev and Alsandair leading the way with five other Esteopian soldiers. We were situated in the order of hierarchy, with Raevon behind the militia, Blekket after her, Seraphina and Demetrio, and then me with Pessy at my side, five other soldiers behind us protecting the rear. Since the sun was obscured by a film of clouds today, Seraphina and Demetrio rode on Ashrays, which looked exactly like regular horses. Seraphina's Ashray resembled an Appaloosa horse with its colourful spotted coat pattern, white with dark spots that flowed out over the entire body. His name was Domino. Demetrio's Ashray was the same shading as a Clydesdale horse, the body a deep mahogany brown with white markings on the face and legs. He'd named his steed Bonnibel, Bonnie for short, after his grandmother.

"If the sun were to come out right now, what would happen to them?" I asked Seraphina as we approached the Dream Forest.

"If we were to see any sun, we'd try to find some shade to step under. If that wasn't an option, they would turn into water, and we'd climb onto one of your horses."

"But what happens to the horses when they turn into puddles? Does it hurt? How do they come back to their regular form?"

"It doesn't hurt them. When it turns nightfall and there's no more light, their mare form is restored. They're trained, if they're not in a close vicinity to their owners, to just turn around and head for the palace."

"That's so cool," Pessy admired.

"I think so too." Seraphina scratched Domino behind the ear, and the Ashray whickered with delight.

Connected to the earth by hoof, Krystal made her way through the forest with ease, now used to the heavy, lethargic fog from our months of traveling to the outskirts. Bonnie and Domino were a tad slower, jolted by the thickness of the haze.

"I forgot how gruesome this forest is to walk through," Seraphina said through a yawn. "It really is quite strong."

"I hope the families made it out alright." I abhorred the thought of the townsfolk struggling through the mist.

"I'm sure the fatigue left them the minute they entered the village," Blekket assured, turning back to flash me an arrogant smile. "I'm usually right."

I leaned in towards him and squinted my eyes, as if I was trying to spot something from far away.

"What? Do I have something on me?" He patted his shirt self-consciously.

"Careful. I think I see a crack in your neck from the weight of your big head." Seraphina barked out a laugh, the sound seeming to fragment the spell of the forest, stimulating the ether.

"That's something Rose would've said," she cackled. "You and my mother have a lot in common, Tympany."

"If that's true, then your mother must've been a wonderful woman."

"*Wow*," Blekket exclaimed. "And you say *I'm* the big-headed one! Is anyone else hearing this shit?"

"I did," Pessy replied, glowering at me censoriously.

"She was a delightful woman," Seraphina confirmed with a slump of her shoulders. "I miss her every day."

"What was your father like?" I'd never asked about her or Demetrio's families.

"Shamus was much quieter than Rose. Rosabella was notorious for her sense of humor. She was one of those larger than life souls. Dad was more reserved, but softer. Mum had quite the temper."

"Were you an only child?" She nodded. "What about you, Demetrio?"

"I have two brothers. Joseph and Dorian. They're both married with their own families in Acadia."

"Are your parents still alive?" He grimaced, shaking his head.

"They both died of old age several years ago. My mother, Ingrid, was very gentle. My father, Frederick, was tougher, but he had a good heart. He taught me and my brothers how to fight when we each turned twelve. I'm the oldest."

"What's your maiden name?" I remembered reading that Demetrio took Seraphina's name when they married.

"Holloway," he responded. "It's been years since I went by that, though. I'm proud to be an Elrod."

"We're proud to have you," Seraphina purred. I had to will my eyes away at the lecherous look that passed between them.

When I glanced over at Raevon, she was pretending to stick her finger in her mouth and vomit.

We escaped the Dream Forest, discovering Tympany's Province shrouded in faces. All the townsfolk were moving their belongings into their homes, the soldiers assigned to them standing guard outside. When the residents caught wind of our arrival, a round of applause swaddled the village in a merry, sweet song, the Esteopians bowing their heads out of respect and admiration for their Queen, King, and for me, the namesake of their new home. The sight of what we'd managed to accomplish finally coming to fruition robbed me of my next breath, replacing it with a sob. I was so proud of all the soldiers' hard work, so proud of how we'd successfully built a village which honoured the ones that came before it, that we made something beautiful out of the ash of what we'd lost.

It was a testament to the resilience of Esteopia, how not even fire could deteriorate their resolve to live.

"Uh oh. Tympany's about to cry. Don't make eye contact." I peered around Blekket to scowl at Pessy.

"I can compel you to shut up without looking at you, you know."

"I'm trembling with fear." She exaggerated a massive shudder, rubbing her hands over her arms, making everyone laugh. I ended up cracking a smile, extending my middle finger.

"I have a surprise for you guys," Blekket told Pessy and Raevon, beckoning them over with a gleaming smile.

While he took the girls away to reveal the cottage he'd built for them, Seraphina and Demetrio went off to intermingle with the townsfolk and offer their assistance. I found myself at the doorstep to my new home, the large Esteopian flag scuffing the clouds and drifting along the current of the wind. I tied Krystal's reins to the porch and took a seat, curling my arms around my knees and peeking up the Geddesia Mountains, where the apex was capped white in the rarefied wintry air.

The mountains stood there like a bold statement of the slowness of time, dropped into a world of ticking human-clocks. It was a reminder of how my life had been stagnant for centuries, the pillar in which all this war and inequity rested upon. I used to perch myself behind the gates of Kylantis and stare at the alpine path longingly, praying for the day I'd get to venture down to the Realm and see what else was out there.

I never dreamt I would find more than just adventure down here, that I'd find myself in addition to love.

I heard Raevon's scream of excitement and turned my head to watch her leap into her brother's arms, exulting in her gift. It was then that I noticed something glint in the distance, a flash of light that flickered like a bulb on the cusp of dying out. It started out tiny, just a twinkle cut into the fabric of space, but then, the spark began to augment as it drew closer, the shape becoming more discernible.

It was a flaming arrow, hurdling towards the town.

I leapt off my feet and sprinted to arrest the missile, Blekket and Pessy calling out to me when I soared past them. I tracked the velocity in which it was traveling at and managed to catch the stem in my hand mid-air. I raised my head, my vision bleary from the smoulder. As the plumes of smoke cleared, the contour of bodies became more distinct, shielded in metal that looked like it was blazing. They were advancing towards us, carrying spears dipped in fire. The Fiery Folk were here.

I screamed, "Everyone, inside *now*!"

I hurled the arrow at the first Sleothian I saw, the flames eating up their screams in unanimity with them crumbling to the ground. Behind me, I heard pandemonium ensue as the Esteopian soldiers rushed the frightened townsfolk inside their houses. I considered for a half second grabbing Krystal and flying up there to see if any drogon accompanied the army, but I figured the Sleothians wouldn't be dumb enough to deploy them when they knew I could easily compel them to leave.

Blekket was at my side within seconds, followed by Pessy, Raevon, Lev, Alsandair, Demetrio, and Seraphina.

"Mum, can you fight?" Blekket asked in disbelief when he saw the sword in Seraphina's grip.

"What? You think just because I'm the Queen and I wear dresses every day that I don't know how to wield a weapon? That's very sexist, Blek." Blekket looked like he'd swallowed his tongue.

"I didn't mean it to be sexist. I've just never seen you fight before."

"Well, you're about to." Seraphina raced forward and swung her sword in the air, dismembering the Sleothian headed towards her. She divorced his arm from his person before she beheaded him with graceful dexterity, shunting his body into the inferno engulfing his former companion.

She kicked his skull to the side, then wiped the blood off her sword with the bottom of her skirt.

"You're my hero," I marvelled, in awe.

"And you're mine," she responded. "Behind you."

I spun around to find a Sleothian with their arm raised above their head, lunging for me. I caught the soldier's wrist, wrenching his arm behind his back. I dislocated his shoulder before slitting his throat, flinging him into the fire to join his friends. I ducked when a female Sleothian attempted to sever my head from my body.

I seized her calf and yanked it. She toppled onto her back, thwacking her head against the earth.

"You bitch," she growled at me. "I'm going to make you regret—" I drove my dagger into her open mouth, slicing through her vocal chords.

Someone grabbed me from behind, dragging the elastic out of my bun and snatching a cluster of my hair. I reached behind me, grabbing hold of the Sleothian's ears, and pitched them over my shoulder, directly into the raging fire. The resonance of a shrill battle cry alerted me of another solider approaching. I readied my dagger, turning on my heel, and plunged it into the Sleothian's chest. I noticed Blekket across the way, trapping a Sleothian in a headlock, the man writhing and jerking his hips to try and free himself. I darted over, Blekket holding him steady, and jabbed my dagger into his heart, clutching him by the throat and chucking him into the pile of incinerated bodies.

"Magnificent." Blekket breathed.

"Is there anything that doesn't turn you on?"

"If it includes you, I'm already a goner." Over his shoulder, I saw a Sleothian running towards us with an axe doused in flames.

"Blek!" I shouted.

Blekket dropped to his knees just in time, while I lurched forward and caught the man by the wrist before the axe made contact with anything solid, crushing his bones in my grip.

He yelped, releasing the hatchet.

Blekket came at him from behind, amputating the Sleothian's head from his body with his sword. He then launched the severed skull into the fire. The inferno vomited more smoke, the head joining the accumulated stack.

"I think we make a pretty good team," Blekket stated with pride.

"I think you're—"

Suddenly, I felt something tickle my spine, the front of my jumpsuit feeling strangely damp.

"Tympany!" Blekket shrieked in horror.

I looked down to try and understand why his face had grown so ashen. I discovered a sword prodded through my back, the tip of the knife-edge poking out of my chest. It didn't hurt—it felt more like an encumbrance on my lungs, like someone was sitting on top of me, then it was painful—but it did send a hazardous rage flooding through my bloodstream. I grabbed the sword by the hilt and skated it out of my back, my shoulders quaking with ire. I spun around to locate the proprietor of this blade.

The Sleothian's face drained of colour. He lost circulation in his legs from fright, tumbling onto the ground.

"Your Excellence," he stuttered, holding his hands up in surrender. "I'm sorry. I didn't realise it was you."

"So it would've been better if you thought I was someone else?"

"No! I mean…ye…I don't…we were told not to harm you."

"Well, you did." I gripped him around the throat and lifted him off his feet, his legs dangling in the air.

"Please don't kill me," the man beseeched. I strangled him a little harder.

"Tymp," Blekket cautioned from behind me.

It surprised me how he was trying to defend this Sleothian, who'd just stabbed me, literally, in the back.

"You will kill no more Esteopians," I ordered, his pupils dilating in response to my compulsion. **"You will leave Tympany's Province and never return. Go back to your own kingdom and stay there."** I flung him onto the ground, taking a step back.

All the Sleothians abruptly stopped fighting, dropping their weapons, just like they had the last time.

In unison, they repeated my words back to me.

"You will kill no more Esteopians. You will leave Tympany's Province and never return. Go back to your own kingdom and stay there." They marched in the direction of Sleotha, the indoctrinated choir echoing my words over and over until the sound faded in the distance along with them.

When they were gone, I peeked down at my now sullied jumpsuit with exasperation. It would take more than one wash to sluice the blood from the fabric, if soap and detergent even did the trick on material this light a colour.

"Are you okay?" Blekket asked, skimming his fingers over the cloth damp with my blood.

"I'm annoyed. I liked this jumpsuit." Blekket's smile was adoring.

"I will have a seamstress make you a thousand more in the exact same colour," he promised, then slanted his head to kiss me.

"Is everyone okay?" Demetrio inquired, surveying the sea of bodies for any of our own. I saw no blue or gold amongst the debris.

"That was amazing, Tympany," Seraphina prided, making me blush.

"The blade really didn't hurt you?" Raevon asked.

"No. It felt like someone was pinching me, only a bit harder than that. I feel normal, just with bloody clothes."

"That's so cool," she admired with a sigh.

I turned to Lev, who was standing a few feet away. "Now that the Sleothian army has been compelled not to return to Tympany's Province, I think the residents will be safe, but we should still have at least one hundred guards stationed here every day, maybe even more. We should never leave it unprotected."

"I agree," he said, holstering his sword in his scabbard belt. "Once Jacinda realises her army won't kill any Esteopians, she will assemble a new army who hasn't been compelled. We should always be prepared for that likelihood."

"What will we do if there's an instance where the Sleothians come, and Tympany isn't here to compel them?" Demetrio wondered.

"Since Blek and I will be living here, I should always be present in case there's an attack, but on the off chance I'm not here, a guard will come find me. I'll fly with Krystal and make sure I'm there to compel them away."

Seraphina and Demetrio's jaws dropped in sync with one another, which happened simultaneously with me realising what I'd just disclosed. I covered my mouth with my hand, looking up at Blekket contritely.

"Blek?" Demetrio faced his son. "Is that true? Do you and Tympany not plan on living in the palace?"

"Uh..." Blekket shifted on the balls of his feet. "I was going to tell you after we moved in all the residents. I didn't—"

The sound of a strangled gasp blanketed the group in a disconcerting chill, engrossing all of us to turn in unison to pinpoint where the noise came from. When I saw who it belonged to, and what caused it, the air was ripped from my lungs.

In the point ten seconds where shock paralysed me, it dawned on me what the strategy had been all along. The army was a smokescreen, a cover for just one Sleothian to creep through the village, hide behind one of the houses, and wait for me to compel the rest of the army away, so we'd believe we won. That false sense of security allowed that one Sleothian to fly under the radar and fire a single arrow.

Into the chest of the Queen of Esteopia.

"MUM!" Raevon screeched, the first of us to react. Her scream fractured the stupor, pouring adrenaline into my numb bones, and propelled me forward. I fell to my knees beside where Seraphina was spluttering up blood, while Pessy wrapped her arms around Raevon's shoulders.

"I'm so sorry," I sobbed, lifting Seraphina's head into my lap with trembling hands. "I didn't see the arrow. I didn't see it. I didn't see it."

"Don't...be...sorry," she choked out, sweat dribbling from her forehead. She raised a hand to cup my cheek. "Don't."

"Mum!" I heard Blekket yell from behind me, crouching to the earth so he could sit next to her. What little control I had over my sanity evaporated at the sight of him crying.

"Sweetheart," she moaned, entwining her fingers with his. "You're...going to be...an amazing king."

"I'm not ready," he stammered, tears torrenting down his cheeks. "Please, don't leave me. I'm not ready."

"You...need to...to be..." She coughed up more blood, her wheezing growing more pronounced.

"Tympany," Blekket gasped. It sounded like it ached him to choke out words. "Help her."

I knew what he meant when he said that. He wasn't asking me to heal her. He was asking me to ease her pain.

I set my hands, which were coated in her blood, on either side of her face, then commanded, **"You will feel no pain. Close your eyes, and go to sleep. Follow the light to where you see your mother waiting for you. When you're with her, you'll know you found peace."**

A single tear trickled down the side of Seraphina's face, dripping onto the soil.

She found my hand and squeezed it. "Take care of...my family, and my...my kingdom."

She then sucked in one final breath, falling very still.

I covered her eyes and whispered through tears, "With your last drop, you are free."

Chapter Nineteen

In the weeks following Seraphina's death, Blekket fell into a deep depression. He refused to come out of his room and interact with anyone who wasn't me. I hardly saw Pessy or Raevon because I spent all my time with his head on my chest, drowning in a silence that spoke volumes as to what was maiming him on the inside.

For him, this loss was layered. He wasn't just mourning the death of his mother and his Queen.

He was mourning his freedom, the life he envisioned we'd have together.

While his official coronation wouldn't happen for another three months, due to the tradition of allowing an appropriate length of time to pass between a monarch's death and holding a celebration to crown their heir, he was technically now the King of Esteopia. Demetrio promised Blekket he would resume his obligations as king for the month of mourning and give Blekket the time he needed to come to terms with everything, though we were all aware of the fact that no amount of time was enough for him to wrap his brain around what he was being forced to do.

When we were together, we didn't talk about it—we didn't talk at all, really. He didn't even have the energy to tease or charm or do anything except lie next to each other in the throes of agony.

I would've assumed he didn't want me there, if every time I tried to get up, he didn't grab my hand and yank me back.

The morning of the thirty-first day was the first time I heard him speak in a month. His head was reposed on my chest, and I was caressing his hair, kneading his scalp with my nails because I knew he liked it.

"It's my birthday next week." He said it so quietly that I first thought I imagined him uttering the words.

"What day?" I kissed his temple.

"The twentieth of March." I brushed a few strands of hair off his forehead. "I would've been expected to be crowned on my birthday. It would've happened right away, if Mum was still here. I guess I got my gift of time after all." He snorted bitterly, then turned his face into my neck, hiding from the world.

I'd tried not to say meaningless shit like *I'm sorry* that would do nothing to assuage his pain, but rather show with actions how I was there for him in any way he needed me.

Still, in moments like this, those words singed my tongue.

"What do you need from me?" was a more supportive and actively constructive thing to say.

"Just don't leave my side, please," he whispered, nuzzling my shoulder.

"Can I leave to go get dressed?" I asked in a playful manner, hoping to beget a smile.

It didn't work, but he kissed my cheek and answered, "Of course," releasing my waist so I could climb out of bed.

Pessy was in our bedchamber when I emerged through the door. She was wearing a dark navy gown with a sultry wrap bodice and long sheer sleeves, which gathered at the shoulder with button deets along the cuffs, all shaped by gauzy woven fabric. A self-tie cinched the fitted waist, atop a full skirt. Her blonde hair was pulled back in a low ponytail, her light blue eyes heightened by the torrent of sunlight pouring in through the open window.

"You look pretty," I told her, stripping off the black slip I had on and climbing into a dark navy jumpsuit made of twilled satin, with a round neckline, short sleeves, and a matching sash belt at the waist.

"Are you bringing your dagger?" Pessy asked, scrambling around the room to find her blade.

"Um...I don't think so. The whole army will be with us. There's no need for it."

"That's what I was thinking. I just wasn't sure where I would put it." She tossed it back onto her cot.

"How's Raevon doing?" I felt bad I hadn't checked on her, but I'd been preoccupied with her brother.

"As well as can be expected." I heard in Pessy's voice the heaviness I was suffering from as well, the burden of knowing, as supportive as we tried to be, there was nothing we could do for the Elrods to mitigate the heartache they were experiencing. For Pessy, it was magnified, because she knew what it felt like to lose a parent. Raevon was lucky she had a significant other who was intimate with this type of loss—I felt completely out of my depth with how to be there for Blekket. "How's Blek?"

"He tried to crack a joke earlier. It was the first time he's talked really in a month. It was a pretty dark joke."

"That sounds like Blek."

"Yeah, but I wouldn't call it progress, especially with the mourning tour today."

In Esteopia, it was custom for the royal family, after the death of their monarch, to travel to each of the villages so the people could pay homage to their fallen leader. We would voyage by horse through the towns, and the Esteopians would touch our legs when we passed to show their support in our bereavement. I thought it was a poignant gesture, but Blekket had been dreading the tour since we'd returned from Tympany's Province.

This would be his first time being presented before the people of Esteopia as their King, not their Prince.

"How're *you* doing, Pess?" I'd been worried about Seraphina's death triggering her, what it might bring up with her dad.

"I'm okay," she said with a shrug. "I just feel so bad for them. They don't deserve any of this."

"I know," I mumbled, shaking my head. It still didn't feel real. It felt like we were trapped in the Dream Forest, crippled by its thick fog, unable to move forward. "Have you seen Demetrio?"

"Only at breakfast. He hasn't really left his room either. Raevon was telling me more about how in love Seraphina and Demetrio were. Demetrio was like half a person before he met her. Seraphina was his whole world."

"This must be killing him." I planned to speak to him before we left for the tour.

Pessy set a hand on my shoulder and asked, "How are *you* doing, Tymp?" Tears pricked the corner of my eyes.

"I feel guilty," I answered, almost choking on a sob. I'd been wracked with shame since we left Tympany's Province. If I was faster in turning around, if I'd sensed that Sleothian sooner and caught the arrow before it reached Seraphina, she would still be here. Blekket did his best to assure me there was nothing I could've done, as well as Demetrio and Raevon, but I hadn't lost the acrid taste of remorse since that day, wishing I could've done more than just ease her pain.

I shouldn't have *had* to ease her pain—that was the point. She should've still been here.

"There was nothing you could do, Tymp. It happened so fast. None of us realised what was happening until it was too late." She wrapped her arms around me and lay her head on my shoulder. I set my hand over her wrist, giving it an appreciative squeeze. "What I was really asking was, how do you feel about Blekket becoming king?"

"I don't really have an opinion about it," I answered. "I know he's struggling, and I want to be there for him in any way he needs."

"What if part of that is you becoming his Queen?" I jerked away from her, stumbling back.

"What do you mean?"

"Blekket is supposed to be married when he takes the throne. While he has some time before his coronation, he has to marry in the next three months. Do you honestly think he's going to choose some random person as his Queen when he has you?" She arched a brow. "You really haven't thought about this?"

"He might not end up on the throne," I argued, panic seizing my throat. "He might find a way out of it."

"No, he won't, Tymp. I'm sorry, but it's naïve of you to think that."

"*Don't* call me naïve," I snapped, my fingers balling into fists. Pessy raised her hands in defense.

"I wasn't calling *you* naïve, but it's naïve to think he can avoid this. He's going to be king, Tympany. You need to make peace with that now, just as much as he has to. He's going to be king."

"Who knows. Maybe Raevon will take the throne, and you'll be the new Queen of Esteopia."

"Oh Gods," Pessy gasped, covering her mouth to quell a gag. "Don't even joke about that."

"I'm not joking. If Blekket declined the crown and Raevon was forced to take the throne, if she asked you to marry her, would you? Would you be the Queen of Esteopia?"

Pessy got quiet as she gave it serious thought, taking a seat at the foot of my bed.

She drummed her fingers on the duvet. "Have they ever had two Queens on the throne?"

"What does that matter? Now's as good a time as any." Pessy dropped her chin into her palm, exhaling a hefty sigh.

"If Raevon had no choice but to take the throne and asked me to marry her, I would say yes."

"Seriously?!" I was *not* expecting that.

"I'm not going to make her do it alone, but we're speaking hypothetically here. That's not going to happen."

"I'm shocked you'd say yes." It proved how much Pessy loved her that she'd even consider the idea. Did my reluctance mean I didn't love Blekket as much as I thought I did?

"I mean, I'm saying, theoretically, I'd say yes, but I honestly have no idea how I would react if that ended up happening. But I'd like to think, if that situation presented itself, I would put my personal fears aside if it meant I could be with the woman I love. If being Queen was the only way I could stay with Raevon, then I'd do it. I wouldn't be necessarily happy about it, but I'd do it." She cocked her head. "Seriously, Tymp. Are you prepared to lose Blek? To see him marry someone else? Cause that's what would happen if he asks you to be his Queen, and you say no."

The thought of losing him, of not spending even a day without Blekket at this point, made me feel like I was dying. The prospect was so painful I couldn't even entertain it, couldn't even let myself go there without sinking into despair. But was being Queen really a price I could pay to insure a future with the man I loved?

I remembered what Blekket said the night of the ball, his reasons for not wanting to be king.

I don't want to be tied down to a throne where everyone expects me to prevail, even when I might not. I don't want to be responsible for people, only to fail them. That's too much pressure for one person.

Would it be any less pressure for two?

"I just don't understand *why* Blekket has to marry anyone to be king," I said eventually. "Why's that even a requirement?"

"It's outdated, I agree, but we're not in a position to judge. It's *their* custom."

"Doesn't matter. I still think it's stupid." I plopped down next to her on the bed, dropping my head into my hands.

"What're you going to do if Blekket proposes to you?"

"I have literally no idea." I groaned between my fingers. "Why is this happening? Why did she have to die? Why did my family let this happen?"

"I think we can blame your family for a lot, but I don't know if they're responsible for this."

I lifted my head to look at her.

"They allowed the Sleothians to attack Tympany's Province, Pess. We were right beneath them, and they didn't intervene. *I* was right beneath then, and they did *nothing*. What if I'd been injured somehow? They didn't care." Pessy's lips knit shut, because even she knew she couldn't argue with that.

When Jaxith refused to heal Cosmina was the first time I felt deserted by my family, but this was ten times worse. I'd been right beneath them, in peril, and they'd done absolutely nothing besides sit back and let the destruction transpire, sit back and let an innocent woman die. I didn't need to know their rationale to know it was baseless—Seraphina didn't deserve to die, just like all the Esteopians in Eveium and Frofsea, and all the Sleothians who were murdered when Esteopia ransacked the countryside on my birthday. None of these mortals deserved to be in this war, and it was my family, particularly my mother's fault it had gone on as long as it had. If they had the power to manipulate simple things, like food or music, or more convoluted matters, like weather, or healing someone's wounds and sickness, then they had the power to solve the enmity between the kingdoms. They were *choosing* to let their people suffer, including their cherished Sleothians, many of whom we'd slaughtered in the attacks on both Frofsea and Tympany's Province. All this bloodshed was on my family's hands.

I would never forgive any of them for that—or myself, for all those years of living blissfully ignorant in Kylantis.

"Hey." She nudged me gently in the arm. "It's not your fault either, Tymp." I frowned at her.

"Did you hear my thoughts through the bond?" She snorted.

"I've known you three hundred years. I don't need to read your thoughts to know what you're thinking. I'm the master of all things Tympany. When you start thinking bad thoughts about yourself, you pick at your hangnails."

"That's what Blekket said," I grumbled, flattening my fingers over my thighs. "Am I really that easy to read? If so, that doesn't bode well for me." Pessy laughed, then stood, proffering her hand.

"Let's get this tour over with," she said, opening the door and letting me go out first.

As we headed down the stairs, I reminded myself that all this talk about marriage and me being Queen was still conjectural. It wouldn't be real until Blekket asked me, until he said the words *will you marry me* or *will you be my Queen.*

Until those words were uttered, I wouldn't allow this to torment me.

I would be the best support system I could be for him today, and let that to be tomorrow's problem.

The Elrods were waiting for us at the bottom of the stairs, all dressed in dark navy. Raevon's dress was made of Georgette fabric, draping alongside a V-neck and back, and laid across a banded waist, the full maxi skirt having a side slit that would make it easier for her to ride.

Her hair was woven in an intricate fishtail braid that tumbled down her back and grazed her waist.

"Am I supposed to wear my hair up?" I asked Blekket, touching the back of my head self-consciously.

"Don't put it up. You look beautiful with it down." He kissed my cheek, stroking his fingers over my hip.

"Hey, Rae." I reached for her the same time she reached for me.

"Hi, Tymp." Her voice was smaller than I'd ever heard it, which was understandable. "You look really nice."

"So do you."

Demetrio was the most distressing to see. He'd lost five pounds and looked tremendously fatigued, as if he'd aged a hundred years in thirty-one days, shifting like each movement was too heavy to bear alone.

The sight of his withered face made me want to curl up in a ball, dissolve into tears, and never leave my bed.

"Can I do anything for you, Demetrio?" I asked, my heart shattering for him.

"It's sweet of you to ask, Tympany, but no. I just want to get today over with."

We all felt that way.

We headed to collect our horses in silence, the air dense with grief. Pessy and I clung to Blekket and Raevon, letting them offset half their weight on us so they'd be able to take the necessary steps needed to reach the stables. Demetrio walked alone.

Every step he took or gust of wind that wafted looked like it might take him down for good.

We started to arrange ourselves into the order of hierarchy when Demetrio brought Bonnie in front of Clarence and Blekket.

"What are you doing?" Blekket snapped at his father. "That's not the right order. Go behind me."

Demetrio exchanged a look with Raevon.

"That's not the proper order anymore," he answered. I imagined it took a lot of will power to say that without retching sorrow.

"Oh, fuck that," Blekket baulked in horror. "I'm not walking in Mum's place. No fucking way."

"You have to, Son. You're next in line. This is what's expected of you."

"Blek," Raevon moaned, on the verge of tears. "*Please.*"

"No! No way!" He turned to me in desperation. "Tympany, compel him to go in front of me."

"I'm not doing that," I refused.

"Seriously?" I'd never seen Blekket so angry. "You compelled Harrison to light himself on fire. You compelled Emilia to get a life, and yet *this* is where you draw the line?"

"*Yes*, Blek," I said sharply, cringing at the reminder of all the ghastly things I'd done since I came here. "I'm not compelling your father. I want to be supportive, but not like that. I'm sorry."

He gritted his teeth, I think wanting to argue further, but didn't have the energy to fight any of us.

"*Fine.* But only if Tympany rides with me." My mouth dropped open.

"If...if I ride with you, wouldn't that...imply..." I held myself back from saying the words *that I'm your Queen* orally, because I didn't want to feed him the idea if it wasn't already in his head.

"I don't give a fuck what it implies." I chewed nervously on my bottom lip, my eyes swooping from the two horses to Blekket. "You promised you wouldn't leave my side today. Please, Tymp. I need you." If I wasn't already moored to him in heart, body, and soul, the sound of him saying *I need you* with such pain would've sealed the deal.

"Do you want to ride on Clarence, or take Krystal?" His facial features softened with relief.

"Clarence, if that's okay with you."

"Of course." I jumped down from Krystal, then leapt off my feet, situating on Clarence's croup behind Blekket. I swivelled around and asked Alsandair, "Will you please take Krystal back to her stall?"

"Of course, Your Grace," he said, gathering her reins from me to lead her back into the stables.

"Thank you for doing this," Blekket whispered. "I know it's a lot to ask, but you have no idea how much this means to me." I wrapped my arms around his waist, snuggling my thighs against his.

"If you need me, I'm there. Always." I nuzzled his back with my cheek, making eye contact with Pessy, who had moved to Raevon's side now that I wasn't riding my own horse. Her smile was a concoction of sympathetic and smug, like she was in on a joke I wasn't privy to.

Her grin said *you're screwed.*

I knew she was right, but I wasn't ready to admit that to myself, or to him. I shut my eyes so I wouldn't have to see her expression anymore, then rested my cheek on Blekket's shoulder blade. He kicked Clarence's side, signaling him to start walking.

Our trek to Acadia was done in absolute silence, but it felt more content then before. The sunlight conjured the most brilliant of mosaics, reflecting off each leaf and wisp of cloud. It was as if there was a pure joy in the light, like it was happy to create art where it shone, warm and steady, something to quench and soothe all at once. It was the balm we all needed to move through the kingdom in harmony, subtracting the tension and giving us each a transitory moment of peace. I took it all in, appreciating, when we passed the Argent Ocean, how the light caused the water to evaporate in slow waves, waves that eddied in the gentle breeze, flowing upward to white-puffed clouds, ships of white in the blue above. No matter how long I lived here or how many times I saw these sights, Esteopia's beauty would never cease to amaze me.

I opened my eyes, having closed them when I angled my face into the sun, and found Blekket staring at me.

"What?" I asked, touching my cheek from embarrassment.

"You're just so beautiful." He stated it like it should've been obvious what he was thinking. "Every time I think I'm going to get used to it, you do something else that just takes my breath away."

Our thoughts weren't so far away from one another, except the object of our esteem had been completely different.

"What was I doing?" I wondered stupidly. He chuckled before leaning in to kiss my forehead.

"You were just being you. Your magnificent self." The tiny smirk that lit up the bottom half of his face was dazzling.

I tipped my chin up, silently imploring for a kiss, which he was more than willing to grant.

"I've stopped myself from saying this the past few weeks because I think these words tend to be overused, and I like to reserve them for when they really count, but I'm sorry, Blek. For all of this. I'm so sorry."

"While I appreciate you saying that, there's no need." He gave my hand that was flat on his stomach a squeeze.

"Told you those words were overused."

"Are you really taking *this* as a moment to be cocky? While we're on the way to tour the kingdom and pay tribute to my dead mother?" He cupped his hands around his mouth and pretended to call out to the rest of our party, "Someone, get me a needle so I may deflate the Goddess's head."

"Are you seriously using *your mother* to try and make me feel bad? That's a new low, *Shamus*."

His lips curled up even further, heightening the allure of his grin.

There was nothing that broke my heart and put it back together more than Blekket Elrod's smile.

"Fuck, you make me so happy, Tympany. Even with all this shit, you somehow make it tolerable. You really are my sun."

I was tempted then to tell him I loved him for the first time, but I wanted to save that special moment for when we were in private. Still, I could say something now that alluded to those feelings.

"And you're my home." I stretched up, kissing his cheek.

"We're here," Lev announced from the front. We were tarrying at the entrance to Acadia. From where Blekket and I were situated in the back of the group, I couldn't see any of the villagers yet.

"Are you ready?" Demetrio asked his son, which I found to be a cruel, useless question.

"Do I really have room to say no?" Blekket spat. Demetrio sighed with frustration.

"No, you don't." He tapped Bonnie with his right foot and trotted ahead. Blekket dithered a moment, stiff as stone.

"Don't let go of me, Tymp," he murmured in a hoarse voice, receding what little was left of my composure.

"Never." I squeezed him tighter for further emphasis.

The villagers were lined up on the fringe of the path, splayed across the terrain like tassels at the end of a blanket. We rode in a single file line, exposed on both sides with no soldiers shielding us. The first Esteopian to reach out and touch me was a ginger female, with messy curls that were thick and trickled down to her hips, shrouding the garish blue cloth of her dress. She placed her hand on my calf, a light gesture, and echoed, "With her last drop, she is free," bowing her head.

The small contact, even through the fabric of my pants, gave me access to her thoughts.

I can't believe she's riding with the Prince. That's a pretty big statement. I'd rather have Emilia on the throne than this outsider.

I gasped, wrenching my leg away.

The woman stumbled back in shock, her lashes whipping her eyebrows at the fast pace they were fluttering at.

"Are you okay?" Blekket asked me, turning back.

"I'm fine," I stammered just as the next one touched my leg, and their thoughts came flooding through my ears.

Blekket Elrod is an immature child. Look at how he broke Emilia's heart, and is now here flaunting this whore around. He's not worthy of being King of Esteopia. I might just have to move to Sleotha.

I squished Blekket's torso so forcefully, he coughed on a breath. "Tympany, what's going on?"

I don't trust her. She's a Goddess. She's just like her miserable excuse of a family who abandoned us.

"When they touch me...I can hear their thoughts." *Blekket is so handsome. Oh, the things I'd let him do to me...*

"Have you always been able to do that?"

I focused on the sound of Blekket's voice to keep myself in the present, to not succumb to all the voices.

"It started when I arrived here. Pessy said it was..." *King Demetrio looks like he's going to faint.* "...my powers evolving, now that I've reached..." *Raevon's riding with that Kylantian girl? What will Dani think?* "...the full age of

302

adulthood." I spoke through wheezes, inundated with all the villagers' judgements.

"Can you read my thoughts?" I shook my head. "That must be annoying for you."

"Annoying?" I laughed. "You think I want to hear your thoughts every time you touch me? I'm relieved I can't."

This never should've happened. I blame the Goddess for not stopping that arrow from hitting the Queen.

"Can you please distract me, Blek?" My throat was clogged by an impending sob.

"I see Emilia didn't bother to show her face," Blekket observed, his eyes skimming the crowd.

"If she's not here, that's messed up." *Raevon has such beautiful, long hair. I wish I looked like her.*

"She should be here. The whole kingdom is required to take part in the mourning tour. Seraphina was her Queen. She doesn't get exempt because she was compelled to get a life and move on. If she lives here, she needs to respect the crown."

"I agree." *Why is the Goddess wearing pants and not a gown? Seems a little disrespectful.* "Should I have worn a dress?"

"What? No." Blekket's brows furrowed together with bemusement. "Did someone say something?"

"That it was disrespectful of me to not wear a gown."

"There's no rule requiring you to wear dresses. You're wearing dark blue. That's the only prerequisite for the mourning tour." He shook his head, spitting, "It amazes me how humans always find something to be critical about."

"You'd be surprised how many people think horrible things under their smiles." *Fuck Blekket Elrod. He's never wanted to be king. Put Raevon on the throne. We'd have an actual chance at winning this war with her.*

"I don't think it would actually," Blekket mused. "I know what it feels like to plaster on a smile that isn't real, to say one thing and really be thinking another. You just don't normally get to hear those thoughts while someone pretends to be sympathetic."

"True." *That's the Goddess Tympany? I thought she'd be taller.* I audibly groaned at that one.

"What?"

"Just someone making fun of my height." Blekket's lips twitched up.

"You are shorter than I expected a Goddess to be. I'm surprised you walk so straight with that small body and big head of yours."

"Fuck you, Blek," I barked louder than I should've, and heard a few gasps from the villagers below us.

"Both of you, *stop talking*," Demetrio hissed, then spun around and squared his shoulders as if nothing had happened. Pessy, Raevon, and Lev were all smirking up ahead.

"Sorry, angel," Blekket whispered, lifting my hand to his lips. "When you hear something in someone's head that's just too much, squeeze me. Pour them into me. Let me be your outlet."

I squashed his ribs then, not because of anything the villagers said, but because I wanted to transfer into him through this precious contact we shared all the love I'd held myself back from verbalising.

The thoughts kept piling on, some of them lovely, and some so uncouth, I couldn't believe anyone had the ability to even think those things. When we reached the end of the line, the last Esteopian in Acadia to touch me had a thought I knew would embed itself in my psyche for the rest of my existence, a thought that sent a perturbing chill down my spine, rocking both Blekket and Clarence.

She really is just like her mother.

We spent the entire rest of the day riding from village to village, so all the Esteopians could pay homage to their fallen Queen. Every time an Esteopian touched us to show their support, they would say, "With her last drop, she is free," a saying my mother originated that was enrooted in the ethos of both kingdoms, voiced in moments of fervency to express commitment, and in times of loss, relinquishing ones soul to Nekropolis. Now, the saying reminded me of that fateful moment when Seraphina died in my arms, when I closed her eyes and sent her off to find peace.

Hearing it over and over again was like being flung back into that moment without my consent, adding a new element to the distress, on top of all the thoughts surging into me from the townsfolk.

I clung to Blekket for dear life, burying my face in his jacket so none of the Esteopians could see me cry.

In the village of Driland was the first time someone referred to Blekket as their king. It was a young Esteopian boy as he was touching Blekket's leg, his large doe brown eyes reflecting the virtue of a child.

He'd said, "With her last drop, she is free, my King."

I felt Blekket clench his muscles so he wouldn't flinch in front of the kid, just nodding respectfully in spite of his discomfort. Just like Pessy, I didn't need to read his thoughts to know what he was thinking.

When we were a safe distance away from the boy and the other villagers, I planted a kiss between his shoulder blades in recognition of his unrest. He squeezed my hand so tightly, I almost lost feeling in my fingers.

By the time we finally returned to the palace, it was well into nightfall, a whisper of perfect black that swelled into a comforting chorus of stars. I was utterly exhausted and itching to crawl into bed, but Blekket had other plans. Before I could dismount Clarence, he took hold of my arm to keep me from jumping down.

"Can we go somewhere that's not the palace?" he entreated with a slight tremble in his voice.

"Of course," I said in spite of my enervation, pecking his cheek and repositioning my arms around his stomach.

Batons of rising branches became dancing silhouettes in the moonlight, swinging in congruence with the current of the wind. We were silent through the journey because we had nothing to say, the quiet not awkward, but relaxed.

"I love dusk." Blekket sighed after a while, tracing the shape of a leaf adjacent to where we were riding.

"Nox always says twilight serenades the day, so the sun may rest with starlit dreams."

"It doesn't surprise me, hearing that, that Nox and Lucius are polar opposites of each other." I agreed with him on that. While sunlight was presumptuous in how it infringed itself upon the world, night-time was a blanket of stillness that ventilated the earth. They were perfect representations of who Nox and Lucius were as people. "Do Nox and Lucius get along with one another?"

"Lucius doesn't get along with anyone," I said. Blekket laughed at that. "Seriously. All my siblings hate him. He makes it very hard to carry a conversation when all he likes to listen to is the sound of his own voice."

"Sounds like someone else I know," he teased, ducking when I tried to flick him. "Are Nox and Luna close?"

"They're twins."

"That doesn't necessarily mean they're close." He had a point there.

"Yes, they are. They both like to keep in the back and never insert themselves in any drama. Luna is a lot more free-spirited, but Nox, in his own way, is unconventional compared to my other brothers."

"What about Benjen?"

"Ben marches to the beat of his own drum. He doesn't give a shit what anyone thinks. I've always admired Ben. I don't think he gets enough credit for his specialty. He's in charge of verifying every person in the Realm has access to nutrients, whether it be through livestock, birds, fish, crops, everything. He has the power to help a harvest flourish, or demolish it completely. He doesn't get nearly enough praise for literally nourishing all of humanity."

"That's an interesting way of looking at it. I guess I never thought of him as having that much influence."

"He's far too underappreciated, unlike Lucius, who's overrated if you ask me. Light and the sun are important, yes, but they're not the only things that sustain life. Each of the Gods has a role to play. Callie isn't just in charge of music, she's also responsible for the happiness and joy of others. Eira and Caspian are just as imperative as Lucius, if not more so, in controlling the weather. Nox and Luna protect the night, Hadestia is the guardian of the dead, and Jax..." My voice trailed off at the debilitating grief that seized me when I thought of my brother. "His job is the conservation of our people's health and wellness, or...at least it's supposed to be."

"And what's your role, would you say?" His fingers traced the veins on the back of my hand.

"I'm not really sure." I frowned. "I've struggled with that for a long time. I don't know what my purpose is supposed to be."

"I think you're a symbol of hope and inspiration," Blekket responded, stroking my forearm that was folded over his stomach. "You represent for humans that, as long as your heart and mind are in the right place, you can achieve anything you desire."

"You think so?" He nodded, my eyes stinging with tears. "Thank you, Blek. That means a lot to me."

"Well, *you* mean a lot to me, so it's only fitting." As if I couldn't love him more, he bent down to plant the most tender of kisses on my nose, pulling my arms even tighter around him.

Halfway to our destination, I recognised the path and realised we were heading to Lake Azrord. The verdant leaves beginning to re-emerge due to the forthcoming spring came as a happy flash mob to brighten up the brook, painting the water in a unique blend of whites, greens, and silvers.

Blekket dismounted Clarence first, then proffered his hand to help me down. While I didn't need his assistance, I would take advantage of any excuse to touch him.

"Look whosssssssss here," Jeka greeted us with a leering smile. "Tympany, you look radiant assssssss alwaysssssss."

"You as well," I beamed.

"My King." Jeka bowed her head gracefully, her smile enhancing in both humor and beauty.

"Don't start with that shit now," Blekket growled. "It's been a long day." All traces of mirth evaporated from Jeka's demeanor.

"I sssssssincccccerely apologise for the lossssssss of your mother. I've sssssseeeeen many queensssss and kingssssss in my time, and Sssssseraphina wassssss one of the besssssst. She wasssssss an incredible ruler."

"Yes, she was." Blekket spoke with no emotion, but I knew it was seething under the surface.

"May our next one be jussssst asssssss formidable." I quickly looked away, pretending I hadn't noticed how she directed that at me.

Jeka ducked under the waves, leaving us alone to revel in the stillness of the night. I leaned against the trunk of a willow tree, twisting my arms across my chest, just staring at Blekket. The moon highlighted the gentle glide of his sharp jawline, accentuating the freckles dusted across his cheeks and the bridge of his nose. His left ear captured the light, his teardrop birthmark taking center stage. He was just exquisite, so much so that it was difficult to speak past the lump in my throat, which surfaced every time I thought about how much I loved him.

"How're you feeling?" I asked. "About everything?" Blekket stuffed his hands into his pockets, closing his mouth, then exhaled, the air forcing itself past his lips and making them flap together like a horse. I let out a chortle, and he raised his eyes to me, smiling softly.

"None of it has really sunk in. Not Mum being gone, or me becoming king. I feel like my brain is refusing to catch up to reality."

"That's normal with grief."

"But how do I *stop* doing that?" He was genuinely asking me.

I stretched out my arms, reaching for his hands to tug him closer, then lifted mine to cradle his cheeks.

"Struggle is pain," I said, tracing his freckles lightly with my thumbs. "The more you fight against your reality, the harder it is to breath."

"Did you hear that from somewhere, or come up with that all on your own?"

"It's a Tympany original, just for you." He laughed, but the smile only lasted a moment before grief caught back up with him. He inclined down, almost collapsing into me, and buried his face in my neck.

"Oh, Tymp," he moaned, his arms curling around my waist. "I'm so scared. Scared I'm not good enough. Scared I'll disappoint and fail everyone. Scared I'll cost us this war by being such a fuck up."

"You won't, Blek," I promised, caressing the hair at the nape of his neck. "You're an intelligent, thoughtful, kind, strong person. You handle yourself with class and brilliance in everything you do. You fight for your people every day, in little and big ways. You will be an amazing king."

"You really think so?"

"I really do." The way he jutted his bottom lip out in a pout was adorable and heartbreaking at the same time.

"I can't do this without you, Tympany," he declared, spiking my heartrate when his hands glided up to cup my face. "I need you with me, not just for right now, but for forever. In just a short while, you singlehandedly turned my world on its head and became the most important person in my life. I can't picture a single day without you, and I don't want to. I love you with every fiber of my being, Tymp, and that love grows with every drop of my blood, every breath I take."

"Blek," I gasped, tears tumbling down my face. Even though I sensed it was about to happen before it did, nothing could've prepared me for the moment Blekket knelt down on one knee.

Time suspended.

He reached into his pocket, his eyes never straying from me, and procured a ring, raising it under the downpour of moonlight.

"This was the ring my father gave my mother," he explained, presenting it to me. It was a large oval sapphire with a white gold, three sided pave diamond band. I'd never seen anything so enchanting. "I've heard the story a thousand times. He got down on one knee and said, 'Ser, you are the light of my life. My pride and joy. My sun. You are the air beneath my wings, and I don't want to live a second of my limited existence on Earth without you beside me'." He stole my left hand, bringing it to his chest. "My angel, you are the light of my life. I've never been more sure of anything. We belong together. You are magnificent in everything you do, and I need you. I need you to tease me about my big head, to keep me grounded and humble, to hold me when I feel lost and never let me drown. I can't imagine anyone I'd rather share my world or my crown with. Tympany, will you do me the extraordinary honour of spending your life with me, and becoming my wife?"

Chapter Twenty

It would've been perfect.

His proposal would've permanently affixed me to him, would've dunked my head as far underwater as it could go, if it wasn't for that one phrase.

Spend *your* life with me.

That meant two different things to Blekket and me. Forever for us meant two different things.

Forever for him was right now, but for me, it was *actual* eternity. I could spend *his* life with him, but he couldn't spend mine with me. Time would always be against us.

The reminder of that left me completely paralysed in what should've been the happiest moment of my life.

"Tympany?"

Blekket was still on one knee, only now, his tears had dried, and he looked ashen. I couldn't begin to imagine how shell-shocked I must've looked for him to turn so pale in only a matter of a few seconds.

"I…" My tongue felt ginormous in my mouth. I couldn't form words around it. Panic caused my throat to cave in on itself, the walls around my esophagus aching with an emergent sob that threatened to tear through my flesh and light me on fire. Before I even realised I'd spoken, I exclaimed, "I can't," and shoved him back, hurdling towards the lake. I fell to my knees and cupped my hands in the water, splashing the cold liquid over my flaming cheeks. My breaths came out as mewls that I tried to regulate, but they showed no signs of abating. The air was like sweltering chains, constricting my ability to respire.

"You *can't?*" he repeated behind me.

I felt the weight of those two words as if an avalanche had collapsed over the top of my head, mashing me into the soil.

When I finally managed to get my wheezing under control, I rose off the ground and spun around to face him. I wasn't prepared for the despondence I found deforming his beautiful facial features into something heartrending, wasn't prepared to be so crippled by horror and guilt that I had trouble standing upright.

"I didn't mean I *can't*," I clarified, still ensnarled in hysteria. "I just mean...I need to think about this."

Blekket blinked at me.

"I'm telling you I love you and want to spend the rest of my life with you, and you're saying you have to *think* about it?"

"I'm not saying I need to think about *you*. I'm saying I need a minute to *breathe*, Blek."

"You think *I've* breathed a second since my mother died?"

I felt more throttled by him saying that then when Lucius had his hands wrapped around my throat.

"I'm sorry," I stammered, strangled by claustrophobia, as if the trees were folding in around us. "I didn't mean—"

"I know," he said more gently, closing his eyes and taking a moment to center himself. "I know." He pinched the bridge of his nose, inhaling paced breaths, then opened his eyes in unison with an exhale. "Do you love me, Tympany? Because if you don't, just say it now and save me the heartbreak later." The pain in his voice was unescapable.

"I do!" I screamed, lurching forward to grab his hand. "I was going to tell you tonight, when we were in private...Blekket, I do. I love you. I love you so much, with every cell in my body, and I love Esteopia too. I just..." I tripped over my explanation. "I know I want to be with *you*, Blek. I don't need to think about that. I need to think about *this*." I gesticulated to our surroundings. "You've had thirty years to know you were one day going to be king of this place. I've been here four months. I spent five thousand years in Kylantis, and I wasn't ready to be queen there. This is a lot to take on after a short time. I just don't want to be the wrong person to lead you all."

"There's no one better than you, Tymp," he whispered, pain replaced with adoration. "You're the best there is."

"I could say the same about you, but you wouldn't believe me, would you?" He grimaced, knitting his lips shut. "Be honest, Blek. Are you asking me to marry you because you actually *want* to marry me, or because you're scared?"

"I'm asking you to marry me because I can't imagine doing life with anyone but you. Yes, that includes being king, but that's not the whole reason." He skimmed my cheek with the tips of his fingers.

"Would you be doing this if you didn't have to take the throne soon?"

"I know I would do this eventually. Would I be doing it right this second otherwise? Probably not, but it doesn't mean I wouldn't still want to." He traced the line of my jaw with the pad of his thumb. "I love you, Tympany. I want you to be mine in every single way humanly possible. If I have to take the throne, I can't do it with anyone else at my side. I won't. I need you."

"I'm immortal, Blek. I don't age from here on out. One day, you'll die, and I'll still be like this."

"What? Are you saying you won't love me when I'm old and grey?" There was a faint teasing lilt, but no humor powered his words.

"I'll love you no matter what you look like. Even if you gained a ton of weight and had a massive gut tomorrow." I splayed my fingers over his chiselled stomach. "I'm just…I'm terrified of what losing you will do to me. If I have to spend an eternity without you…" The prospect made me sick, "…that's the closest to death I will ever get."

"Sweetheart," Blekket moaned, dropping his face into the safety of my neck, twisting his arms around me. "You can't let fear stop you from living life. If you fixate on the future, then you miss out on the present."

"I know," I mumbled, a new batch of tears surfacing. "I'm trying. It's just…harder to remember than I thought."

"Having something worth fighting for, even with the chance you might lose it, is still better than not having loved at all."

"Did you get that from somewhere, or come up with it yourself?" He raised his face out of my neck, his lips twitching upward.

"A Blekket Elrod original, just for you." He tucked my hair behind my ear. "I love you, Tympany."

"I love you, Blek. I love you." In his arms, I felt secure. In his embrace, the thought of being queen didn't seem so daunting. But the minute his arms left me, that fear would be stifling again. "Can you please give me a day to think about it? To just wrap my head around all of this? It doesn't mean I don't love you, or that I don't want you. I just need a day to process what being your *wife* really means."

He was silent for too long. I worried I lost him…until he finally bobbed his head in a nod.

"I'll give you as much time as you need," he promised, smudging a tear from the corner of my eye.

"I'm sorry."

"I thought you said sorry was an overused word."

"It feels appropriate at the moment." I sniffled, wiping snot on the back of my hand. As if he couldn't be more of a gentleman or make me feel any worse about myself, he offered me his jacket to smear my tears.

"Let's go back to the palace," he said, draping an arm around my shoulders and steering me over to where Clarence stood.

"Are you okay?" I asked, which was a stupid question.

"No, Tympany. I'm not okay. My mum just died, I'm being forced to take the throne in three months, and the woman I love just said she has to think about whether or not she wants to marry me."

His candor throbbed like a stab wound. "I'm sor—"

"If you apologise again, I'm not letting you on this horse." He smiled to show he was kidding, but I wasn't entirely sure he was.

The ride back to the palace was completely silent, laced with awkward tension. My arms were wrapped around his midriff, but it felt like hugging a statue, a million leaps away from relaxed.

We went our separate ways without saying a word. I fled to my bedchamber, and he trekked to the stables to deposit Clarence.

When I opened the door, I found Pessy in there. She was drowning in one of her father's large tunics, pacing back and forth. She sprinted across the room, reaching for my left hand, and felt around for a ring that wasn't there.

"What happened?" she demanded.

"You *knew?!*" I couldn't tell if I was appalled or enraged.

"Raevon told me during the tour. I wasn't sure if I should tell you or not."

"Um, a head's up would've been nice!" I ripped my hand out of hers and marched over to the bed, unbuckling my sandals. She spun around, her lips wilting.

"You said no?"

"No, I didn't say *no*. I said I needed to *think* about it. I need…UGH!"

I chucked my shoe across the room with a loud scream. I once again underestimated my own strength, as the sandal pitched into the window and fractured the pane, shards flying everywhere.

"Tympany!" Pessy flew in front of me, shielding me from the airborne glass. "Are you okay?"

I crumbled into a ball on the floor, buried my face in my hands, and dissolved into violent tears.

Pessy sunk to her knees, snaking an arm around me. She hauled me to her chest, where she rested my head on her shoulder and began stroking my hair from the root down, letting me slobber all over her shirt.

"Let it out," she said. "Just let it out, Tymp."

The release was a strange combination of cathartic and devastating, of revitalising and draining. I wasn't sure if, through it, I found clarity or more problems, but once the dam was broken, I couldn't stop. I cried for me, for Blek, for Seraphina, for the kingdom that lost its monarch, because none of this would be happening if I'd been fast enough to catch that fucking arrow.

I cried for hours, just wept and wept and wept, until my sobs bled into yawns, and my bones enfeebled with exhaustion.

Pessy helped me crawl into bed, and I was already passed out when she turned off the lights.

I dreamt that night I was back in Kylantis as Queen of the Gods.

The bulk of the gilded crown on my head felt like a prison, the throne tingling unnervingly against my spine. There were manacles attached to the arms of the chair, snug around my wrists, trapping me. When I tried to pull myself free and stand, the clouds encompassing the seat saturated my skin in a blazing fire that travelled the length of my body, cementing me to the chair. The conflagration slithered around my throat in the form of fingers, asphyxiating my windpipe. I couldn't see, through the inferno, where my skin started, and the throne began. I was becoming one with the chair.

"Help!" I screamed before my lips were eaten by the flames. "I don't want this! Help me! Help!"

A monsoon suddenly doused the throne in water, exterminating the flames and liberating me from its clutches. On the other side of the smoke was Blekket, holding a metal bucket in one hand, with the crown of Esteopia in the other, the aqua jewels spangled in the sunlight. He set the bucket down on the ground, then offered me his hand.

"Until my last drop," he murmured, placing the pink crown on my head, "you will always be my Queen."

"Tymp. Tymp, wake up," a voice from outside my fantasy said.

"Blek?" I shot up out of bed, startling Pessy enough to knock her off the mattress. I heard the loud thwack of her head hitting the marble floor, followed by a groan. "Pess!" I dipped over the edge to grab her hand and yank her up. "Are you okay?"

"Peachy," she replied, rubbing the sore spot on her forehead where she'd collided with the ground. "Are *you* good, though? You started screaming *help me* in your sleep. What were you dreaming about?"

"I was back in Kylantis, being forced to take the throne. I tried to get up, but the chair caught on fire and wouldn't release me. Blekket was there. He poured water over the flames to free me, then took the Kylantian crown off my head and replaced it with the Esteopian one."

"Hm. Sounds interesting. I think you should listen to what your dream's telling you." She arched a brow, smirking.

"You're enjoying this way too much," I accused. Her smile vanished.

"I'm not enjoying seeing you suffer, Tympany. It kills me to see you struggle, and I especially don't want to pressure you into doing something you don't genuinely want. You know I'd never do that to you."

"I know." Our fingers crept across the mattress, finding each other.

"The only reason I keep saying any of this is because I know you. Sometimes better than you know yourself. And I see how much you love Blek. I see how much you love Esteopia. I haven't seen you fight this hard for anything, and that includes how you've fought for yourself over the years. You've stepped up here and taken charge on numerous occasions. You're a leader, Tymp, through and through. You never had the chance to explore that side of yourself in Kylantis, but here, you've prospered. They would be lucky to have you as their ruler, and Blekket would be lucky to call you his wife and Queen."

"Pess," I whimpered, struggling not to cry.

"Don't let me, or anyone else, tell you what to do. Let the decision be entirely your own. Whatever you decide, I'm there. If you choose to say yes, then you know I will support you through this in any way I can. If you choose to say no, then we'll grab Belgian and Krystal and leave Esteopia tonight."

"What?" That shocked me. "You would really leave Esteopia? Leave *Raevon?*"

"Home isn't home without you, Tympany. You're not just my bonded. My love and devotion to you has nothing to do with my duty. You're my best friend. Nothing could ever come before that." She stretched across the bed to smudge a tear from the corner of my eye with her knuckle.

"I would never ask you to leave Raevon, or Esteopia."

"I know. But you wouldn't need to ask. I go where you go. Always." I squeezed her hand so tight, I would've crushed her bones if she was mortal.

"I love you, Pessoranda Halynn Whitereaver."

"I know. I'm easy to love." She flipped her blonde hair over her shoulder with a haughty shrug, making me laugh.

After we dressed for the day, we headed to the dining hall. I had a feeling Blekket wouldn't be there, and that hunch was confirmed when we arrived to find only Raevon and Demetrio seated, Lev and Alsandair perched in the corner like always. I saw Raevon's eyes swing to my hand, her lips downcast and shoulders sagged when she saw nothing seated on my left ring finger.

Demetrio was sipping his water, staring blankly at the pastry on his plate to avoid looking at me.

"Good morning," I said to the table in greeting, though it was anything but.

I hunkered down into the spot next to Demetrio, across from Pessy. I made eye contact with the empty chair at the head of the table, which Seraphina habitually occupied. It would now be expected to be filled by either Blekket, or me, if I said yes. I wished for the ground to swallow me up as I shoved a sushi roll into my mouth, just so I would have an excuse not to talk to anyone.

"I take it, from your empty left hand, you said no." I choked on the rice, coughing up fish and avocado.

I was stunned Demetrio decided to state this publicly, with Lev and Alsandair present, but I also gathered, from everyone's facial expressions, that this was already common knowledge.

"I didn't say no," I refuted, wiping my mouth with my napkin. "I told him I needed to think about it. It's a big decision, and I don't want to make it lightly." Demetrio looked impassive, until he nodded his head and smiled.

"Good. It is a big decision, and you shouldn't jump into it carelessly. I'm happy to hear that."

"Are you happy to hear I'm thinking about it, or happy to know there's a chance I might say no?" I snapped, causing both Raevon and Pessy to lift their heads in shock at my sudden belligerence.

"I would be thrilled if you said yes and became our Queen, Tympany. I would also be thrilled if you said no, and Blekket married someone with Esteopian blood. I have no opinion on this matter, as long as my son ends up on the throne."

"Right, because you've already made very clear where you stand. Blekket's happiness means nothing to you."

"Tymp," Pessy cautioned.

"You would be just as satisfied seeing him marry someone he doesn't know or love then see him with someone who genuinely makes him happy. Do you understand how wrong that is? Since Seraphina died, you haven't given him a moment to breathe. He hasn't had a second to even mourn his *mother* because you've imposed all this on him. He's had no choice. You're confining him to a throne he doesn't want, and you don't even care how it will affect him mentally to take on the burden of an entire kingdom at *war,* on top of *grief.* What kind of parent does that?"

"You know nothing about what it means to be a parent," Demetrio argued.

"You're right. I don't, but if being a parent means pressuring your child into a life they don't want, then what's the fucking point of even having children, letting them grow into their own people, only to dictate everything they do and say later? What's the point in gifting them independence, only to rip it away from them when they need it most?"

"Sounds an awful lot like what you planned to do here, offering us support, only to take it away at the last minute."

"Dad," Raevon warned.

"The difference between you and I, Demetrio, is I never followed through with that plan. You have. In his weakest moment, you took Blek's autonomy away. You gave him space over the course of his life to form his own opinions and personality, and now expect him to just abandon everything he believes, as if he never lived those thirty years. What I came here to do was wrong, but what you're doing is worse."

"I think you've made your point," Demetrio said coldly, leaning back in his chair.

317

"I don't think I have," I hissed, my fingers balling into fists under the table. "How many times does your son need to tell you he's not ready for it to sink in to that thick skull of yours that being king might *actually* kill him? I can't be the only one who wants to see Blekket happy, and if I am, then screw you all."

"Tympany," Pessy gasped aloud, then reprimanded, *Tymp, stop it*, through the bond.

"If I don't advocate for Blek, no one will."

I threw my napkin onto my plate and rose, the legs of my chair scuffing the floorboard aggressively.

"Where are you going?" Pessy shouted.

"I need some air. **Don't follow me,**" I ordered Alsandair when I saw him start to move from his stationary position on the wall. I marched through the door, shutting it behind me with a loud grunt of exasperation.

My feet led the way to the stables, the wind whipping my hair around my face. Krystal buzzed with excitement when she saw me approach, lifting up on her hind legs and neighing with delight.

"Let's get out of here," I said, leaping onto her back.

I didn't really have a plan when I lightly tapped her side, signalling for her to unfurl her wings. All I knew was I needed distance between me and the palace drama to process this big decision.

It'd been a month since the battle at Tympany's Province. I felt saddened by the anxiety and melancholy visiting there brought me, such a contradictory feeling to the overwhelming pride I felt the last time I was there. It was a comfort to see all the townsfolk going about their everyday lives as normal, as if no tragedy had occurred, but the air was hefty with calamity, thick with heartache, the opposite of what we'd wanted to capture with this town. I hated that our vision for Tympany's Province would be forever tarnished by Seraphina's death, and hated even more that the disaster stood at the bottom of the Geddesia Mountains, a reminder of how my parents had been right above us and did nothing to stop the devastation. While this village would forever be associated with that loss, I hoped it would one day stand again for the strength of Esteopia, how even when the Sleothians attempted to annihilate it, it remained victorious in the face of adversity.

I tied Krystal's reins to the porch and entered our house. I glided my fingers over the velvet chairs, tracing the light fixture on the ceiling that looked like pendulous bubbles, plopping down on one of the plush couches. I kicked my sandals off, curling my arms around my knees, and rocked back and forth, lowering my chin between my legs.

I wished in this moment I could speak to my mother, ask for her advice separate from her personal feelings about Esteopia. I wondered if she'd like Blekket as a stand-alone person, if she would welcome him into our family despite what he was and where he came from.

Then, I thought, *is that one of the reasons I'm having trouble wrapping my brain around marrying him?*

Because I know I won't have my family's approval?

Not that I needed it—I knew that, but I'd spent five thousand years melding my life around their dogmas. My family's opinions on the Realm, mortals, and each other, influenced every decision I made, shaped me into who I was, regardless of if I wanted them to or not. I wasn't really given the space to have my own personal beliefs because everyone around me shared the same values, and it would've been strange for me to differentiate mine from theirs. While I felt forced to uphold the ideals my mother set out for us, I carried with me for five thousand years the feeling that the words coming out of my mouth weren't my own, that I didn't belong there, that I was a fraud. I was never sure what my purpose was, and lugged shame over that confusion with me everywhere I went.

I wasted each new day itching to leave Kylantis, taking for granted the wonder of life, the years blending together into a callous monotony.

Down here, I'd finally found variety and excitement and love. The tedium of immortality ruptured into bursts of colour. I finally found a purpose in Esteopia, in being a symbol of hope and inspiration for them. They trusted me with their home and their lives, and I'd actually been able to protect them. My failure in saving Cosmina and Seraphina came to mind, weighing heavy on my heart, but I knew, deep down, those deaths weren't my fault.

I also knew, when it came down to it, I'd been strong enough to defend these people. I would continue to draw that strength from the Esteopians' faith in me. I'd be a just ruler, who pledged to prioritise the equality for all and the well-being of Esteopia before anything else. I could help them win this war, and I would be happy to do so, because Esteopia was my home now, too.

Then, I thought about Blekket, my *real* home.

I never felt safer than when I was in his arms, never felt more free to be completely myself without fear of judgement. I had no doubt, when things got to be too complicated or too stifling, Blekket would always be there to lighten the mood with a joke, would always be there to hold my hand and tell me everything would work itself out.

I couldn't imagine not being with him, and yet, I knew eventually there would come a time when I'd lose him to the clutches of sickness or old age, and be forced to endure an eternity alone.

As a Goddess marrying into the royal family, I would usurp Raevon, or even mine and Blekket's kids, since I'd never die. If I agreed to be his Queen, I was agreeing to be the Queen of Esteopia *forever*, with or without Blekket.

Was my love for Esteopia contingent on Blek? Would I grow to resent these people if I had to lead them alone? I didn't think so, but then again, I couldn't predict how I'd react when the time came.

But I also knew I couldn't live so far in the future that I missed the present moment. Time would always be hovering over us, but maybe that was okay. It would give me the chance to appreciate human life the way mortals do, to truly value the time we were given together, even if it was limited.

I had to stop thinking of time as the enemy, and treat it as a gift to be cherished.

I would've been lying to myself if I said I could fathom a world where Blekket and I didn't end up together. When I thought about the potential sixty plus years we could have with one another if I said yes, I knew I'd rather spend every day of that limited time we had blissfully happy, then give up and spend an eternity alone, having never lived those years with him by my side.

Blekket was right—loving someone, even with the chance of losing them, was better than not having loved at all.

I could handle being Queen, as long as I had him as my King. With that realisation, there was no more fear.

After I finally found the courage to peel myself away from the cottage and begin making my way outside, I found Lev waiting on the porch beside Krystal, feeding her haylage from the palm of his hand.

"Sorry," he stammered, jerking his arm back when he spotted me at the threshold. "Pessy sent me after you to make sure you weren't here alone."

"It's okay. No need to apologise. Do you want to sit?" He nodded, crouching down to the ground and taking a seat on the porch next to me. "I still can't believe he built this without me knowing," I marvelled, admiring the cottage.

"He can be very resourceful, that Blekket," Lev said with a smirk.

"How long have you been the Elrod's first in command?"

"Almost twenty years, since I was thirty." He ran a hand through the ginger curls settled atop his head. "Seraphina hand-picked me herself. She and Demetrio introduced me to my wife, Marisa. I owe everything to them." He spoke with such a profound sadness that it tugged at my heartstrings.

"I'm sorry you lost your friend."

"You have nothing to be sorry for. Her death wasn't your fault. There was nothing you could've done, Tympany."

"I'm trying to believe that, but it's hard. If I'd just been fast enough turning around, none of this would've happened."

"Maybe it wouldn't have. Or, maybe it would've, just in a different way. You can't know for certain you catching that arrow would've changed the course of events. We may have ended up here regardless." I rested my chin in my palm, glaring at the Geddesia Mountains as if they were to blame for all this strife, which, in a way, they were, considering what existed above them. "I apologise for speaking out of turn, but I need to say this. It's hard for me to fathom anyone besides Seraphina as Queen, but if I have to fill that image with someone, it's you, Tympany. Since the moment I met you, I knew. You were born to be our Queen, to lead us to victory against Sleotha. It can only be you."

"What makes you think that?" Lev was quiet a moment, scrubbing a hand down his dimpled cheek.

"Just a feeling," he said after a moment. "I'm a firm believer in fate. So was Seraphina. I think her death needed to happen, in a way, so Blekket would be forced to step up, and you could take your rightful place on the throne. Destiny cannot be avoided, no matter how hard we may try to outrun it."

"Well, you can tell your precious fate that this was a cruel twist, and I would like a do-over."

He smiled. "You can tell fate yourself."

"I'll make sure to stick my middle finger high up in the air to show my censure." Lev's cackle was a lovely, gratifying sound, the kind that spilled honey into your veins and made it impossible to think there was anything wrong with the world.

"Do you have any clue what you're going to do?" he asked tentatively, in case I wasn't inclined to answer.

"I do...but I'm not ready yet to say it aloud." I rested my head on his shoulder. "Can we sit out here for a little longer?"

"We can sit here for as long as you want," he promised, linking his arm with mine.

Lev escorted me through the Dream Forest back to the palace, which took roughly an hour to get past. By the time we reached Esteopia, night-time had graced the sky once more with its ambient deep hues, the moon bathing the land in her comfortable splendor. Lev offered to take Krystal back to the stalls, aware I had somewhere I needed to be. I walked through the palace with perspiring hands, until I was standing in front of Blekket's bedchamber with sweat dripping down my forehead.

I took a deep, preparing breath, wiped my palms on my leggings, and knocked on the door.

It flew open.

Blekket appeared behind it wearing nothing but a loose pair of trousers that hung criminally from his hips. The deep delineation of the V-shaped muscles that ran diagonally from his hip bones to his pelvic region robbed me of the ability to breathe, let alone to form words.

"Tympany? Eyes up here," he teased.

"S-sorry," I stammered, mortified to have been caught drooling over his beauty. "Can I come in?"

"Of course." He stepped to the right, gesturing me inside.

I twisted my fingers together, standing at the foot of his bed, where I waited for him to join me. He shut the door, sauntering over, and loomed above me with his arms crossed over his chest.

"To what do I owe this honour?" It was relieving to see he'd revived his sense of humor.

"I'm gonna say some things. You'll get to speak after, and then, we will each have a chance to rebuttal what the other said."

"Okay," Blekket replied with a tiny smirk, waving his hand.

"Before we officially met on my birthday, I stole a peek down at all the humans who came to Kylantis to celebrate me. I saw you. In a crowd of thousands of mortals, I saw *you. Only* you. You were all I saw. You are all I've seen since I left Kylantis. You are *it,* Blekket. You're it for me. I've never been more sure of anything in my whole life either." Blekket's jaw dropped to the floor.

The words burned on my tongue, pleading to be unfettered. I no longer had the restraint to hold them back.

"I love you, Blek," I continued, my eyes watering with tears. "I love every single thing about you. I love your massive head, and even bigger heart. I love the way you make me feel. I love the way you always ask me if what you're doing is okay, and how you keep asking to see if the answer's changed. I love how you tease me. I wouldn't change a single hair on that obnoxiously handsome head of yours. I love you, Blekket Shamus Elrod, and I will spend the rest of my life loving you more and more every single day. I didn't need a moment to think about *you.* I needed a moment to accept all this that comes with you, but once I took that second, I knew what my answer was, what it's always been. My answer is *yes.* Yes, I will marry you. I'll be your Queen. I can't imagine my life without you in it, and I don't ever want to. I love you, Blekket. I love you. I lo—" My speech was cut off by Blekket's lips.

He crashed into me, backing us up against the wall, cupping my face in his hands as if it were delicate glass. I curled my arms around him, tasting both mine and his tears between us.

When I was finally given a moment to breathe, I said, "Was that your rebuttal? If so, it was a really good one."

"I definitely win this round," he declared with overarching pride.

"Let's get something straight. You're going to be my *husband.* I'm going to be your *wife.* I win every round from here on out."

"Is that a promise, sweetheart, or a challenge?" He angled his hips against mine, trapping me beneath him.

"Both." I raised my pelvis, the friction making both of us gasp.

"Fuck, Tympany," he groaned, scraping his teeth along my jaw. "I need you so fucking much."

"You have me. You will always have me."

I would always be his, for however many lifetimes I saw come and go. I would never not be his.

Chapter Twenty-One

"I need you," he said again, only this time, he began walking us backwards, lowering me down onto the bed beneath him. He'd crawled on top of me before I took my next breath, wedging his knee between my legs at the same time he gripped my chin and plunged his tongue between my parted lips, taking a long, fervent sip from me.

He slipped his other hand inside my leggings, skimming my pelvic bone, then slid his middle finger inside me.

I lifted my hips, grinding down on his palm, and let out a guttural moan, throwing my head back on the mattress.

"*Fuck,* Tymp. You're soaking. Is this just from saying yes? If so, I'll propose to you more often."

I wasn't the least bit embarrassed, though maybe later, I would be. Right now, I just needed him closer.

"Blekket," I groaned when he added another finger, curling them inside me and stroking the interior walls, in unison with his thumb massaging my clitoris. Sparks of heat and energy discharged from his touch and set the rest of my body on fire, rendering me a writhing mess on the bed. "Please."

"Please what, angel?" His teeth grazed my chin, licking down my throat. "Tell me, and it's yours."

"I…" He rubbed the outer folds of my labia in circles with the same fingers he'd had inside me, coating me in moisture and drawing another raucous moan out of me. I whimpered, "I want you, Blek."

"You've got me. You've had me since I saw you in that corridor, with no chance of ever losing me."

I decided I couldn't wait any longer and reached for his trousers, tugging them down his thighs and to his knees. I cupped the back of his neck, dragging his lips back to mine. I curled my toes over his behind, just as I had in Lake Azrord, and wrenched him down so he was as close to me as he could be.

"Tympany, I swear to the Gods, if you do that again, I'm going to come right now," he warned.

"Is that a promise, or a challenge?" Blekket's eyes flared with desire.

"Both. Always both with you, sweetheart." I squished his butt cheeks again, scraping my nails down his back. He groaned, "You are dangerous for my soul, Tympany. I need you naked. Now."

While he worked my leggings down my legs, I yanked the tunic I had on over my head, chucking it to the side. I'd worn the white long sleeve with the grey and aqua gems that belonged to Seraphina's mother, the one she'd complimented me on before the battle at Frofsea. She said Rosabella would've been honoured to see me wear it. It was strange to seek the approval of someone who was dead, but I hoped that was the case, that she would approve of me marrying her grandson and ascending her throne.

"What're you thinking about?" Blekket asked, making me realise I'd zoned out when I saw how he was looming over me.

"Your grandmother. I hope she would've liked me."

"You're thinking about my grandmother right now? Really, Tympany? That is the worst mood killer ever."

"I'm sorry! I can't help where my mind goes!" We both burst into gales of laughter, the sounds fusing together in perfect harmony before flowing into a crackling tension when we locked eyes. My giggles concluded under the intensity of his stare.

"Let's get something straight." He skidded a hand up my abdomen at a leisurely pace, as if savouring the whole process of touching me, leaving goosebumps in his wake. "None of our family members belong in our bedroom. When we're in here, it's just you, and me. No one else exists past these walls." He fondled my breast, skating his thumb over the pebbled peak of my nipple. "Do you agree to these terms?"

"Absolutely." I sighed, then arched my back, pushing my breast even further into his hand.

"You are such a sensual creature," he praised. "I'm the luckiest bastard alive."

He kissed me like he was starving, floating his other hand down my leg, coiling it around his waist to hoist me up.

"Wait," I said, setting a hand on his chest to halt him. "Don't we need…protection?"

325

"We're good," he swore. "I drink the contraceptive root everyday with my morning coffee."

"Why are you drinking a contraceptive root when you're not even having sex?" His lips warped into a wicked smile.

"I needed to be prepared, just in case I managed to charm the pants off a certain Goddess."

I rolled my eyes. "I hate you."

"No, you don't. You love me." I melted into the mattress from how true that statement was.

"I do. I so do." His eyes softened like a cloudless dawn.

"I love you so much." He kissed the corner of my mouth. "You sure you want to do this? We don't have to."

Him saying that made me love him even more. "I'm sure."

"I won't lie. It may hurt at first, but if you need me to stop at any point, just say so, and I will. I promise."

"Stop making me love you more. I don't want your head to explode if I have to keep telling you how great you are."

Blekket chuckled, then trailed a sequence of searing kisses down the side of my face, like he was marking his territory. He left no patch of skin untouched.

"Ready?" he asked. I nodded. "With words, angel."

"Yes," I pledged, and with that, he thrust his hips forward, inching his way inside me with such a gentle, slow tenderness that it brought tears to my eyes, tears that had nothing to do with feeling any discomfort.

"Are you okay?" he rasped out through a shaky breath.

"Yes," I gasped. It pinched at first, and I felt a slight sting at the foreign intrusion, but the languid warmth that ensued was far more prominent than any pain. He shifted his hips, pushing in a tiny bit farther. I pre-emptively dug my nails into his arms, expecting it to hurt, but all I felt was liquid sunshine writhing through my bloodstream, pouring light into all the hollowed places of loneliness I'd never experience again.

The feeling of fullness was just exquisite, like a part of me had been missing until this very moment.

"Gods, you feel amazing, Tymp," he groaned into my neck, suckling at my throat. "Is this okay?"

"If you stop right now, I'm rescinding my acceptance of your proposal."

"That's a very big statement," he laughed, his warm breath on my neck adding a whole new layer of fulfilment.

My hips tilted up at their own accord, meeting him in the middle, pleasure radiating out from the act.

Blekket shuddered. "Do that again."

I repeated the motion, welcoming the friction as he grinded down in opposition, driving into me slowly with each piston of his hips. My fingers tangled in his hair, guiding his mouth to mine so I could drink from him. I tasted love and gratitude, which I tried to reciprocate in turn.

I curled my legs around his waist, tying myself to him in every humanly way possible, in body, heart, and mind.

"Fuck. I need you, Tympany. I need all of you. I need every single part of you." In that moment, I knew I would let him take whatever he wanted willingly if it meant I could have this intimacy with him forever.

"Take it all," I said with no shame. "It's yours."

"Fuck, Tymp. You're everything."

He picked up the pace of his thrusts, threading his fingers in my hair and cradling the back of my head, kissing me everywhere: my eyelids, my cheeks, my lips, my jaw, my neck. I felt the liquid sunshine dribble down and pool between my legs, the burn increasing with the upsurge of speed and force. With our breaths and movements in sync, I felt more connected to him now than I ever had before, just when I thought there wasn't room left in me for all these feelings to swell.

"I love you, Tympany," he moaned. "I will always love you, until the last drop of my blood."

"I love you so much, Blek," I cried, a tear dripping down the side of my face, which he was quick to kiss away.

The mounting pressure and heat rear-ended, shattering inside me in the form of a scream that was purifying in its power, accompanied by a series of spasms that made me feel like I was being pitched into the clouds. Blekket meandered his arm around me, hauling me closer so no part of our bodies weren't touching, slipping and sliding against one another due to accumulated sweat. He dropped his head into my neck, trembling around and in me. His muscles flexed, and then, he let himself go, emptying his heart and soul until there was nothing left of his that wasn't mine. I took it all greedily, clinging to him like a limpet with no intention of ever letting go.

He laid his cheek against my chest, listening to the sound of my heart pounding beneath my ribcage.

"How was that?" he asked, his eyes wrought with a strange anxiety I didn't entirely understand.

I gave him a sated smile and answered, "Magnificent," appreciating the way his face lit up with amusement.

"Magnificent, eh?" He kissed my chin, my cheek, then my nose and lips. I winced when he pulled out of me, which caused his forehead to wrinkle with worry. "You okay? Did I hurt you?"

"Never better," I swore. My muscles ached, but in a way that felt satiated, not painful. "How was that for you?" I wasn't sure why I suddenly felt self-conscious, but I needed to know it had been as life-affirming for him as it was for me.

"Every part of the last ten minutes, you agreeing to marry me and then *this,* was the highlight of my existence thus far," he replied. "Seriously. I've peaked. I could die happy right now."

"Please don't make jokes about dying after I just agreed to marry you. It really puts a damper on me trying to live in the present." Throwing his leg over mine, he snuggled close to me, nuzzling my hair.

"You have nothing to worry about, my love. You're going to be stuck with me for a long, long time."

"Good." I rested my cheek in the crook of his neck. "So…what happens now?"

"Whatever we want." He kissed my forehead. "We don't have to marry right away if you don't want to."

"I don't see why we'd wait." Now that I'd said yes, it didn't make sense to put off the inevitable.

"I might enjoy watching my father squirm for a little."

"You're terrible," I admonished, but grinned at the idea of torturing Demetrio. The man could stand to be knocked down a few pegs. It was clear where Blekket got his ego from. "Pessy is going to lose her mind when she finds out."

"That we're getting married, or that we had sex?" If my glower was fire, he would've been reduced to ash. "You're so easy to tease," he chuckled. "Probably because not many people had the nerve to do so back in Kylantis."

He had a point. I wasn't really treated like a being in Kylantis—I was viewed as more of an object you worship than a person who could withstand a little bantering every now and then. Besides Pessy, everyone walked on eggshells with me and all the Gods, fearful of upsetting Roara or infuriating one of us.

"I have a theory about why your abilities don't work on me," Blekket said randomly after a moment of silence.

"Let's hear it." I waved my hand, granting permission.

"When others look at you, they see their own desires reflected back at them. That's why your presence inspires people. When *I* look at you..." He tucked a strand of hair behind my ear. "When I look at you, I just see *you*. Not the Goddess of the Heart and Mind. Not the Muse of all mortals and celestials. Just the woman I love." I swallowed the knot pressing against the walls of my throat, fiddling with his hand.

"But you didn't love me when we first met."

"One might argue I've loved you since the second I laid eyes on you," he disputed. I narrowed my eyes in a scowl.

"I have a counter theory."

"Let's hear it." He mocked me with an authorising nod.

"Maybe you're just my soulmate." Blekket shut his eyes, absorbing my words, and moaned.

"Tymp," he groaned, leaning over to kiss me. "I like your counter theory."

"Me too." I nestled against his chest, wishing I could be even closer to him than I already was, that our skin could blend together so we'd be one entity instead of two separate beings. I'd never felt more complete then right there in his arms, the calm after the storm.

"You remember the night we met, how I was able to hold you down against that wall in the corridor?"

"How can I forget?" It was a bruise to my ego, though I wouldn't put it quite like that if Blekket asked.

"I think the reason you didn't tear me limb from limb was because you didn't *want* to. You know you're stronger than me. I've seen you in action. You're a freaking Goddess. You didn't overpower me in that corridor because you didn't want to. If you had, I wouldn't be here right now. I'm certain of that."

"Huh." I'd been so perplexed as to why he was able to incapacitate me, thinking it must've been because he caught me off guard, or because he was a Neraid. I'd never considered that perhaps the reason he'd done it so seamlessly was because I *let* him do it, because I didn't actually fight back. "Maybe I loved you since the moment I saw you too," I mumbled, and regretted it instantly after the most obnoxiously wide smile expanded across the bottom half of his face.

"I snagged you since day one," he declared proudly, curling a strand of my hair around his finger. "Lucky me."

"Yes. Lucky *you*." I beamed.

"Hold on a moment." Blekket crawled out of bed, and I admired the sway of his hips, his strong legs and plump, bare behind. He opened one of his drawers, rummaging through his folded shirts.

He returned, no longer empty handed. He was now holding Seraphina's engagement ring.

"I want to make this official," he explained, then dipped down to one knee at the foot of the bed. I swung my legs over the side, my eyes glazing over with tears. "I'm only going to ask this one more time, so *please,* don't change your answer." He held the ring up. "Tympany, will you marry me?"

"Yes, you worrywart," I whispered, proffering my hand for Blekket to slide the engagement ring onto my left ring finger. It glided into its forever resting place with ease, as if it knew it belonged there.

"A perfect fit," he marvelled to himself. "Saves me a trip to get it resized."

"I love it." I flexed my fingers, and the oval sapphire caught the moonlight, reflecting a silvery blue beam onto Blekket's cheek. "I'm never taking it off."

"You better not," he growled, launching himself at me.

He knocked us both back onto the mattress. I squealed, twisting my arms around his neck and hooking my ankles around his torso, holding on as if my life depended on it. He consumed my laughter in a kiss so earth-shattering, everything else ceased to exist beyond the pressure of his lips.

And then, we lost ourselves to love.

"Sweetheart. Wake up."

The sensation of teeth tugging at my earlobe replaced the cobwebs of sleep, my eyes fluttering open with a gasp.

I was on my stomach, naked and curled around a pillow. Blekket was hovering over me, his front to my spine.

"Good morning, *fiancée*," he cooed softly, kissing my jaw, then nipped at my bottom lip to coax another moan out of me. I felt his swelling bulge dig into my lower back, igniting my libido. I grabbed his hand on the mattress, then moved it between my legs.

"Morning, *my King*," I mumbled, my hips rolling in a circular motion to match the rhythm his fingers had commenced.

"Fuck, you calling me that in your sexy morning voice is going to be my undoing. I'm sure of it."

"More," I whined, rocking against his hand.

He increased the force, drawing out a long, throaty moan. I twisted around, clasping the back of his neck, and yanked him down to meet my lips, our tongues wrestling for dominance of the shared space. He swallowed my next moan, lapping up ever pant he extracted from me.

"I'm addicted to you," he groaned into my mouth when I reached behind me and found his cock, stroking him from the base up, like I'd done in the shower. He massaged his fingers back and forth, then skated his middle finger inside me, stroking the interior walls in a come-hither motion while persecuting my clit with his thumb.

"Blek," I groaned, throwing my head back against his shoulder. I couldn't believe I'd been asleep only a few moments before.

I dragged my hand up and down his length, coordinating our movements so we followed the same inaudible cadence. The pressure began to rise, tossing me into a fever pitch that made me feel like my skin was made out of flames rather than flesh. He inclined down, capturing my lips, and kissed me deeply, the rest of the world crumbling away.

Nothing mattered except for the move of his fingers, except for the impression of his lips over mine, educing sounds I never thought would've been possible for me to make before I met Blekket.

The tension snapped. I buried my face in the pillow, screaming a garbled version of his name as my orgasm flooded through me in waves. The sound of my climax was enough to send Blekket over the edge. He collapsed on top of me, moaning my name into the cloud of my hair.

While he kissed the same spot on my neck over and over, I thought, *I can get used to waking up like this every morning.*

"Will you marry me?" he asked after we'd each had a moment to come down from our spiral.

I shifted back around to look at him. "I can't. I'm already engaged."

"Who's the jackass? I'll fight him for you." He kissed the corner of my mouth, resting his chin on my shoulder.

"How'd you sleep?" I asked, running my nose down the slope of his.

"I slept amazing, in spite of your sleep talking."

"You make it sound like I shriek in my sleep, which I know I don't." I twisted onto my back beneath him.

"I think it's adorable. You kept saying *ring, ring,* I think talking about your engagement ring."

My face couldn't have been hotter. "What else did I say?"

"You said my name a few times, and always with a smile. My favourite was when you said *I love you, Blek.* That did me over." He stroked my face with the tips of his fingers. "I don't think I've ever been this happy in all my thirty years of life. I wish my mum was here to see this. She would be thrilled." I started to say *I'm sorry,* but he cut me off. "Don't even think about saying what I think you're about to say, Tymp. You have to stop blaming yourself. No one else is."

I bobbed my head in a nod, rather than utter words I didn't mean. I knew myself well enough to know, no matter how many times Blekket or Raevon or Pessy told me I wasn't responsible for Seraphina's death, it would never fully sink in. There would always be a part of me that wondered what would've happened if I'd been fast enough turning around to catch that arrow.

"As much as I want to stay here," he kissed my shoulder, "in bed," another kiss on my neck, "with you," one more on my chin, "all day," he nuzzled me behind my ear, kissing the spot beneath it that triggered shudders and made me giggle, "we should probably go get something to eat."

"Can we come back here when we're finished?" His impish smile grew to new heights of perfection.

"I thought that was implied." He kissed my cheek, then crawled out of bed.

Blekket accompanied me to my bedchamber so I could change out of my tunic and leggings from yesterday. I put on a white and light blue sleeveless jumpsuit, the stripes thin, which was tailored into a cinched waist, with a v-neckline, side seam pockets, and a matching sash belt.

"I love it when you wear pants," he mused, bending down to kiss my bare shoulder.

"I hate dresses. I need full range of motion." I tucked my blade inside the belt, slipping on my sandals.

"Always need to be prepared." He plucked my left hand off the hilt of my dagger, twiddling my new ring. "It's funny. Mum wore this ring every single day I knew her, and yet, now that it's yours, I can't remember what your hand looked like before you had it on your finger."

"I know." I felt similarly.

The minute he put this ring on me, I felt whole, like I'd been incomplete without it.

We headed down the stairs to the dining hall in comfortable silence, Blekket fiddling with my engagement ring, stroking his thumb down the oval sapphire. I thought about what he said earlier and couldn't recall a time when I'd felt happier, or more whole, then I did right then. Now that I'd made the decision and felt confident in that choice, the thought of being Queen wasn't as fear-provoking. There were a lot of factors we still needed to consider, like what our next move against Sleotha would be, those judgements now falling to us as the reigning sovereigns, but I knew Blekket and I could handle anything, as long as we did it together. Esteopia would forever be in the hands of two people who not only loved each other with every fiber of their being, but loved this kingdom as well. We would do everything in our power to protect our people, and each other, at all costs. I couldn't fathom a world where anything could commandeer that kind of devotion.

Entering the dining hall, we were assaulted upon arrival by thundering applause. Pessy, Raevon, Demetrio, Lev, and the rest of the staff, were congregated in the room, screaming, "Congratulations!" at the top of their lungs, filling my heart with so much love that it was bursting.

"How do you already know?" I shrieked, falling into Pessy's arms and squishing her ribs.

"Um, sorry for being crude, but you guys were not quiet last night." She pulled back to flash me a roguish smile. "Everyone could hear you, so it was pretty easy to put two and two together."

I'd never flushed so violently in my life.

"Let me see the ring!" I spread my fingers out and offered Pessy my left hand. She examined it with wonder, her garish blue eyes twinkling. "I'm not going to say I told you so, because that's beneath me."

"You just did," I said with a disapproving frown.

"Give me the win, Tymp. I need this."

I tried to feign dissatisfaction for a little while longer, but I ended up laughing in spite of myself.

"Thank you," I whispered, swathing her in my arms again.

"I'm so proud of you," she murmured, my eyes stinging with the threat of tears. "You're going to be an amazing Queen." She released me, peeking up at Blekket. "You're a lucky man, Blek. Just don't screw it up, or I'll have your head on a silver platter faster than you can say the words *I'm an idiot*."

"I genuinely believe that." He bent down to kiss Pessy's cheek.

"We're going to be sisters!" Raevon squealed, leaping on me from behind.

"Sister!" It was impossible not to be swept up in ecstasy with all the enthusiasm in the air.

When I made my way over to Demetrio, he stunned me by enfolding me in a tight embrace, going a step further and kissing my hair.

"I'm thrilled you said yes," he whispered in my ear with a surprising amount of sincerity. "I prayed you would. I truly couldn't imagine a better person to call our Queen, or to have as a daughter-in-law." I leaned back, my throat clogged with emotion.

"I'm sorry about what I said yesterday. I shouldn't have been so critical. I know you love your son."

"There's no need to apologise, Tympany. We're going to be family. Sometimes, families fight."

When he smirked, he looked just like Blekket.

As we took our seats around the table, Lev appeared at my side, placing a plate of yellowtail and avocado sushi in front of me.

"For you, Your Majesty," he announced.

"Lev, you don't have to call me that. Please, just call me Tympany."

"I'm afraid I must call you that, Your Majesty…in public anyway." His dimpled face blushed like a rose.

"Thank you for yesterday," I said, taking his hand and giving it a grateful squeeze. "For sitting with me, and everything else you said." He returned the pulse I sent up his arm with an appreciative smile.

"Congratulations again." He bowed his head respectfully, then turned on his heel and stalked off towards the kitchen.

"So. What's on the agenda for today?" I popped a roll into my mouth, leaning against the back of my chair.

"Well, now that you've officially said yes, before we start planning a wedding, we must have an engagement proclamation," Demetrio replied.

"Engagement proclamation? Is that a party?" I groaned.

"*Not* a party," Blekket assured, plucking my hand off my knee so he could play with the ring. "It's basically just us standing on a terrace and having the kingdom below welcome us as their new rulers. Very low key."

Low key my ass, I thought to myself. "So, no party?" I asked a second time for confirmation.

"No party," he swore. "I get you all to myself tonight." He grazed my knuckles with his teeth.

"You get me to yourself every night."

"I'm glad to hear it." When he looked at me with such unabashed desire, I completely forgot we were with company.

"I want to make a toast." Raevon lifted her glass of water, gesticulating for all of us to follow her lead. "To Blekket and Tympany. There are no two people who are better suited for one another. May you continue to make each other and everyone around you laugh until our bellies ache, and may you always remember how magnificent you both are, both individually, and together as a unit. I adore you guys, and am honoured to call you our King and Queen, and my family."

"Rae," Blekket whispered, stretching across the table to kiss the back of her hand. "I love you."

"I can't wait to call you my sister," I said. Her answering smile looked like it had been molded by magic.

"To Tymp and Blek!" Pessy concurred, raising her chalice of Argent Ocean water in the air. "And a lifetime of battling each other's egos!" That made me cackle, the room soon teeming with everyone's delighted laughter.

"Thank you all," I choked out, Blekket leaning over to kiss away the tear that dripped down my cheek. "Thank you for accepting me into your kingdom and your family. I promise, I won't let either one down."

"We know you won't." I could've sworn I saw Demetrio's bottom lip tremble when he spoke.

That irresistible joy carried on throughout the remainder of breakfast, dousing everyone in its sweet ruddiness. There was no room to feel anything but euphoria, no room for doubt or stress or fear. We talked through the meal like we never had before, Demetrio sharing stories about Blekket and Raevon growing up—like how Raevon used to steal all of Blekket's things before he started hiding them under his mattress, which he had to stop doing when he developed an ache in his back from sleeping on top of his toiletries. He told us about his own life, growing up with his two brothers, Joseph and Dorian, who used to gang up on Demetrio because he was the eldest. They would pull pranks on him, like pouring a bucket of ice water over his head while he was sleeping, or the time they iced his birthday cake with toothpaste, and he ended up vomiting all over their mother's favourite carpet. That story made Pessy laugh so hard that juice shot out of her nose, which had me rushing to the bathroom so I wouldn't urinate all over the fancy velvet chairs.

It was the first meal we shared where we felt like a real family.

While happiness looped us together, Seraphina's absence was still evident, an encumbrance on each of our shoulders. I imagined it would haunt us for the rest of our lives, the missing piece to our perfect family puzzle, but maybe someday, the dearth of her presence wouldn't feel quite as heavy.

When we finished eating, Blekket's intentions were clear once he knit his fingers with mine and started leading me in the direction of the bedchambers.

"Your Grace? May I have a word in private?" Alsandair interrupted before we could begin ascending the stairs.

"Of course." I met Blekket's frown and assured, "I'll just be a moment," kissing his cheek.

"If you're not back in five minutes, I'm coming to get you," he said, squinting his eyes at Alsandair in warning. After Blekket traipsed up the stairs and disappeared from sight, I turned to face Alsandair, folding my fingers together in preparation.

"Is everything okay?" I asked.

"Your Grace…forgive me for speaking out of turn, but I would be remiss if I didn't say this at least once."

My heart fluttered with anxiety. "Okay?"

"I understand you and the Prince are…romantically involved, but before you commit to all of this, I advise you to remember your duties in Kylantis. Your mother intends to make you Queen, and I imagine she will be very displeased to know you plan to take the throne here instead of there. I don't think it's worth inciting her wrath over. She may cause irreparable damage to Esteopia if you do this. Just consider what the consequence of these actions might be, not just for you, but for the people you love." While I knew subconsciously he meant well with this advisement, that what he was saying also had validity, all I felt in that moment was irrepressible rage.

"You will *not* tell me what *my* duties are," I snapped. "If you are to stay in Esteopia, then you serve *me. Not* my mother. If you disagree with what I'm doing here, you should return to Kylantis. Do I make myself clear?"

"Yes, Your Grace." He dropped his head to avoid looking at me, shifting on the balls of his feet. "I apologise if I've offended you. I just couldn't stand by and not speak my truth."

"Well, you've said your piece. Now, please, don't say it again." I flicked my wrist, signalling for him to go. He barrelled down the hall, rushing to get away from me.

I exhaled a hefty huff, then marched up the stairs, grumbling as I went. When I entered Blekket's—now *our* bedchamber—I found my future husband sprawled out on the bed, resting against the headboard with his hands behind his skull, completely naked from top to bottom. He was the epitome of temptation and arrogance.

"I've been waiting for you," he greeted in a husky voice.

"I can see that." I kicked off my shoes and crawled onto the bed with him, straddling his waist. Blekket placed his hands on my hips, gliding them around to my behind.

"Everything good with Alsandair?"

"Everything's fine." His eyes narrowed.

"You sure? You're not usually so brusque."

"Let's not talk about him right now. No one exists in here except us, remember?"

His lips curled up in a lecherous smile. "That's my girl."

Before he could say anything else to kill my libido, I dove down, my teeth finding his ear.

Lev sent word to all the villages that there would be an engagement proclamation tonight, which called for every Esteopian to travel to Acadia for the celebration. They would be escorted to the anterior of the palace, where they would stand below us as we walked out onto the terrace to be received. Pessy, Raevon and I spent the afternoon picking what I'd wear for tonight, ingesting far more champagne then our bodies could withstand while I tried on a million different gowns. We ended up unanimously agreeing on a white dress with a v-neckline and thin straps, encrusted with opal and crystal embellishments. The twinkling beads and lustrous imitation pearls danced across the slender bodice and onto the soft and billowy tulle skirt, flowing down to the ground like rivulets of water.

When I finally started getting ready, I was drunk, so much so that I couldn't hold the curling iron without my hands trembling.

"Pess? You still here?" I called out.

Blekket appeared in the doorway wearing the same trousers he'd been in the night before, sans a shirt.

"Oh. It's you."

"Yeah. Me." He cocked his head. "Are you drunk?"

"Merely buzzed," I replied, enunciating every word so I could avoid slurring.

"If *you're* smashed, then I'm concerned what state Pessy and Raevon are in right now." He strolled over to where I stood at the vanity, wrapping his arms around my waist from behind. "Did you pick a dress for tonight?"

"I did." His lips started at my temple, trickling down my cheek, then pecked the corner of my mouth.

"Can I see it?"

"You can see it when I put it on."

"Now I want to see it even more," he groused, making me laugh.

He undid the sash of my robe, slipping his hands inside the silk to flatten his fingers over my stomach.

"You are entirely...distracting." I sighed, moaning at the swipe of his tongue on my throat.

"Why else do you think I came in here?" He grinned against my neck, gliding his hands up to fondle my breasts.

"You need to go," I groaned, but arched my back and shoved my breasts farther into his dexterous fingers. "I have to do my hair for tonight."

"I can do your hair for you." I jerked my head back to look at him, his hands dropping to my hips.

"No, you can't."

"Yes, I can. I used to do Raevon's hair all the time."

"You calling yourself a barber now?" Blekket rolled his eyes before releasing my torso. I redid the sash around my waist when he let me go, aware that, if I kept everything exposed, we'd both get distracted again.

"I'm a jack of all trades," he declared, grabbing the wand off the vanity. "Now, let the master show you show it's done."

"I already regret this decision."

Blekket situated me in front of him and began winding a tendril of my hair around the iron, holding it to the heat so the ringlet would cement in place. His brows were furrowed adorably in concentration while he did this.

"What made you decide to cut your hair short?" he asked.

"I was inspired by Luna," I answered, watching him work through the mirror, giving each strand an equal amount of attention. "Her hair's even shorter than mine. I just…I didn't want to look like all my other sisters anymore. I wanted to stand out."

"How long did your hair used to be?"

"It was down to my hip, like Raevon's." Blekket whistled through his teeth.

"I can't imagine you with long hair."

"Do you like it short?" I traced a wisp with my finger when it dribbled over my eye, brushing it to the side.

"I love this length on you. It's sexy."

Sexy had never been a word used to describe me once in all my five thousand years—until now.

"Would you still love me if I had no hair?"

"Sweetheart, I would still love you if you were bald, missing all your teeth, and had warts all over your face. I don't love you because of how you look. Your looks are just an added bonus to what's already on the inside." My heart yelled with adoration.

"As if you couldn't be more perfect," I said with a shake of my head.

"You think I'm perfect?" His smug grin was blinding.

"Forget I said anything. Your neck's looking unstable enough as is. No need to add more weight to it."

"Oh, so now you're calling me fat?"

I sunk my teeth into my bottom lip to detain a laugh, which was challenging with how nonplussed he looked.

"You said in your proposal you need me to humble you."

"I should've known I needed to be careful with my wording. Everything I say with you bites me in the ass." I laughed, then rotated around so he could curl the front pieces.

Blekket was very quiet as he worked, absorbed in his task, extremely focused on not messing up a single lock. My hair splattered over my eye, and he tucked the strand behind my ear, tracing his thumb down the line of my blush.

"I just want to make sure it's perfect for you," he said, melting my heart.

"I don't care how they look. I'm not the one who has to stare at myself all the time. You do."

"True. Though I think you're perfect with or without styled hair. But you already know that."

He inclined down until we were at eye level with one another, raking his fingers through the curls to separate them, so they'd be less rigid in shape. Up close, I noticed, sprinkled into the dark blue hue of his eyes, were flecks of cerulean, the same lighter shade circling his pupils before bleeding back into midnight.

"You have really pretty eyes," I blurted, and felt like a complete idiot after the words escaped.

"So do you. Sometimes, they look really green, like the colour of a Granny Smith apple. Other times, like when you compel someone, they look like caramel. And sometimes, they look almost yellow. I can always tell if you've been crying when they look kind of like a bleached lemon."

His cheeks flushed an endearing shade of red, leading me to believe he hadn't meant to go into such detail.

"Very observant," I teased, trying to lighten the mood, since I now felt just as self-conscious as he did.

"Only when it has to do with you." He kissed the tip of my nose. "Okay. I think you're all good. Let me know if you like it."

I twirled around, facing the mirror, and inspected his handiwork. For all the grief I gave him, he certainly knew what he was doing. The curls framed my cheeks like a diadem of chestnut, each one immaculate and identical. When I looked past the bouncy ringlets at the woman underneath them, I saw a light in her eyes I hadn't seen in ages, if ever, a natural glow in her cheeks that emanated outward due to her inner contentment. She was radiating bliss, and that joy wasn't contingent on the magnificent man standing behind her. She'd finally found herself in this land, in these people, in trusting her gut and not being ashamed of what it told her to do.

Her skin no longer felt wrong around her bones, less like camouflage and more like a cape of pride.

That self-love made her more beautiful than ever.

"Thank you," I stammered past the lump in my throat, but I wasn't thanking him for the curls.

I was thanking him for not only seeing me, but helping me to really see myself.

"Tymp," Blekket moaned, sensing there was more behind those two words then a simple thank you for curling my hair. "I should be the one thanking you." I spun in his arms, setting my hands on his chest.

"You can do that for the rest of time, if you like."

"Oh, I plan to. Everyday." He slanted his head, cajoling my lips to split so his tongue could explore my mouth, pouring gratitude down my throat with every moan. When I kissed him back, I tried to communicate all the feelings I possessed that words just weren't enough to adequately express. I strived to prove with each lick of my tongue and inch I moved closer that I was tethered to him, that while I may be his sun, he was my moon, my center, my peace, my home.

"I love you," I gasped when I was given the chance to breathe, overwhelmed with the depth of my commitment to him.

"I love you more," he declared.

"Nope. Not possible."

"Are we really about to have a battle over who loves the other more? Is this what our life together is going to be like?"

"This is what you signed up for. Get used to it, Shamus." I patted his cheek, then crossed the bathroom and headed into the bedchamber.

It took some convincing for Blekket to finally leave the room so we could both start getting ready. I clambered into the gown, gliding the straps to my shoulders, and tried to reach behind me to button the back myself, but it was too far for me to reach.

"I'll do it, Tymp," I heard Pessy say behind me as she entered the room, shutting the door. When she approached, she marvelled, "Did you do your hair yourself? If so, I'm impressed."

"Blek did it." Her eyebrows shot up.

"*Blek* did this? I'm doubly impressed." When I glanced behind me, I saw that Pessy was wearing a navy blue dress with a v-neckline, wrap front, tie waist, and a dipped hem, the design lined and the dress midi length. Her hair was also tailored to perfection, spilling down her chest like kinks of melted butter.

"It's annoying how you look good in everything," I said, causing the corners of her lips to quirk up in a smile.

"I'd say the same about you, but you'd hit me if I tried." I cackled up at the ceiling, Pessy's smile enlarging at the sound. "I don't think, in all the time I've known you, I've ever seen you this happy."

"Me neither," I mumbled, flushing.

"I know I said it earlier, but I'm really proud of you, Tympany. You're making the right choice, not just for you, but for everyone."

"I hope so." I thought about what Alsandair said for the first time in hours. "What do you think my mother will do when she finds out?"

"I certainly don't want to be there to see that." My shoulders sagged. "Hey, it's okay. She'll be upset, obviously, but she'll have to get over it. It's your life, and you're allowed to live it however you want to."

"I know that. I'm just worried she'll retaliate against Esteopia in some way."

"If she does, we'll make sure we're prepared for any sort of attack. We will never leave Esteopia unprotected."

Her assurance slackened the tension my muscles. "You know what else this means, right?"

"What?" I smiled.

"When you marry Raevon, we'll be sisters." Pessy's eyes glittered, her lips mirroring mine in a shit-eating grin.

"Our dream!" She kissed my cheek, engulfing me in a bear hug.

With our arms linked, we descended the hallway towards the passage connecting the third and fourth quadrants of the palace, where Blekket and I would stand under the arch to be received by all of Esteopia. Blekket, Raevon, Demetrio and Lev were waiting for us by the corridor, turning in unison when they heard our footsteps. Raevon looked exquisite in a light blue mermaid gown that had a beautiful embroidered floral overlay, her hair pulled away from her face in an elegant bun, permitting her collarbones, freckles, and cobalt eyes to be on full display. Around her neck was a gorgeous diamond necklace, the gems precast in the shape of teardrops.

"That necklace is beautiful," I complimented her.

"It was my mother's," she replied in a low voice, then shook the brief despondence away and beamed at me. "You look gorgeous, Tymp."

"She's right," Demetrio concurred, clearing his throat to speak.

I looked over at my fiancé, whose jaw had dropped so low, I worried it would dislodge permanently from the socket.

"Having trouble breathing?" I taunted, which woke him from his trace. He grew all at once cocky.

"Just needed a moment of well-deserved pride."

"Like you'd only take a moment," I spat, making everyone laugh. Drinking him in, I realised he was wearing the same apparel he had on the night we met, same petticoat, black slacks, and grey vest with a white dress shirt underneath, minus a tie. The sentiment was not lost on me.

"You really are so magnificent, Tympany," Blekket said in earnest, lifting my left hand to kiss my engagement ring.

"So are you," I whispered, taking my rightful place at his side.

Raevon reached for Pessy's hand, then asked. "Will you walk out there with me?" This was a big deal, to be presented before the entire kingdom together as a couple. I thought it would daunt Pessy, but she smiled wider than I'd ever seen her grin before and laced her fingers with Raevon's.

"Always," she vowed, kissing Raevon's cheek.

Sisters! I squealed to Pess, who just rolled her eyes at me.

While Pessy and Raevon situated themselves in the front, ready to lead the group, Blekket leaned over and whispered, "I have to say, as beautiful as you look in that gown, now all I can think about is how I can't wait to get it off you." I raised my eyes to him in slits.

"Is that a promise, or a challenge?" His answering grin told me all I needed to know.

Raevon and Pessy strode down the corridor together hand in hand, welcomed by the crowd below with an outstanding tumult of cheers and screams. The vociferous volume demonstrated how much the people of Esteopia adored their Princess, and how now, that love was being transferred over to her partner. It filled my heart with joy to see Pessy accepted by the Esteopians, to see her thrive in the spotlight when usually, she preferred to hide behind me. She looked right at home at Raevon's side without an iota of nervousness, oozing confidence, like the princess I had no doubt she would one day be.

"Here." Demetrio removed the crown from atop his head and handed it to Blekket, who glared at it as if he'd been offered sludge.

"I'm not wearing that," he objected, shoving it towards his father.

"You have to. You're being received by the people as their ruler."

"I'm not wearing that crown until the wedding," Blekket snarled. I knew, from that tone of voice, he wouldn't be changing his mind. Demetrio raised his hands in surrender, backing up.

"Tympany? Will *you* wear it?" I eyed the crown nervously.

"I mean…it doesn't really make sense for me to wear it and not Blek. I'll just wait until the wedding too."

In truth, I said no because I'd been so level-headed and composed about all this, and was worried that the moment I put the crown on my head, everything would become too real, and I'd splinter into panic.

"Alright," Demetrio said with a disappointed sigh and a shake of his head, passing the crown to Lev.

He fixed the lapels of his jacket, squaring his shoulders, then stepped out onto the terrace, assailed by what I gathered must've been an enormous standing ovation from the deafening roars of the townsfolk.

"You sure you'll be okay out there?" I joked, tipping my chin towards the terrace. "You know, with your fear of heights."

"Good thing I've got you as an anchor," Blekket crooned, curling an arm around my waist. "You ready to do this, angel?"

"Ready as I'll ever be," I said, but the truth was, I felt more ready for this than I ever had before.

I'd chosen my life—it was time to start living it.

Timing my steps with Blekket's, we made our way out, halting in the center of the long corridor. We exchanged a look and a synchronised breath before turning our bodies to face the…*our* people. The degree of approbation we received, the way the crowd hollered with delight down below, was inundating, so much so that it stripped me of my next breath, as though I'd been kicked in the stomach. Tears pricked the corner of my eyes, threatening to topple over onto my cheeks.

Blekket leaned down, his lips at my ear, and whispered, "They love you, but not nearly as much as I do."

I elevated my head, beaming at him. "I love you more."

"Your head just grew three sizes." I laughed, gazing back down at the congregation of Esteopians, hailing us as their new rulers.

It felt like the kingdom had waited eons for a fresh heart to beat a new rhythm into the matter that made it.

I just happened to be the lucky owner of that heart.

Chapter Twenty-Two

I stepped through the dimly illuminated hall with a black silk robe draped over my sheer nightgown, creeping into the kitchen. I'd woken up starving after all the madness of the engagement proclamation and didn't want to wake Blekket, so I just slipped out of bed and tiptoed out the door. I opened the fridge and grabbed the container of yellowtail and avocado rolls, setting it down on the wooden countertop.

When I went to lift the lid, moonlight bespattered over my ring, projecting beams of blue light onto the wall.

I raised my hand under the torrent, flexing my fingers. There was a poeticness in being gifted Seraphina's ring, like I was carrying a piece of her wherever I went. I wished she could've been there to see us adoringly received as the new rulers of Esteopia, to see her wish come true of Blekket becoming king. I would've loved nothing more than the honour of calling her my mother-in-law.

"It's a beautiful ring," a voice admired from behind me.

It sent a landslide of shudders down the length of my spine, because that voice shouldn't have been there.

"Mother?"

I spun around, dropping the container of sushi on the floor, the rolls spilling out onto my bare feet.

There she was in all her glory, looking stunning in a metallic gold maxi dress. Her reddish brown hair was blow-dried over her shoulders, curled at the ends, and her brown eyes appeared as black as coal in the obscurity of night. The gilded crown to Kylantis sat atop her head.

"You should get that," Roara said, leaning against the wall with her arms crossed over her chest, looking down at where the sushi had collapsed at my toes. "I taught you better than to wait for the help to clean up your messes."

"How're you here right now?" I demanded.

In all my five thousand years of existence, Roara had never once set foot outside of Kylantis.

"I have my ways," she answered elusively with a shrug. "I thought it was time I had a chat with my youngest."

I lunged forward, sprinting to the door, and rattled the knob, startled to find it was locked.

"You seriously tried running from me?" Roara leapt from her immobile stance. She flew across the room, landing in front of me, and shocked me by encircling her fingers around my throat, garroting me just like Lucius had on my birthday, only ten times stronger. She lifted me off my feet and thrust me against the wooden door so ferociously, I heard the wood crackle under the weight of my skull.

"Mum!" I shrieked, tugging at her fingers to try and rip her off me.

"Tympany, wake up!" I heard Blekket shout, but when I looked around, I didn't see him in the room.

That's when I realised—she wasn't really here. She was coming to me in a dream.

Roara used to do this when I had nightmares. She'd infiltrate my mind so whatever illusion was tormenting me would be vanquished by her presence, and I'd fall back into a peaceful slumber. It was the part of her powers mine derived from, her ability to bend the mind to her will and make you see whatever she wanted you to see. She once told me, when I was older and my abilities had fully matured, I'd be able to do what she did. I'd been so excited to learn from her.

If she was permeating my dream, it meant she was back in Kylantis, in the safety net of her bubble.

Her fingers weren't *actually* around my neck.

Which allowed me to take control once more and seize her wrist, turning it back so she was forced to release me.

I dropped to the floor like the spilled sushi rolls, wheezing. She stood over where I was crumpled on the ground, frowning with contempt.

"Tymp? Tymp, it's okay. It's not real," Pessy assured from outside the reverie. She must've felt through the bond I was in trouble somehow and came running. The sound of her voice was a comfort.

Roara shook her head at me.

"I hate to admit it, but Lucius was right." I rose to my feet when I felt confident my knees wouldn't give out, caressing my enflamed throat. "I thought

347

sending you here without any preconceived ideas would make you appear more genuine to the Elrods, but it was a mistake. You're too impressionable. It only took them three days to weasel their way into your head before you switched sides. I thought you were stronger than to fall victim to the first person who gave you attention."

"Being impartial is different than being impressionable," I argued, clenching my muscles so I wouldn't flinch at what she'd said about me and Blekket. "I formed my own opinions based off fact, off what I was seeing with my own eyes. I was in the thick of the battle at Frofsea. I saw what the drogon did to Eveium. I was there when the Sleothians invaded Tympany's Province. They are ruthless, and cruel, and I don't understand why the Gods favour them over the Esteopians, who, if you bothered to get to know, are kind, *good* people. *Seraphina* was good. She was an amazing Queen, and you allowed the Sleothians to murder her right below you, in front of her children and husband. You let Jax refuse to heal a five-year-old girl and left her to die just because she was Esteopian. It's wrong, and sick. You're *sick.*"

Roara suddenly snapped, as if someone had taken a bat and shattered the glass in her head. She realised quarrelling with me wasn't the way to get me to listen to her and fluctuated from aggression to earnest desperation. She reached for my hand, pointedly not my left one.

"Come home, angel. Just come home, and I'll explain everything. I'll tell you anything you want to know. I promise."

"I'm not coming home," I roared, wrenching my hand out of hers. "Kylantis isn't my home. And *don't* call me angel. That nickname no longer belongs to you." She recoiled as if I'd struck her.

"So you'd rather stay *here?* With *these* people, then be with your *actual* family?"

"*These* people *are* my family," I sneered. "They accept me for who I am. They don't shut me down when I try to speak or treat me like I'm small because I'm the youngest. They haven't once tried to pressure me into a role I didn't want. They let me make my own choices. They trust me to take care of them and give me the strength to actually meet those expectations. I've never felt stronger than when I'm with them. I love them, and I won't leave them."

"Them, or *him?*" She wrinkled her nose at my left hand.

"*All* of them," I asserted, wishing my blood didn't boil in my cheeks to display my embarrassment.

"All those years you said you didn't want to be Queen, it wasn't a throne you were averse to. It was just mine specifically."

"Gee, I wonder why I want to be nothing like *you*." I instantly regretted saying that when her face pinched with rage.

She slapped me so hard, I felt the blow ripple through my entire body, launching me at the wall with a harsh crash. Part of the partition crumbled with me when I nosedived to the floor.

"Tymp!" I heard Pessy scream.

"It's okay, angel," Blekket consoled in reality. "We're right here, sweetheart." I couldn't imagine what I was doing to make Blekket's voice tremble like that.

I must've been convulsing uncontrollably, or screeching.

"You will not speak to your Queen that way!" Roara bellowed, marching across the room and fisting a handful of my hair, yanking me to my feet. She clutched my chin, cementing me in place, so I was forced to meet her incense head on. "When you are in my presence, show me some respect."

"You're in *my* home now. This is *my* territory." I grabbed a hold of her forearm and twisted it behind her back, her bones making a satisfying crunching sound when they yielded to my control. Her hips bucked forward as she tried to break the entrapment. "You abandoned these people for centuries. You have no standing in Esteopia. *I'm* the Queen here. When you're in my presence, show *me* some respect."

I kicked at her lower back, punting her to the ground to join the sushi. Roara flicked a grain of rice off her cheek and raised her eyes, scrutinising me like she didn't recognise what she saw staring back at her.

"I always knew you'd be an amazing Queen," she muttered, unsure if she should be in awe, or frightened of me.

"Just not of *your* domain," I spat.

"Let me make myself perfectly clear, Tympany." She articulated every word very prudently. "You *will* come home and face me. You will not hide out here forever. If you don't, the consequences for Esteopia and your precious Elrods will be dire. If I have to smoke you out with more slaughter, with starvation, with having Eira freeze the ocean, or Lucius make the sun so blistering that it scalds your skin when you step under it, I will. No matter what you do, you are coming home."

And then, I woke up.

I lurched upright in bed with a gasp so loud, it pricked the walls of my throat, my hand flying up to where she socked me in my dream. Pessy, Blekket, and Raevon were all standing over me, faces etched with concern.

"What happened, sweetheart?" Blekket asked, smudging his thumb through the streaks of tears collecting on my cheeks.

"It was my mother," I explained, peeking up at Pessy. "She reached out to me through my dream."

"Like what she used to do when you were little?" I nodded. "What did she say?"

"She wants me to come home. She threatened the welfare of Esteopia, and you guys, if I don't."

"Was she hurting you?" Raevon asked worriedly, hugging her shoulders. "It sounded like she was."

"She strangled me, then slapped me when I was rude to her."

"She *strangled* you?" Pessy uttered in horror.

"That bitch," Blekket snarled, causing all three of us to inhale sharply. "I don't care that she's the Queen of the Gods, or that she's your mother. I don't care if she smites me for disrespecting her. *No one* lays a hand on my wife."

All the anxiety, distress, and pain that throttled me a minute ago vanished at that single word.

Wife.

His wife.

There was no greater honour.

"I'm so sorry, Tymp," Pessy muttered, taking a seat next to me on the bed to lie her head on my shoulder.

"How did you know I was in trouble?"

"I felt it through the bond. It's hard to describe, but it was like someone, maybe you from afar, stuck a needle in the back of my neck, where the mark is. I just knew I had to come to you."

Raevon crawled onto the mattress and positioned herself at my other side, resting her cheek on me, so both my shoulders were occupied by heads. Blekket sat across from us, glaring at the wall, silently seething.

I captured his hand, splaying his fingers out over my cheek, and angled my face into his palm.

"I'm okay," I assured him. I wasn't concerned about myself—I was far more concerned for everyone else.

He bobbed his head in a nod, but didn't look entirely convinced.

"What're you going to do, Tympany? You can't just *not* listen to your mother," Raevon said.

"Watch me." I wasn't afraid of Roara. Somewhere, beneath her indignation, I knew her partiality for me remained. She'd only wounded me in the dream because it hadn't been real. "At the end of the day, Roara wants me to take the throne of Kylantis. That will never happen if she ostracises me completely. I have the power here, not her. I don't believe she would do anything to actually hurt me. I'm more concerned about what she plans to do to Esteopia, if she follows through on having Eira freeze the ocean so we don't have access to the fish. I think tomorrow, we should travel to Jopolis and speak to Solara, warn them about Roara's threat and make sure we gather as much fish as we can in case that happens. We should be prepared for anything."

"That's a good idea," Blekket agreed, giving my hand a squeeze.

"What happens to Floatsim in the winter, when the waters are frozen?" Pessy asked Raevon.

"The merfolk move to Jopolis when the temperatures drop, because otherwise, they'd be trapped under the ice."

"And the Hippocampi?"

"They hibernate in the palace in Floatsim for the off season." I cringed, loathing the thought of Alexandria and Calypso entombed in frozen temperatures for several months.

"What will we do if Roara has Caspian stop nourishing the harvests?" I could hear Pessy's escalating anxiety.

"Caspian wouldn't agree to deny Esteopia rain," I disputed. "There's no way. He'd never do that to Solara."

"What about Benjen?" Raevon enquired. "Can't he intervene in the harvests just as much?"

"I don't see him agreeing to that either. Ben wouldn't refuse anyone food. If they were to implicitly starve the people of Esteopia, they'd do it through freezing the ocean and through the sun. Ben and Casp would never agree to that, but Eira and Lucius would." In fact, I bet Lucius offered the idea up himself. "I'm worried about Lucius making the sun blister. On particularly warm days, I think we should mandate a quarantine to protect the townsfolk from burning. We can have soldiers bring them necessities in the meantime from the palace, until it's safe for them to leave their houses."

"Can you do that?" Pessy stammered.

"We're the King and Queen," Blekket said, stroking his thumb over my engagement ring. "We can do whatever we want."

We're the King and Queen. I was surprised by how those words thrilled, rather than frightened me.

"The villagers won't be happy about it, but if it insures their safety, they'll have to endure it," Raevon approved.

"Right now, all of this is conjecture, until my mother actually follows through with one of her threats, but it's important to be prepared no matter what, even if she's just bluffing. It's far better to be safe than sorry."

"I agree." Blekket ran his hand down the back of my hair. "I think we should let Tympany sleep some more. We'll plan to reconvene in the morning and leave for Jopolis before noon."

"Okay." Pessy crawled off the bed, then asked me, "You sure you're okay?" I nodded. "Reach out if you need anything."

"I promise. Thanks for coming."

"I always will." She and Blekket exchanged a nod before she laced her fingers with Raevon's.

"See you guys in the morning." I waved goodbye to Raevon and Pessy as they exited the room.

"Come here," Blekket pleaded once we were alone, opening his arms for me. I fell back into them, melting against his chest with a relieved sigh. *This* was my home. "You scared the shit out of me," he whispered into my hair.

"What was I doing? Was I talking?"

"We heard your side of the conversation, like you were speaking to us. We just couldn't hear hers."

"You heard what I said to her?" He nodded. "All of it?"

"All of it. Even the part where you told her she couldn't call you angel anymore. Not going to lie, that made me ridiculously happy." He kissed my hair, and I snuggled closer, squishing his ribs.

"I don't care what she does to me. I just don't want her to hurt any of you."

"Well, *I* care what she does to you, and I'm fucking pissed she hit you. It doesn't matter if it was a dream or not. For as long as I live and breathe, until the last drop of my blood, no one lays a hand on you that you didn't want there. Not even me. I pledge that to you, Tympany, now and forever." My heart felt like it was deliquescing around my ribcage.

"I love you, Blek," I squeaked, the corners of my eyes stinging.

"You don't understand the depth of my love for you," he groaned. When I turned my head, I saw tears welling in his eyes. He traced my cheeks with the tips of his fingers, gushing, "I need you more than I need to breathe. If you go back to Kylantis, I'm terrified you'll never come back. I can't lose you. I just found you."

"You won't," I swore, placing a kiss on his jaw. "You won't. I'm not going anywhere. Not now, not ever."

He lay his forehead over mine. "I love you so much. More than anything. More than myself."

"More than yourself? I'm shocked." He narrowed his eyes in a scowl.

"Alright, you. Time for bed." He rolled me over by my waist, spooning me from behind, his thighs snuggling around mine.

"Blek?" I whispered in the dark.

"Yeah, Tymp?"

"We're going to be okay?" I'd meant that to come out as a statement of assurance, but it escaped in the form of a question.

I felt his breath tickle the back of my neck before he rested his cheek against mine, kissing the corner of my mouth.

"We're gonna be okay," he promised. "Because we have you."

Splotches of red stained my vision, inveigling my eyes to open.

I welcomed the new day by twisting onto my back, unfurling my arm over the mattress. It took me a moment of staring at the oval sapphire of my engagement ring, drenched in sunshine, to realise I shouldn't have been able to sprawl my arm out with Blekket lying next to me.

He wasn't in bed.

"Blek?" I called out, kicking away the duvet. I scampered into the bathroom, finding it empty as well. I quickly stripped out of my nightgown and pulled on a blue jumpsuit with tiny white polka dots printed on the fabric. I twisted my hair into a low bun, knotting it away from my face, and tucked my blade into my pocket before slipping on my sandals and scurrying out the door.

Lev was waiting in the hallway, wearing his customary blue armour with his hands folded in front.

"Good morning, Tympany," he greeted with a sweet smile.

"Morning, Lev. Where's Alsandair? Is he late waking up?" Lev grimaced, not the reaction I was expecting. "Is something wrong?"

"I'm afraid Alsandair departed for Kylantis early yesterday evening, before the engagement proclamation."

"What?" I gasped. "Are you sure?"

"Augustus saw him leave. He travelled alone. I'm sorry."

I wasn't sure why I was so stunned—I'd told Alsandair to leave if he couldn't accept my decision to marry Blekket. I guess I just didn't expect him to actually go.

"Their loss is our gain, Your Majesty," Lev avowed when he saw my face fall, setting a hand on my shoulder.

"Thank you, Lev." I squeezed his hand. "Have you seen Blekket?"

"I believe he's down in the utility room, where we keep the weapons. I can walk you there, if you'd like."

"Please." I gave his hand another squeeze before we departed.

As we made our way down the stairs, I thought of all the Kylantians who'd accompanied me on this quest, who were missing their families and thousands of miles away from the only home they ever knew. Now that I was to be Queen of Esteopia, I had the entire Esteopian army to guard me. I didn't need the Kylantians anymore, and it wasn't fair of me to keep them from their other duties or lives. I decided, after we returned from Jopolis, to sit down with each of the Kylantians and offer them the choice—they could either stay here with me and fight for Esteopia, or return back to Kylantis.

I'd make it clear there would be no ill will against anyone who decided to return home. They'd been instrumental in getting us this far, with all the work they put into Tympany's Province, and would have my eternal gratitude no matter what they chose to do.

Lev left me at the entryway of the utility room. I knocked on the door first. Then, when I heard no answer, I shoved it open with my elbow and stepped inside. Blekket was there, shirtless and wearing his night trousers, practicing his swordsmanship. I stood in the doorway, my fingers wrapped around the doorknob, watching him slice through the air in awe. He wielded his weapon as if he were following a soundless melody, his movements as fluid and agile as water. It almost looked like he was dancing.

I didn't know a man of his height and bulk could be so graceful.

Blekket's eyes oscillated to the door, finding me there. He ceased all activity, his arm falling to his side.

"Don't stop on my account," I said, feeling guilty for interrupting his rhythm.

"It's better to practice with a partner anyway." He beckoned me over with a beautiful smile.

"You want me to fight you?" I spluttered.

"Why? Afraid you might lose?" He gripped the hilt of his sword in one hand, the other sweeping hair damp with sweat off his forehead.

"No. I'm afraid I might accidentally cut your head off, which will be easy since your neck is already so unstable from all that extra weight." He rolled his eyes, scoffing.

I reached for my dagger, positioning myself across from him. He readied himself in a fighting stance, knees bent, clasping his sword in both hands.

"Don't go easy on me, angel."

"Not in my nature, Shamus." I gestured with my index finger for him to come closer.

Blekket came at me full force, raising his weapon as he charged. I stood perfectly still, tracking his velocity, then dipped low when he swiped the sword through the air in an attempt to disunite my head from my neck. While I was still leaned back, I caught his wrist and flipped him onto his back, disarming him at the same moment I dove onto the ground and dug my knee into his chest. I pressed his own blade into his neck, brushing my lips lightly against his.

"Is that the best you can do? I thought my future husband was a better fighter. This is just sad."

He caught me around the waist and rolled us, so I was on my back beneath him. He plucked my dagger out of my hand and jabbed the tip of the blade into my throat, over where my pulse had risen from both surprise and arousal.

"You underestimate me, sweetheart," he said with a show of his criminally white teeth. "Must be that God complex of yours."

"I don't have a God complex," I objected.

"Yes, you do, but it's okay. We won't hold it against you." He kissed the air where his lips hovered over my mouth, successfully piquing my competitive side.

Now, I *really* wanted to show him up.

I head butted him, whacking him off me, then found where he dropped my dagger and jumped to my feet. I stampeded towards him, dropping to the floor to wrap my foot around his ankle and tug him back onto his ass. Blekket anticipated this and seized my foot mid-air, wrenching me forward so I was leaning into him on one leg, his crotch rubbing against mine in just the right spot.

"You should really learn another move. Don't want to become a one-hit wonder," he whispered in my ear.

"Is that so?" I reached up, cradling his face in both my hands, stroking his cheeks with my thumbs in a gentle manner.

I leaned in so my lips were a whisper away from his. Then, while he was distracted, I wiggled my leg free from his grasp. I raised it in conjuncture with slamming his head down, his forehead colliding with my knee.

"Fuck, Tymp!" He backed away from me, rubbing the spot I'd smacked him. "Are you trying to give me a concussion?"

"I'm sorry, I thought you said you *didn't* want me to go easy on you. My mistake."

His eyes narrowed in slits. "Oh, it's *so* on."

He spun on one foot, the bottom of his boot connecting with my stomach, then ducked to avoid the swing of my dagger when I pounced. He caught my wrist, twirling me around so my back was to his front, twisting my arm behind me and nearly dislocating my shoulder. I tried to buck my hips forward in an attempt to escape, but he held the blade of his sword to my throat, effectively trapping me.

"You're going down," I growled, pissed he'd been able to do that so quickly. His lips trailed my jaw as he let go of my arm, his other hand flattening over my stomach, pushing me back against him so I could feel his growing erection.

"Yes, I am. On you, after I win."

"In your dreams," I spat, elbowing him in the dick. Blekket gasped, releasing me and his weapon to cup himself between the legs.

"I fucking worship you," he marvelled when he looked up.

"Like I said," I declared, whirling my dagger between my fingers. "I win every round from here on out."

"Like *I* said," he responded haughtily, "I win every round just by looking at you."

"What's going on in here?" We turned to find Pessy and Raevon in the doorway, dressed for our excursion to Jopolis.

"We're practicing our swordsmanship," I explained, adding, "Blekket needed a bit of work on his craft."

"Not the least bit true," he snapped, straightening up once the ache between his legs subsided.

"Ooo, I want to fight Tymp!" Raevon reached for her sword, darting into the room.

"You sure about this, little sister?" I gripped my blade. "I'll take it easy on you, if you like."

"Don't insult me," she barked, making me love her even more.

I heard Pessy when she took a seat against the wall whisper to Blekket, "I'm not sure who I'm supposed to root for."

"I'll take my girl, you take yours," he replied. The two shook on it.

Raevon and I stared each other down, daring the other to make the first move. I'd been expecting her to advance with her sword, like Blekket always did, but she surprised me and charged head first, catching me in the stomach with the crown of her skull. She straddled my waist once she had me sprawled out on the floor, raising her weapon up over her head. I managed to elbow her in the stomach before she could bring the sword down, knocking her off me. I seized her ankle, dragging her forward, and pressed the pointy end of my dagger into her throat.

"She's got better instincts than you," I threw at Blekket over my shoulder.

"Who do you think taught her everything she knows?" Raevon shifted her head to glower at him.

"Now I want to fight *you*," she hissed, shoving me off her and rising to her feet.

I crawled over to where Pessy sat on the ground, twisting my arms around my knees as I watched the Elrods begin their showdown. Raevon's fist hurdled towards Blekket's face, but he caught it before it made contact with his striking features. He tugged her into him and started poking at her ribs, taunting her with evil chuckles, which only enraged her more. She plunged her knee into his stomach and lobbed him with the shaft of her sword, drawing blood from the corner of his mouth.

"You got this, Rae!" Pessy shouted.

"Strike him down!" I cheered.

"Is no one rooting for me?" Blekket asked, then stooped low when Raevon swerved her blade near his eye.

"Are you okay? After last night?" Pessy whispered.

"I think so," I answered with a shrug. "I'm just worried about Roara's threats, what she might do to Esteopia."

"I think preparing for every possible scenario is smart." In front of us, Blekket and Raevon start arguing over who had better form. "Arming yourself with as much information as possible and laying down groundwork is the only way to get through the unknown, especially in a war."

"I know. I'm glad we're going to speak to Solara today. Maybe they'll have some suggestions on other ways we can protect the kingdom. That's all I care about. Protecting the people of Esteopia."

"Look at you, being all monarchy. You're such a queen." She nudged me, giggling when I rolled my eyes.

"Pess," Blekket declared through laboured pants, pointing at her. "My favourite. You and me. Let's do this."

"I don't know, Blek," she heckled, standing up. "Tympany will murder me if I ruin that pretty face of yours."

"So you're admitting you think I'm pretty?" He grinned sinisterly at his sister. "Uh oh, Rae. Looks like you've got some competition."

"See, this is why no one's rooting for you," I said, making everyone except Blekket laugh.

Just as Pessy and Blekket were getting ready to fight, we heard a rowdy clatter barrel down the stairs.

Then, Olivette appeared in the doorway.

Her ashen expression caused my muscles to constrict with worry. Raevon and I rose immediately to our feet.

"What happened?" Blekket enquired, slipping on a shirt before curling his arm around my waist.

"There's someone at the gates," she explained while wheezing. She must've sprinted here. "Demetrio sent Lev down there to scope them out. He still hasn't returned. It's been almost thirty minutes."

"Where's Demetrio?" I asked.

"He didn't want to send anyone else down there if it wasn't safe. He wants you to check them out." She directed that at me, the only person in the group who could compel a potential threat away.

"We'll leave now."

I reached for my dagger as I followed Olivette up the stairs, Blekket, Raevon, and Pessy trailing behind me.

We didn't bother stopping at the stables to retrieve our horses, running at full speed down the pebbled path to the elaborate gates of Esteopia. In front of the cylinders of water stood a woman. As we got closer and her contour became more distinct, I saw she was dressed in gold Kylantian armour, long blonde hair surging down her chest.

I knew who it was just by the way she carried herself before I even saw her hair or face.

"Mum?" Pessy whispered.

She then staggered back, smothering a hand over her mouth to stifle a scream.

In one hand, Mergona carried her sword, the blade saturated in fresh blood. It's what she had in her other hand that robbed me of my next breath.

It was Lev's severed head.

Chapter Twenty-Three

Pain.

It was everywhere—under my skin, knotted in my hair, clogging my throat, lodged in my stomach, compressing my lungs. Everything hurt. The air was dense and chockfull of grief, the anguish emanating out from where Lev's head dangled inside Mergona's grip.

No one moved.

No one breathed.

It was Mergona who shattered the silence, speaking first. "Your mother warned you, Tympany."

Pain was then exchanged for blistering ire.

It swamped every nerve end in fire, the tingle in my fingers begging me to grab my dagger and start running towards her, ignoring the screams I heard behind me from Pessy. I raised my hand in opposition, charging at Mergona, but she sidestepped me with ease, dropping Lev's head on the ground. It rolled a few feet away, joining his crumpled body on the pavement.

"I don't want to hurt you, Tympany," she said, holding her hands up in surrender before setting her sword down as a show of good faith.

"You killed him," I snarled, shaking with rage. "You killed our friend."

"It was the only way Roara could get the message across."

"What message? That you're all sadistic sociopaths? If so, message received, loud and clear."

"That you need to come home. You've spent far too long here with these people, and you must return to where you're needed."

"You don't know anything about *these* people," Pessy cried, retrieving everyone's attention.

Mergona's eyes dipped to where Pessy was grasping Raevon's wrist, standing half in front of her protectively.

"Pessoranda," she said with a shake of her head. "I'm disappointed in you."

"Yeah? Well *I'm* disappointed in *you*, Mum! You just killed a kind, innocent man. Lev didn't deserve to die!"

"I agree. This could've all been avoided, if Tympany heeded Roara's warning sooner."

"Don't try and blame this on Tympany," Blekket snapped, setting his hands on my shoulders when he saw me gearing up to lunge at her again. "You're the one who did the deed. His blood is on *your* hands."

"More innocents will die," Mergona continued, as if Blekket hadn't spoken, "if you don't come home, Tympany. This is your last warning. I pray you come to your senses, so no more mortals have to suffer."

"You can tell my mother to go fuck herself," I sneered.

"You can tell her that yourself." Mergona glanced over at her daughter. "I hope to see you both again soon."

She turned on her heel, ambling over to where her Thoroughbred horse named Giles was waiting for her, and mounted the steed with impressive skill. We watched her lightly kick Giles in the side and begin trotting off in the direction of the Dream Forest without looking back at us once.

"Pess," Raevon whispered, draping an arm around her.

"No one touch me!" Pessy shrieked, shaking Raevon off.

She hugged her arms around her shoulders in an effort to bring herself some reprieve, sobbing hysterically.

I wanted to go to her, but my eyes singled in on where Lev's discarded body and amputated skull lay a few feet away. My feet brought me over there at their own accord, my knees bending as I knelt on the ground beside him. I ran my fingers over his unruly ginger curls, always nestled atop his head like a crown of autumn leaves. Lev had been there since day one. He was the first Esteopian I met who'd been nothing but gracious, who'd opened my eyes to the possibility of there being goodness here, unlike what I'd been taught to believe about Esteopia.

Lev was there for me when I struggled over Blekket's proposal. He encouraged me to follow my heart and overlook the doubt afflicting my mind, to not be afraid of being in a position of power, but to embrace it. He'd believed in me, trusted me, and protected me, until the very end.

I couldn't even utter the words, "With your last drop, you are free," without tasting bile on my tongue.

I thought about his wife, Marisa, and their sweet four-year-old daughter, Charly. They didn't wake up today expecting their world to be crushed. They didn't deserve to have the heart of their family excavated. They didn't deserve to now have to grieve someone who should still be here. This loss would map out the rest of Charly's life, dictate every action she made in the future, just like Zion's death plagued Pessy. Charly would lose her sense of innocence the moment she found out. It would permanently change her into something harder than the sweet, warm child I met at the ball. She'd go through life forever feeling like something was missing, like her home, which should be an oasis for her, wasn't complete.

Marisa would have to raise their little girl without her husband, spend the rest of her life without the man she loved, a concept that made me feel like I was drowning when I tried to fathom living even a second without Blekket. This could've been so easily avoided, if I hadn't acted so stubborn and thought I was better than the Queen of the Gods. Blekket was right—somewhere, embedded in my psyche, I did have a God complex, like all the Gods did. And hubris cost Lev his life.

"Tymp?" Blekket jostled me from behind. "You still there?"

"We should've been here," I stammered.

"There was nothing we could've done."

"We could've *been here*, Blek." I swatted his hand off my shoulder so I could stand. "While we were fooling around in the utility room, Lev was getting his *head* chopped off. We should've been here. *I* should've been here. I could've stopped this...stopped her...and now, he's gone. Lev's gone." My bottom lip trembled with an inbound sob, my heart plummeting into my stomach.

"Tymp," Blekket whispered, reaching for me. "This isn't your fault."

"He's right," Pessy agreed. She'd begun to calm down, her breaths more regulated and her tears dried on her cheeks. "Don't listen to my mother. It's not your fault, Tympany. This is Roara's doing, not yours."

"She warned me. She said she'd smoke me out with more slaughter." I thought she meant through starving the nation. I never imagined she would send Mergona here to personally murder one of our own. "I can't let this go any further."

"What are you saying?" Blekket rocked with anxiety.

"I'm saying, I need to go there. Back to Kylantis. I can't let any more innocent civilians be killed."

"No. Absolutely not," he objected. "Not happening."

"She's just going to keep killing people, Blek. I don't have a choice."

"If you go back there, she's never going to let you leave, Tympany. I'm never going to see you again."

My voice grew softer. "You don't know that."

"Yes, I do!" he screamed, making everyone flinch at the volume. I'd never heard him so emphatic. "Look what lengths she's already gone to just to get you back. Do you really believe she's going to let you walk out once she has you again?"

"He's right, Tymp," Raevon murmured.

"I can't let more Esteopians be killed! I just can't!" I wasn't sure how I hadn't burst into tears yet.

"We'll come up with another solution." Blekket seized my hands so I couldn't bolt, which he'd been smart to do, since I'd considered it. "We'll mandate that all Esteopians can't leave their houses for the time being. We'll have the Kylantians you came here with guard the gates. We'll have half the Esteopian soldiers bring supplies and necessities to the villagers, while the other half guards us and Tympany's Province."

"For how long can we sustain that, though? We can't force people to stay in their houses forever. It's not a durable solution."

"It's better than you going back to Kylantis and never coming back," Blekket growled, his eyes tiny slits of fire.

"I can compel Roara to let me leave Kylantis after she's said her piece."

"You've never compelled your mother before," Pessy reminded me. "You don't know it will work."

"You don't know it won't!" Why was everyone being so difficult?

"Tympany, please. Listen to me." Blekket cupped my cheeks, turning my face so I could see his desperation. "There are other ways we can combat your mother's threats without you jeopardising your freedom."

"I just don't see any other way," I squeaked, my throat aching with sadness. I didn't know how else to convince them that this was the only appropriate solution to our problem. Roara would just find new ways to torture Esteopia and the people I loved if I didn't swallow my pride and hear what she had to say. It wounded my ego to be submitting to her out of fear, but my hand had been forced here. I wouldn't let Lev's tragic fate befall anyone else I cared about.

"I'm sorry, Tympany, but I forbid you from going."

"You *forbid* me?" I rolled my eyes. "What century are you from? You can't forbid me from doing anything."

"You want to test me, sweetheart? Try and get past me. I dare you." We glared each other down, urging the other to surrender or strike first. The air between us crackled with tension, the invisible string that was our love personified stretching out to remind me once again that this man was my heart and my home.

It was impossible to be even the slightest bit angry with him when I could see the blatant fear in his eyes.

"This arguing is getting us nowhere," Pessy said, and thank the Gods she did, because it broke Blekket's spell.

"How does going back to Kylantis actually benefit you, Tympany? Tell me, and I won't be a dick about you going."

Because I loved and respected my fiancé, I gave it actual thought before opening my mouth again.

"Besides saving all of Esteopia from Roara's torment, I can finally get some answers as to why the Gods favour Sleotha. Maybe I can trick Roara into telling me some incriminating information about the Sleothians or about Queen Jacinda, so we can plan our next move against them more methodically."

"She's not just going to offer you the key to winning this war."

"Not intentionally, but I can test my compulsion and see if it works. If it does, I can compel whatever information she's hiding out of her."

"And if it doesn't?"

"I'm quite the charmer when I want to be. It worked on you, didn't it?" For the first time in minutes, a smile fiddled with the corners of his lips.

"It certainly did," he replied, "which is why I don't want you going anywhere I'm not, with the chance you won't come back."

"I'll go with her," Pessy intersected, Raevon's face falling, "and make sure she gets back to you and Esteopia."

"Why do you have to go?" Raevon asked, her shoulders slumping.

"I'm Tympany's bonded. I go wherever she goes." I nodded to Pessy in recognition, silently thanking her.

"Here's the final plan. Pessy and I will go back to Kylantis, while you guys go to Jopolis and speak to Solara. I still think we should prepare for the worst, in case Roara follows through with those threats anyway. We will meet back here by nightfall and begin planning our next steps against Sleotha."

Neither Blekket nor Raevon looked happy about it, but they bobbed their heads in conceding nods.

"What should we do…with Lev's…body?" Pessy stuttered. The four of us looked down at our fallen friend.

"I think…for now…we leave him." Blekket cringed. "When we get back to the palace, I'll let Dad know what happened. He can have…someone…come clean him up." I imagined it took a lot of strength not to gag or bawl when he said that.

"Lev must be given a proper burial," I asserted, losing the fight against bursting into tears. "He deserves to be put to rest in peace, with Marisa and Charly present. Don't let them burn him, Blek."

"Okay." Blekket wrapped his arm around my waist, hauling me to his side. "I'll make sure no one burns him." When he kissed my hair, it felt like he was apologising.

We made our way back to the palace in complete silence. Raevon was nuzzling Pessy's neck, and Pessy was stroking Raevon's hair, exchanging their own silent promise. Blekket kept his arm around me, but he was tense with frustration. I could feel his fury imparting off him in waves. I didn't have the bandwidth to sympathise or try to assuage his anger, not while I was trying to wrap my brain around facing Roara and my siblings. Although I'd put on a brave face in insisting I could handle my family, manage Roara, and find a way to return home, even if my compulsion didn't work, I was just as concerned as Blekket that the minute I stepped foot in Kylantis, I would been prohibited from leaving. The thought of living another five thousand years in that place felt like torture, but living there without Blekket would be the quintessence of death.

I couldn't go back to an existence of half-living, not when I'd finally gotten a taste of what it felt like to be truly alive.

Demetrio was waiting in the foyer for us, pacing back and forth with worry. He saw each of our faces and knew instantly.

"No," he gasped, his hand flying to his mouth. "No…no…"

"I'm so sorry," I mewled, surprising even myself by raising my arms and folding them around him.

"He's gone?" Demetrio dropped his face into my neck, just like Blekket would, and burst into tears.

I couldn't imagine what he was feeling, losing his wife *and* his closest confidant in the span of a couple weeks. I felt each wretched sob as it rampaged through his body and clung to him, forcing myself to endure the agony as punishment for my truancy when Lev needed me most. I would do the same when I saw Marisa and Charly, make myself carry half that burden so they wouldn't have to stomach it alone.

"Lev was a bright light in a sea of darkness," Demetrio snivelled, leaning back to wipe snot on the back of his hand.

"He was," I agreed. "The world will never be the same."

"Who was it? Down at the gate? Who did this?"

Pessy winced, then responded contritely, "My mother. She was following Roara's orders."

"Roara?" he stammered in horror. "Why would Roara send your mother down here to kill our best solider?"

"Because she wants me to come home," I answered, saving Pessy from having to further explain. "Which I plan to do. Pess and I are going to leave right now and return back to Kylantis."

"Are you sure that's a good idea?"

"It's a terrible idea," Blekket grumbled from behind me.

"No, it's not." I spun around to shoot him a glower. "I don't see any ending where we stay here, and more blood isn't shed. Roara threatened to freeze the ocean and make it so we can't walk outside without burning. I can't let anyone else die because of me."

"While I appreciate that sentiment, Tympany, and it shows how much you care, going back to Kylantis is a big risk. She might not let you leave once you're there, and Esteopia can't afford to lose another queen."

"You won't," I swore, squeezing Demetrio's hand. "I'll be back by nightfall."

"Don't make promises you might not be able to keep." My fingers slipped out of his, retreating to my side.

"I will do everything in my power to return home to you all. That is a promise I'll make. That I will try my damn hardest to make it back here, if it's that last thing I ever do." I stared at Blekket when I said that, pledging this to him. His eyes glazed over with tears.

"Dad," he choked out at the same moment he tangled his fingers with mine. "Could you have someone go down to the gates to…collect Lev? And make sure no one burns his body before we have a chance to bury him."

"Of course, Son," Demetrio replied grimly with a nod.

"Come, Tymp," Blekket whispered, tugging on my arm and practically dragging me up the stairs with barefaced determination.

I had a suspicion why he was lugging me so fast, which was confirmed when we entered our bedchamber.

Blekket was on me before I took my next breath. He threaded his fingers in my hair and tipped my head back, consuming me in a kiss. His tongue plunged through the opening and found mine, the two intermingling in the middle of the shared space, coming together the same way our bodies and hearts did.

"I need you," he burst after we crashed into the wall.

"You have me," I promised. "You will always have me."

He stooped down, cupping his hands under my knees, and hoisted me up, tying my legs around his waist.

"Blek," I moaned, fisting my fingers in his hair.

He carried me over and deposited me on the bed below him, our entangled limbs sinking into the pillows.

"I worship you, Tympany," he gushed, licking up the column of my neck to my chin. "I'm going to prove it to you."

And he did.

After several minutes of relishing our post-coital fog, I crawled out of bed and made my way over to the dresser, selecting what to wear for the trip to Kylantis. I chose an emerald green one-shoulder jumpsuit made of polyester, with a unique draped front and sash. Blekket was sprawled out in bed, hands behind his head, studying how I shimmied the fabric up my body, the polyester clinging to my curves.

"Aren't you supposed to wear grey in public?" he asked. "Won't your mother be upset you're wearing green?"

"I know. That's the point." The smiles that unfurled over both our faces were equally wolfish.

"I love you," he laughed, making me beam.

"I know. You did a fine job proving it."

"Fine? *Fine?* Don't insult my skills, Tympany." I giggled, wrenching the elastic out of my hair, then raked my fingers through the short strands, unravelling the knots. When I raised my eyes to the mirror, Blekket was now behind me, slithering his arms around my torso and drawing me back against him.

367

"You know I love you, right?" I was worried I hadn't made this abundantly clear, that my propensity to tease him would lead him to believe I didn't feel as strongly for him as he felt for me.

"I know," he murmured, resting his chin on my shoulder.

"Do you? Because I know I don't say it a lot, and I know I like to tease you…it's just, back home, with my family, we weren't big on proclamations of love or public displays of affection. We never really told each other that often that we loved each other, since it was always just…implied. But I don't want you to think, just because I don't always say it, I'm not thinking or feeling it, because you're my everything. I just—"

"Tympany." Blekket set his hands on my shoulders and spun me around, cradling my face between his palms. "I know. I know you love me. I see it every time you look at me. When I notice you searching for me in a crowd. When your hand just naturally gravitates towards mine. When you say my name in your sleep. I see it in the little things, and the big things, like how you agreed to be my Queen when being a sovereign was something you were always adamantly against. I've never questioned your feelings for me, and I never want you to question how *I* feel for *you,* or the depth of my commitment to you. You come before anything else, before this kingdom, before my family, before everything. You're my sun, Tymp, and I'm forever grateful I met you and get to be in your orbit for the rest of my life. I don't worship you because of *what* you are. I worship you because of *who* you are, the goodness in your soul that inspires me to be better."

"Blek." A tear toppled over the edge, trickling down my face, which Blekket kissed away.

"I'm not going to make you promise to return to me, because I know there's a very real possibility you won't be able to keep that promise, no matter how hard you try. So I'm only going to ask one thing of you. Just promise me you won't forget me. I can live here, ruling over Esteopia, as long as I know you're up there still thinking about me, the way I will always be thinking about you."

"There is no universe where I could possibly forget you, Blekket Shamus Elrod." I stroked my thumb over the freckles sprinkled across his cheeks. "You're a permanent tattoo on my soul."

"Good." He kissed my forehead. "Then I have no regrets."

We walked to the stables in a distraught silence, our grip on each other's hands asphyxiating. Pessy, Raevon, and Demetrio were waiting for us outside, Pessy clutching Krystal's reins.

I made a beeline for Raevon when I saw her dissolve into tears, gathering her in a tight embrace.

"I love you, Tympany," she whispered, hugging me with all her might. "You're the most amazing person I've ever met. You're my hero. You've brought my brother so much love and joy, and you're the reason I found Pessy. No matter what, I will forever be in your debt for all you've given us."

"Rae. You're going to make me cry." She leaned back, her cobalt eyes amplified by the tears. "I always wanted a little sister. You're better than any dream I could've conjured up. I can't imagine anyone I'd rather see with my best friend. We will always be family, and you'll always be way cooler than the rest of the world."

"Always." She giggled, kissing my hand.

I shifted to face Demetrio, whose fingers were intertwined and squeezed together so tautly that his knuckles were white.

"Seraphina adored you," he told me, his voice hoarse. "She loved you so much. She already looked at you as a daughter, before everything. I allowed my personal prejudgments about your family to mold my perception of you when we first met, and for that, I will always be sorry."

"There's no need," I said with a wave of my hand. "It's water under the bridge."

"You and I don't always see eye to eye, but I respect you greatly, Tympany. You're independent, strong, kind, intelligent, beautiful, and fierce. I'm honoured to have gotten the chance to know you and see you grow into the remarkable Queen you've become. I pray we'll have more moments together in the future, so I may get to know you even better, and so our kingdom can thrive under your influence."

"You have no idea how much I appreciate that," I squeaked past the lump in my throat, which was burrowing painfully into my esophagus. "I loved Seraphina and will never forgive myself for her passing."

"I hope one day, you do. No one here blames you for it." He tucked a strand of hair behind my ear. "Make me a promise I know you can keep. Promise me you won't revert back to letting others take center stage. That if, Gods forbid, you end up stuck in Kylantis, you will continue to be the leader I know you are, and not allow your family to shut you down or pressure you into changing your beliefs. You have a voice, Tympany, and when you let yourself use it, you inspire a world of good. This universe needs you to be a guiding light. We've suffered for too long without it."

The threatened tears began to fall.

"I promise." I stepped inside his open arms. "Thank you for coming around and accepting me."

"Thank you for making that an easy decision in the end."

She better fucking come back. I don't want to know what will happen to Blek if she doesn't.

He let me go, scratching the back of his neck shamefacedly, as if he knew I heard his thoughts.

Blekket stood there with his hands stuffed in his pockets, forcing them to remain at his sides so he wasn't tempted to haul me over his shoulder and lug me upstairs.

Knowing that brought a small smile to my face.

"If I hug or kiss you again, I won't be able to let you go," he declared when I stepped forward to embrace him.

"Oh. Okay." Despite how badly I itched to touch him, I reined it in. "I love you, Blekket Elrod."

He shifted on the balls of his feet, vibrating with the strength it took to hold himself back, then finally gasped, "Oh, fuck it," and leapt forward. He took advantage of my gasp to slip his tongue into my mouth, absorbing the sound. He slurped every moan he coaxed from me with a groan of his own and a flick of his tongue. He tasted of love and appreciation and desperation, a heartbreaking, life-affirming combination. My hands glided up the length of his chest, feeling every chiselled sinew, my fingers scorching from the heat oozing out of his skin beneath his dress shirt. I clutched his biceps and arched my back, our chests rubbing against one another in unison with our breaths synchronising. A single seed of desire planted itself deep in my belly, blossoming with every twirl of his mouth around mine, every scrape and clash of his teeth. I let the yearning resonate through my veins, following the tempo it hummed as I moved against his body, enticing him closer.

What began as a kiss of urgency turned into an expression of gratitude, each of us communicating our thankfulness for the other's existence through this precious contact we shared.

When we broke apart to breathe, Blekket rested his forehead over mine. "You're the love of my life, Tympany Elrod."

"And you're mine," I whispered back breathlessly when he called me what would hopefully one day be my official name, if all went according to plan. "Good luck with Solara. Tell Sterling I say hello, and make sure to duck when he throws that trident. I want that pretty, big head to stay on your unstable neck a little while longer."

"I will," he chuckled, then mustered the courage he needed to finally let me go.

I coerced my feet to take the necessary steps towards where Pessy and Krystal were waiting, going against their instinct to rush back to Blekket. Pessy's cheeks were swollen from abrasive crying. Her goodbye with Raevon had to have been just as emotional as mine was with Blek.

"Are you sure you want to come with me?" I asked. "You don't have to."

"We're a package deal, Tympany. Neither one of us does anything alone, for the rest of our lives."

My eyes watered anew. "You're the greatest friend there ever was, Pessoranda Halynn Whitereaver."

"I'm actually looking forward to finally flying on Krystal with you. I've waited three hundred years for this moment."

I burst out laughing in a much needed moment of levity, then sprang off my feet and mounted Krystal. Pessy took my proffered hand and allowed me to tug her onto Krystal's back, situating her feet in the stirrups behind me.

"Okay, you two," Blekket said, touching my leg gently. "Take care of each other out there. Tympany, pay attention while you're flying. I expect you both back here by nightfall, or I'm going to be fucking pissed."

"Alright, Dad," I teased with a roll of my eyes, while Pessy grabbed his hand and brought it to her face.

"Take care of Rae for me," she mumbled in a low voice, so Raevon wouldn't hear from a few feet away.

"Of course." He kissed her knuckles. "You know you're secretly my favourite."

"I wear that as a badge of honour," she answered, then released his hand to curl her arms around my waist.

Blekket backed away, joining where Raevon and Demetrio were huddled together. I glanced over at the Elrods, at my new family, and waited to feel the same strangling sense of loss I'd felt when I first left Kylantis. Fortunately, it never came. I took that as a sign I would return to Esteopia, that I wasn't already mourning because deep down, I knew I'd be back with them tonight.

I would cling to that premonition until I was standing in front of my fiancé once more, breathing the same air as him.

"You ready?" I asked Pessy, and she nodded.

"Kylantis, here we come," she muttered under her breath.

I inclined down, stroking Krystal's mane to retrieve her eyes. She elevated her head, waiting for permission.

"Let's do this, Kry," I told her, lightly tapping her side.

I felt her power pulsate through her before Krystal unfolded her wings, leapt off her feet, and hurled us towards the clouds.

Chapter Twenty-Four

The sky was a brilliant blue-grey brindle with the softest accents of white, expanding before us like a carpet of vapor and sunlight. Pessy clung to me as we soared through the clouds, the air swirling and eddying around us.

"Are you okay?" I asked her while we flew.

"Amazing," she answered, studying a seagull with wonder when it squawked and tumbled beside us.

"I don't mean about flying. About your mother." I felt guilty I hadn't rushed to comfort her after Mergona left, but I'd been in shock over Lev. Pessy tightened her arms around my waist.

"Um...I don't know how I feel." She rested her chin on my shoulder. "In all my life, she's never once told me she was disappointed in me."

"You know you've done nothing wrong, right? Being with Raevon, fighting for Esteopia. It's her problem, not yours."

"I know. It just made me wonder...would my dad be disappointed in me, too?"

"Even if he was, it still wouldn't be your problem. You're allowed to be you, Pess, to want things for yourself, to love who you love. That's what you told me when I was on the fence about Blekket. Anyone who stops looking at you the same when you decide to stand in your truth are not people worth having in your life, even if they're blood. If she can't accept who you are and the things you care about, then it's her loss." Pessy snuggled closer, pressing her cheek into my neck.

"I love you, you wise old geezer."

"Did you actually just call me a geezer? I will toss you off this horse and never look back."

"Blekket's right," she chuckled. "You're way too easy to tease. You need your head deflated every now and then."

"Calling me a geezer won't make me humble. It'll just make me mad. Now, no more talking. I need to focus."

We didn't speak for the remainder of the flight.

We galloped over the Geddesia Mountains, the rocky peak dotted white, sculpted by the raindrops of eons. The further up you got, the luxuriant leaves transmogrified from verdant to variegated, the trees spouting each of the colours of the Gods in iridescent, clean brush strokes. I wondered, seeing Kylantis from a bird's eye view, if that was the reason Roara hadn't made my signature colour green—green represented the earth, exemplifying humanity. It was how we differentiated the land of Kylantis from the Realm, when the canopy of leaves we existed below were no longer the shade of emeralds, but painted as if a rainbow had barfed on the world. I was proud to be walking into this confrontation wearing the colour of the mortals, proud to be defending the Esteopians' right to exist.

I steered Krystal towards the palace, hurdling down at an alarmingly fast rate. Pessy gripped me tighter in anticipation, but there was no need to fear. Krystal evened out her stride and matched the pace of the wind before disembarking the clouds and docking in front of the citadel.

"That was awesome!" Pessy squealed, slipping off Krystal's back and landing on her feet.

"I was disappointed Blekket didn't enjoy flying."

"Yeah, well, Blek's a wuss." I threw my head back and cackled, not noticing right away that someone was approaching us.

When I spotted the figure from the corner of my eye, I shifted my head to the side and found Alsandair standing a few feet away, dressed in his customary Kylantian uniform, hands clasped in front.

"Your Grace," he greeted me with a peculiar nervousness. "Welcome home."

"You told Roara about me and Blekket," I realised the moment I saw him. The timing of him leaving Kylantis and Roara showing up in my dream made sense.

He hung his head in shame, corroborating my hunch.

"I sincerely apologise for any harm I caused, but I felt the Queen deserved to know what was happening."

"*Harm* you caused? Do you have any idea what you've done? Lev's *dead* because of you. Mergona chopped his head off. Your friend is dead, and it's *your* fault. You have to live with that for the rest of your life, knowing you cost Charly

374

her father, that you took Marisa's husband away from her, all because you couldn't keep your mouth shut. His blood is on *your* hands." Alsandair's lashes fluttered in horror, which lead me to believe he had no idea what Roara did to Lev. When he took a step towards me, I bellowed, "If you put your hand on me, I will cut it off." He immediately retreated. "Make yourself useful and let my mother know I've arrived. **While I'm here in Kylantis, don't talk or even look at me. You will not utter a single word about your time in Esteopia or anything you heard about our plans for Sleotha to my mother or anyone else from here on out.**" I prayed he hadn't already, but this would protect us in the future.

His pupils dilated in absorption, then shrunk in submission.

"Yes, Your Grace." He bowed his head in an effort to be respectful, but it honestly felt insulting.

"Leave, now." He turned on his heel and stalked off, scampering in the direction of the palace.

"You're magnificent." Pessy breathed, making me roll my eyes.

"Let's get this over with, so we can go back to our *real* home."

"Let's do it." She linked her arm with mine, and we coordinated our strides into the citadel.

Loitering inside the foyer were eight out of nine of my older siblings, all except Hadestia, garmented in their signature colours. Lucius, of course, led the pack, wearing the same gold jacket he'd worn the night of my birthday over his yellow tunic. I wondered if this was a meditative move on Roara's part in an attempt to make me jealous, or if he wore gold because he was actually being groomed, now that I was gone, to take the throne. Either way, Roara wouldn't provoke the reaction from me she wanted.

All eight of my siblings' jaws dropped when they saw me, like they didn't recognise the woman entering the palace.

"The prodigal sister returns," Lucius sneered. It had only been a second, and I already wanted to slap him.

"Asshole," I spat, his lips parting in surprise at my flagrancy. I then looked at Jaxith, who was cowering in the corner. "Coward." His shoulders caved in, his head dropping. I glanced at Caspian and smiled. "Brother."

"Sister." He grinned. "You look good in green." He knew this was a deliberate power play against Roara.

"Hi, P," Calliope said to Pessy.

"Hey, Callie," she replied sort of awkwardly.

Calliope blinked, dumbfounded that she didn't acquire the coquettish reaction she normally got out of Pess.

"Shall we head in?" I pranced ahead, enjoying the sound of them all scrambling to follow me.

As we strolled to the throne room, I murmured to Caspian, "Have you spoken to Solara recently?"

"I have," he whispered back, his voice just as low as mine. "I'm sorry about Seraphina. I always liked her."

"Yeah…me too."

"How's Blekket handling being king?" I looked around, making sure our other siblings weren't paying attention.

"*We're* handling it swell."

I fluttered my fingers so Caspian could see my engagement ring, sitting loud and proud on my finger.

"You're kidding," he gasped, tracing the oval sapphire. "You wanted this, right? You weren't pressured into it?"

"Not at all. I couldn't be happier." A beautiful smile fissured the bottom half of my brother's face.

"Good for you, Tymp. Don't listen to anything I say in there in front of our family. Know that's how I really feel."

"Thank you, Casp." I was so grateful to have him going into this meeting, knowing someone was on my side.

"What're you two whispering about?" Lucius interrupted. I twisted around to narrow my eyes in daggers.

"Only worthy people can hear it," I hissed.

"You always sucked at comebacks, Tymp."

"And you always sucked at being picked first, *Luce*." Luna cracked a smile when Lucius's face fell.

Mergona was perched outside the throne room, her blonde hair twisted in an intricate braid, adorned around her shoulder. Her eyes swung right to Pessy, her features contorting with regret.

She tried to touch her daughter in an attempt to reconcile, but Pessy stepped out of Mergona's reach before she could.

"Pess—"

"Don't waste your breath," Pessy protested, all of my siblings behind me gasping in surprise. They'd never heard Pessy talk back to Mergona before. Neither had I, but I was ready for the spectacle. "You said you were disappointed in me. For what? For following my heart and falling in love with a beautiful girl who accepts me for who I am? For fighting for what I believe in? All I've done is everything you and Dad taught me. You have no standing to say *you're* disappointed in *me,* when *I'm* not the one who killed an innocent man in cold blood for no reason. You robbed a four-year-old girl of her father. As someone who knows what it feels like to lose her dad, to lose the heart of her family, for the first time in my life, I am *ashamed* to call you my mother." I was so proud of Pessy that tears welled in my eyes.

Outwardly, Mergona looked unruffled, but I could see the breakage of her heart reflected in her eyes.

"Pessy—"

"If you try to come near me again, I'll have Tympany compel you away." She took a step closer to me, looping her arm through mine to show where her allegiance lay.

Mergona bobbed her head in a nod, withdrawing.

I gaped at my best friend and gushed, "*You're* magnificent," never meaning that word more.

Entering the throne room at the front of the group was a new experience. I'd spent the majority of my life lingering in the back, far more comfortable blending in than standing out. Now, I sauntered inside with poise, radiating a confidence that came entirely from within and wasn't spawned by anything external. Roara sat in her throne composed of clouds, with Isaias positioned at her side. She wore a gold dress with a deep V-neckline, blouson bracelet sleeves, a beaded waistband, and a column silhouette, the hem trickling down to the floor like melted gilt. Her hair was woven back in an immaculate bun, exposing the gentle glide of her jaw. Her large brown eyes were on full display, outlined by succulent lashes that fluttered when she saw me enter with my siblings.

"Tympany!" she cheered. "You're here!"

"I wouldn't celebrate if I were you. This will be a quick visit." Her smile teetered as she sunk back into her throne.

I stood in the middle of the room, while all my siblings situated in their respective limestone chairs around me. I eyed the two chairs that were technically mine, the one at Roara's right, and the one across from Jax, which had my butt imprinted in it from centuries of use. Neither one of them felt like mine now.

The only chair I knew belonged to me was the throne to Esteopia.

I looked over at my father, a lump forming in my throat. I wanted to feel joy at seeing him again. Isaias had always been someone I felt I could depend on to advocate for my right to choose, but this conflicted with the knowledge that he was the root cause of the strife between the Gods and Esteopia.

"Father," I said brusquely.

"Darling," Isaias replied, his voice heady with affection. "You look beautiful. How have you been?"

"Never better," I replied. "I feel alive for the first time in all my five thousand years."

Roara flinched.

Isaias circled in on my engagement ring, his brows hoisting up. "What's *that?*" he demanded, switching from tender to terse.

"Oh. You didn't hear the good news from Mother?"

"Tympany," Roara warned, gripping the arms of her chair like she was holding herself back from lunging at me. I raised my left hand and spread my fingers for everyone to see.

"I'm engaged," I announced. "To Blekket Elrod." Isaias's eyes were so wide, they looked on the verge of tumbling out of his head. "That's right. I'm going to be the new Queen of Esteopia." Roara was about to stand up before I commanded, **"Sit down, and don't stand up until I tell you that you can."**

She lowered back down, capitulating to the order. I no longer had to wonder if my compulsion worked on her.

Thank fuck, Pessy exhaled through the bond.

"Here's how this meeting is going to go," I explained, now that I held the upper hand. "I'm running things. **If you want to speak, you raise your hand. If you are not called on by me, then you cannot speak.** You're going to see what it was like for me to live here for five thousand years. **When this meeting is over, Pessy and I are going to walk out that door, and no one is going to stop us. You will not freeze the ocean, or make the sun blister the Esteopians. We are going back to Esteopia, and you will do *nothing*. Now, repeat my words back to me, so I know everyone heard them."**

My entire family in unison echoed, "If you would like to speak, you raise your hand. If you're not called on by Tympany, then you cannot speak. When this meeting is over, Pessy and Tympany are going to walk out that door, and no one is going to stop them. We will not freeze the ocean, or make the sun blister the Esteopians. We will do nothing." Pessy breathed a sigh of relief at my side.

We were safe from being trapped here.

Roara was the first to raise her hand. I granted her permission with an authorising wave, then clasped my hands in front.

"I see your powers have matured," Roara complimented.

"That's not the only thing that's matured about me. Now, to business." I wanted to be in and out of there as fast as possible. "The only reason I came here is because I want to know why the Gods favour Sleotha. Either you will tell me that willingly, or I will compel it out of you. If I were you, I'd take the easier route and be honest the first time I ask." I waited a moment to see if anyone would just start prattling, but as expected, no one wanted to be the first to fess up. Blekket was right about us all having God complexes. "Now, the first story I heard as to why the Gods favour Sleotha was that Queen Jacinda is Sleotha and Lucius's daughter. The thought of Lucius procreating is probably the most frightening concept ever, so I was thrilled to hear that wasn't true." Lucius's hand shot up over his head. "No, Lucius, you may not speak. **Put your hand down.**"

Lucius looked like he wanted to scream. Under my compulsion, he couldn't, so he just flipped me the finger.

"Then I heard the reason the Gods favour Sleotha is because of you, Father." I faced Isaias. "Is that true?"

He forgot he couldn't speak without permission and tried, but his lips were glued together.

"You may speak," I granted.

"Yes, that's true," he finally declared.

"Why?" I gasped in horror. "What could you possibly have against Esteopia to convince Mother to turn her back on her own people?" He exchanged a look with Roara that was riddled with angst. "If you don't tell me voluntarily, I will just compel it out of you," I reminded him, tired of all this secrecy.

"Before I died, I was next in line to the throne of Sleotha," Isaias confessed, and it sounded like it pained him to do so. "Sleotha and Rafferty, the original Queen and King, were my parents."

"What?" My eyes strayed to Pessy. *Isaias was a Sleothian royal?*

"I was murdered in an Esteopian attack on the capital." Roara took his hand and sent a supportive pulse up his arm. I fiddled with my engagement ring, a mechanical impulse that made me feel like Blekket was standing here with me. "My mother and father were murdered as well. It was a horrendous devastation for Sleotha. They killed thousands of Sleothians that day. Thousands."

"Sounds an awful lot like what happened in Eveium and Frofsea." Isaias balked, his shoulders twitching.

"They murdered three members of the royal family, Tympany."

"Yeah, and the Sleothians murdered Seraphina right in front of her husband and children. Look, I'm sorry that happened, Dad. What they did to you and your family is truly awful, but the actions of Alden and Lavinia don't reflect who Esteopia is today. If you actually bothered to get to know them, you would see they are good people. Demetrio and Seraphina never would've done the things Lavinia and Alden did."

"They are *not* innocent, Tympany," Isaias roared. "Demetrio and Seraphina had their army invade Sleotha on your birthday and kill seventy Sleothians to steal their livestock and crops, leaving even more wounded."

"Which I told them to their face I disagreed with, but they only did that as a counter attack to what the drogon did in Eveium. Do you know how many Esteopians were killed in that village? Forty thousand. Do you know how many were killed in Frofsea? Ten thousand, if you want to start comparing numbers. I fought in that battle alongside them. I saw the Sleothians in action. They were *ruthless*. They burned Esteopians alive. They slaughtered children." I gesticulated to Jaxith, who slid down in his chair. "Sleotha objectively has done more damage to Esteopia than Esteopia has done to them, and it's because *you guys* have given them the tools to do so."

Roara raised her hand to speak.

Once permitted, she said, "None of us are saying Sleotha is irreproachable, but no one is blameless in a war."

"Yet for thousands of years, you've held the actions of the original King and Queen against these people, who have done nothing since then to warrant your hatred. Instead of getting to know them and see how they've changed, you've harboured these resentments without stopping to think that maybe they've learned from their past mistakes. Maybe they've grown. Maybe they're not these deplorable fiends who deserve to be abandoned for centuries. Their conflict has been with Sleotha over the land, but *you've* made it a war against the Gods by ignoring their prayers. Did you know the villagers started a rumor that the Gods were asleep to try and justify why they never heard from you all? How sad is that? They *still* worship you, and you just turned your backs on them."

"You make them sound like they've always been upstanding citizens," Roara pushed, as if I hadn't spoken a word. "They're just as involved in this war. They've killed innocent people over the years too, Tympany."

"Yeah? How are you any better? You murdered Lev."

"Lev? Who's Lev?" That sent a murderous rage rampaging through my body, heating my blood to a boiling point.

"You didn't even bother to learn the name of the man you had Mergona kill?" Roara's cheeks drained of colour. "The solider she murdered at the gate, the one whose head she chopped off, was named *Lev*. He was our friend, and he was kind. He was *good*, and *you* killed him. You don't even get to blame the Sleothians for that. *You* did it." I saw Lucius about to raise his hand and screamed at the top of my lungs, "DO I LOOK LIKE I'M DONE TALKING, LUCIUS? **PUT YOUR FUCKING HAND DOWN!**"

Lucius surrendered to the order, while Caspian concealed his mouth behind his hand to hide his smile.

"Clearly, we're going to agree to disagree here, since I won't be able to convince you all in a matter of minutes that the Esteopians are good people. The last thing I want to know, before I walk out of here and never come back, is about Queen Jacinda. I want to know why she's lived as long as she has."

"No one answer," Roara ordered, glowering at everyone in the room.

"Are you forgetting she can compel it out of us?" Jax said. "Just tell her what she wants to know."

I felt a fleeting sense of gratefulness, but I couldn't latch onto it without remembering what he did to Cosmina. Isaias exhaled in surrender, raising his hand to speak.

"Jacinda is my sister," he explained when I granted him permission. "When she died of old age, we had Hadestia revive her. She's lived as long as she has because she's technically not alive."

My jaw nearly dropped to the floor.

I'd thought Jacinda could be my niece—never in a million years did I think she'd be my aunt.

"Do the people of Sleotha know that?" He shook his head.

"As far as they know, she's immortal. Jacinda has no godly powers. She just can't be killed."

She couldn't be killed—that didn't bode well for us. But she had no godly powers—that would make things easier.

Oh my Gods, Pessy exclaimed through the bond. *Blekket was right about Jacinda being dead.*

We can't tell him that, though, I warned her. *It'll just go to his head.*

"Where did the drogon come from? Are they linked to her?" Roara tensed, while Isaias again shook his head.

"I have no idea where the drogon came from. Honestly, no clue. You can compel me if you don't believe me."

"I do." I felt the tiniest bit of shame at his blatant fear of me. "When did they first appear? Were they around when you were still human?"

"No. They showed up after Hadestia resurrected Jacinda, but I can't say for certain they're linked to Jacinda. Their appearance just coincided with her revivification."

Okay.

So even if we couldn't kill Jacinda herself, the drogon were still fair game. It honestly worked out better for us that her lifeline wasn't interrelated to the drogon, because without them, she was basically mortal. They were her only leverage against us.

If we got rid of the drogon completely, conquering Sleotha would be easy with a Queen who had no powers.

Leaving here, I knew what our next move against Sleotha should be, and I felt confident in that decision.

"That's all the information I needed to know. Pessy and I will be going now." I stared at my mother and ordered, **"You will not terrorise the people of Esteopia, and you will stop visiting me in my dreams. You will accept I'm going to be Queen of Esteopia and let me go."**

Roara gripped the arms of her throne so powerfully, I worried they would snap off.

"If you would like to bend your legs, now you can," I threw over my shoulder, Pessy and I making our way to the exit.

When we were out of earshot, we both covered our mouths with our hands at the same time to suppress screams.

"Tympany! That was unbelievable!"

"I can't believe that just happened." I didn't recognise myself, but in a good way. I'd never been so assertive, especially not with my family. It felt right, like how I was always supposed to be. "I can't wait to tell Blek everything. I think we should—"

"Tymp? Can I talk to you?" I spun around to find Jax with his head poking out into the hallway.

"Of course."

Before he closed the door, I could hear the eruption of panic from inside the throne room in response to my visit. It was sickeningly pleasing to know I had this much influence.

"What was it you wished to say?" His eyes flicked over to Pessy, who was affixed to my side. Her hand gripped the hilt of her sword to show Jaxith he was being regarded here as an enemy, not a friend.

"I wanted to apologise for what happened in Frofsea," he began, not what I was expecting to hear. "I've felt horrible about it ever since. You and I used to be so close, closer than any of our other siblings. I've really missed you, and I just couldn't stand the thought of you hating me anymore." His blue eyes glazed over with tears, which he did his best to quell.

"Are you apologising for what you did because you acknowledge it was wrong, or because you miss me?"

He frowned. "What difference does it make?"

"It makes all the difference in the world," I snapped. "You refused to heal a five-year-old girl just because she was Esteopian. If you don't comprehend why that was wrong, then you and I have nothing to talk about here."

"Tympany—"

"You're supposed to be the God of Kindness, Jaxith. You're supposed to be fair to all, or, at least that's who I always believed you were. I was so disappointed in you, but I also felt betrayed by the person I thought you were, the brother I always looked up to. I'm not going to forgive you just so you can feel better about yourself when you don't even understand why what you did was wrong. You can't call yourself the God of Kindness if you're not going to extend that to everyone."

I didn't give him the chance to say anything else before I turned on my heel, Pessy following behind me.

When we were finally outside, we both exhaled as though we'd been holding our breaths the whole time we'd been here.

"That was heavy," Pessy said.

"Thank you, Captain Obvious."

"You're such a bitch," she laughed, shoving me. "You and Blekket deserve each other with your big heads."

We approached were Krystal was stationed, neighing with delight and lifting up onto her hind legs when she saw us.

"Down, girl," I giggled, caressing her side. "You ready to go home and see your main man, Clarence?"

Her whinny of exultation was answer enough.

I mounted Krystal first, then tugged Pessy up. She wrapped her arms around my waist, snuggling her thighs around mine.

I gathered Krystal's reins and sighed. "Let's go home."

Chapter Twenty-Five

Blekket, Raevon, and Demetrio were waiting behind the gates when Pessy and I flew overhead. Even from so high up, I could feel the communal relief interleave between them, amplifying the closer we got to the ground.

"Thank fuck," Blekket exclaimed after we'd landed, rushing forward. While Pessy sprinted to Raevon, I dismounted Krystal and flung myself into Blek's open arms, curling my arms, legs, and entire being around and into him. He buried his face in my throat, gasping like he hadn't breathed in hours.

"I'm home," I assured him, over and over, stroking the hair at the nape of his neck. "I'm home. I'm home."

"I love you," he cried, and I felt his sobs writhe through his whole body. "I love you so much, Tympany."

"I love you more," I whispered, my throat bunged with emotion.

My limbs became something buoyant in the comfort of his embrace, like a weightless cloud hitched in the sky, floating above the earth in search of a home base. When my heart fastened itself to his, it felt like my center of gravity had shifted to orbit around this magnificent man. He clung to me as though his life depended on it, as if he was being ravaged internally and I was the only life raft able to rescue him from the boisterous sea that was his mind. The thought of being someone safety net would've scared me four months ago, as I'd been convinced I wasn't capable of carrying the weight of someone else's love, but now, I knew it was the role I was born to take on.

Here in his arms, I had no purpose other than to be exactly who I was. I didn't need to be the Goddess of the Heart and Mind, Muse to all mortals and celestials, or even the Queen of Esteopia.

Here, I was just Tympany, and there was a beauty in that name just as much as all my other titles.

It took finding Blekket for me to recognise that.

When we broke apart, I glanced at where Pessy was standing a few feet away, her arms around Raevon.

She looked just as thankful to be back in Esteopia as I was.

"Welcome home," Demetrio said to us. From his earnestness, I knew, if I touched him right now, I'd hear a million different profane words, spewing gratitude over how we made it back here alright.

"It's good to be home," I replied, and meant it.

"We have much to discuss, I'm sure. Let's convene in the dining room, so we may eat while we talk."

"Sounds like a plan." Blekket slithered his arm around my waist, cementing me to his side.

"How was Solara?" I asked on the way.

"It went well. They appreciated the heads up and agreed to amass as much fish as they could for the villagers."

"Did you remember to duck?" Blekket smirked arrogantly.

"My pretty head wouldn't be on my unstable neck if I hadn't. Sterling says hi, by the way. He was much less accommodating without you there."

"Next time, I'll make sure I'm present."

"Let's hope there won't be a next time." His eyes warmed with a piquant mixture of love and lust.

"By the way, Blek, I thoroughly enjoyed flying on Krystal," Pessy said, flipping her hair over her shoulder so Raevon could kiss her neck.

"I like flying on Krystal," he argued.

"No you don't," I laughed. "Every time we fly together, you squeeze me so hard, you nearly cut off my circulation."

"Being a tiny bit frightened doesn't mean I don't enjoy it."

"A tiny bit? That's cute." He squinted his eyes in slits. "What do you have to be afraid of, anyway?"

"Um, crashing?" he offered, which made Raevon snort.

"Scaredy cat," she mumbled.

"Fuck off, Miss terrified of bees." Raevon stuck her tongue out at him.

"I've been flying Krystal for more than a thousand years," I said. "You really think I could crash?"

"You spend most of the time while you fly just rambling. How can I tell if you're actually paying attention to where you're going?"

"I talk while I fly because I don't need to be looking where I'm going. It's like second nature to me."

"Uh oh. I think I see a crack in the Goddess's neck. Someone, get me a net so I can catch my fiancée's big head when it falls."

I chortled loudly, then entwined my arms around his waist and squished with all my might, trying to pour all my love into him for safekeeping. I let the relief of knowing I'd never have to leave him again swim through me, resting my head on his chest, above where his heart sung a mellifluous tune.

As we situated around the glass octangular table in the dining room, I dithered a moment, my eyes passing between the chair I would normally take, and the one that used to be occupied by Seraphina. In my heart of hearts, I knew which one belonged to me.

I plopped myself down at the head of the table, Blekket flanking my left, and Raevon flanking my right.

"Finally," Demetrio murmured, causing a diminutive smile to materialise on the bottom half of my face.

"So, tell us. How was Kylantis?" Blekket's hand found mine under the table, toying with my engagement ring.

"Tympany was extraordinary," Pessy began. "You should've seen how she took charge. It was—"

"Magnificent?" Blekket smirked at me.

"It really was," she verified.

"Tell us everything." Raevon popped a grape into her mouth, her other hand clasping Pessy's thigh.

"Clearly, you were able to compel your mother, since you're sitting here right now," Demetrio guessed.

"That's true," I confirmed. "I was able to compel everyone, in fact."

"She made them raise their hands if they wanted to speak," Pess continued. "If they weren't called on, they had to be quiet. It was so badass."

"That's my girl," Blekket praised, kissing my knuckles. My skin had never felt so feverish.

"I also compelled my mother not to harm the Esteopians through the sun or freezing the ocean, so we won't have to worry about any of her threats anymore."

"Oh, goodness," Demetrio gasped, which sounded almost like a wheeze. He folded his hand over where his heart was most likely pounding in his chest, exhaling a pleased sigh. "That's a relief to hear."

"What were you able to find out?" Raevon asked.

Augustus strolled into the room, setting a plate of yellowtail and avocado rolls in front of me. I longed for those hands to be Lev's, so much so that it made me lose my appetite.

I pushed the plate away and cleared my throat.

"Isaias *is* the reason the Gods favour Sleotha," I told them, and noticed Demetrio's fingers ball into a fist on his knee under the table. It made me realise that all the times Blekket and I held hands, trying to be discreet in front of Seraphina and Demetrio, they probably saw us do so through the glass. "Isaias is the son of Rafferty and Sleotha. He was next in line for the throne when Lavinia and Alden murdered him and his parents in an attack on Paramore. Jacinda is his sister."

"His *sister?*" Demetrio stammered. "How has she lived this whole time? Is she a God too?"

"No. When she eventually died, Roara and Isaias had Hadestia revive her. She's lived as long as she has because she's technically not alive."

"I was right!" Blekket leapt onto his feet and danced around the table victoriously, whooping.

"You're such a dweeb," Raevon chided with a shake of her head.

"A dweeb *you* said was stupid for suggesting she was dead." Blekket shook his fists in the air in celebration.

"This would be adorable if it wasn't just sad." Even Demetrio laughed at my joke. "And you were only half right. You thought she was dead, and the Fiery Folk were covering it up from the Sleothians. That's not true."

"Tymp's right. Sit your ass down." Raevon swatted at him when he shoved his middle finger in her face.

"I'm taking the win anyway," Blekket announced, hunkering down in his chair once more and regrasping my hand.

"No one is surprised to hear that," Pessy giggled.

"So Jacinda isn't a God," Demetrio reiterated, trying to steer us back on course, "but she *is* immortal. What's her connection to the drogon?"

"My father didn't know, and I believe him. He said the drogon showed up around the same time as her resurrection, but he wasn't certain if their lifelines are linked to hers."

"Okay." He stroked his chin. "That could be good for us."

"Without the drogon, Jacinda is basically mortal. If we get rid of the drogon, conquering Sleotha should be easy."

"What're you saying?" Raevon sounded nervous.

"I'm saying, I think we should bomb Khidayle." Demetrio's eyes glittered with triumph, as this had been his original idea back when we'd first discussed next steps against Sleotha.

"I thought you were against that plan because you didn't want any innocent civilians to get hurt," Blekket reminded me.

"That was before they murdered Seraphina. At this point, more casualties are inevitable. The only leverage the Sleothians have against us is the drogon. Without them, Jacinda is completely vulnerable. However, I don't think we should rush into this. We need to do some research first. I would like to, either tomorrow or a few days from now, fly above Sleotha and scope out Khidayle, locate exactly where the drogon are kept and figure out how far that is from where any civilians live. If possible, I'd like to limit the destruction strictly to where the drogon are, but if that's not feasible, then I can accept those losses if it means we annihilate the drogon race."

Or, at least I *hoped* I could wrap my head around it.

"You know I support this plan," Demetrio said with a smile. He even winked at me.

"I don't want you flying there alone," Blekket objected, "in case someone spots you and sends the drogon. I'll accompany you."

"Or Pess can, since she handles being on Krystal better."

"I can handle it," he snapped, bringing a grin to my face. Blekket liked to say I was easy to tease, but his ego was far more fragile.

"Tomorrow, I can show you where we keep our firepower," Demetrio offered.

I ripped at a loaf of bread and slathered some parmesan cheese on top of it, shovelling it into my mouth.

"That would be amazing," I spoke through my chews, then swallowed. "Where do you keep everything?"

"The arsenal is located deep in the heart of Acadia, where our arms and ammunition are made, maintained, stored, and repaired, in the cases of damage."

"How much ammunition do you think we'd need to bomb Khidayle?" Raevon queried.

"To kill one creature of that size would take a bunch, but for several, I imagine we'll have to use all of it. Or, at least most of it."

"How difficult is it to make a nuclear weapon?" I asked.

"Difficult," Demetrio replied. "You cannot make a bomb without an oxidiser, which provides the oxygen needed to sustain the reaction. You'd need a mixture of ammonium nitrate and fuel oil, both of which are hard to come by, especially in rural areas like this. To successfully create a nuclear weapon, you'd also need weapons-grade uranium, another substance that's not common around here. We've managed to make enough weapons with what we have, but our supply is already limited."

"How did Esteopia get these materials? They sound like something that would come from Sleotha."

Demetrio tensed. "I imagine Lavinia and Alden stole them from Sleotha when they invaded all those years ago. Otherwise, I'm not sure where we would've gotten such provisions. Now, Sleotha has the drogon, which are far more deadly than any bomb, so they don't need it anymore."

"Huh. Interesting." Maybe that's how the drogon came to be, because the Sleothians needed something to replace the firepower they lost. "Will nuclear weapons even work on the drogon?"

"If we catch them by surprise, so they have no time to react, then yes, I believe it will work."

"How many drogon does Jacinda have?" Pessy enquired.

"We already know she has at least three, but that's something Blek and I can find out when we fly over Sleotha." I took a sip of water in between speaking. "Once we know how many drogon she has, we can try to calculate how much firepower we'll need to destroy them. Since our supply is already limited, we should use it sparingly, so we can save it for any future attacks. If we have to use all of it, it's not a waste if it works, ridding Sleotha of their only source of power."

"I agree with Tympany." This was the first time since I'd been in Esteopia that Demetrio and I agreed on something so seamlessly. It was strange to be on the same side as him. "It won't be a waste if it works."

"If it doesn't, then we lose all that firepower," Blekket said negatively.

"Stop being such a worrywart," I griped. "Let's just see how many drogon there are in total, then decide how much ammunition to use." Blekket's eyebrows shot up, his lips coiling with mirth.

390

"It's been a long day for us all." Demetrio sighed, suppressing a yawn. "I imagine you guys must be exhausted from your trips to Kylantis and Jopolis. We should get some rest, then resume this conversation in the morning." Before any of us had a chance to rise, he added, "I'd just like to say how thankful I am you both made it back here safely. You would've been greatly missed if you hadn't, and our family would've felt incomplete in your absence." Pessy and I were both touched.

"We're thankful to be home too," Pessy whispered shyly, giving his hand an appreciative squeeze.

As we began separating for the night, Blekket tangled his fingers with mine, tracing the oval sapphire on my ring.

"Are you tired?" he asked me, and I heard mischief in the underbelly of the question.

"Why? What're you thinking?" His smile was libidinous, drawing me close to snake his arms around my waist.

"How about a bath?" he murmured huskily in my ear at the same moment his hands slid further down, cupping my behind.

"How could I ever refuse such a proposition." I stretched up on my tiptoes to kiss him.

Blekket asked me to wait in the bedroom while he set up the bath for us. I slipped off my sandals and removed my jumpsuit, folding it in the laundry basket before twisting my legs into a pretzel on the mattress.

"Okay, it's all—" He paused in the doorway, his jaw falling open.

"What's wrong?" His expression suddenly softened, as if he was seeing sunlight for the first time.

"*That* is a beautiful sight," he marvelled. "You sitting on our bed, completely naked beside your engagement ring. There is nothing more magnificent than that." I wanted to pretend like his words didn't warm me from head to toe, but I imagined that was already obvious in my blush.

"You're required to say that, because you're my fiancé."

"I'm not required to say anything. I am many things, Tympany, but I'm not a liar. I only speak the truth when it comes to you."

He proffered his hand, and placing mine in his was the easiest decision I would ever make.

Entering the bathroom, tears pricked my eyes. Blekket had lit candles around the room, which secreted a pungent vanilla scent that swirled through the air and embraced everything it encompassed. In the bath itself, the water was swathed in a stratum of soap bubbles, which foamed above the surface and ponged of citrus.

When I peeked up at Blekket, his cheeks were endearingly red.

"In celebration of you returning home safely, I felt like pampering my girl," he explained with a shrug.

"Well, as it just so happens, your girl feels like being pampered." Blekket cackled from behind me as I stepped into the bath and sank down below the bubbles, melting inside the froth. The warmth of the water made me moan.

"Scoot over. I'm coming in."

I opened my eyes, crawling forward so Blekket had room to join. He stooped down into the water, his limbs consumed by bubbles. I felt his hands flatten over my stomach before he tugged me backwards, his thighs snuggling around mine. I shut my eyes, leaning my head against his shoulder, and sighed. Soaking in that heated water, feeling it hug every inch of skin so gently, breathing in the aroma of the bubble bath with Blekket wrapped around me like silk, it was paradise, a place for us to breathe deeply and let our inner peace return after a trying day apart.

"I could get used to this," I blurted, and felt him smile against my throat.

"Well, we're going to be married soon, so you might have to." He placed the most tender of kisses on my fluttering pulse.

"So, tell me. What do you *really* think about the plan to bomb Khidayle? It's just us here, so you can be honest."

He rested his chin on the top of my head, contemplating his response. "I like the idea of us scoping out Khidayle first and figuring out the best approach, so we don't slaughter any civilians. If we have no other option, than that's that, but I think it's important we try not to harm as many innocent Sleothians as possible. After all, when we eventually conquer Sleotha, they'll be our people too."

I wished I could've captured this speech of his in a bottle and showed it to my family to prove the Esteopians were considerate, generous, good people, who deserved the same treatment as Sleotha.

"It's crazy to think of them as *our* people," I mumbled, kissing Blekket's forearm when he slithered his arms around my shoulders. "That we're actually the King and Queen of this place."

"Well, not officially for another three months, but pretty much." He kissed the crown of my head.

"I thought I'd be more scared, being responsible for this many people's lives. But it all just feels…right."

"I'm thrilled to hear you say that, Tymp. Fucking thrilled." He nuzzled my damp hair. "I feel the same way."

"You do?" I twisted around so I could look at him.

"I do," he repeated, sounding mystified. "Before you, I couldn't fathom being king. The thought made me feel sick, but that was when I imagined doing it alone, or doing it with someone I didn't love or trust. With you…everything just comes so easily. Since the moment I met you, I've never felt like I had to try to be myself, or try to love you. I just did. Maybe that's part of your influence as a muse, I don't know, but loving you feels like it's been in my genetic makeup my whole life, just waiting for you to awaken it in me. I look at my life now in two parts, the pre Tympany Blek, and the post Tympany Blek. Pre Tymp Blek would've cowered in the corner and transferred the burden onto someone he thought was more capable. Post Tymp Blek knows his worth, and believes he's the right person to lead. You give me the strength to do the one thing I never thought I could do. I will spend the rest of my life making it up to you for lighting that fire under me."

I placed my knees on either side of him, so I was straddling his legs, then threw my arms around his neck. Tears leaked down my face, which Blekket was quick, in his peerless, sweet way, to apprehend with his lips, gripping my hips under the water and pulling me closer. Some of the soap bubbles trickled over the edge of the bathtub and onto the marble floor with a loud splatter.

"I will never be able to repay you for all you've given me, Blek," I squeaked, not recognising the sound of my own voice. "For trusting me when I didn't deserve it. For letting me into your heart. For loving me in spite of my downfalls, in spite of what I am and where I come from and why I first came here. For never giving up on me, and never letting me give up on myself either. I love you with every fiber of my being, and I promise, I will love you for the rest of eternity and whatever exists beyond that. I can't wait to be your wife. It will be the proudest title I ever wear."

"Tympany," he moaned, sliding his hands up my back and fisting them in my hair. "I need you."

"You have me," I swore, our lips coming together with the joining of our hearts and souls.

I woke to the sun splotching my vision, and an empty bed beside me.

"Blekket?" I shouted, sitting up against the headboard. My limbs were fatigued from yesterday's travel, plus mine and Blekket's passionate reunion last night.

"In here," I heard him holler from the bathroom.

He strolled out with a silver tray, which had on it a dish of yellowtail and avocado rolls, a chalice of Argent Ocean water, a wine glass filled with champagne, and a skinny, aqua ceramic vase, housing a singular white rose.

"Blek!" I squealed, covering my flaming cheeks with my hands. "You did not!"

"Just trying to win the title of best future husband." He carried everything over, situating it in front of me on the bed.

"This might be the sweetest thing you've ever done," I said, tears welling in my eyes. "Next to building me a house, of course."

"If that's true, we need to up our game." He smoothed a napkin out over the duvet, then placed the plate of sushi on top of it, balancing the two cups on the tray before setting them down on the nightstand.

"Only you would try to outdo yourself." I shoved a roll into my mouth, moaning. "No matter how many times I eat this, it will never not be delicious."

"Really thought you'd be sick of them by now. I guess we'll give it another hundred years before you move on to something else."

"Hey. Don't yuck my yum." I seized his hand and raised it to my lips. "Thank you for doing this."

"No need to thank me," he replied, fiddling with my ring. "You're my Queen. Whatever you want, I will crawl to the ends of the earth to make it happen."

"That sounds like a life well lived." He laughed, then sloped down and captured my lips right after I'd sipped some of the champagne, lapping up the liquid before I had a chance to swallow it myself.

"Tastes better off you," he crooned.

"You're the worst."

"By the worst, you mean the best."

"I don't believe I misspoke." I went to drink more champagne, nearly choking on it due to Blekket's pout making me giggle.

"I would be annoyed, if the sound of your laugh wasn't the most magical fucking thing I've ever heard."

My cheeks scorched. I'd never met someone who had the capacity to infuriate and disarm me in a matter of a few seconds. Maybe that was the gift, that he could spark so many different emotions in me at once, but when those feelings dispersed, they left nothing but bliss in their wake.

"I love you," I whispered.

"I love you more," he pledged, stealing my glass of champagne from between my fingers and downing the rest.

"I thought you got this for me?"

"You weren't fast enough." Just when I was about to lunge at him, Pessy barged into the room.

"Sorry to interrupt," she exclaimed, breathless from rushing, "but there's activity at the gate."

Blekket and I exchanged a look, then crawled out of bed.

I threw on a pair of leggings under Blekket's oversized tunic, grabbing my dagger on the way out the door. Raevon was loitering in the hall, sword in hand. She joined the fold as we flew down the stairs and marched outside, sprinting to the gate.

Demetrio was already there when we arrived. On the other side of the water bars stood a man.

He was garmented in blue rags, which, upon first glance, made him appear as though he was Esteopian, but the iron sword he was gripping had the emblem of fire on the hilt, representing Sleotha.

He must've masqueraded as an Esteopian to make it through Tympany's Province without being stopped by the militia.

I took a step forward and ordered, **"Go back to your kingdom."**

Shockingly, the man stood completely still, not heeding the command. His expression was empty, as if his head were a hollow sphere rather than something containing a functional brain.

"It didn't work," I gasped. Then, the man spoke.

"Queen Jacinda requests the presence of Goddess Tympany and Prince Blekket in Sleotha this evening," he announced in an orchestrated manner, as though he were reading off an invisible scroll. "She would like to discuss a potential ceasefire face to face. If you are not in Sleotha by nightfall, she will take that as an act of war, and the consequences for your kingdom and people will be dire."

"A ceasefire?" I repeated. "What does she—"

I didn't get a chance to ask another question before the Sleothian raised his sword to his neck.

"With my last drop—"

"Wait! Stop!"

"I am free." He slit his own throat, disintegrating into a pile of powder and smoke on the pavement.

Chapter Twenty-Six

"What the fuck?" Blekket spluttered.

"Took the words out of my mouth," Pessy mumbled, while I just stared at the heap of steaming ash that a few moments ago had been a living person.

"My compulsion didn't work," was the only thing that came out of my mouth. Blekket approached me from behind, cupping my shoulders.

"It's okay, Tymp," he assured me, kneading my tense muscles.

"No, it's not, Blek. My compulsion didn't work." It was as if the Sleothian man had already been compelled. "The only person my compulsion doesn't work on is you. What does this mean?"

"I don't know," he answered, sounding just as helpless as I felt. "I don't know."

I turned to Demetrio. "Has Jacinda ever requested you and Seraphina's presence in Sleotha?"

"Never," he responded. "The two times we travelled to Sleotha were us requesting a meeting with her, and even then, we never met with her personally. She always sent a proxy. She's never invited us there to speak face to face." I let that sink in, flooding me with more confusion and questions.

"She wants to discuss a potential ceasefire?"

It was hard to believe, after everything the Sleothians did in Eveium, Frofsea, and then in Tympany's Province, Jacinda would just turn around and now suddenly want to talk peace.

"No way that's true," Blekket stated with a shake of his head. "This has to be a trap. I say we ignore the bitch and go on planning our attack on Khidayle."

"She said if you don't go, the consequences will be dire, which I assume involves the drogon," Pessy interjected.

"All the more reason to continue with our plan to destroy them," he pushed back.

"I agree with Pess. I think we should go." Blekket's brows lifted in surprise at me. "Maybe she's serious about an armistice."

"What do we have to agree on? Both of us want to be the sole sovereign of the entire Realm and watch the other kingdom be annihilated. That hasn't changed. We have nothing to truce on."

"Aren't you curious what she has to say?"

"No, and I'm surprised you are." I flinched at his curt tone, taking a step back from him.

"She's my aunt. Of course I'm interested in what she has to say."

"Don't you think the timing of this is strange? You guys return from Kylantis, and she suddenly wants to meet us?"

"All of it is strange, but that's all the more reason to go. It's better to know what she has to say than to keep guessing. If there's a chance she's interested in an actual ceasefire, then we should take the opportunity to hash things out. If not, we should still know what she's thinking, so we can plan accordingly for it."

"I agree with Tympany," Demetrio said.

"Wow. Twice in the span of two days?" I quipped. "Who are you and what have you done with Demetrio Elrod?"

"Very funny," he grumbled, narrowing his eyes.

"You call me a worrywart, but it's because I'm the only one who allows myself to go to the worst case scenario," Blekket continued. "Best case is, she's serious about a truce and we're able to finally settle centuries worth of strife, but there's a very slim chance that's why she wants to meet us."

"I acknowledge that. Really, I do, which is why we will come equipped with weapons and make sure we're prepared in case this is a trap. But we have to hear what she has to say." I leaned back. "Let's put it to a vote."

"There's no point voting when we already know you're going to win," Blekket snapped, rolling his eyes.

"That's not true."

"Yes, it is, Tympany. You're a fucking muse. I may be arrogant, but I'm not dumb. I wouldn't bet against you influencing someone to agree with you." I hadn't thought about that. Most of the time, I completely forgot I posessed the ability to inspire someone's decisions, which was separate from me compelling them. When I got Solara to deploy the merfolk as protection detail for the villagers while the Esteopian army built Tympany's Province, the mermaid said I was very persuasive.

I'd inspired Solara to consent, which was almost the same as me taking away their choice through compulsion.

"I'm sorry," I choked out, which, from his stunned expression, I could tell was clearly not what Blekket expected me to say. He fluctuated from tense to soft in a matter of seconds.

"What're you apologising for, Tymp?"

"I don't want you to think I'm not hearing you, because I am. I see the risks. I just believe it's better to be armed with all the information than to keep guessing. If she's willing to sit down with us, I think we should do it, even if the offer isn't genuine, but I don't want to make you do something you don't want to. If you're not comfortable with this, then we won't go. It's completely up to you, Blek."

His lashes fluttered, his mouth popping open, then sealing shut. "Um…I think…I think we should go."

"Are you saying that because you genuinely feel that way?" I wanted to make sure he didn't feel pressured, that this was a choice made from his own free will and not influenced by me.

"You're right. If there's a chance she's serious about a truce, then we should hear what she has to say, but we should also be prepared for the possibility she's not, and this is a trap. We shouldn't walk in there blindly."

"I agree." I took his hand, kissing his knuckles. "Thank you." He looked bemused, but squeezed my hand back.

"Let's head back to the palace," Demetrio suggested, scowling at the Sleothian's remains. "I'll have someone…clean this up."

We agreed we would bring one hundred Esteopian soldiers with us to Sleotha. If they weren't permitted into the kingdom, then we would deny Jacinda her meeting and turn back around. Pessy would accompany us, but Raevon would stay in Esteopia. This took some convincing, as Raevon loathed the idea of the three of us going without her, but we needed her to remain safe in case this plan were to go awry—if, Gods forbid, we needed her to assume the role of monarch.

"You're the designated survivor," Blekket teased, which caused her bottom lip to jut out in a pronounced pout.

"Don't make jokes like that," she groused. "It just makes me want to go with you guys even more."

Blekket and I returned to our bedchamber so I could change into something more appropriate for a meeting with the Queen of Sleotha. I selected a sleeveless, light blue printed ruffle jumpsuit with an elastic waistband, leaving my hair down, the waves tickling the tips of my collarbones. It had grown in the four months I'd been in Esteopia. When we returned home, I would have Pessy cut that extra inch off.

"You're sure about this?" Blekket asked me for the seventh time, slipping on the same petticoat he'd worn the night we met.

"No," I repeated for the seventh time, "but I think it's the right thing to do. We have to hear what she has to say."

As I wrapped my leather holster belt around my waist and sheathed my dagger, I wondered what Queen Jacinda would be like. Would she look like Isaias? Would I feel any sort of kinship to her because we're blood? Would she be more agreeable to the terms of a ceasefire because I'm her niece? What would a ceasefire between these two kingdoms even look like? Blekket and I had discussed our conditions, what we'd ask of her if this turned out to be a diplomatic negotiation. We would demand she stop sending the drogon to burn down our villages, and that we continue to peaceably trade Argent Ocean water with Sleotha for vegetables and meat. They will leave Tympany's Province alone, and if anyone wishes to travel up the Geddesia Mountains to visit the Gods, they must ask permission from the crown of Esteopia to pass through the village.

Blekket came up behind me, snaking his arms around my waist, and lay a sweet kiss on my bare shoulder.

"I do love you in pants," he murmured, his lips grazing my throat. "Please wear a jumpsuit to our wedding."

"Don't I have to wear a gown?"

"You don't *have* to do anything, Tymp. Not with me." He kissed the spot beneath my ear that always beget shudders.

"Then pants it is." I raised his hand to my lips, kissing his left ring finger knuckle. "Can't wait to see a ring here soon."

"Me too, sweetheart. Me too."

Augustus and Olivette had already procured Clarence and Krystal for us when we arrived at the stables. The two horses looked as though they were in their own little word with one another.

Clarence nuzzled Krystal behind her ear, and Krystal purred, her mouth warping into a flirtatious smile.

"Alright, you two. Break it up," I said, gathering Krystal's reins and leaping onto her back.

"Don't be such a buzzkill, Tympany," Blekket accused. "They love each other. Let the horses be, for fuck's sake."

"Did you actually just call me a buzzkill, worrywart?" He positioned his foot in the stirrup, swinging his leg over Clarence's back. He situated on Clarence's croup before scooting forward, now more centered.

"I like buzzkill more than idealist. I'm gonna keep it."

"I will slice your head off if you call me that again." In that moment, I meant it.

"Is it better or worse than when I called you a geezer?" Pessy asked, kicking Belgian lightly so he'd begin trotting.

"You called her a geezer?" Blekket tossed his head back and cackled. "I would've loved to be there to see that."

"I actually hate you both," I grumbled.

"No, you don't. You love us. We're lovable." Pessy flipped her hair over her shoulder, simpering at Blekket.

He grinned back. "*This* is why you're my favourite, Pess."

Demetrio and Raevon were waiting for us at the gates. Raevon immediately zipped over to Pessy, snatching her hand.

"*Please* make it back here okay," she begged emphatically, "because if something happens and I end up being queen of this place without you, I'm going to be fucking pissed."

Pessy melted with unconditional love, her hand raising to cup Raevon's cheek.

Raevon kissed the center of Pessy's palm.

"I love you, Raevon Audrey Elrod," Pessy whispered softly for the first time in my presence.

"Tell me that tomorrow," Raevon replied, backing away.

"Be careful," Demetrio counselled, giving my hand a squeeze. *Let's pray this isn't a trap*, he thought, then let me go.

"We'll be back tonight," I assured, then regretted promising something I had no power to control.

Demetrio curled his fingers around one of the cylinders of water, a beam of silvery light swimming up the stream and broadcasting to the rest of the bars, the gates parting in response to the inaudible order.

"Good luck," he shouted as we began heading in the direction of the Dream Forest.

There were fifty Esteopian soldiers traveling in front of us, and fifty behind, so we were protected on all sides. I rode between Blekket and Pessy, never feeling more claustrophobic. My view ahead of me was hampered by heads, the shadows obscuring the sun, before Esteopia too dissolved behind the breadth of trees, so all I saw around me were limbs and faces and blue armour.

"I wonder what Queen Jacinda will be like," Pessy speculated, bouncing on Belgian when we scampered over a patch of jagged rocks.

"I'm sure she's lovely and cooperative," Blekket said, dripping sarcasm.

"I wonder if she'll look old, like the age she was when she first died, or if she'll look younger," I added.

"I imagine," Blek mused, "if she's lived ten thousand years, she wouldn't have kept the body she withered in."

"Good point." His brows shot up.

"That's the first time you've ever said that to me."

"And it'll be the last," I teased. His smile faded into a scowl before he stuck his tongue out at me.

At this point, I was impervious to the Dream Forest's incantation, as were Blekket and Pessy, but that didn't stop the steeds from falling victim to the hex. They slowed down through the thick glittered fog, dragging their limbs as if they were encircled by weights. We reached Tympany's Province an hour later, the sight of the bustling, fully thriving settlement a sight for sore eyes.

"I haven't been back here since..." Blekket's voice trailed off when a tremor overtook his ability to speak.

I stretched over, grasping his hand. "Seraphina would be proud to see how Tympany's Province is prospering."

"I know. Thanks to you." He winked.

We were exuberantly welcomed by the villagers, the soldiers peeling off our sides and shuffling back so the Esteopians could have space to reach out and touch us in greeting, like they did on the mourning tour.

"Goddess Tympany. King Blekket," an Esteopian esteemed, while in their thoughts, I heard, *the bitch who failed to save our* real *Queen, and the chicken boy Seraphina would be disappointed in if she still lived.*

"Let go," I ordered, the Esteopian releasing me at once. *"Respect your King and Queen."*

"Your Majesty," they declared, bowing their head respectfully before withdrawing into the throng.

"What was that about?" Blekket asked after I caught back up with him.

"I didn't like what I heard in their thoughts." I wouldn't elaborate further. I didn't want to burden Blekket with the slander, as it would only enrage him to know what the villagers were thinking.

"Augustus," Blekket called out. "Bring the soldiers back around to cover us, please."

"Yes, Your Majesty." Augustus signalled to the militia, and we were once more swathed in bodies, the villagers' range thwarted.

"I'm sorry, angel." He kissed my engagement ring. "I forgot about your ability to read thoughts. I shouldn't have let them touch us."

"Don't apologise. Not all the thoughts are bad. You just have to filter out the negative ones to let in the good."

"A skill I have not yet been able to acquire."

I mockingly gasped, "Blekket Elrod admitting he's lacking in a certain area? I never thought I'd live to see the day."

Blekket rolled his eyes, scoffing, while Pessy giggled, "I love you guys," beaming with pride.

This was my first time seeing the Sleothian gates up close, and they were as miraculous and striking as the gates to Esteopia. They were constructed entirely of fire, the flaming iron pipes excreting a dangerous heat that was palpable even from several feet away.

I had no desire this time to reach out and touch them.

A Sleothian guard advanced from the other side of the gates, sword in hand, while the Esteopian soldiers cleared a path for me, Blekket, and Pessy to step through.

"Goddess Tympany," the Sleothian stammered, as if he couldn't believe I was really there.

"Alert Queen Jacinda of our arrival," I commanded, watching the man's pupils dilate before shrinking in submission.

His lips twisted into a menacing smile.

"You can tell her yourself." My jaw dropped. "Please, follow me towards the palace."

The Sleothian wrapped his hand around one of the fiery poles, which didn't burn him.

The gates unfastened for us to enter through.

I didn't move right away, even though everyone else had already begun making their way inside the city.

"Tymp," Blekket called out, gesturing me over.

"It didn't work, Blek," I whispered, fragmenting into a panic. "*Again.* Are my powers failing?"

"Try it on me," Pessy suggested.

I shifted to her and ordered, **"Raise your hand in the air."** She capitulated immediately, her arm heaving up. "I don't understand," I griped with frustration, nibbling on my thumbnail. "What's happening?"

"I have a feeling we're going to find out soon," Blekket mumbled, then pulled my hand out of my mouth to give it a supportive squeeze.

The edifices in Paramore resembled that of Jopolis, made of brunet stone that looked damp, even though it was balmy and dry. Seeing it in person, I understood why Blekket's perception of Sleotha when he was little had been that the kingdom was red and light. Without the fastidiously dispatched torches and ignited lampposts lining every street, the city would be quite dark, but instead, it was blindingly bright. As we passed through, I made a mental note of all the Fiery Folk I saw stationed in the village, wondering why they were necessary in the city as opposed to in the palace protecting the Queen. I got my first glimpse of the citizens of Sleotha, garmented in red, similarly to how the Esteopians all wore blue. I wasn't sure what I expected to see, but I hadn't been prepared for the way everyone's eyes latched onto me, for the looks of terror that invaded their faces.

I first assumed those expressions were directed at me because I was a Goddess, but that was soon disabused.

One of the Sleothians lunged, grabbing a hold of my ankle, which allowed me access into her head.

Help us, the woman implored, as if she knew I would be able to read her thoughts.

A Fiery Folk member lurched forward, seizing the woman by the back of her shirt, and wrenched her away from me. He battered the villager in the face with a flaming rod, searing her skin.

"Hey!" I screamed, jumping down from Krystal and inserting myself between the solider and the civilian. **"Stop it!"**

"Make me," the Fiery Folk hissed.

"Gladly." I caught the man's wrist, twisting it around so his hand was sticking out in a way that was abnormal, forcing him to drop the rod on the ground. I squished my fingers around him even tauter, his bones making a satisfying crunching sound as they pulverised beneath his skin. "Was that clear enough for you, or do I need to squeeze a little harder? You don't really need this hand."

"C-Clear," the solider whimpered in a trembling voice, writhing to try and break my hold.

I liberated him, shoving him into the soil, then sprinted across the terrain and offered the injured woman my hand to help her up.

"Are you okay?" I asked her.

"F-fine," she stammered, smearing the grime of the earth on her already sullied pants. "Thank you."

"Of course." I set my hand on her arm and thought, in my head, *I will find a way to free you. I promise.*

The woman gasped, then raised her large chocolate eyes to examine my face, her expression one of veneration.

She heard me.

I scuttled back to where Blekket, Pessy, and the Esteopian army were waiting, mounting Krystal once more.

"Magnificent." Blekket breathed in awe.

"The Fiery Fok are sadistic," Pessy muttered after we picked up our stride, heading towards the palace.

When I'd asked Seraphina about the quality of life for the Sleothians, she said she didn't know, but that she assumed it was poor due to how frequently they prayed to the Gods. Now, I understood the villagers' dependency on my family.

It was more than just having an unreliable monarch who they never saw and who wasn't transparent with them.

I had a hard time believing my family was oblivious to the maltreatment of the Sleothians by the Fiery Folk, given the amount of time my siblings spent here versus Esteopia. If Sleotha was so precious to them, why weren't they, or my father specifically, who once lived amongst them as their future sovereign, doing more to assist these people? Why leave them here to be abused?

Unless, for some reason, they really didn't know this was happening.

"I heard the woman's thoughts," I told them in a low voice, since we were surrounded by Sleothians. "She asked me to help them."

"And we will, angel," Blekket swore, kissing my hand. "When Sleotha is ours, we will."

"I communicated back to her, kind of like when you and I speak through the bond," I said to Pessy.

"That's different. You've never been able to do that before."

"Or, at least you've never tried it." Blek added, "That could be useful for us down the road."

"True." If this newfound ability allowed me to communicate with others in a covert way besides Pessy, I could see how it would be beneficial later on.

The Sleothian palace was a colossal structure of stone, bordered by a moat of fizzling orange lava that effervesced and susurrated below. We trotted in a single file line, since the rock-strewn bridge was narrow, and made it onto the cement pavement in front of the castle unscathed.

"Goddess Tympany," a blonde haired Sleothian guard greeted while stepping forward. "Welcome to Sleotha. I'll take your horse for you."

"Yeah, that's not going to happen." I handed Krystal's reins to Augustus. "Please stay with Krystal and make sure no Sleothians touch her."

"Yes, Your Majesty." The corner of Augustus's mouth quirked up.

Blekket and Pessy handed their horses off to Olivette, who joined Augustus in following the Fiery Folk to where they kept their steeds. We had half our soldiers trail after them, while the other half escorted us inside.

The interior of the palace was a strange juxtaposition of murky and bright. The décor was all dark wood furniture and red velvet draperies, which would have made the design of the place gloomy, if it weren't for the luminosity provided by the lit torches. We were brought into what looked like a sitting room, where a woman was waiting for us with her hands folded in front. The minute I saw her, I knew it was Queen Jacinda—she looked like the female version of my father, same pale blue eyes and thick blonde hair that framed her heart shaped visage like a wreath of sunlight. Her features were soft and youthful, just like his, and her smile was surprisingly tender. She wore a red pleated gown in lamé chiffon, with cape-like sleeves and a shirred bodice, the skirt spilling down to the floor.

I was surprised to see the top of her head empty, not bearing a crown. Seraphina and Demetrio were never seen without theirs.

Where's her crown? Pessy wondered in my head.

"I present before you the Goddess Tympany of the Heart and Mind, accompanied by her fiancé, Blekket Elrod, Prince of Esteopia," the Sleothian solider announced when we entered the room.

"Fiancé," Blekket repeated under his breath, then whispered in my ear, "I like the sound of that, but I think I'm going to like *husband* even more." I turned back to beam at him.

"Me too."

"Niece," Jacinda greeted, stepping forward. Her voice sounded much older than her appearance led on. "It is an honour to finally make your acquaintance."

"I wish I could say the same," I replied, which she disregarded.

"I'm so glad you decided to come. You look so much like my brother, it's like he is standing here with me."

I was used to being told I was a replica of Roara, so hearing I had any resemblance to Isaias was different.

"You wanted to discuss a ceasefire," Blekket said, switching gears to business. "So, we came. Where do you want to do this?" Jacinda grimaced, shaking her head.

"While that *is* the purpose of your visit, it is not *I* who wishes to speak with you today."

Blekket and I exchanged a worried look. "If not you, then who?"

"Allow me to lead you into the throne room." She spun on her heel and darted off through the gallery without giving us another glance, like she was being guided by an invisible thread.

"What the fuck?" Pessy muttered, looking just as confused as I felt.

"I knew coming here was a mistake," Blekket grumbled. "I will gladly rub this in your face later."

"Both of you, stop. Let's just see where this goes." I rushed to follow Jacinda down the hall.

We entered through a massive wooden ingress, which lead us into a gargantuan chamber with beige marble walls that had black bleeding through the stone. There was a sitting area with a wooden table and matching chairs, and then, in the center of the room, was the throne to Sleotha. It looked like it had a bunch of wooden spikes sticking out the back, the tips of the thorns doused in fire. A woman occupied the throne, dressed in a black sequin ball gown with long sleeves, a floral embroidered overlay, and a beaded waistline. Her pitch-black hair was woven away from her face in an intricate braid, and sitting atop her skull was an elaborate crown, painted black with red gems adorned on the sides.

Jacinda halted a few feet away, lifting the skirt of her gown as she curtsied.

"My Queen," she said. "I brought our guests to you, as requested." The woman who inhabited the throne tipped her chin up, her brown eyes that felt strangely familiar skimming the throng.

When they found me, they lit up.

I couldn't understand it, but the minute I saw her, I felt like I knew her, like I'd know her my whole life.

"Hello, little sister," the woman greeted, wiggling her fingers in a wave. "I've been *dying* to meet you."

Chapter Twenty-Seven

My oldest sister was everything, and yet nothing like how her portrait portrayed her in Kylantis. Her brown eyes were as if Roara's had been copied and pasted onto her face, and her nose was identical to Isaias's with the same low bridge. There was a ruggedness to her features that was more bitter, though, which I gathered came from living most of her existence in Nekropolis, away from the luster of Kylantis.

"Everyone always says you look like Roara's twin," Hadestia commented, cocking her head. "I don't see it."

"I take that as a compliment," I replied, which made her grin. There was a hint of Luna in her smile, and a trace of Calliope in her dark hair.

She stood, crossing over to the sitting area in the corner, and waved us over. "You don't have to stand so far away. I won't bite."

I shifted back to look at Pessy and Blekket, who were frozen in place with what seemed like permanent shock.

I was the first to move, ambling over to the round oak table and taking a seat beside her. Hadestia poured herself a glass of some liquid that was the same colour as her eyes, then passed it to me.

"What is it?" I asked, sniffing the substance.

"Scotch. You've never had scotch before?" I shook my head. "Right. You've probably only tried nectar."

"I've had other drinks," I said tersely, feeling like I needed to defend myself against the assumption that I hadn't expanded my horizons past the amenities of Kylantis.

I waited for Hadestia to take a sip from her glass first, so I knew it was safe, then tasted the liquid. It was quite strong, that first mouthful making me cough. It had a malty aftertaste, but I didn't mind it on the second sip.

Hadestia raised her head when Blekket and Pessy advanced. Her eyes flew to Blekket before she flashed my fiancé a smile that was bordering on molestation.

"Hi, Blekket," she purred. "It's nice to see you."

"I'm sorry, have we met before?" he stammered.

"You wouldn't remember me, but I remember you." She situated next to me, leaning her spine against the back of her chair, and swirled her scotch in her glass. "And who are you?" she asked Pess.

"Pessoranda Whitereaver," Pessy replied, her voice slightly trembling. "Tympany's bonded."

"Oh. Nice." Hadestia's eyes trickled down, over my left hand on my thigh. "I hear you're getting married," she said, then asked with a teasing lilt, "Was being a Goddess not enough for you?"

"I could accuse you of the same thing," I snapped, her lips twisting into a wicked, wolfish smile.

"I knew I was going to like you," she muttered, sipping her liquor.

"So *you're* the Queen of Sleotha?" Pessy inquired first. We all had so many questions, but that felt like a good place to start.

"Does *this* not make it obvious?" Hadestia pointed to the crown, shaking her head like she was disappointed in the question.

"Why are you here and not in Nekropolis?" I asked.

"Nekropolis doesn't need a guard dog twenty-four-seven. I got bored down there, so I decided to come up here. I check back in every now and then, but it's quite…dark there." I could only imagine.

"How come you've never returned to Kylantis?"

"I was tired of being under Mother's thumb. I know Roara planned to make you Queen. You understand, better than anyone, how she can be, and how confining that place is. But I still keep tabs on everything that happens there. I have spies on the inside, kind of like what you tried to do to him." She tipped her chin towards Blekket, whose hand I was crushing. "I have to say, I was impressed when I heard you'd been the mastermind behind that scheme. I knew it was time we met after I heard how you compelled our whole family to raise their hands if they wanted to speak. I bet Lucius liked that a lot. I would've loved to see him silenced for once in his gods-damned life." She laughed to herself, picturing it, then took another sip of her scotch.

"They don't know you're actually running things here?"

"Nope. You see, when Mother and Father had me revive Jacinda, what they didn't realise was, since she's technically not alive anymore, she's under my control. I have authority over everything that either *is* dead, or *was* dead. Jacinda does whatever I say. Don't you, Jaci?" She peeked over at where our aunt was perched in the corner.

"Yes, my Queen," Jacinda said with an acquiescent nod.

"So, when I decided I was tired of living down in Nekropolis, it was easy to supersede her as monarch."

"You use her as a smokescreen," I presumed, "so Mum and Dad don't know you're here?"

"Exactly. If Roara knew I could leave Nekropolis, she'd haul my ass back to Kylantis. It's safer for me if she thinks I'm trapped down there. Jacinda keeps my identity secret and allows me to rule here without being spotted."

"I take it that also means Jacinda isn't the one who controls the drogon, but you," Blekket ventured.

"Pretty *and* smart," Hadestia admired. "You're a lucky girl, Tymp." I shifted uncomfortably in my chair, closer to my fiancé. "Yes, I control the drogon. I create them from the ravaged souls that enter Nekropolis."

"*You* created them?" She nodded. So the appearance of the drogon didn't coincide with Jacinda's resurrection, but with Hadestia conquering the throne of Sleotha. "How many drogon are there?"

"I can't tell you all my secrets," she chuckled, tracing the mouth of her glass with her index finger. "At least, not until I know we're on the same side."

"Same side? Of what?" If *she* was the ruler of Sleotha, then we could never be on the same side.

"Of the *real* war. It's not between Sleotha and Esteopia, Tympany. It's between *us*, and Kylantis."

"Kylantis? You want to go to war with *Kylantis?*" Pessy gasped. "I mean this with the upmost respect, but…are you insane?"

"A little." She brought her index finger and thumb closer together, nearly letting them kiss. "The Gods have had too much sway over the Realm for too long. They are the root cause of all the strife between the two kingdoms. They've egged on this rivalry and allowed for millions of mortals over the centuries to die in the name of the "land," but really, it's because our family didn't bother to give a shit about these people they claim to love. It's time we fought back. They have lost the right to be in power anymore."

"So, what? You want to kill our entire family?" I couldn't believe it.

"I just know, as long as the Gods remain in power over both kingdoms, there can be no peace between Sleotha and Esteopia. If destroying them is the only way to achieve that, then I don't see another option."

"They've turned their backs on Esteopia, but they still aid Sleotha," Blekket interjected. "Isn't that what you want, for Sleotha to be the sole nation?"

"It's true I'd like to see the Realm belong to Sleotha, but I want peace for *all* our citizens, not for some. I think the Gods' treatment of Esteopia is deplorable, and reflects how little they treasure humanity as a whole."

"If that's true, that you want peace, then why attack Esteopia at all? Demolish countless villages and slaughter thousands of lives, one of which was our Queen?"

I felt bad for making Blekket flinch at the mention of Seraphina.

"Because I still wanted Sleotha to conquer the entirety of the Realm, but my hope *now* is that Sleotha and Esteopia can come together to subjugate Kylantis, so we can end centuries of conflict and all live in congruence." She downed the rest of her drink like it was water, then stretched across the table to retrieve more. "I never would've even considered a ceasefire between Sleotha and Esteopia if not for you, Tympany," she continued, pouring herself more scotch.

"I'll take the credit," I said, "but I'd like to know why first."

"When I sent the drogon to Frofsea and my army came back brainwashed clones, which, thanks for that, by the way, I realised you'd arrived in Esteopia. When I heard you and the Prince," she gestured with her glass to him, "were romantically involved, I knew I needed to get you on the throne to carry out my plan." She turned to Blekket and said, with a surprising amount of sincerity, "I apologise for the loss of your mother, but it was a necessary feat in a much larger scheme."

"My mother was not a necessary feat," he spat, his fingers that weren't clasping mine balling into a fist. "She was a *person*."

"Yes, she was, and after we purge ourselves of the Gods, her death will not be in vain." She faced me once more. "If we're able to do this harmoniously, Tympany, then I see no reason why the two kingdoms can't coexist in the future. If that isn't feasible, then Esteopia must go, but I hope that's not the case. I'd much rather work *with* you than against. I've seen what you can do. After I heard your compulsion worked on our parents, I knew we needed to team up. With the two strongest Gods on each of the thrones, with my drogon and your abilities, we're unstoppable. Kylantis wouldn't stand a chance against us."

I had to agree our odds against the rest of our family were great if we banded together, and while a lot of what she was saying had merit, I wasn't ready to concede yet. I needed more facts.

"If we agree to this, what would the next steps be?"

"Well, first would be you and Blekket marrying, of course, so you assume your rightful place as Queen of Esteopia. Then, I'd like to pick your brain a bit, learn everything I can about Kylantis. It's been years since I've been back there, and I don't know our siblings or parents as well as you do. I don't want to rush anything, but I'd also like to move quickly, before our family catches on to our plans."

"If we do this...help you *destroy* Kylantis...you will allow Esteopia to exist?" Blekket asked again. "You won't try to extinguish us anymore?"

"No offense, but I'm really asking for Tympany's help here, not yours."

"Tymp and I are a package deal," he stated, fiddling with my engagement ring under the table. "You don't get my Queen's help without my involvement too."

My heart liquified in my chest.

The three squeezes I gave his hand said *I love you.* The four I got in response said *I love you more.*

"I can see that," Hadestia said with awe, glancing at our joined hands. "There are worse conditions to have than needing to look at your pretty face every day. But yes, if you agree to do this, and we *succeed,* I will leave Esteopia alone. Cross my heart and hope to die." The irony of her words made her snort.

Maybe she is *insane,* I said to Pessy.

"How much time are you giving me to make a decision?" Hadestia slurped her scotch, licking her lips.

"I'm feeling generous today, so I'll give you a week to decide. But after that point, I will take your silence as a no. My offer of a ceasefire will disappear, and I'll come at you ten times harder than ever before. Now that my army is no longer susceptible to your compulsion, you'll have nothing to defend yourselves against me."

That piqued my interest. "What do you mean, your army is no longer susceptible to my compulsion?"

413

"I'm *so* glad you asked." She sat up. "When you managed to compel the Fiery Folk not once, but twice, it was because they were still living. So, I remedied that." It took watching her lips whorl in a sinister smile to realise what she meant.

"You *killed* the entire Sleothian army?" I uttered in disbelief.

"I brought them back to life, didn't I?" She said that like it justified mass murdering her entire military. "With them not technically living, they're no longer vulnerable to your compulsion. The dead cannot be influenced, little sister." She cocked her head. "Why else do you think your abilities don't work on your fiancé?"

Blekket's hand went flaccid in mine.

In a room of kindled torches, where the walls were molded by fire, all I felt was ice in my veins.

"What…what are you talking about?" I asked for Blekket, who had turned to stone next to me.

"When you were seven," she told him, "you got sick with a nasty influenza. You died. Your mother and father prayed for me to revive you, and I did."

"Why would you help your enemy?" Pessy pressed.

"Because I knew having a puppet who was next in line for the throne to Esteopia would be of use to me down the road." I cringed when she called him that.

He wasn't a puppet, and he would never be one for as long as I lived and breathed.

"I don't believe you," I declared stubbornly.

"What, you want proof?" She shrugged. "Fine. Just remember, you asked for it." She shifted to Blek, then said, in a voice that was kitten soft and silky as butter, "Blekket…attack Tympany."

I waited for it.

I waited for Blekket to tell her to go fuck herself, waited for him to lunge at her and not at me.

But refusal never came.

Instead, Blekket's eyes suddenly glowed silver, causing me to release his hand and shuffle back.

Then, he pounced on me.

Surprisingly durable fingers twisted around my throat, garroting my windpipe as we crashed to the ground, Blekket on top of me. I clawed at his hand,

414

attempting to pry him off me, but he was channelling Hadestia, his strength resembling that of the Gods, which was impossible to contest.

With his other hand, he fisted a handful of my hair and raised my head, smacking my skull into the floorboard.

Black splotches bleared my vision.

"Blek!" I shrieked through wheezes. "Blek, it's me! Let go!" Blekket didn't appear to hear me. His midnight eyes were slits of coal, his humanity quarried. He wasn't Blekket in that moment.

"Stop him!" Pessy screamed at Hadestia.

"Alright, Blekket, enough," she ordered with a wave of her hand. Immediately, he let me go.

"Tympany," he gasped, his soul returning to him. Horror pervaded his eyes at the realisation of what he'd done. "Tymp, I'm so sorry. I'm so sorry, sweetheart."

"It's okay," I assured him, stroking my enflamed throat with one hand while the other cupped the side of his face.

Blekket helped me off the floor, then frowned down at his fingers, like he was questioning whether or not they were his.

"You will *never* do that again," I commanded Hadestia, praying my compulsion affected her.

"Sorry, little sister. That's not going to work on me. Like I said, the dead cannot be influenced. Not by you anyway."

"But you're not dead," Pessy pointed out.

"My connection to the dead makes me invulnerable to Tympany's abilities." She had a quick answer for everything, it seemed. "I've been generous in allowing you to fall in love with my puppet, Tympany, but I can take him away as easily as I gave him to you. If you agree to help me destroy Kylantis, then you and Blekket can live happily ever after forever. And I do mean *forever,* since Blekket is technically not alive. As long as he isn't killed again, once he turns thirty and assumes his role as King, he can live for eternity, just as Jacinda has. I didn't want to have to do this, but if you don't agree to my terms, then I will take back what's mine."

"Blekket is *not* yours," I roared, standing in front of my fiancé, as if I could shield him from her influence with my body. "He never has been, and he never will be."

"I don't want to take him from you, Tympany, but I will if I have to. Take that into consideration when you're making your decision." I would've slap her if I thought it'd do me any good. It would only enrage her, and I didn't want to see her take out her ire on Blekket again. "Jacinda," she exclaimed, glancing over at our aunt, who'd been a silent voyeur through this discussion. "Please escort our guests out now. It's dinnertime, and I wish to feast alone."

"Yes, my Queen," Jacinda responded, then gesticulated to the door. That was our cue to leave.

Blekket couldn't have gotten out of there faster. He sprinted out the door, his movements so rapid that he didn't even make a sound. Pessy and I exchanged a concerned look before she darted after him.

"Tympany?" I spun back around. Hadestia was standing over me, leaning in so close that if I tipped forward a fraction of an inch, our lips would've met. "It was a pleasure to finally meet you," she said, finishing the last of her scotch. "I hope you come to the right decision, but regardless of your choice, I will see you soon."

She proffered her hand as a show of good faith. I was tentative when I slipped mine into hers.

I can't do this without her, I heard in her thoughts. *Sleotha has no chance against her if she doesn't agree.* I bit my tongue so I wouldn't make it obvious what I'd heard in her head.

I just shook her hand and plastered on an agreeable smile.

She flicked her wrist, a motion she adopted from our mother, and dismissed me from her throne room.

We rode back to Esteopia in absolute silence.

So much went unspoken, but Blekket didn't want to talk, and both Pessy and I respected that. I spent the majority of that ride thinking about what I'd heard in Hadestia's thoughts, wondering how it was possible I could enter her mind, but not compel her. Maybe she wasn't as impenetrable as she thought, and that was something I could take advantage of down the road, if we agreed to work with her. We'd always be one step ahead of her, and we could gauge whether or not she was telling the truth when she swore not to harm Esteopia—*if* we succeeded in vanquishing Kylantis.

There were pros and cons to this plan. A lot of what Hadestia said was true. Roara and Isaias had micromanaged the two kingdoms for centuries and allowed them to essentially destroy each other. There could be no peace between Sleotha and Esteopia with the imbalance of treatment from the Gods, but at the same time, I had to wonder if this could be achieved another way, separate from slaughtering them. I didn't know if it was even possible to kill them, or, if it was, what the ramifications of annihilating all our siblings and parents would do to the foundation of the Realm, once Roara's magic was no longer fuelling it. There was also the question of *after*.

After we destroyed Kylantis, then what?

Would we really be able to live in peace?

Was Hadestia serious in saying she would allow Esteopia to exist if we aided her plan?

Then, I thought about my beloved fiancé. If I agreed to do this, Hadestia wouldn't harm Blekket. We could be together forever, *actual* forever. I'd never have to fathom a life without him, which had been at the crux of my resistance in agreeing to marry him.

We'd be immortal together.

But if I decided I couldn't go through with destroying our family, I would lose him.

I glanced over at my brooding man.

My heart felt heavy. I couldn't begin to imagine what form of anguish he was experiencing internally after discovering he wasn't exactly *alive*. I didn't need to read his thoughts to know he was beating himself up for what Hadestia made him do to me.

Demetrio and Raevon were waiting in the dining room, rejoicing when they saw us come around the corner.

"Thank goodness you're back." Demetrio breathed a sigh of relief. "We were getting—"

Blekket marched forward, seizing his father by the shirt, and shoved him up against the wall.

"Blek!" I screamed.

"How could you not tell me?" he cried, shaking Demetrio so hard that he made his father's teeth chatter. "How could you not tell me I'm DEAD!" Demetrio's face drained of colour.

"What?" Raevon rushed out of Pessy's arms to stand at her brother's side. "What're you talking about?"

"We met Hadestia while we were in Sleotha," I explained, retrieving both Raevon and Demetrio's undivided attention. "She told us what happened. That when Blekket was seven, he…he died, and you prayed for her to revive him."

"Dad!" Raevon shrieked. "Is that true?"

"We never thought you'd need to know," Demetrio said, tears welling in his eyes. "I'm so sorry, Son."

"What? You thought I wouldn't notice when I stopped aging?" Demetrio's brows furrowed.

"What do you mean?" he demanded, turning to me.

"As long as Blek isn't killed again, because he's not technically alive, he will live forever, like Jacinda."

"That's great news, isn't it?"

"It would be," Blekket growled, "if Hadestia didn't have the power to control me and make me do whatever she wants!" He grabbed one of the dining room chairs and chucked it at the wall.

It clattered into the marble, the wooden limbs splintering apart and scattering across the room.

"Can you please not ruin the furniture?" I groaned, plopping down at the table.

"Because I'm technically *dead,* she can control me," he continued, his cheeks flushed from exertion and rage. "She can make me do whatever she wants, when she wants it, which includes attacking the love of my life."

Everyone's eyes flew to me, while I rubbed the spot on my forehead where a migraine was forming.

"Blekket, we never meant to cause harm in keeping this a secret from you. Your mother and I just weren't ready to lose you, so we prayed to Hadestia, and our entreaties were answered. We never questioned what that meant. We were only grateful we got to keep you a little while longer. I'm sorry, Son."

Demetrio placed his hand on Blekket's shoulder, but Blekket wasn't quite ready to accept the apology.

He walked over to where I sat and stole the spot next to me, reaching for my hand under the table.

"What did Jacinda want, Tympany?" Demetrio asked after clearing his throat, taking a seat at the table with us.

"It wasn't Jacinda," I replied. "Hadestia is the Queen of Sleotha. She uses Jacinda as a smokescreen, so our parents won't find out she's not in Nekropolis. She wants us to destroy Kylantis together. She says once we get rid of the Gods, Sleotha and Esteopia will live in peace, but that's contingent on me helping her. If I don't agree, she will destroy Esteopia and take…take Blekket away from me." I evaded his eyes when I said that, but his hand twitched in mine anyway.

"Destroy Kylantis?" Raevon spluttered. "What does that even mean?"

"I don't know. I have no idea if that's even feasible, or how getting rid of the Gods might affect the Realm. I don't think Hadestia has thought that far ahead either. I couldn't compel her, but I was able to read her mind before we left." Pessy and Blekket's heads turned to me, eyes bugged out. "She can't do this without me. She's scared. She said Sleotha doesn't stand a chance against me if I decide not to help her."

"You read her mind?" Blekket asked. I nodded. "How is that possible when you couldn't compel her?"

"I don't know. Perhaps she's not as invulnerable as she thinks. Or maybe my mind reading abilities are different from my compulsion. She said I can't influence the dead, but that doesn't mean I can't read their thoughts."

"Wait a second. You can read thoughts?" Demetrio gasped. I'd forgotten that wasn't common knowledge.

"You can't read *my* thoughts," Blekket reminded me.

"Yeah, but Hadestia isn't actually dead, so maybe she's exempt from that. This is all guesswork, but having the ability to read her mind will come in handy for later. We'll always be one step ahead of her."

"If Hadestia's scared, it means we have a chance here." Demetrio leaned back in his chair.

"If you agree to do this and she turns on you regardless, then all that destruction was for nothing," Pessy pointed out.

"Which is why I need to determine how serious she is when she says she'll leave Esteopia alone if we help her. Reading her mind will help me do that. I won't agree to anything if she's not sincere about that promise."

"What about the Sleothians?" Blekket added. "If we focus on destroying Kylantis instead of conquering Sleotha, are we really just going to leave them there to be abused by the Fiery Folk?"

"You should've seen how they terrorised this woman," Pessy told Raevon and Demetrio. "It was appalling."

"After we deal with Kylantis, once we've gained her trust, we can speak to Hadestia about the treatment of her people. It's possible she doesn't even know how the Fiery Folk behave in the streets, since she spends all her time cooped up in the palace, hiding from our parents. If she's really all about peace, then it will bother her to know what they're doing to her people. If it doesn't, if she knows and is just not doing anything, then we'll have to do something about it, but we can worry about that after we've successfully destroyed Kylantis."

"Are you actually thinking about doing this, Tymp?" Raevon asked. "Destroying your whole family?"

"I'm…" My words mingled with a vigorous yawn. I wasn't about to make that decision now, when I was struggling to keep my eyes open, so I rose from my chair and announced, "I'm going to bed," leaving the four of them in the dining room.

I dragged myself up the stairs and into our bedchamber, stripping off my jumpsuit and crawling into one of Blekket's oversized tunics. I pulled my hair into a dishevelled bun, then lugged myself into the bathroom to wash my face. While I scrubbed my teeth clean, my eyes were drooping shut, so I didn't notice Blekket enter the room. I only realised he was there when I felt his arms wrap around my waist, causing me to gasp in surprise and tense, since I didn't know he was in here. He removed his arms immediately and took a step back from me, his eyes brimming with tears.

Seeing his heartbreak woke me from my stupor.

"Blek? What's wrong?" I set my toothbrush down and rushed over to cradle his face in my hands.

"You tensed," he choked out, a tear dripping down his face. "You tensed when I touched you. Is it because of what I did? Tympany, I cannot begin to tell you how sorry I am. I never would've strangled you if I'd had control over my actions. I know I told you I would never lay a hand on you that you didn't want there, so if you can't trust me anymore—"

"NO!" I screamed, now wracked with guilt. "Blekket, no. I tensed because my eyes were closed, and I didn't see you enter the room. Not because I don't trust you." I smudged the fallen tears off his cheeks. "Blek, what happened wasn't your fault. That wasn't you. I will not allow you to blame yourself for this. That was Hadestia, not you."

"I'm so sorry," he gasped, collapsing in my arms and burying his face in my neck. "I'm so sorry."

"You have nothing to be sorry about," I promised, stroking the hair at the nape of his neck.

"I love you so much, Tympany." His body trembled around mine.

"I love you more." I kissed the tip of his nose when he leaned back. "I love you more than anything in this universe, which is why I've made my decision. I'm going to help Hadestia destroy Kylantis."

"What?" I swept the hair off his forehead when he jerked his head back. "Tympany, you can't be serious."

"I am. I don't have a choice."

"Of course you have a choice, Tymp. You don't—"

"How many times do I have to tell you I can't live without you before it sinks in to that beautifully large head of yours that you *are* my life?" His eyes enlarged to the size of saucers at the volume of my declaration. "I just found out there's a chance you and I get to be together forever. *Actual* forever. I'm going to do whatever I have to do to insure that future."

"You can't do this for me."

"Besides, Hadestia's right. The Gods are the reason these two kingdoms have lived in conflict for centuries. Roara never did anything to stop the fighting when it was just her, and after she married my father and had us, she made everything worse by turning her back on Esteopia. I don't see a universe where either kingdom lives in peace with one another if the Gods remain in power. I don't know what that looks like yet, but it's worth finding out. And I'm *especially* not going to let my psychopath of an older sister take you away from me. I would rather work with her than against if it means I get to keep you forever, so no, I'm not doing this for *you,* Blek. I'm doing this for *me.*"

"Tympany," he moaned, kissing my forehead before fitting his mouth over mine. "You're magnificent."

"I'm not the magnificent one," I claimed, tracing the tips of my fingers down the side of his face. "That's all you."

"So, we're really doing this? We're going to help that lunatic destroy Kylantis and all the Gods?"

"If it means you and I get to be together forever, that Esteopia can exist in peace, then it'll be worth it." I set my hand over where his heart pounded beneath his ribcage. "Do you feel that, Blek? Your heart beating? It means you're *alive.* And as long as you're alive, you don't belong to her, or anyone else. Well, besides me."

The smile that bloomed across his face was glorious, impregnated with so much more love than I deserved.

"Until the last drop of my blood, my Queen," he whispered, planting a kiss over the ring that would remain on my finger for eternity.

CPSIA information can be obtained
at www.ICGtesting.com
Printed in the USA
BVHW032254061222
653631BV00006B/38

9 781398 480117